"I was told you

Sage didn't have anything to say to that. Disagreeing would be weak and agreeing would be arrogant. Arrogance was a fine thing in a soldier, but like every weapon, it had its time and place. This wasn't the time and the general's office would never be the place.

"Looking at your field service report, I can understand why you were mustered back to a training position."

Sage hadn't understood that then, and he didn't understand it now. He was a soldier. He'd chosen to fight for the Terran Alliance, and he'd die for it if he had to.

"Soldiers like you are hard to find: men who have survived continued combat with the Sting-Tails." Whitcomb eased himself out of his chair and walked stiffly to the wall behind the desk. He pressed his hand against the surface and an image opened up.

Makaum floated like a fat green fruit against the blackness of space. Other space stations orbited the planet in geosynchronous positions, and support flitters traveled between them. Whitcomb stood with his back to Sage and peered out at the planet.

"They should have left you at the training facility. You're going to be wasted out here."

MASTER SERGEANT

The Makaum War: Book One

MEL ODOM

HARPER Voyager
An Imprint of HarperCollins*Publishers*

HARPER Voyager

An Imprint of HarperCollins*Publishers*
195 Broadway
New York, New York 10007

Copyright © 2014 by Mel Odom
Cover art by Gregory Bridges
ISBN 978-0-06-228442-6
www.harpervoyagerbooks.com

First Harper Voyager mass market printing: February 2015

Harper Voyager and ⟩ is a trademark of HCP LLC.

Printed in the U.S.A.

10 9 8 7 6 5 4 3 2 1

*For my sons, Shiloh and Chandler,
who enjoy a good war story set in
outer space*

ACKNOWLEDGMENTS

For my amazing editor, Kelly O'Connor, who made this a much better book.

And to my agent, Ethan Ellenberg, for always having my back.

MASTER
SERGEANT

ONE

The official report stated that Master Sergeant Frank Nolan Sage, 3rd Battalion/Fort York/Loki 19 (Makaum), acted with "impaired judgment" before he reached planetside. Other military personnel who witnessed the incident stated that Sage had "perhaps enjoyed one refreshment too many" while "adjusting to the native hooch."

And there were others—one of the hostesses at the Azure Mist Tavern—who insisted he was a hero.

Personally, Sage knew his give-a-damn meter about rules regarding engaging the corporation security sector had cycled dry after he'd gotten a bellyful of the crap spewed by one of DawnStar Corp private sec bashhounds. He'd come to Makaum to get back in the fight against the Phrenorian Empire after a six-year assignment training troops. The bashhound had just ended up as collateral damage along the way.

What really happened was this:

"YOU KNOW THEY got other names for Loki 19 than Makaum. That's just what the natives call it." Corporal Trevor Anders dangled a brown bottle of local beer between his fingers as he watched one of the serving girls hustling drinks. Anders was young enough to be Sage's son and had a narrow face, intense blue eyes, and short blond hair. Like Sage, he wore camo-colored ACU pants and a beige ARMY tee shirt. "The corp's zenobiologists call the place 'Macabre' because of all the weird plants and creatures. Any soldier that's been on the ground in those jungles calls it the 'Green Hell' because most of those plants and creatures try to kill you."

Sage grinned at that and tipped his bottle back. The beer had an odd mushroom-and-wood-pulp taste that had taken some getting used to, but it was growing on him. The alcoholic effects were stronger than anything he'd had outside of Sergeant Welker's home brew on Ganatol. One batch had caused temporary blindness in four soldiers that had required some creative paperwork and help from the medical teams to keep the incident under wraps.

Sage and Anders sat at one of the small round tables packed into the Azure Mist Tavern, supposedly named after the rainy season planetside. The décor was a mix of highly polished black and blue-green tiles. The tables and chairs were flat black. Nearly three hundred people sat inside the bar, and the cumulative conversation bordered on deafening, taxing the capabilities of the white noise generators at each table.

Anders looked at Sage again. "They have lizards on Makaum that are as big as dinosaurs. I heard Terran scientists got excited when they first heard about them, then got disappointed when they found out they weren't much different than what we had back home."

"Just bigger."

"Exactly. A whole lot bigger." Anders grew more animated in the telling, leaning in closer. "And a whole lot more predatory. Then there's the bugs. They say a saber spider can take out an attack chopper, and that you'll never see one of them coming."

Sage shrugged, a small movement but one that was easily read. As sergeant, he'd learned body language shorthand. Troops had to pick up screens of information from small movements. Combat required economy. Sparse movements. Sparser words. He knew his craft. "Guys on the ground always tell newbies horror stories."

"Yeah, but there's vid floating around out there on MilNet. Shows a helicopter fighting off a saber spider. You seen that?"

"A lot of other things are on MilNet too. Not all of those things are true either." The military ComNet kept the Terran Army rolling, but even the top encryption specialists couldn't keep canny and bored grunts from cannibalizing bandwidth for personal projects, porn, and the grapevine.

"How many planets you been to, Top?"

It was a question Sage had often been asked. The greenies were always curious, but he couldn't blame them. They didn't realize that war zones tended to blur after a while when a soldier stayed juiced on adrenaline and combat sense enhancers while wearing an AKTIVsuit. The Armored-Kinetic-Tactical-Intelligence-Vestment boosted strength and speed, and had an array of chemstims. "Kid, you learn to stop counting."

"But you've never been here before?" Anders squinted, like he was trying to work some really hard math problem.

"Nope." Sage shifted in his chair, trying to get comfortable and failing. There were too many moving parts around him, too many voices, and the zone hadn't been clearly defined or secured. He didn't much care for being around the corp muscle. Those guys always lit up his personal security radar.

The corporal hesitated. "Makaum is a backwater, Top. Why would somebody with your field-service record be assigned to a nowhere place like this?"

"I volunteered. You greenies need somebody to keep you alive." With a friendly grin, Sage tilted his bottle back and took another sip. The pleasant buzz rolled in his head and he didn't intend to talk about why he was there anymore. His options had been limited, by the military and by his own sense of honor. Makaum was the only destination available on his particular career path at the moment. He was hoping to change his luck. If not, going primitive for a while suited him. There would be less top brass to worry about.

Looking disappointed, Anders shook his head. "I volunteered too. But not for this. For the Khustal System worlds. The war with the Phrenorians is hot out there. Since the Pagor System fell, we need a toehold somewhere out here. Somewhere that we can push back against the Sting-Tails. I wanted to make a difference."

"The Phrenorians are here too, kid. Don't forget that. You forget that, you're next door to dead." Sage was serious, and his flat, hard voice captured the younger man's attention instantly. "You don't have to travel far to find enemies this far out in the Systems. And you can make a difference no matter where you are." That was Mil-speak. He didn't believe it anymore himself, but the words came to his lips without his even thinking about them. He still wanted to believe them, and he didn't know if he was being innocent or desperate. It amounted to the same thing, he supposed.

"Guess not." Anders rolled his empty bottle between

his palms and shot an irritated glance around the bar. "I need another beer. Tomorrow I get dumped planetside on a dropship. The long fall. I hate that ride. Always makes my guts churn. I'd rather not spend my last night here sober."

Because he knew he'd spoken gruffly and probably a little harder than the corporal was ready to deal with, Sage nodded and placed his empty on the table. "Me neither. This round's on me."

Anders looked around glumly. "Got better service last night, but tonight the bashhounds and corps execs are slumming."

The servers had focused on the corp execs and their bashhound security teams. Everyone in the space-station bar knew the private sector had all the big creds. Developers and merchants were making a killing in pharmaceuticals discovered on the planet. They spent cred like water among the little people.

The bar crowd sat in separate camps. Private enterprise hung on one side of the room and outnumbered the Terran Army soldiers on the other side by nearly three to one.

Sage watched the two groups while he waited to catch the eye of a passing server. Both camps had uniforms. The Terran military forces sported light and dark green AKTIVsuits meant for disappearing in Makaum's jungles. DawnStar, Silver Spin, Tri-Cargo, and other corp entities wore a lot of black. The sec teams also wore their guns in shoulder holsters because they went armed all the time.

The military wasn't allowed to do that because the space station was built by the private sector, DawnStar Corp to be exact. As a result, the Terran Army was there by invitation, and the invitation meant not having to construct a geosynchronous habitat themselves. The various corps had provided funding to DawnStar, then had taken out long-time leases. According to the rules of engagement, the Terran Army was there as a peacekeeping force to aid in the civil strife racking the planet's populace. But they were paying a long-term lease as well. Contact with an interstellar species wasn't going swimmingly on Makaum.

Less kind observers would say that the Terran military was on Makaum to safeguard corps and their financial investments from hostile elements on the planet. Bashhounds handled personal protection for the execs and regular army maintained law and order. And maybe they protected the planet from the Phrenorians. The StingTails had exhibited interest in the planet on several occasions, and there had been some bloody exchanges.

Sage turned his attention to the large trid displays behind the bar. The three-dimensional broadcasts showed a football game and an ultimate fighter competition from Terra that were months old. Sage didn't have any interest in those. He'd seen the football game live back on Terra before he'd been reassigned to Loki 19.

The other screen showed the verdant planet below, interrupted by documentaries regarding various corps, market interests and advertising. The space station stayed in geosynchronous orbit directly above the large, sprawling urban maze that was Makaum. Only one true city existed on the planet, but dozens of pocket communities existed, barely staying one step ahead of the planet's predators and the verdant growth that spewed from the jungle and required incineration at least every other day.

Humans weren't the dominant species. In fact, humans hadn't even evolved on the planet naturally and their continued survival had been difficult. The "native" human race comprised the descendants of a generational colony starship that had crash-landed there more than four hundred years ago. The survivors had thrived and established a civilization and now numbered too many to simply relocate. They were an obligation for the Terran Alliance, a target for the Sting-Tails, and a convenient market and cheap labor force for the corps who were after the rich natural resources.

Jungles consumed the planet to the point that it seemed all the plant life would suck the world dry. However, the oceans ran deep, the rivers and swamps were plentiful and contained myriad botanical marvels, and the northern and southern poles regularly calved glaciers that floated down into the oceans that could be harvested for fresh water. Loki 19 ran according to its own bio clock, and everything that thrived there learned to kill prey while remaining alive. It was an ongoing exercise of Darwin's Law: survival of the fittest.

The lack of human or otherwise sentient habitation rendered the planet one fat prize for the corporations that had the capital to invest in the recovery of natural resources. The only fly in the ointment was the spillover from the continuous war with the Phrenorians. The hauls the corps took from Makaum tended to be vulnerable to the Sting-Tail space vessels. The military was on hand to keep the peace and manage assets on the ground and keep the Phrenorians from plopping down illegal planet bases, which translated to making sure they kept their cut of those assets earmarked for military use. That didn't stop the corps from trying to shortchange Terran military taxes.

One of the primary exports from the planet was oxygen. Loki 19 was oxygen rich and the starships used fresh oxygen whenever they could get it because scrubbers could only extend oxygen so far. Gypsy traders hauled oxygen out from Loki 19 and traded it to asteroid miners working near Loki 27, the gas giant that kept the Loki system primarily swept of space debris because of its gravitational field. The asteroid belt around Lodestone, as it was known in the vernacular, was thick and rich with heavy metals.

Sage had fought on jungle worlds before, but he'd never faced anything like Loki 19. On Terra, right after he'd enlisted, he'd fought in South America. His mother had been born in one of those war-torn countries, brought away by his father when he'd been in the Terran military. As a result, Sage's skin was a rich walnut color, his eyes even darker, and his hair—high and tight—was as black as a raven's wing. His Norwegian father had given him his size and heft, 195 centimeters and 113 kilos, broad shouldered and narrow waisted.

One of the serving women shrieked in protest and backed away from a black-suited sec guard, who laughed at her. His friends joined in. Sage watched with interest but hadn't seen the inciting incident.

One of the young privates spoke up from a nearby table. "Hey, keep your hands to yourself. The lady's just here to do her job."

Thick bodied and in his late twenties, the bashhound swiveled his gaze to the young private. "Maybe you should keep your nose in your own business, junior."

The young private's face turned red. "Just leave her alone."

"You got a crush, junior? Is that it?"

Sage sat up a little straighter in his chair and shook off some of the effects of the alcohol. He wasn't sober, but his blood beat a little faster and his body warmed.

The private turned away from the bashhound.

Scowling, the bashhound got up from his table and crossed over to the table where the young private sat with two of his buddies. "I'm talking to you, snowflake. You broadcast pretty loud when I was sitting over there. Maybe you aren't quite as brave up close."

Sage waited to see if one of the bashhound's companions would stand him down. That was what should have happened. There was no need for the situation to turn physical. But they smelled the blood in the air and they were looking forward to it like jackals waiting for a fresh kill.

"Just calm down." The petite server was back and made the mistake of stepping between the two men. "Let me buy you a drink, mister."

"I don't want a drink. I want soldier boy here to apologize for raising his voice to me."

The server tried to take the man by the arm. Before she could blink, the bashhound slapped her hard enough to make her stumble back. Blood showed at the corner of her mouth and trickled from her nose.

Anders cursed.

Sage waited for the bar's bouncers to do something. But the three men hung back. Either they were afraid of mixing it up with the bashhound or they drew part of their pay from the corp he represented.

The young private vaulted up from the chair and took up a fighting stance. He didn't even have his feet set before the bashhound swept his guard away with one hand and punched him in the face with the other. Bone broke with an audible *snap* and blood rained in droplets over the surrounding area. As the private fell backward, the bashhound stayed on him, hitting him two more times in the face before the private's friends tried to jump him.

Moving so swiftly and smoothly that Sage knew at once the man was cybered up, hardwired with programmed reflexes, the bashhound turned and pirouetted on the ball of his foot. He kicked one soldier in the head and put him down, then caught the other one by the wrist when he threw a punch. Spinning again, the bashhound hurled the soldier over one hip and broke his arm.

By then Sage was out of his chair and crossing the floor

in long strides, blood humming in his temples. He'd never tolerated bullies.

The bashhound looked at Sage and grinned. "You want something, Grandpa?"

Sage ignored the insult and stopped just out of the man's reach. He had maybe fifteen years on the man, not enough to be his grandfather. "I just came to get these men out of harm's way."

"You looking for trouble?"

Sage stood there, arms at his sides, feet comfortably spread, well balanced. He kept his voice low, nonthreatening and emotionless. "No. Two of these men need an infirmary."

"What if I tell you that you can't have them? Maybe I'm not through with them."

Sage didn't say anything.

Lost in an alcoholic haze and preening, the bashhound looked back at the table where his friends sat. "Terran mil. Bunch of gutless wonders is what we have here."

Taking advantage of the bashhound's momentary lapse of attention, Sage hammered the man in the side of the neck hard enough to take his breath away. The bashhound stumbled and almost went down, but the cyberware kicked in and kept him upright. He even took another step back and dropped into a crouch as his programming moved him into an attack position.

The martial arts the bashhound was programmed with needed space to operate. Sage stepped into the man, bumping into his opponent and taking that space away. He headbutted the man in the face, breaking the guy's nose, then rocked his opponent's head back with a solid jab that fired off his shoulder, followed it with two more that were on target as well.

Dazed and nearly unconscious on his feet, the man staggered back, fighting the cyberware now and trying to retreat. That was the problem with the programming: it didn't let a man think for himself when his faculties were partially off-line. And programming didn't react to survival instinct or feel pain. Survival became a second-ary thing and winning was the only strategy. If that didn't happen, a programmed warrior died.

The other bashhounds stood at their table and Sage knew things were about to turn even uglier. The man in front of him managed to set himself and unload a back-fist.

Sage slapped the blow aside, took one step to the side, then lifted his foot and stomped down against the side of the man's knee. The joint came apart with multiple snaps. A lot of cyberware came with amped reflexes but not knee-joint reinforcements. That cost extra because those joints tended to be vulnerable. Corp muscle was often cheap.

As the man lurched sideways on a leg that no longer held his weight, Sage spun him around and stepped behind him. He roped one arm around the man's neck and secured a chokehold with his fingers digging into the flesh of the man's throat. He caught hold of the man's trachea, ready to tear it out if he had to, but stopping as he realized more bashhounds were in motion. At the same time, he snaked a hand up inside the man's black jacket, freed the high-capacity Gatner semiautomatic fletchette pistol, and pulled the weapon out. Luckily, the pistol didn't have a biometric lock that prevented others from using it.

Before any of the bashhounds could reach them, Sage had the pistol's safety flicked off and aimed the weapon's vicious snout at the approaching men. "Stop right there or I'm going to rip out his throat and start killing you." He spoke in his command voice, flat and unforgiving.

Some of the men hesitated for just a moment, listening to the authority in his words, then pulled weapons of their own and pointed them at Sage. His large size and broad shoulders made it hard for him to take cover behind his captive, but he succeeded in keeping his head out of the way of the red laser targeting sights that flared across the man he held.

One of the bashhounds lifted a hand. The laser sights winked out of existence. The man was tall and rangy. He wore his blond hair brushed back and neat, polished with platinum-white definitions. He was clean shaven and handsome. He smiled calmly. "Who are you?"

"Just a man trying to take care of his buddies. Call off your dogs or I'll put them down."

A small blurred spot opened up in the man's retinas and Sage knew the man was accessing an integrated on-line camera that broadcast images through his eyes. The residual blurring was a dead giveaway.

"Master Sergeant Frank Nolan Sage of the Terran Army. You've got quite an interesting history, Sergeant."

Sage ignored the comment. Corp execs getting into military files wasn't surprising. They got into everything the military did, and most of the time the motivation was to find planets like Makaum, places they could weasel into and rob blind while Terran soldiers spilled blood protecting those worlds.

At that moment, a group of blue-suited space-station law-enforcement officers in riot gear arrived on the scene with stun batons and pistols. They separated Sage from the bashhounds and he surrendered his captured weapon.

"You're under arrest for disturbing the peace, Master Sergeant Sage." A woman wearing lieutenant's chevrons at her collar grabbed Sage's wrist and expertly pulled his arm behind his back. She was in her thirties and experience stamped her tight features.

"Yes, ma'am." Sage placed his other hand behind his back before she had the chance to reach for it. The cold metal bit into his wrists. "If you could do me a favor, Lieutenant?"

"I'm not in the habit of doing favors for those that I arrest."

"Make sure those soldiers get taken care of. They weren't asking for trouble tonight."

The lieutenant's face softened a little, but she remained professional. "I'll make certain of it myself, Sergeant."

"Thank you."

She led Sage through the bar's front door. The blond man's gaze bored into his back the whole way.

"My names Velesko Kos, Sergeant Sage," the bash-hound called out behind him. "Remember that name. Our paths will cross again."

Sage ignored the threat and kept moving.

TWO

Sage. Frank Nolan."

Hearing his name, Sage drifted out of the doze he'd willed himself into through long years spent waiting in hostile conditions. He sat on the narrow cot in gen pop that he'd claimed for himself in the space station's holding center. He raised his voice as he leaned forward and got off the cot. "Here."

Conditions in the brig's general population holding area weren't aimed at creature comforts. Malcontents that had broken the law and spent the night in the brig sat scattered around the five-meter by five-meter cell. Disinfectant masked the stink of hungover men, blood, urine, and vomit, but the chems didn't eradicate the odor. The noxious sour stench stung Sage's nose, but it wasn't any worse than some of the barracks he'd been assigned to.

The other men in the holding cell glared at him. He hadn't made any enemies, but everyone had gotten the message to keep their distance from him. Ignoring them, he walked to the bars. None of them made a move on the cot, not certain if he would return.

Four jailers stood in the hallway. A young first lieutenant in full Terran Army dress stood with them. He referred to the wristcomm he wore. For an instant Sage saw the small reproduction of his image from the field service record illuminated on the vidscreen. Then the lieutenant looked at him again without expression.

"Put your hands through the bars and turn them palms up." The jailer held an oval scanner not much larger than his hand.

Sage shoved his hands through and turned them up. The scanner pulsed blue light that slid across his palms. Visual ID was never enough.

"Fingerprint analysis, handprint analysis, DNA analysis all confirmed." The jailer returned the scanner to a holster on his belt. "This is Sage, Frank Nolan, Master Sergeant Terran military." He looked at Sage. "Stand back from the door."

Sage pulled his hands back through the bars and took a step back.

A meter-wide section of the bars yawned open, retracting back into the ceiling with a smooth hum. Sage waited, knowing better than to walk through without permission. The space station had a lot of volatile people on board at the moment, and the security people were antsy. All four of the jailers had their sidearms at the ready in case the incarcerated people decided to stage a coup.

"Walk through."

Sage did and came to a stop at the lieutenant's side. He stayed in step with the officer as the containment cell door yawned closed behind them and they were escorted from the holding area. A scuffed blue line painted on the steel deck led from the cells to the security department's administration offices. Sage had followed such lines before, in other places.

THE LIEUTENANT HAD already made all the arrangements, signed off on all the necessary edocs, so all Sage had to do was leave a thumbprint for his personal effects. Once he had his ID and MilCard back, he put them in his pockets.

"That it?" The lieutenant looked at Sage expectantly. He was in his early twenties, probably fresh out of the academy and still full of spit and polish that hadn't gotten worn away yet.

"Yes sir."

"You don't carry much."

"Not much to carry, sir."

"I'm Lieutenant Flynn."

"Good to meet you, sir."

Flynn smiled mirthlessly. "We both know that's not true."

"Yes sir."

"We also both know you're in a lot of trouble with the brass."

"Yes sir."

The lieutenant led the way to the door. "Have you ever served under General Whitcomb?"

"No sir. I've never had the pleasure."

"See? That's your mistake, Top. The general is only pleasurable to work for when you're not embarrassing him."

"Yes sir. I'll keep that in mind, sir."

Compartment 683-TAOP HQ (Terran Army OffPlanet
Headquarters)
0943 Hours Zulu Time

Uncomfortable, hungover, hungry, and irritated that he
was kept waiting, but knowing that the brass dragged
their feet to remind a disobedient non-com of the chain of
command, Sage sat in the lobby and tried to think about
other things. Instead, he thought about the fact that he'd
missed breakfast and how much work he had ahead of
him on Makaum. Part of him looked forward to the challenge of the posting, but the other part still felt offended
that he'd been sent to the planet instead of the front lines.
As Anders had pointed out, someone with the amount of
time he had in deserved more preferential treatment.

The challenge wasn't just that the planet was green.
Nearly all the soldiers onplanet were green as well, because anyone with experience was on the front lines of
the war. Getting chewed to bits on a regular basis by the
Phrenorians. Not many soldiers lived these days with
the experience he had. Young soldiers looked at him like
he was something out of myth, or like he was a pariah
from the apocalypse. He was alive because he was good
at what he did—and because he was lucky. Young soldiers just interpreted that any way they wanted. The
brass didn't want to field a man others would follow
because they thought he was supernaturally protected,
and soldiers didn't want to follow a man who had whole
squads around him killed while he still lived.

Sage blanked that out of his mind. Thinking like that
only made him more dissatisfied with his posting.

A collection of campaign booty occupied the walls.
Three-dimensional images of battle scenes from Kauld,
Nostan, Valeek, and other places shared space with

pieces of Phrenorian armor. Closer to MilHQ, such things wouldn't have been allowed. But out here in the fringe systems, the rules were different. Things got more primordial. Soldiers reverted to a more savage state. That came with living with the constant fear of getting killed. Other tri-D images showed soldiers fighting the massive hordes of the Phrenorians.

Seeing the huge bipedal scorpions covered in blue and purple scales, sporting four "lesser" arms along with the two main ones that ended in pincers—the resemblance to the Terran insect made even more uncanny by the long, wicked tails they had—reminded Sage of all the battles he'd been in. Phrenorians were humanoid at first glance, but that wasn't their true nature. They were insectoid and had very little comparable DNA to Terrans. Their culture resembled colony insects as well, developed into stratas and substratas based on pecking orders PsyOps still hadn't completely deciphered.

The Phrenorians were chitin-covered killing machines, some of the best Sage had ever seen. He'd survived confrontations with them by being smart and lucky. He was one of the most learned hand-to-hand combat people he knew, and that was just the simple truth of the matter. He'd learned though battle and by being observant. He'd fought hard, gave war everything he had, because he didn't want to die and didn't want to see his men killed around him.

No matter how hard a sergeant tried, he couldn't teach that to guys in boot. A Sting-Tail's barb was poisonous and caused general incapacitation and probable death for anyone not equipped with an antidote. Fighting one of them was like fighting a man with an extra limb. The only training a soldier could get for that was fighting one of the enemy. Then it was just a matter of adjusting quickly or dying.

The young corporal manning the front desk of the general's office was only mildly distracting. She was blonde and pretty, little more than half Sage's age, and extremely efficient as she plowed through subspace transmissions and wormwave communications that fired through Oakfield Gates and provided almost instantaneous communications back to Terra when the stars— literally—lined up. The subspace communiqués were easy, but the Gate dispatches required a deft touch. An unskilled operator often didn't get the whole message reassembled after being Gated.

A bright blue dot flared to life on the fade-monitor in front of the corporal. She reached up and dragged the blue dot down to the bottom of the see-through screen, sliding her finger through the three-dimensional image of the monitor to make contact.

"Yes, General." She adjusted her micro-headset and glanced at Sage. Her green eyes sparkled with interest. "I'll send him right in, General."

Sage stood and waited some more.

The receptionist waved him toward the general's door. "A word of advice, Top?"

Sage paused and smiled hopefully. "Intel is always appreciated when approaching hostile territory, Corporal."

"No matter what the general says, or how vicious he gets, *don't* say anything to excuse your actions. He doesn't buy into excuses."

Tight lipped, Sage nodded. He wasn't a man to give them.

"And the general *will* get vicious. He hates this backwater planet and everybody on it. After the festivities last night, as far as he's concerned you're wearing a gold-plated reticle."

"Sure."

Her eyes held his for a moment, and she hesitated, as if uncertain. Then she spoke her mind. "But the men are proud of you. What you did made a difference. Soldiers are getting tired of the bashhounds kicking dirt on them. Those corps sec people will think twice in the future about starting something with us."

A crooked grin twisted Sage's lips. "Good enough then. Worth a night in the brig. Have you heard anything about those boys that got hurt last night?"

"They're going to need medical treatment, but they'll be fine. Broken bones. Some light reconstruction. Lacerations. Nothing they haven't dealt with before. We're a tough bunch."

"We are. What about the girl?"

"She's fine. More scared than anything."

Sage twisted the knob and let himself into the general's office. He gave the receptionist a wink.

She smiled at him, then turned back and focused on her work.

THE GENERAL'S QUARTERS were spotless and kept to a minimum, like a man there on temporary assignment. General Howard Whitcomb had served as Makaum's Terran military leader for four years. A few personal trophies—images of the general with politicians and other decorated soldiers, as well as Sting-Tail knives and blasters—hung on the walls. Since every cubic centimeter of space was precious aboard a space station, the fact that the general had a large office and a place to hang his personal things spoke volumes. Behind the desk, a huge screen filled the wall.

Sage strode briskly to the front of the polycarbonate desk polished to a high black shine, whipped his cover under his left arm, and drew his right hand to his forehead in a crisp salute. He'd been doing that for more than half his life and the movement was automatic.

"Sir, Master Sergeant Frank Sage reporting as ordered, General Whitcomb, sir." Sage kept his gaze above the general's head.

Whitcomb saluted back in a perfunctory fashion.

Sage finished his salute and stood at attention, thinking more about his breathing and planning his lunch than the trouble he might be in. Whatever the general said, Sage didn't much care. There was nothing he would have changed about his actions the previous night. And there was no other posting he could be regulated to that would offer more punishment. He was going planetside. Nothing would be done to prevent that.

The general was old by Terran standards, a heavyset man who had obviously been put out to seed playing nursemaid to Makaum. His short-clipped gray hair stood out like wire bristles and gray gleamed along his chin. One of his cheeks held an ancient scar that had almost disappeared in the seams of his face.

"At ease, Sergeant."

Sage dropped into parade rest but wasn't at ease.

"Got anything to say for yourself?"

"No sir."

Whitcomb glanced up at Sage with a trace of irritation. "Not even an apology, Sergeant?"

"Would you like an oral or written apology, General?" Sage didn't care. If desired, he'd knock one out either way—or both—and be done with it. He'd delivered a few apologies over the last six years while trying to make his case to his superiors to break him out of training and support assignments.

"Neither. I don't get the impression that it would be heartfelt."

Sage didn't respond. There wasn't a question in the general's reply.

Whitcomb laid a hand on the desktop and tapped his fingers. In response, a trid image opened up a few centimeters over the desktop.

The trid showed Sage taking out the corp exec and holding the captured weapon on the other men.

"It's a wonder those men didn't ventilate your head, Sergeant."

"Yes sir. I suppose I wasn't thinking straight at the time, sir." Sage didn't think those sec guards would have killed him. He'd felt certain then that he could have taken all the men out if he'd had to. Looking at the trid from the corner of his eye, he still believed that. They would have died, he would have lived. No other equation worked for him. A soldier who doubted himself in a confrontation was a dead man.

But that wasn't what the general wanted to hear.

"We're not here to jeopardize the working relationships we have with the corps. Without them, we wouldn't have our present HQ." Whitcomb gestured at the frozen image and frowned. "Your actions last night were stupid."

Sage wanted to point to the two soldiers lying on the floor at the man's feet, but he didn't. Generals only saw what generals wanted to see. "Yes sir."

Whitcomb looked at him and anger glinted in his pale eyes. "You're just going to stand there and agree with me, Sergeant?"

"Yes sir." Sage resisted the impulse to ask the general if there was someplace else the man would rather he stand while being so agreeable. That would have landed him in the brig again and he didn't intend to end up there without getting around a decent meal first.

Whitcomb cursed and tapped the desktop again. The trid image vanished. "Why do you think you've been sent to Makaum, Sergeant?"

"Sir, I've been tasked to assess the Makaum troops and

bring them into line with Terran military standards for at least the next Terran year."

"No, the way you got here was by petitioning training command to the point that they knuckled under."

That was true. But it had taken six long years to get back anywhere near the front, and Makaum was practically outside the bubble. Sage didn't say anything because he knew the general wasn't expecting a reply.

"Let's get back to those *standards* you were talking about," Whitcomb said.

"Yes sir," Sage said, because a response was in order, from the general's tone.

"Do those standards include bar brawling?"

"No sir." But those skills did translate.

"Good to hear that, Sergeant, because the next time you're brought before me for something like this, you'll be in the brig for a month on bread and water."

"Yes sir." Sage tamped down the anger that filled him. No officer he'd served under before would have been so quick to punish a soldier for defending other soldiers from outsiders.

Whitcomb was evidently different. He didn't want his house rocked.

"My orders here are to interface with the Makaum people, liaise with the corps that have trade rights on-planet, and keep the Sting-Tails at bay—diplomatically, if possible—so they can't use the natural resources here. In addition to that, I have to continue a nonconfrontational relationship with the (ta)Klar in the area."

That was news to Sage. He hadn't known the (ta)Klar had come sniffing around. Makaum was a good find, though, attractive to any star-traveling species that didn't mind skating off the main gateway grid, which described the (ta)Klar to a T. With the Phrenorian War expanding, Makaum wasn't as far from the action as it had been. In their own way, the (ta)Klar were as threatening as the Phrenorians—just not as direct.

"I was told you were a good soldier, Sergeant."

Sage didn't have anything to say to that. Disagreeing would be weak and agreeing would be arrogant. Arrogance was a fine thing in a soldier, but like every weapon, it had its time and place. This wasn't the time and the general's office would never be the place.

"Looking at your field service report, I can understand why you were mustered back to a training position."

Sage hadn't understood that then, and he didn't understand it now. He was a soldier. He'd chosen to fight for the Terran Alliance, and he'd die for it if he had to.

"Soldiers like you are hard to find: men who have survived continued combat with the Sting-Tails." Whitcomb eased himself out of his chair and walked stiffly to the wall behind the desk. He pressed his hand against the surface and an image opened up.

Makaum floated like a fat green fruit against the blackness of space. Other space stations orbited the planet in geosynchronous positions, and support flitters traveled between them. Boxy dropships occasionally streaked planetside, their jets flaring orange and red as they burned off acceleration and fought gravity.

"Most soldiers don't survive to get the kind of experiences you've had, Sergeant." Whitcomb stood with his back to Sage and peered out at the planet. His reflection in the screen showed hostility and Sage knew that not all of that emotion was directed at him. The general obviously despised his posting. "They should have left you at the training facility. That's where you're needed. You're going to be wasted out here. We both know that."

Quietly, Sage released a pent-up breath through his nose. One way or another, he'd been determined to leave the training facilities. He had experience fighting the Sting-Tails. That was dead certain. But the turnover in the training centers had stepped up the pace, increasing the numbers in the units while cutting training time shorter. At the end, Sage knew all he was doing was producing semi-educated targets suited to delaying the war but not taking care of themselves and their units.

He hadn't had the stomach to do it anymore. He needed to fight at the sides of those men he trained to die.

"But somehow you ended up here, Sergeant, and you've already become a complication in my job. DawnStar Corp is planning to sue the Terran Army for the damage you caused their employee. Repairing one of their cybered secs is expensive."

Sage thought about the soldiers the bashhound had put down, knowing those boys would require operations and weeks of rehab before they were comfortable and fit again. Healing human bodies was a lot cheaper than repairing a cybered bashhound, but they took time. And if soldiers couldn't be repaired, they were just sent home with a stipend that barely kept them from starving. At least if they died in battle, their families got death benefits.

"I'm going to have to deal with DawnStar, Sergeant." Whitcomb turned back to face Sage. "Not only that, but now I should be worried about you as well."

Sage refused to ask the question that had been dangled out in front of him. He figured he knew what was coming.

"This far out-system, the corps figure they're a law unto themselves, Sergeant. If one of those men decides he has a grudge against you, all he has to do is wait until you're out in the brush—and believe me, at some point you will be—then burn a hole through your head. And there won't be a thing I can do about it." Whitcomb shook his head.

"If that happens, I won't do anything. One man isn't worth jeopardizing the relationship we have with the corps."

Letting out a long, quiet breath, Sage forced himself not to say anything. Personally, he thought there was a lot that could be done, and a lot he would do if it were left up to him.

But it wasn't.

"I've moved you up in the dropship rotation, Sergeant, just to clear you off this station. As long as you're up here, you're a target."

Don't do me any favors. Sage thought that, but he didn't say it. Getting slammed into the brig while the Dawn-Star bashhounds were gunning for him could have been a death sentence. He was surprised no one had made a run at him last night, but the brig had a lot of soldiers hanging around off-duty.

"You'll be planetside by this evening. I've already informed Colonel Halladay that you'll be coming early. He'll have someone meet you to get you squared away."

"Thank you, sir."

"Let's get something straight, Sergeant." Whitcomb glared at Sage from the other side of the desk. "If you cause any further problems for me or this operation, I'll drop a rock on you somewhere out in the Green Hell. Do I make myself clear?"

"Crystal, sir." Despite his bottled anger, Sage spoke civilly. He'd had years of experience talking to brass who had no idea of what went on in the front lines.

"Get out of my office, Sergeant, while I'm still in a mood to leave you those stripes."

"Yes sir." Sage saluted smartly, waited as Whitcomb gave a perfunctory response, then turned and walked from the general's office.

"BAD?" THE YOUNG corporal looked up at Sage as he emerged from the general's office.

Sage just smiled and winked. If he was lucky, he had time to grab a meal before he had to take his berth on the dropship. And he intended to shower the brig stench off him too.

THREE

A-Pakeb Node
BioLab
Makaum
3728 Akej (Phrenorian Prime)

Zhoh GhiCemid, captain in the Brown Spyrl of the Phrenorian military, did not like feeling weak, but he knew that upon occasion he had to suffer through such indignities if he was to evolve. He had recently succumbed to his latest *lannig*, the moulting process during which a Phrenorian shed the exoskeleton to grow a larger one, and was not at liberty to put off the process. That would have been physically harmful, perhaps potentially lethal, and moreover, foolish. The moult rebuilt him, made him more than what he had been.

The *lannig* could not always be planned. The rebirth came upon a Phrenorian whenever the time arrived. Sometimes it was a result of successfully feeding in an environment for a time. At other times the process was instigated by constant stress on an individual, a reaction to physical or mental pressures. Zhoh had been through three *lannigs* since he had signed on with his *spyrl* upon attaining adulthood. His brothers and sisters in arms had welcomed him as a soldier, then again as a gifted leader among them.

Once he had known the *lannig* was upon him, when the first true split had shown along his upper shoulders, Zhoh had retreated to his quarters and soaked in the waters of his homeworld to keep his skin soft and pliant, and his body hydrated. Hydration was key, otherwise the body fed on itself to the point of self-termination. The *lannig* demanded a lot. His people had come from the Issgar Ocean and those ties would never be completely severed.

Now, as he lay in his private tank, he felt along his back for the split and ripped it larger. The pain was excruciating but he did not want to put off the process. He wanted to expose and revel in his new self. The sooner the old skin was separated from him, the sooner the new skin beneath could harden.

Zhoh did not like being away from his duties. And he had many enemies among his own people. The fact that he had been taken from the Kustal System was proof enough of that. Taking another breath, suspended in the nutrient-rich liquid, Zhoh tore again at the split, widening it further still. He stifled his cries of pain and hung onto his consciousness with savage fury.

The tank occupied a corner of his quarters, allowing his bed and his personal armory to share space. The small computer that kept him in contact with his *spyrl* sat against the wall. The liquid gurgled and bubbled as it slid through the recovery system and heating unit.

Zhoh's chelicerae, the segmented arms at the front of his face, twitched involuntarily as he steeled himself against the fresh agony. With a final effort, he succeeded in shoving his broad shoulders from his moult, then wriggled out of it entirely. Angrily, he thrust the limp mass from the tank and onto the floor.

Immediately, the three *krayari* beetles he kept in his quarters scurried out from under the bed and tore into the cast-off skin. The *krayari* were as long as his arm, black as night, quick, savage, and had limited intelligence, but they were trainable. They ate any organic matter that had not been deemed desirable by him and kept the room clean. They also kept watch over him, ensuring the privacy of his quarters. They chittered at each other, trying to get the biggest parts of the moult.

Satisfied that he had freed himself, Zhoh lay back to enjoy the soak. He reached out to trip a new flood of nutrients into the tank. These were designed to help harden the new skin. He felt calm, weightless, as he waited for his new body to move toward its final shape. Already his lines and dimensions were filling out. His tail contracted and extended restlessly, slipping between limpness and rigidity as it took on the new scales. The tail always hardened first, a biological survival mechanism. The tail was a Phrenorian's first and most deadly line of personal defense.

The *krayari* chirped and fought over the moult, tearing it to pieces as they devoured it. Some of the younger Phrenorian soldiers did not care for the beetles because they were afraid they would one day turn on their masters for sustenance if not properly cared for. It had happened, but not until after their master had died from wounds received in battle, old age, or an unmanageable moult.

Having the beetles live with him, inside his personal quarters, made Zhoh a subject of discussion among the lower ranks of his *spyrl*. Any distinction among his bloodline was a welcome thing. He had killed and eaten any *krayari* that dared attack him, and others in his unit had watched him take his grim repast in disbelief and awe. The beetles had enough intelligence to wish to live, so the others that survived learned, though they sometimes forgot themselves.

That was forgivable. Predators lived to kill or to conquer and stake out territory. This, too, was ingrained in the Phrenorian DNA, so Zhoh accepted it. *Krayari* flesh tasted terrible and didn't provide much true protein, which was why they were bred and kept to dispose of waste instead of used as a food source.

Zhoh closed his eyes and pushed away the pain, dreaming only of the Terrans he would kill once he was given the opportunity. He thought of his past victories and looked forward to those that would come.

THREE HOURS LATER, Zhoh clambered from the tank and walked toward the full-length mirror next to the computer desk. Water ran down his body and pooled on the floor, but the *krayari* lapped it up, following right up to his heels till he kicked one of them away. The creature hissed and righted itself, stood for a moment like it might attack— most things born on Makaum did—but then lowered its mandibles and scurried away. The other two carrion beetles retreated and chittered among themselves.

Zhoh glared at the image that showed in the mirror. His new skin was pink and pathetic, obviously soft and vulnerable. He willed it to turn quickly, to take on the deep blue and purple color of a fully healthy exoskeleton. His legs and arms felt weak and distant from him, almost as if they belonged to someone else. That would change, though, and quickly enough if he took care to allow himself time to heal.

He waved one of his lesser hands in front of a light switch, hating the look of the appendage because it had three fingers and a thumb and looked far too human for his liking. No Phrenorian had ever wondered where such hands had come from until they had encountered the humans. Until then they had simply accepted that the lesser hands were part of the tool development necessary to the race. His primary hands were almost as large as his head, and they were powerful enough to shatter the bones of humans. He had crushed the skulls of his opponents many times and always derived enjoyment from the ability.

Powerful ultraviolet lights came on around him and dried out his skin. As they did so, the pink hue of his new skin gave way grudgingly to the purple and blue.

"Mirror," Zhoh spoke.

"Awaiting orders."

"Growth chart comparison."

"Confirmed growth at eight percent."

Eight percent? In the reflection, Zhoh watched as his chelicerae flexed and flicked at his enjoyment. Eight percent was the largest growth he had ever had. He surveyed his larger frame with eagerness. His weight still wasn't up much, but he knew he could easily put on more now that he had the frame to support it. He would be stronger and faster than he had ever been.

He itched to be in battle, to prove himself and to explore his new capabilities.

Soon, he told himself. He hadn't come all the way to this backwater planet to remain idle.

He continued to bathe in the ultraviolet rays, getting harder and more certain of himself. Phrenorians had always been predators. A host of worlds knew that. The people of Makaum would soon know that as well. Then they would cower in fear as the *krayari* beetles in his quarters did. Zhoh would make certain of that.

The Phrenonian Empire desired the planet, and Zhoh was there to get the world under control.

FOUR

Dropship VDS Chalker
Docking Hub
Space Station DSC-24L19
Loki 19 (Makaum)
LEO 332.7 kilometers
1341 Hours Zulu Time

"Prepare for flight. T-minus three minutes."

The familiar engine vibration thrummed through Sage's body as he leaned back against the dropship bulkhead and buckled himself into the restraints. He was freshly showered and pleasantly sated from a Thai diner he'd found on the space station, and he was thankful to be putting the place behind him. Not powered up at the moment, his AKTIVsuit felt loose and cool. That would change in a heartbeat when it went into battle readiness.

The prospect of spending four more days inside the station's steel hulls hadn't appealed to him. He liked wide, open places, no matter how civilized or how dangerous. After a month of being Gatestreamed through the systems, he was ready to get his boots muddy.

"Flight?" One of the privates down the line snorted a curse and shook his head. "Dropships don't fly. They fall. If you're lucky, they don't fall really hard."

Another private picked up the dialogue like it was an old routine. "It's not the fall that kills you. It's the sudden stop at the end."

Sage leaned his head back against the bulkhead, absorbed the vibrations that ran through the dropship, and closed his eyes. There was nothing to look at. Only blank bulkheads and cargo crates, barrels of liquids, and sacks of dry goods occupied the storage section. Some of the soldiers around him were nervous. He felt that emotion mixed in with the adrenaline surges.

Being in the dropship with the men felt like coming home, and Sage was surprised to note how much he had missed that feeling. Training exercises with men in relative safety just weren't the same. He'd missed the adrenaline, missed that sharp edge of fear that spun through every moment. This was where he belonged. Why couldn't the top brass understand that?

After a final countdown, harsh clanks sounded overhead as the umbilical supports providing water, air, and power blew free and recessed. Cargo ships ferried those things to the station from Makaum. The pilot continued his countdown. When he reached zero, the side thrusters powered the ship out of the station's docking bay and into space.

The momentum pushed Sage out of his comfort zone and rocked him in his seat, but he took a deep breath and relaxed again. Free of the space station's rotation, artificial gravity faded and the feeling of falling filled Sage's gut. He'd never gotten used to that feeling. The AKTIV-suit's altimeter and gyroscope functions pulsed across his vision, tracking through the biosystems wired into his eyes since he wasn't wearing his helmet.

One of the privates gazed around at the blank walls. "Wish we had a scanner to see what's going on. I hate being blind like this."

Sage silently agreed, but he'd gotten used to the helpless feeling that came from being inside a dropship. He knew enough to operate one, get it up and running in case of emergency or attack, but he spent nearly all of his time aboard one in the cargo area. Army pilots handled the equipment.

A short time later, the pilot warned of the impending descent planetside. Shortly after that, gravity returned and Sage felt every nasty bump of the angled arrival through Makaum's thick atmosphere. The straps pulled on him and held him stable.

After long minutes, the "fall" leveled out into weightlessness again, then hammered him back into the restraints once more as the descent jets kicked to full burn. A few of the soldiers grumbled and cursed, but Sage just concentrated on breathing till it was over.

Fort York Military Spaceport
Loki 19 (Makaum)
1508 Hours Zulu Time

The dropship touched down with a jar that Sage felt in his back teeth. He waited a moment more to make certain the vessel was fully at rest, then pulled the straps free and stood. He reached into the nearby cargo compartment and hauled out his gear. He opened the duffel and took out his protective vest and helmet. He slapped the vest onto the AKTIVsuit, which powered up and adhered it in place as extra protection, then pulled on the helmet.

Once the helmet was in place, the AKTIVsuit's power cells fired to life and the faceshield shimmered for just a second and elevated the dim light through light multiplier refraction. A second later, a green dot flared to life in the lower right quadrant tucked at the edge of his vision to let him know the helmet's reception of photon-directed magnetic energy broadcast from the post was reaching him, swapping over from the satellite feeds.

Staying within the perimeters of Fort York would keep the helmet and armor powered. Outside the post, the armor drew energy from transport vehicles and geosynchronous satellites. Theoretically, the gear could interface from nearly anywhere on Makaum.

As Sage strapped his Birkeland coilgun to his hip, the visor interface acknowledged the link with the weapon through the biometric link grain in his palm and briefly flared a red reticle into his vision. When he picked up his Roley gauss rifle, a violet reticle flared to life. He added a Smith and Wesson .500 revolver in a shoulder holster and thick-bladed fighting knives in both boots. If he got separated from the power broadcast or his armor was damaged, he was fully prepared to go old school. He held the rifle in his right hand across his body as he got ready to debark.

For the first time in six years, Sage felt complete. He belonged on the front lines. He'd been born on a battlefield, and he never felt more alive than when he was headed into hostile territory. Makaum, so far off the beaten path, wasn't a war zone, but the enemy was here. He was closer to the fight.

Only a few of the other soldiers had their helmets in place and their rifles in hand. Sage let out an impatient breath through his nose and curbed the urge to command them to gear up that automatically came to him. Until he was presented to the men, he wasn't going to assume control over them. Chain of command had to be followed. If he tried to pull rank before he was acknowledged, they'd resent him.

They'd probably resent him anyway, on principle.

A few of the soldiers saw him, noted the sergeant's chevrons, and pulled their helmets on and their rifles off their shoulders. Others saw them, looked at him, and walked by without suiting up.

Sage didn't take offense. He'd known some of the men stationed at Makaum would be discipline problems. They lacked the cohesive nature of being in a firefight together, or being steadily drilled. He was there to take care of the latter.

"Stand clear of the exit ramp." The pilot's voice reached Sage through the helmet's aud receptors.

Sage stood at the forefront of the soldiers, his rifle canted across his body. Hydraulics wheezed and the dropship shivered as the massive ramp opened outward and thumped hard against the tarmac.

Increased sunlight polarized the helmet's faceshield before Sage could narrow his eyes. Instantly the glare of the harsh sun went away, but the heat baked into him as the cool air mixed with the native atmosphere.

"This place is a sweatbox." A soldier with a broad face and pale skin scowled. "The racks better be cooled."

"Or what?" Another soldier shoved the first man. "Nothing you can do about it, Donaldson. Gonna have to toughen up."

The first man swung a lazy fist toward the second, who only laughed and quickly stepped out of the way.

Sage strode out of the dropship and swept the tarmac with his gaze. Only military personnel occupied this section of the spaceport. The corps held other sections. As he walked, sleeker dropships touched down on the other side of a long row of warehouses and the blowback from the engines threw a spray of dust and debris that peppered him. A few military aircraft flew aloft, but most of the aerial traffic came from private enterprise. Thunder cracked around them as the vessels broke the sound barrier. The port was busier than Sage had thought it would be.

Small cargo ferries flitted around the newly arrived military dropships like bees working a clover patch. Several of the units looked like they'd been rescued from the scrap heap.

"Master Sergeant Sage."

Tracking the voice, Sage turned toward a lean man in his early thirties. The man stood at attention and fired a quick salute. He was nut brown, wide in the shoulders, and watchful. His faceshield cleared so his features showed.

"Sergeant Richard Terracina."

Sage recognized the name. Terracina was 3rd Battalion's First Shirt, the first sergeant and top non-com at the fort. Technically, at the moment Terracina didn't have to salute him. That he did so now was a sign of respect. Sage was going to be taking over for him. "At ease, Top. We're both working men here."

Terracina smiled. "We are." He nodded at the dropship. "Give you a hand carrying your gear?"

Sage shook his duffel. "Got everything here."

"You travel light."

"Got what I need."

"Figured maybe I'd run you around the base, give you a look, then treat you to dinner."

"I came down early. I don't want to waste your time." Sage also preferred to do his own looking.

Terracina looked a little embarrassed. "I heard about what happened in the Azure Mist. Gotta admit, I enjoyed listening to how you handed those bashhounds their heads. There isn't any love lost between the corps and our people down here."

Sage wasn't surprised, but the hostility concerned him. Especially if his actions exacerbated the situation. "That much of a problem?"

"It can be." Terracina shrugged. "They've got their agendas and we have ours. We try to stay out of their way and we bulldoze them out of ours when we need to. Here in the sprawl, we hold our own, but out in the bush, it's a different story."

"How different?"

Terracina's face hardened into a scowl. "Out in the Green Hell, you gotta worry about the local critters, the crime cartels that sprang up from civilian support when they got introduced to the idea, the occasional Phrenorian scout team, and the anti-gov locals who don't like us being here in the first place. But the corps do a lot of business out there too, and most of the time they don't want us to know what they're doing. Makes the whole situation volatile." He jerked a thumb over his shoulder. "I got a crawler. I'll give you a lift."

"Sure." Sage followed the younger man.

THE CRAWLER WAS a four-man transport unit with an open square cargo area. Painted a bright orange that had dulled and showed dozens of scars from past impacts and abuse, the crawler sat on six wide tires that came up to Sage's waist. The two rows of seats were back to back and barely covered by a sunshield.

Sage tossed his duffel in the rear compartment but kept his rifle with him. "No armament?"

"Nope." Terracina slid in behind the wheel and shook his head. He locked his rifle into the brackets beside his seat. "No air conditioning either. And a really rough ride if you get onto Makaum's side streets. Keeping everything clear of vegetation is almost impossible." He pointed.

Sage slid into the passenger seat, locked his rifle into the brackets, and followed Terracina's forefinger. Four men equipped with backpacks walked a grid over the spaceport. As they walked, they blasted sections of the tarmac with solvent.

"Defoliant." Terracina pushed the ignition button on the dash. The crawler quivered to life as the engine caught. "We have to devote a lot of manpower to keeping the Green Hell beat back, and the jungle just figures new ways and DNA strands to beat what we throw at it. This planet is nothing if not adaptable. Got a big budget for defoliation, and some of the corps even have R and D funding earmarked for genetic research to make the local flora more controllable. That's part of what makes us unpopular with the anti-Terran movement."

"The locals don't want the jungle contained?" Sage looked out over the rolling green density that surrounded the city. Trees and brush ringed the city like an emerald ocean that wouldn't be denied.

"Some of them wouldn't mind it so much, get more living space and arable lands without breaking your back, but most of the Makaum people have accepted the ongoing battle with the environment as part of the price they have to pay for survival. They've found interesting ways to make it work for them." Terracina shook his head. "Others believe that the existing balance in nature shouldn't be tampered with. Something this big but tightly ingrained, if an outside change is introduced, they're afraid it could start a chain reaction of falling dominoes, maybe kill off everything here."

Aware of all the jungle on the other side of the military base to the south, Sage nodded. "That would be a lot of dominoes."

"Yeah, but I don't think it will ever happen. This whole planet is just too mean and nasty." Terracina maneuvered around a group of cargo handlers offloading a dropship of supplies.

"How much of a problem is the local resistance?" Sage had read up on that as well.

Terracina drove through the spaceport. "More annoying than difficult. We're limited in how we can interface with the locals. Usually you can depend on a sizeable civilian population to shore up noncombat positions. The mess. Janitorial. Services. That way we don't stretch the combat units thin with comfort care and day-to-day. We provide jobs for the locals, a new way of living, an economic infrastructure they didn't have before we arrived. You know the score."

Sage did. The army and civilian camps had to grow together in populated areas. Usually the gestalt was mutually beneficial because the local civilians provided a much needed labor force the military couldn't muster and the fort enhanced the local economy with government creds and soldiers' pay. That practice was usually deemed a win-win scenario. But it also allowed a lot of areas for civilian and military personnel to get "creative."

Unless the solder was in a war zone. Then everything was kept more separate, more carefully monitored.

"The resistance is more disgruntlement than hostility." Terracina negotiated a pass around another newly arrived dropship. "We keep the fence up just to keep the honest people honest." He waved in the direction of the city. "At the other end of Makaum, the corps' spaceport sector does the same thing, but with better equipment and more men."

"Local looters?"

"Negligible. And we're safe from the corps vultures because they have better equipment than we do. We don't have anything they want." Terracina gave a sour smile, then wiped it from his face with a big hand. "Do I sound whiny?"

Sage grinned. "Maybe a little."

"It's deserved, trust me. I've thought about a cushy corp job running sec somewhere."

Most Terran soldiers had. The military had lost a lot of good soldiers to the corps.

"So what's holding you back?"

"I got kids." Terracina answered soberly. "When I get back to them, I want to be proud of what I do. Even if I don't beat the face off some poor guy just trying to lift enough cargo from a fat corp to make life a little safer or easier for his family, I want them to know I worked to make lives better. Not enhance some corp's bottom line."

"Yeah." Sage had turned down several corp headhunters over the course of his career. "The corps take many personnel from the fort?"

"Every now and again, if they run short of bodies. Hire our people with fat bonuses. Technically, those soldiers are AWOL, but we don't go after them. Not cost effective, with everything else we've got going on. And the last thing we need is to create a hostile force in our own brig. We've got enough enemies outside the walls." Terracina shook his head angrily. "You've seen our stats. The guys we get out here are bottom-of-the-barrel soldiers, or they've broken under fire on some other planet, or they're too green to know much more than which end of their weapon is dangerous. When you *don't* have manpower the corps want to steal, you know you're working in the sewer." He paused. "Sorry. Didn't mean to make this posting sound any harder than it is, but it's plenty brutal."

"I appreciate the honesty." Sage had already come to that conclusion. Whoever had put the intel package together had all but spelled out the lack of experienced soldiers with boots on the ground in Makaum.

Five vertical meters of fence separated the spaceport from the city on the other side. On the military side, the tarmac lay relatively level, marred by chips and stains, and jumpcopters, crawlers, powersuits, and drones, while ATV Razorback fighting transports occupied neat rows.

On the other side of the fence, Makaum lay disheveled. Even some of the cobblestone streets next to the spaceport had been buckled and broken by rampant undergrowth. Vines and roots twisted through the walls of stone buildings. Most of the nearby flora had curled up in brown and ash-gray death and near death. Evidently defoliant had been applied, or had drifted from the military area.

"You get out farther from the biz sector, you'll find people living in structures formed from trees and brush." Terracina shrugged. "The people who live and work there don't fight against encroaching growth. They just adapt to it."

"Learned to live with it?" Sage was fascinated, wondering what those buildings looked like. Intel had been sparse regarding the intermediary area between the fort and the Green Hell.

"More than that. Some of the Makaum people have a real knack for cultivating the growth. Can almost get it to grow—or not grow—any way they want to. They can make shelters, grow crops, transplant different branches to trees so they grow separate fruits. Several of the corps are exploring those abilities but they haven't discovered much yet. Some of them think it's some kind of psi talent that was either latent in the colony ship or a self-preservation mechanism that developed once the people were onplanet. That jungle also helps them hide from the larger predators out there, and there are plenty of those. You get out far enough from the sprawl, the natives are like ghosts—can't be seen or heard unless you're teched up." Terracina batted at a large, brightly colored bug that resembled a butterfly. It fluttered around his faceshield.

The insect was larger than both of Sage's hands together. Scarlet wings edged in yellow held violet spots in the upper centers. When the insect abandoned Terracina and came for him, Sage slapped it to one side and was surprised at how meaty and heavy the butterfly was. Astonished, Sage watched the insect flap away.

"Weird, huh?" Terracina smiled. "Get used to it. Makaum throws curveballs at you all day long when it comes to insects and lizards. Planet grows stuff that you wouldn't imagine ever seeing. Our imagination is limited compared to what comes out of the Green Hell. Just when you think you've seen it all, you see something new. Some of the corp biologists think that's because the planet is constantly mutating, creating new species, but always lizard or insect, no mammals or avians. One of them told me Makaum is in a state of 'creative flux,' whatever that means. Like the planet is fighting a battle against itself."

The butterfly disappeared behind the immense hulk of a battle tank. The four-man crew huddled around the armor was talking more than working. For every hour used in the field, heavy armor required three hours of maintenance. Sage made a mental note to have a word with the armored cav unit commander.

"You'd be surprised how many of those insects and lizards are edible, too." Terracina smiled. "That Crimson Granny—the thing that just passed us by—was named because of the color and of the curious way it hangs around. It's tasty if you roast it up."

"You've eaten them?"

Terracina grinned. "I have. When I had to."

During his tours on other worlds, Sage had eaten many vegetables and animals not native to Terra. There had been a lot of insects as well, toasted, roasted, and raw. He wasn't looking forward to eating anything Makaum had to offer, but it was good to know the possibilities existed.

"Wouldn't recommend the Grannies." Terracina grimaced. "Leaves you with the worst cottonmouth you've ever had."

"I'll keep that in mind."

FIVE

A-Pakeb Node
BioLab
Makaum
3817 Akej (Phrenorian Prime)

Clad in his battle armor now because he did not want his troops to realize he had undergone a recent moult, Zhoh walked through the bio lab. His disappearance from his tasks would also lead some to suspect that he had undergone *lannig*. Despite his fairness, there were some in his unit who wanted his rank, who chafed under his command. Officers only maintained their positions as long as they were physically capable. Phrenorians hated weakness and were genetically coded to kill individuals that were deemed too weak to live. The gene pool had constantly evolved, pushing the species toward perfection.

Zhoh pulled at his combat armor, a bare latticework that protected the softer abdomen, shifting it so it didn't wear against his developing exoskeleton. He was pleased with the work going on in the labs under his command.

He had been tasked with discovering as much as possible of the local flora and fauna.

Most of the genetic work continuing there was legal, made in accordance with the agreements with Makaum people, and he was in charge of it. Even if he didn't understand everything the scientists were doing, he knew it was profitable. The Phrenorian Empire ran on lifeblood and credits, which could be wielded as a weapon to buy loyalties and spies.

But the work in Lab 9 was off the books and aggressive. Technicians labored there to deliver the secrets of the planet to the Phrenorian Empire. And to come up with weapons to strike against the Makaum people and the creatures that shared the planet with them. The checkpoints the Terran military kept around the world prevented the Phrenorian Empire from bringing weapons of mass destruction onto Makaum, but no one could prevent the Phrenorian labs from constructing one if they found the proper resources.

Guards along the individual labs stood up smartly as Zhoh passed, and he took great satisfaction in that. He was an excellent leader; the troops under him knew that. He led them in battle and did not command them from the relative safety of battlescreens. He spilled blood with his troops, and together they dined on the bodies of those who had fallen before them, despite the Honor Pact that existed between the Phrenorians and their enemies.

War was not for the weak. Only lesser species tried to restrict it.

Zhoh peered in the tall windows of Lab 9. He knew the schedules of the people under his purview. Geneticist Nhez Chofisia would be on duty now. His chelicerae unfolded from his face and touched the thick acrylic observation window, feeling the tremor of movements vibrating through the surface. He closed his eyes and experienced the room on the other side of the acrylic through tactile sensation rather than sight, feeling his way through what he had seen. He could not place everything, but the vibrations touched him on a primeval level that he felt linked him with his ancestors.

The lab held a number of crates filled with captured insects of all sizes. The smallest were fruit flies and the largest were the saber spiders, easily the apex predator out in the jungle. The large cages containing the saber spiders were on the other side of the wide room. The massive arachnids, physiologically similar to the Phrenorians in many ways, battered the force walls again and again, causing small tremors to run through the lab.

Zhoh pulled back his chelicerae and opened his eyes.

Technicians labored at several of the tables. Most of the subjects were still alive at that moment, but others lay dissected in trays while nanobots plundered secrets from the corpses. Nanobots had been one of the best technologies the Phrenorians had gotten from contact with the Terrans. The species was quite inventive, spurred by that innate curiosity so many of them exhibited.

Getting the technology from the black market had been well worth encountering the Terrans. With help from the nanobots, the Phrenorians had been able to better understand their moulting process and manage a quicker turnaround to hardened exoskeletons. Their evolution continued at an accelerated rate. They became taller, heavier, more powerful, and their exoskeletons turned thicker and harder, making them more difficult to kill in combat. These were good things.

Besides the stolen science, there was the satisfaction of killing the Terrans in combat. Phrenorians tended to be territorial and combative. They had bred for those traits, and Zhoh was the culmination of those efforts. Even after the shame of his brood, several females hungered for his spermatophore to ensure a higher standing in the Phrenorian hierarchy.

Mating could be pleasurable, but Phrenorians were not as oblivious to the gene pool as the Terrans and other human cultures. Bloodstock on Phrenoria was important. Families rose and fell on who they had been and who they would be.

Zhoh's own family had lost some of their power because his mate had delivered ten ill-formed offspring that had all died soon after birth. He had mated up from his station, therefore the responsibility for the failed brood had fallen on him. His mate's father had bought off the geneticists and ensured their reports reflected the same finding.

If he had lived thousands of years ago, before the Empire had emerged to allow the Phrenorians access space, as their homeworld was drowning in overpopulation, Zhoh would have killed his mate for failing him, cracked open her exoskeleton, and eaten her, then excreted what remained into the nearest ceremonial dung pit.

Those times were not now, and Zhoh sometimes felt that the Phrenorians were less because of it. So he had borne the shame that was not his own, and his family was forced to bear it with him.

In addition to the public knowledge of his failed family, Zhoh had been reduced in rank and sent to Makaum with strict orders to make himself over into the warrior he was destined to be, to salvage himself from the ashes of his shame. He could be successful in his mission—or he could die.

Leaving the large observation window, Zhoh walked to the access door. The guard on duty instantly let him into the lab. Zhoh passed through the air barrier that ensured no flying or crawling insects made it out into the rest of the building.

Nhez Chofisia, the lead scientist in the department, stood hunkered over a scanning device. The medical tool had been another Terran invention that had been appropriated through the black market, then reverse engineered for use throughout the Phrenorian Empire.

Nhez was tall and lean but she barely came up to Zhoh's shoulder—he was larger than most Phrenorians, something he took pride in, and something that instantly marked him as a desirable mate. Her exoskeleton was primarily a dark blue with a hint of dark green threaded through it. Those colors made her a desirable mate for many because color was a valuable trait among Zhoh's people; she could hide and strike in the night and in the jungle.

She wore a dark green vest with a multitude of pockets containing various instruments and chemicals. Her primary hands hung at her sides and occasionally twitched, useless for fine motor skills necessary for the instruments she employed in her experiments. Her lesser hands managed the scanning device and the large insect that lay in the specimen tray.

A young male stopped on the other side of the table, opposite Nhez. He held several specimen trays in his hands. "Geneticist Nhez, you have a visitor."

Nhez looked up at the young man, who pointed his chelicerae at Zhoh. Turning, Nhez spotted Zhoh standing only a few feet away. Her chelicerae flickered, though whether in surprise or annoyance Zhoh did not know, then finally settled back into her face, closing off whatever emotion she might have been feeling.

"Captain Zhoh, you have come for a report?"

"No, I came merely to observe you working, Geneticist Nhez."

"Why?"

"You have skill, and watching you proceed so methodically allows me diversion to think my own thoughts." It was the truth. Zhoh had always appreciated a being that was so careful, so exacting in procedure. He had been that way since he'd been a youngling.

"Do you have time for such frivolity in your schedule? I would think someone as busy as you would not have a spare moment."

"Knowledge is a weapon on this world. The more I can learn of my enemy and of the environment, the more familiarity I will have with Makaum." Zhoh knew that was true, and he had reminded himself of it daily. The Terrans claimed to be here to protect the Makaum people, but Zhoh knew they wanted the world's resources as much as the Phrenorian Empire did. The Phrenorian primes, the heads of state, had made clear their intentions for such things. "I want to make certain my weapon is as sharp as I can make it."

Nhez's chelicerae flickered again, more calmly this time. A faint scent of pheromones filled the air around her, further indicating her pleasure at such a response. "It is good that you seek to extend yourself and your understanding, Captain."

"Don't let me interrupt you. Carry on with your labors."

For a moment, Nhez regarded him closely. "You are bigger than you were."

"Talk carefully." Zhoh put an edge on his words and resisted the immediate impulse to strike her for speaking so directly. He passed pheromones that gave a warning to all around him. "The life you save may be your own."

Her chelicerae quivered in distress this time, and the pheromones surrounding her gave that off. "Of course. I am tired. I did not think." That was not all of it. Part of her observation had been the result of her own DNA. The geneticists were bred for their curiosity and eye for detail. She trembled slightly, and Zhoh knew that an observer might well notice that response and take note.

Stepping close to her, Zhoh seized her by one arm and leaned in close enough that their faces almost touched. His chelicerae whipped out and snatched hers, then his pedipalps, his smaller mandibles, seized hers as well. He injected just enough venom into her to dull her distress and panic, infecting her with a small euphoria of intoxication. Her eyes dilated slightly. Her distress pheromones thinned and her trembling ceased.

Confident that he had succeeded in calming her, Zhoh drew back. She would have been receptive to him then. Her pheromones indicated her sexual interest, though he had none of his own. He would mate only to further his family's holdings, and then only with someone he knew he could trust and depend on. He had learned that lesson and would not ever forget.

"I am sorry." She looked up at him, obviously sensing his lack of pheromone response.

"I want the reports on the new narcotic." Zhoh had been amazed to learn how much stock the Terrans and the Makaum people had put into drugs that diminished them on so many levels. The Phrenorian people had their own problems with members who became addicted to pheromone stimulation. When discovered, those members were always immediately put to death. Phrenoria brooked no weakness, no strain that could be carried down through families and generations and dilute the warrior spirit.

She talked then, and he listened to the toxicology of the hooded toad, thinking that he would soon have another means to earn credits while on Makaum that would help him influence political events on the planet.

She took him to a cage where a dozen hooded toads sat confined. They were as large as one of his primary hands. As they sat in the relative cool dampness provided by the cage, the toads' camouflage abilities turned their wart-covered skins a multitude of subtle colors, running from violet to red. Folds of skin covered their wide heads, cowls that masked the toads' more vulnerable eyes.

When attacked, the hooded toad, called the *crazathi* by the Makaum natives, concealed its head and secreted fast-acting poison from every pore of its skin. The poison killed even the *khrelav*, the large flying lizards that sailed through Makaum's skies and tree canopies and were large enough to take down jumpcopters.

"We have come far in our research," Nhez said. "We have succeeded in creating doses of the *crazathi* venom that will cause euphoric reactions in the Makaum natives as well as the Terrans." She must have sensed Zhoh's frustration in his scent. "This is a great success, Captain, I assure you. The *crazathi* venom is extremely potent. Getting it diluted to this level has been exceedingly difficult."

Zhoh curbed his irritation. "I understand. The Terran corps and the indigenous population have not been able to do this?"

"No." Nhez leaned forward and her chelicerae unfurled, delicately stroking the acrylic barrier that kept the *crazathi* imprisoned. "The poison's potency has desirable attributes for the Terrans and those species like them. In addition to that, since the resulting drug is nearly all bio materials, like the mushrooms that have been found on this planet, it will take time for enforcement agencies to learn a way to track shipments."

"The venom extract will be discovered." That always happened.

"Yes, but that will take time. We will be able to offload large shipments, relatively speaking, since not much of the venom is necessary to induce the desired euphoria. It is highly hallucinogenic. One of the potential distributors,

a Piradian named Aniyol that I believe you have an ac-
quaintanceship with, tells me that test subjects are often
convinced that they can see the future while under the
venom's influence."

Aniyol was a disgusting creature, as all Piradians were.
Squat and fat, covered in tough leathery skin, and possess-
ing long faces that all too often looked alike, members of
the Piradian race were only a step up from the *krayari*.
Like the carrion beetles, the Piradians slid through the
Gates feeding on the offal of other, stronger species. They
were mostly criminals and beggars, slave laborers on several planets.

"Can they see the future?"

Nhez pulled back from the cage and looked at Zhoh. "If
so, they would have foreseen their own deaths, wouldn't
they?" Her chelicerae curled in to her face. "No, they do
not see the future. Instead they ask for more of the drug.
Addicts are foolish and weak."

That was one of the reasons the Terran military tried
to control the drug cartels on Makaum. Species that were
not biologically designed for the continued struggle that
true evolution required grew weary and afraid of war.
Their soldiers gave in to substance abuse. The *crazathi*
venom would only be one more weapon in the Phrenorian
arsenal.

Two of the toads launched spiked black tongues at
Nhez's face but the acrylic barrier stopped them, deflect-
ing the long organs. The barbs insured that if the tongues
penetrated flesh, they would not easily be removed. They
could strike over a three-meter distance, uncoiling from
the toad's squat body. The tongue attack was a last-ditch
offense and often resulted in the toad's own demise, but
not before it pumped venom into its aggressor. The hardwired response was something Zhoh appreciated.

"You have done well, Geneticist Nhez. Send me a full

report and I will forward it to the primes so that you may be recognized for your work."

Her chelicerae pulled in more tightly to her face in an effort not to quiver in excitement and her pheromones filled the air again, eliciting a small feeling of arousal in Zhoh that he quickly quashed. "Thank you, Captain."

MIND OCCUPIED WITH plans, Zhoh was not aware of the attack until it was in full motion. He was almost to his quarters when Lieutenant Yuburak stepped from the doorway on the other side of the hall with his *patimong* naked in his right primary. The honor blade was made from thickened orange-red resin drained from *daravgane*, the sacred primordial predators on Phrenoria. A full meter in length, the *patimong* remained flexible and had nano-thin edges that could cut through nearly everything.

Zhoh dodged back, barely able to avoid the lethal blade. The point still scored the right side of his face, almost severing one of his chelicerae. Stepping back in the wide hallway, Zhoh set himself and swept up his *arhwat*, the electromagnetically enhanced buckler that was also part of the Phrenorian traditional weapons arsenal. He flicked the power on with a lesser hand, feeling the electromagnetic charge dance through the buckler and his primary.

Yuburak's second attack beat down on the *arhwat*. The resulting dissonance buzzed in the hallway.

Three sec guards sprinted down the hallway and drew their laser pistols.

Yuburak crouched and held the *patimong* over his head, displaying the blade for all to see. "I claim *Hutamah*! It is my right!"

The guards instantly stood down, holstering their weapons. The sergeant, Chantaf, a female that had impressed Zhoh with her diligence and skill after he had arrived onplanet, nodded. "You have the right to challenge, Yuburak, and I think you are a fool to do so."

"For that outrage, Sergeant, I will demand your death after I have dealt with Zhoh." Yuburak moved languidly, his chelicerae twitching and twisting as he tasted the vibrations in the air. He was not as big as Zhoh, but he was younger, perhaps faster. His exoskeleton was mostly a lackluster brown and purple, colors that had forever doomed him to a lesser rank within the Phrenorian Empire. Only proving himself on a battlefield could improve his standing, and being stationed on Makaum wasn't going to permit that.

Zhoh drew his own *patimong* and stood ready. Still, the commander in him was loath to lose a soldier. "It is not too late for you to walk away, Lieutenant."

"Do you fear me then, Zhoh?" Yuburak's chelicerae quivered in anticipation.

The reaction caused Zhoh to more thoroughly taste the lieutenant's pheromones. Although Yuburak would deny it, he tasted of fear—and something else. For a moment Zhoh was lost in the mystery standing before him, lost in seeking knowledge. Then he recognized the trace of the alien scent that clung to Yuburak.

"You have lain with a Terran female." Disgust filled Zhoh at the realization.

Although the two species did not share sexual congress, there were Terrans and Makaum natives and other species that viewed Phrenorian venom as a drug. When it didn't kill them. The Phrenorian chemistry likewise reacted to other species' secretions. Simply licking sweat from the alien bodies could bring on bliss. Such a thing was dangerous, though, because a Phrenorian locked in bliss often could not defend himself or herself.

Growling incoherently, Yuburak threw himself into

the attack. Zhoh blocked the lieutenant's sword with his buckler, feinted with his own sword, then turned it to intercept Yuburak's whipping tail, batting that attack aside as well. Still in motion, Zhoh curled his own tail around the lieutenant's *patimong*-wielding primary and pulled it away, then he smashed the edge of the *arhwat* into Yuburak's face, slicing off three of the chelicerae.

Yuburak howled in rage. Facial disfigurement was an insult to a Phrenorian. To do so, even accidentally, was to invite lethal retribution. He wiped at his face with one of his lesser hands, smearing the black viscous blood that dripped from the wounds.

"I would have given you a quick death, Zhoh, though Sxia did not wish that, but now I will torture you before I end your life. You will beg me for mercy."

The name of his mate on Yuburak's lips surprised Zhoh. He shut down the response before all the pain and anger flooded through him. He offered no return words. His sword and his skill would speak for him.

Hand-to-hand combat was a potentially dangerous thing. If a warrior was not in complete control of the engagement, any outcome was possible. Ending a fight quickly was preferable to a sustained encounter.

Yuburak tried more finesse this time, but Zhoh battered his opponent's attacks aside, blocking the *patimong* with his *arhwat*, allowing the lieutenant to knock his tail aside with his own *patimong*. As they closed, Zhoh dropped his *patimong* and grasped Yuburak's tail, set himself, then yanked the lieutenant into his chest.

Instantly, Zhoh shoved his face into Yuburak's, then uncoiled his pedipalps and chelicerae and clamped onto the lieutenant's face. Triggering his injectors, Zhoh spewed venom into Yuburak, stopping just short of killing him, but not before Yuburak raked a knife across the left side of Zhoh's face.

Paralyzed by the venom racing through his body, Yuburak collapsed to the floor.

Zhoh stood over his vanquished foe and felt the precious blood weeping down the side of his face. "How do you know Sxia?"

Yuburak panted as his body failed him, leaving him more dead than alive. "You are no longer favored by the primes, Captain Zhoh. You have enemies here."

That surprised Zhoh. Personal vendettas were not allowed within the Phrenorian Empire by the will of the primes. Any personal problems were immediately dealt with or dropped so the Empire could continue moving forward.

Zhoh drove his *patimong* into Yuburak's thorax, deliberately missing both of the warrior's lungs. Sitting next to Yuburak, Zhoh cracked open the lieutenant's exoskeleton to reveal the pinkish gray flesh within. He scooped out a handful, watching as Yuburak's eyes widened in terror and pain. The venom paralyzed him, but it did not dull his pain receptors.

"I'm going to eat my fill of you, Yuburak," Zhoh said, "then I'm going to give what's left of you to the *krayari* that live in my quarters. When the time comes and you leave me, I will excrete you onto a dung hill and there you will remain till you dry out and blow away." He pushed the lieutenant's flesh into his maw, feeling the blood run down his face.

SIX

Mostly what you're going to have at Fort York is soft service. You watch, you keep the peace when it comes to military ops—and that's mainly hardcases out in the Green Hell that don't let a body count stand in the way of profits from looting and illegal drugs—and you drill." Terracina sipped from the longnecked bottle he held.

Sage held a bottle as well. They didn't come out of a manufacturing plant. Uneven brown glass marred by imperfections, slightly bulbous, the bottle had been hand-blown in a local business. He liked the weight of the bottle in his hand because it felt more solid than those in the space station, and more welcoming than the bulbs soldiers drank out of in the field.

The local brew wasn't beer. It was some kind of fermented fruit or nut, maybe a blend of both, but it was just as heady as he remembered from the night before. His senses were already buzzing and the edginess he'd had since planetfall was a step back.

He and Terracina sat at a table outside a small café in the heart of Makaum's downtown sector. Three- and four-story buildings filled the narrow streets, and all of the structures had plants and roots knotted through their walls that provided part of the infrastructure.

The Makaum people traveled on foot, on bicycles that were obviously corp trade, and on *dafeerorg,* domesticated lizards the size of Bengal tigers. Serrated teeth filled the long mouths. Occasionally motorized vehicles shot by the locals, and most of those were driven by corps sec teams or by natives hired by offworlders to pilot groundcraft for them. Only a few of the vehicles belonged to Terran military.

Mosquito netting hung over the outdoor area of the café and a veritable cloud of insects that Sage didn't recognize clung to the mesh. Clicks, whistles, scratching, and humming filled the air despite the white noise generator that Terracina set on the table, but the cacophony was diminished. Small winged lizards half the size of a human flitted through the space above the netting and dined on insects as large as Sage's fist.

"Want my advice?" Terracina lifted an eyebrow.

"Sure." Sage shifted his gaze from one of the domesticated lizards ridden by a young woman, who looked away when she realized she'd been caught staring at the diner. Like most of the populace he had seen, the Makaum woman possessed green-hued skin with shifting tints.

According to the military's reports, the Makaum people had developed some chameleon-like abilities. Some of them, it was said, could disappear in the jungle without making a move, just fade right into the background. Mostly, they were human-looking, but they maintained a distance when it came to offworlders.

"First thing you do, you go to provisions and get you a white noise generator." Terracina tapped the squat, fist-sized cube sitting on the table. "These babies have been spec'd out to manage ambient noise on industrial worlds like Dithor 9 where iron mining goes on around the clock. They provide peace and quiet there, but the best you can hope for on Makaum is to deaden the constant noise of the insects."

"I'll do that." Sage had already grown tired of the incessant barrage of noise. He'd been to Dithor 9, protecting the mining site from the Phrenorians. In addition to all the constant noise, the mining site had been in one of the continual sunlight regions. Darkness and silence had come at a premium.

The café was near the fort, so it was primarily frequented by soldiers and civilian support staff, as well as the port personnel. The young soldiers swapped games, media packs, and lies as they sat at the tables. They acted like they were back in primary education, and the fraternization between the male and female soldiers was obvious.

Other patrons kept themselves apart from the soldiers, but they watched them with curiosity and caution. Many of the nonmilitary personnel wore Terran clothing, but others were dressed in shirts and pants made with lightweight material, corp grunts who handled the daily work of keeping the business flowing. Only a handful of Makaum people sat inside the café, and they kept their own counsel. Sage got the feeling the Makaum people were there primarily to watch the offworlders.

"Something else you want to get for your down time is local clothing." Terracina tilted his bottle at Sage's armor. "Even ACUs will get hot. Locals make their outfits out of spider silk and plant fiber and don't bother being too creative with it. They got tailors here that will make your clothing custom fit for next to nothing. Not as durable as offworld stuff from the corps, but it's cheap." He smiled. "You can do your bit to help stimulate the local economy and keep the profits from the corps."

Sweltering inside his armor, Sage took in the fit of the native clothing and how the shirts and pants hung easily. Most of what he saw was gray or brown, but here and there bright colors stood out, though those were primarily offworld clothing.

"They choose the muted colors on purpose." Terracina grinned. "Allows them to step into the shadows easier out in the jungle or in the dark alleys here in Makaum. A lot of the lizards and the big spiders can see color. That ability makes the Makaum critters hunt the Phrenorians because some of the Sting-Tails tend to stand out in this environment with their bright colors. Those exoskeletons come in a lot of different reds and yellows, as well as blues and greens that are a lot safer. Black and brown tend to blend right in, but the Empire doesn't much care for those colors."

Curious but trying to remain polite, Sage studied the Makaum people at the scattered tables around him. As a general rule, the indigenous population kept to themselves, but they kept eyeing the soldiers and offworlders around them. Most of them were male, but there were a few females. All of them were tentative and watchful.

Terracina continued telling stories. He was good at it, and he had a lot of them to tell since all he had on his mind was waiting out his return home. That kind of energy expended while waiting made a soldier talkative. Suddenly that other world, the *real* world, was coming back into focus. A lot of soldiers had trouble getting back to normal even though they believed that was what they truly wanted.

A lot of them didn't make that transition.

As Sage listened, he separated the knowledge from the color and kept what taught him about the planet, the fort, and the people he was going to be around. While he listened, he ate, not really paying attention to the food. Terracina had ordered the meal. Sage didn't really care what he ate. It was all fuel to keep him going. Some fuels were better-tasting than others, and he did have his favorites, but those weren't necessary.

He also watched the young soldiers in the café, silently irritated at the way they had their guards down. They were there for socializing, for entertainment, for a chance to get away from the fort. They had stepped away from being soldiers. On one hand, Sage didn't fault them, but on the other they needed to remember they were in hostile territory. An unwary soldier was a near-dead soldier just waiting for the bullet, beam, or bomb that would make that final change.

"This is part of the DMZ." Terracina pointed with his fork. "You go farther north, you hit the region claimed by the Phrenorian and (ta)Klar embassies. They each cut themselves out a nice-sized piece of real estate, but I can't blame them. We dropped a fort into place on our end of town."

"The Phrenorians aren't fortified here?"

Terracina shook his head and took a sip from the long-necked bottle. "No."

"You're sure?"

A look of irritation showed on Terracina's face. "We check the jungle regularly. The Phrenorians have their embassy and a few outlying areas according to the agreement with the Makaum government. They can't establish any kind of fortification—outside of the embassy. Not permitted under the treaty we and the Makaum have with them. The Phrenorians get to negotiate trade, which at the moment leaves them primarily in the red. They want the resources Makaum has to offer, but they don't have much the Makaum people want in return." He shrugged. "That's pretty much true with the Terran corps too, but they're happy passing the cost of doing business on to the consumers at the other end."

"I don't like the idea that the Phrenorians are getting supplies here, under our noses, to use in the war."

"The treaty shortlists Phrenorian trade same as it does us. They're limited to air, water, and food. No mineral resources to make weapons or armor, no pharmaceuticals other than what the Makaum people want to let go of."

"We can control that?"

"With the help of the corps, yeah. Between the military and corp assets, we can monitor most of what the Sting-Tails do. Maybe."

"Maybe?"

"You've been in situations like this. It's hard to manage everything unless you control it all. Bottom line? We don't."

"It would be easier if we kept the Phrenorians offplanet."

"You've got my vote, but the Makaum people don't want to take a stand like that. They're not sure whether they should fear the Terrans or the Phrenorians more."

"So they allow both of us here."

"Yeah. Kind of managing an uneasy balance, I think. And the (ta)Klar." Terracina frowned. "Now there's a shifty bunch I don't care to trust. The (ta)Klar are only about doing good for themselves. No one and nothing else hits their balance sheets."

Over the years, Sage had few dealings with the (ta)Klar. That species tended to stay away from active battlefronts and negotiate their business behind bunkers. Better yet, from orbiting spaceships. The only ones Sage had seen all fit the general physiques: bodies small enough to be Terran children, skin as blue as mold and covered in the same kind of short, wispy fuzz that sprouted on cheese, and wearing clear bowls over their heads because they tended to be an aquatic species. Portable rebreathers kept the liquid oxygenated.

"What do the (ta)Klar get?"

"Trade. Same as the Phrenorians. Terra and (ta)Klar haven't gone head to head so far, but they've given hard stares at each other over the same cesspools." Terracina grinned. "I guess you already knew that. You've been at some of those cesspools."

"Yeah." Sage didn't care for the (ta)Klar. He'd never met a more self-serving and secretive race in his life. At least the Phrenorians were up front about their hostility. The (ta)Klar liked the passive-aggressive game and tended to cause hardships wherever they went.

If it hadn't been for the way the (ta)Klar had factionalized Nogdria 7, that planet would have had a chance of surviving against the Sting-Tails. As it was, the world had been decimated and left in ruins six years ago, when a Phrenorian phalanx arrived.

That had been the last active duty Sage had seen. Medics had scraped up what had been left of him, gotten him offplanet, and rebuilt him. He'd been offered a medical discharge, but he'd grimly suffered through the DNA rebuild and stood on his own two legs—more or less—at the end of three months. He'd come back in good shape, better than the doctors had thought he would.

"So far," Terracina said, "the Phrenorians have played by the rules. Generally."

"It's hard to enforce a treaty with somebody you're at war with."

Terracina grinned. "Gets easier when you have a fort to negotiate with. Terran ambassadors negotiated that before the (ta)Klar got involved. It's made all the difference."

Sage sliced into some kind of tuber, forked it into

his mouth, chewed, and then swallowed. The taste was starchy and sweet.

"For now," Terracina went on, "the treaty stands. Phrenorian soldiers and Terran soldiers can go to the same bars and restaurants, the same bordellos—in staggered shifts so they're not there together, but they can't invade the other's territory."

Sage cocked an eyebrow at that. "Bordellos?" Places where a soldier could get a sex partner for a price carried even more potential problems than a business that sold hooch. Soldiers would fight over sex partners. Phrenorian biology was different from Terran biology. Despite the general human build, the Sting-Tails fit the arthropod makeup more than mammalian.

"Sex doesn't work between Phrenorians and humans," Sage said.

"I didn't think so either. But Makaum is as close as we've gotten to the Sting-Tails in a relaxed environment. What we've discovered is that the Phrenorian males do have a taste for human sex pheromones."

Sage digested that, thinking it wasn't the strangest thing he'd ever heard, but it was unexpected. "How many bordellos?"

"Three places."

"Locals do the work?" Sage had to ask because a fight over a local girl would extend past the two military powers involved. Getting the locals riled up when a prostitute's blood was inadvertently spilled made things more difficult. The balances were hard to keep in a DMZ.

"No local guys or girls. Weird thing. The Makaum women will sometimes fraternize with us, and I've even heard a few of the soldiers have gotten into intimate relationships with the male Makaum, but none of the locals work the cathouses. Everybody in the bordellos was brought in by the corps." Terracina grimaced. "*Entertain-*

ment ventures, they call them. At least the *entertainment* is professional. That helps some. Those guys and girls will kill a client that gets out of line without hesitation. They laid down that message when they first arrived. Two corps bashhounds who thought they would take liberties ended up laid out in front of Ruby Lights. In pieces. No one knows if the sec people at the bordello did the chopping or if the prostitutes did it. But the message was clear."

"Yeah. It would be." Sage sipped his brew. "Is the community against citizens working in the bordellos?"

For a moment, Terracina paused, then shook his head. "I think it's just that the Makaum in general have a higher sense of self than that. Kind of sounds lame to say that out loud, but that's what I think. The Makaum put up with us, and they like some of the toys we bring along, maybe some of the otherworldliness, but they don't want to be used by us. If they could have put up a wall and kept everyone out, I think they would have. As it is, I think they're resigned to just trying to make the best of a bad situation, now that we've found them."

That was interesting. None of the places Sage had been had taken the moral high ground and held it. Military occupation was too pervasive, and there were too many things offworlders could bring to planets that didn't have space travel. He took another bite of tuber and the spices it had been cooked in exploded inside his mouth. For a moment it felt like his mouth had been firebombed. He took a sip of his drink to quench the flames.

"What about the (ta)Klar?"

Terracina shook his head. "As usual, they keep to themselves. They work with the council, but they don't . . . *partake* of the available entertainment."

Sage chewed and thought about that, building a mental construct of how things worked in the streets. Demilitarized zones were pretty much the same everywhere. Soldiers didn't kill each other when they were in town only because they didn't want their privileges restricted. They grudgingly traded tolerance for the illusion of freedom and safety. Civilizations did that on a planetary scale as well.

The Phrenorians had amped-up passions and the sense of unease in the area. They were death out in the field and aggressive once they'd decided to establish themselves or take a planet.

The (ta)Klar, on the other hand, seemed to live only to do business. All of their social conventions were directed toward that end. They didn't interface with others unless there was a deal to be made. Romantic relationships were part of the deal, so no (ta)Klar man or woman was going to marry down. Or *fraternize*. They gave themselves only when benefits could be worked out.

"The fact that they're choosing to keep a low profile doesn't make the (ta)Klar any less able to defend their embassy, though. We and the Phrenorians know that."

Sage nodded, taking it all in. "You've been working teams in the brush?"

"Yeah. Based on intel we get from the local hunters and trappers, and there's precious little of that, we've gone out and taken down some drug labs and fields. Enough to keep us busy, but not enough to keep us sharp."

"Resistance?"

"Limited for the most part, but I think that's changing, becoming more aggressive. The drug traffickers we've taken down lately have had increasingly heavier firepower."

"Somebody's investing."

"The corps claim their field-study groups have 'lost security equipment' while exploring." Terracina cursed. "Nobody believes that."

"But it's hard to disprove."

"Yeah."

"Who do they say is taking the equipment?"

"Deserters from the civilian population. People the corps have brought in." Terracina cursed again. "You think they'd screen their people better."

"They probably do. These 'deserters' were probably chosen just for the purpose they're serving."

"They are. There are chem cookers working out in the jungles, brewing up mindblowers for the civilians, guys in our unit who use—though we weed them out when we find them—and Makaum people who decide to be more experimental in their recreation."

"Business is good for those folks, I take it."

Terracina nodded and smiled unhappily. "All these bio-pirates here ripping off plants and local medicine savvy, you'd think they wouldn't have enough time to start up a homegrown drug franchise."

"Maximizing profit potential through an available on-site revenue stream." Sage had seen that happen before on other worlds.

"The corps probably look at it that way. The thing is, busting the drug suppliers isn't the greatest danger."

"Then what?"

"The contraband seeds and plants they bring in to do their business present a lot more problems and potential for disaster. We spend more time doing slash and burns around a drug camp than we do putting the operators down. Some offworld plant gets loose in the environment without a natural predator in play, it can take over and destroy some of the food chain. We've already had to go after some environmental disasters. Here and there, you can find burnouts we've staged where nothing grows. And nothing probably will for years."

"The corps don't care?"

Terracina shook his head. "They're here to make money,

steal what they can't buy, and leave as soon as they're done. They don't have a long-range plan. Sooner or later, all good things come to an end. You follow a corp's back trail, you can find a lot of planets that have been cherry-picked. Most of them never recover, and when they do, the corps come back in to suck it all dry again."

A trio of bashhounds entered the café. They strode confidently into the room and talked in loud voices as they took a table off to the side. One of them saw Sage, and Sage thought he recognized the guy from the previous night.

Throwing Sage a mocking smile, the bashhound made a gun with his forefinger and mimed shooting, then blowing smoke off the barrel.

Terracina nodded toward the bashhounds. "Looks like you've already got a fan club."

Sage didn't reply.

"You know any of these guys?" Terracina nodded at the soldiers sitting at the surrounding tables. The tension in the air had shot up by degrees.

Sage didn't bother looking around. He didn't know anyone on Makaum. Most of the soldiers he'd gotten to know during the last training session were on the front lines. Where he should have been. "No."

"Then I'd suggest getting to know a couple of them. Somebody that will have your back when you're in the DMZ. A guy who drinks alone out here and has enemies? They usually turn him to mulch for one of the Makaum gardens."

"I'll keep that in mind."

AFTER THE MEAL, which Terracina paid for, they returned to the crawler. The bashhounds watched them leave the café, but nobody said anything. They studied Sage, though.

The city looked different in the moonlight, darker and layered in shadows. The air hummed with the sound of insect wings. Darting bodies, some of them longer than Sage's arm, flew through the streets.

"Welcome to the nightlife." Terracina chuckled. "If you think there's a lot of bugs in the daylight, it gets worse at night. Those things big as your arm? They're *elhtho*. That's Makaum terminology, though. The grunts were already calling them hellbeetles when I got here. Don't know who came up with the name, but it fits. They're carrion feeders for the most part, vegetable and animal, but they'll take a bite off someone living if they get hungry and get the chance."

One of the hellbeetles hovered less than a meter away, turning its ugly face on Sage and Terracina. The thing's proboscis was at least twenty centimeters long and looked as sharp as a knife. Its wings drummed the air so fast they were invisible and the humming was so loud it felt like a physical blow.

"Those things are dangerous. Most things on Makaum are. A hellbeetle's proboscis can penetrate body armor. Not very far, but far enough. You go down, get enough of them on you, your life expectancy drops to minutes as you bleed out. You don't have battle armor on, you can cut that time down to less than a minute." Terracina whipped out the fighting baton at his hip, telescoped it with a flip of his wrist, and crushed the hellbeetle's head into mush.

The dead creature dropped to the ground.

Terracina kept the baton in his hand, then took a button-sized device from his vest pouch. "Need to give you this. Clip it to your shirt collar when you're out of your armor."

Sage took the small device and slipped it into his chest pouch. "What is it?"

"Ultrasonic generator. We call them whistlers. The bugs don't like the frequencies." Terracina led the way to the crawler. "One button is good for twelve hours. There's a bin back at the post where you can toss it so it can be charged again. You wear them during the day, they power up from solar energy or from your armor."

"Also marks you for anybody who knows to look for the ultrasonic frequencies. Even with a rolling frequency, a tech-savvy opponent can track it."

Terracina nodded and hauled himself up behind the steering wheel. The vehicle started with a rumble. "When you're out in the field on a cover op, you don't wear them. But you'll wish you could."

Loud voices across the narrow street drew Sage's attention. A lot of what was said was in the Makaum language he'd learned from datachips while Gating to the planet, but there were English and Spanish words in there as well. He took a fresh grip on his gauss rifle.

Terracina gripped his rifle and cut the crawler's engine. He automatically pulled out his helmet and put it on. Sage already had his helmet tabbed into place and the night-vision program was queued up. Transparent numbers floated into his view, marking off the street and the distance to the buildings, defining the potential battle zone.

"Peacekeeping." Terracina took the lead, holding his gauss rifle canted before him at the ready. The maneuver was second nature to him, everything properly in place. "Just another one of the services we provide. You have to watch out, though. A lot of the locals don't like it when we get involved."

SEVEN

Sage followed on Terracina's six, far enough back to have a good field of fire around the other man. Terracina headed through a short alley between buildings that looked like they were on the verge of falling over. Roots, resembling fibroid veins, crisscrossed the walls of the structures, curling out of the native rock and mortar, then tunneling back in. More of them laced the ground in confusing tangles.

Evidently the defoliants couldn't keep Makaum's vigorous plant life from growing into the walls of buildings. The mortar of the structures lay in the alley and didn't look more than a few years old. Maintenance on the planet had to be cost prohibitive. Upkeep would have meant tearing the buildings down and starting over. That explained why there was so much urban decay. It was easier and cheaper to erect new buildings on top of newly defoliated areas than to tear down older structures and start over.

Terracina paused at the other end of the alley. Sage automatically fell into place on the opposite side of the alley with his rifle tilted down across his body in the half ready position.

"Bashhounds." Terracina cursed under his breath, but the helmet mic transmitted his words.

Fifteen meters away, on the other side of the street, ten Terran soldiers stood confronting four corps secmen. On the surface, the situation seemed to favor the soldiers, but Sage knew the cyberware the bashhounds carried counted in a big way.

A dozen or so Makaum people shifted in the shadows of the buildings. None of them appeared armed, the onboard suit security didn't identify any weapons, but that didn't mean they weren't carrying. It didn't have to be high-tech. Sharp and pointy could kill a soldier just as dead.

On Sage's faceshield, the ranks and identification of the ten soldiers floated up in transparent script. The fort's database had been downloaded to his system on the dropship trip.

The squad of Terran soldiers was assigned to Sergeant Greg Wireman. According to the field service record Sage glanced through, Wireman was young and somewhat inexperienced, only three months on the ground locally, and without true combat experience. His promotions had come through attrition while at a training fort.

"Sergeant Wireman, what's your sit-rep?" Terracina asked.

Wireman's head swung slightly so his field of vision picked up Terracina. "Top, we've got smugglers. These guys are unloading contraband to the locals."

One of the bashhounds turned to Terracina and held

up a hand. Sage's friend/foe programming kicked in and swept the ecard in the bashhound's hand. The digital information contained on the ecard funneled into Sage's faceshield.

"Security exec Bao Fong of Green Dragon Industrial Trade." Fong was in his middle years, average sized, with short-cropped black hair and a goatee. Not much more information was provided. He'd been with Green Dragon for nine years. At least, that what was digitized onto the ecard.

Fong's heart rate was 47 percent lower than average, and Sage surmised the man's cyberware probably included replacements for his arms and legs. The reduced circulation paths increased the heart's efficiency. Or maybe the heart itself had been replaced or augmented. Either way, the man—and his associates—were loaded with potentially deadly surprises.

Fong glared at Terracina. "Who's in charge here?"

"Top?" Wireman stayed locked on his weapon, aiming dead center at the bashhound's chest.

"Where's the contraband?" Terracina stayed where he was.

"Guy's still got it."

"What is it?"

"Drugs of some sort. Maybe some hardware. We didn't get a good look."

Fong shook his head. "Incorrect. You misinterpreted what you saw. I'm telling you for the last time to disengage."

"What about the rest of you people?" Terracina addressed the Makaum onlookers in their language. "What did you see?"

A few of the onlookers at the back of the crowd chose that moment to wander away.

One of the young men in front crossed his arms and shook his head. He wore dark, lightweight clothing that bagged around his body. Milspec boots gleamed dully and were worn down enough Sage suspected they were junked gear. "We didn't see anything, Terran. You people need to take your argument somewhere else."

"You think so?" Terracina spoke calmly. "Maybe we should collect you, take you in to see the council reps, see what they think about you being here with these people. If I run your identification, what am I going to find?"

The young man snarled a curse. "You offworlders weren't invited here. You've got no right to tell us what to do. And your identification does not define who I am."

"I've got treaty rights. I'm here as a peacekeeper. Your council doesn't want your people to have access to off-world drugs."

One of the soldiers in the back of the squad spoke up. "I recognize this guy, Top. His names's Krol. Brought him in twice myself for distribution. He works as a spotter for drug labs out in the Green Hell."

"Let's bring him in too, then."

Two of the soldiers stepped forward. One of them held a pair of plastic cuffs. "Get over here, Krol."

The young man lifted a small burner from the loose folds of his shirt. He brought the weapon up like he knew what he was doing, extending his arm as he took aim at the young Terran soldier.

Sage fired and a blue bolt twinkled from the gauss rifle's muzzle. The piezo-electric shockround smashed into Krol and blew him backward, wrapping his body in crackling blue lightning for a moment. The stench of ozone filled the street. Keeping the rifle ready, Sage watched the crowd and the downed man. The rifle had been set to stun. The Roley could fire the shockrounds or steel ball bearings.

The electromagnetic charge had lifted the young Makaum from his feet and short-circuited his nervous system. When he recovered, in an hour or two, he'd have a headache and be relatively unharmed.

Unless the charge stopped his heart. That was always a possibility. But Sage's suit sensors confirmed that the man's heart was beating and respiration was taking place.

The crowd reacted at once, becoming more threatening but at the same time frightened.

"The boy's alive," Sage said over the suit comm. "I didn't shoot to kill."

"Put your weapons down," Terracina ordered over his suit's loudhailer. His amplified voice ricocheted from the buildings along the street, sounding alien and cold. "He is not dead, just stunned. Put down your weapons before someone does get hurt. We will not allow the distribution of contraband."

For one frozen moment, Sage felt the violence hanging over the scene. Things were about to defuse or blow up in the blink of an eye. He felt certain the bashhounds would make the first move.

Instead, the four bashhounds seemed to come apart, blood spurting, and the explosive detonation of automatic weapons filled Sage's hearing, instantly blunted by his helmet's suppressors.

Bao Fong yanked a laser pistol from his hip with the arm that remained to him, but he couldn't stand on the shredded metal that heavy-caliber bullets had reduced his cyberlegs to. Still, even on the ground, he struggled to raise his weapon and take aim. A single shot cored between his eyes and evacuated his brain in a rush. The bashhound lay back, permanently offline.

Swinging the gauss rifle around, Sage located the shooters. He was already barking orders to the soldiers. "Get out of there! Get to cover! Get those civilians clear!"

The men should have already been in motion, but it didn't take them long to get moving. They flooded into the alley on the other side of the street. The few Makaum people still standing there got swept along by the first two soldiers, who waded into their midst with their arms spread wide.

"This is the Terran military! Put your weapons down!" Sage peered over his rifle at the seven figures spread out on both sides of the street a block away. The nightvision programming lifted the shadows from Sage's vision.

They were Phrenorian. The curling tails that moved restlessly behind them were a dead giveaway. They stood, on average, a head taller than the Terran soldiers. Their blue and purple exoskeletons offered a lot in the way of natural protection, but they'd reinforced that with segmented body armor that glinted dully in the moonslight. Instead of rounded helmets like the ones worn by the Terrans, the Phrenorians' helmets were angular, wider at the top than at the bottom, and had an elongated faceshield to accommodate the six twenty-millimeter mandibular "arms"—chelicerae—that jutted out from their faces.

For a moment, Sage felt certain the order was going to be ignored. A cool burn covered the back of his neck as he held his position, his finger poised over the trigger. Using his thumb, he flicked the rifle's setting to lethal, readying the ball bearing ammo.

Then the largest of the Phrenorians waved to his companions. His voice, gruff and raspy through the vocal modulator he wore to approximate human speech, held a note of derision. "This is not the reaction I'd expected to receive for saving your lives."

The nuances the Phrenorians had learned to enunciate still perplexed the modulator designers, as well as the xenopsychologists. The Phrenorian society wasn't a hive mind, like that of bees. They operated more like ants, everyone knowing his or her place within the society but still capable of independent action.

Derision was a human emotion, but the Phrenorians had learned to use it like a weapon. After it had first manifested, that fact alone had astonished the military's PsyOps division. The Phrenorians could radically and speedily evolve, always changing as they adapted to resistance. That was the biggest threat they posed, because they'd proven more flexible than the Terrans.

"You didn't save anyone." Terracina's voice was hoarse. "You executed those men."

"Truly?" The Phrenorian snorted, something that should also have been physically impossible for them. "That is how you choose to view what just happened here?"

"That *is* what happened."

The Phrenorian shook his head, then reached up and unfastened his helmet. "Four high-level bashhounds against the twelve of you?" He laughed. "You would have all died."

Sage didn't see it that way, but he didn't argue. If the bashhounds had chosen to attack, things would have gotten bloody. Looking at the pieces of the corps secmen scattered across the street, he amended his assessment. *Bloodier.*

With the helmet dangling at the end of one double-jointed arm, another facet of Phrenorian physiology that benefited them in combat, the alien glared at Terracina with the three pairs of black eyes above his mouth. He had another pair on the back of his head. All of those eyes were capable of seeing more of the color spectrum than a human and in low light. His face was sharp and angular, faceted rather than rounded, flat like it had been smacked with a plank to knock everything into place. Coarse reddish-brown hair was scraped back from his high forehead and pulled back in twin tails wound with bright red bands.

"Accept our generosity, Terran, and don't presume to give me orders again." The Phrenorian boldly lifted his rifle once more. "Your time here is up. We have run of this part of the city now. It's best if you move on. Unless you want to break your treaty with us—and with the Makaum."

The rest of his men lifted their weapons as well.

Sage's stomach tightened and he didn't drop his sight-line. Thoughts of all the young men and women he'd trained for the war ricocheted inside his skull. He didn't know how many of them still lived, or how many of them were dead or maimed or otherwise broken fighting the Sting-Tails. But there in that moment, he knew all he had to do was twitch his finger just the fraction of a centimeter and the score would be a little more balanced.

"All right, people. Relax." Terracina dropped his rifle to rest in front of him and stepped out of the shadows. He nodded toward the pile of dead bashhounds. "You killed them. This is your mess to clean up."

The alien's *chelicerae* twitched and formed an eerie semblance of a smile. Expressions weren't native to the Phrenorians either, but they'd learned to read those of humans and to mimic them. "Of course."

"I'm going to report this."

The *chelicerae* twitched again. "My name is Captain Zhoh GhiCemid of the Brown Spyrl. For your report."

Sage studied the alien, marking the creature's profile and taking in the wound on the left side of his face. That would take time to heal, and by that time—if Zhoh insisted on being around—Sage would know his enemy better. In time, he would get to know them all.

"Sure." Terracina waved to his men while he and Sage kept them covered. Once they were safely in the alley, Terracina assigned a pointman and wings and someone to walk slack. He and Sage stayed in the center of the group.

The Phrenorians ignored the pile of human scrap in the middle of the street and continued on. Reluctantly, Terracina ordered his men to sort out the dead. They took IDs and contraband, and notified the Green Dragon corp before leaving.

The private walking beside Sergeant Wireman spoke quietly. "So that was Zhoh GhiCemid?" She shook her head. "You ask me, he didn't look like much."

"You're green, Private. You got a lot of years ahead of you before you can start making calls like that. GhiCemid's got a rep as a killer. One of the Phrenorians' top warriors."

Sage pulled up the Fort York database and accessed the Phrenorian intel. Zhoh GhiCemid was a known entity. An acknowledged warrior among the Phrenorians and a veteran of several of the bloodiest battles in the war. Sage logged onto a private frequency with Terracina. The files must have been out of date or wrong because they identified GhiCemid as a major. "Did you know GhiCemid was here?"

"No. But now that we know he is, you can bet a lot of the brass is going to want to know what he's doing here. We've heard about him, but he's never been on the ground here, or anywhere near Makaum." Terracina shot Sage a mirthless grin. "Your tour is already looking interesting."

"Yeah." Sage kept focused on the shadows around them as they headed back to the crawler.

EIGHT

Sage woke before Terracina reached his bunk. They'd assigned him personal quarters in the Quonset hut Charlie Company occupied. His quarters were next door to Terracina's. For the next few days, they would be sharing an office while Terracina transferred responsibilities over to Sage and managed the transition prior to rotating home.

"You awake?" Terracina's voice was calm, controlled, but there was a hint of tension in his words.

"Yeah." Sage lay still and didn't take his hand from the revolver under his pillow.

"I know it's just your first night here. Thought about letting you sleep in. Then I considered how maybe you'd be miffed if we rolled without you tonight."

The blood sang in Sage's head. The only thing that had

ever made sense to him had been going into battle. Whenever he'd been in combat, he'd felt most alive, felt most sure of himself. Living or dying didn't leave much room for confusion, and not a lot of missed opportunities. It all played out right there. "I would have been."

Terracina grinned in the darkness and his teeth flashed white in the soft glow of lights in the outer room. "How long will it take you to get ready?"

"Two minutes." Sage threw his feet over the side of the bed and reached under for the go-bag he kept packed with equipment. Then he was moving, getting prepared to go into the fray with the old rhythm that he would have thought he'd forgotten after being locked down in training for so long.

God help him, he was looking forward to whatever was going to happen.

Fort York Military Airport
0312 Hours Zulu Time

Dressed in his AKTIVsuit, info flickering across his faceshield as more data dropped into place, Sage jogged toward one of the waiting jumpcopters. His heart beat low and controlled and the air tasted sweeter as he breathed it in. Maybe it was the higher oxygen index onplanet, but he didn't think so. The doldrums from the long trip sloughed off him and his blood whispered through his veins. He was here to make a difference.

The boxy aircraft were the mainstay of the Terran military onplanet deployments. Stubby wings equipped with jets to assist in quick takeoffs and firmpoints for an array of armament stuck out on either side of each jumpcopter. Capable of transporting fifty soldiers at a time, or sixteen heavy powersuits that were the equivalent of walking light tanks, the jumpcopters also broadcast continuous power to the AKTIVsuits and the weapons.

Sage stayed a step behind Terracina, listening to the man bark orders. The troops reacted, but they didn't have the crispness of combat readiness that Sage would have wanted. He divided his attention between scrambling onto the jumpcopter and pulling up maps of the area Terracina had designated as their destination.

The target site was 157 klicks from the fort, a 314-klick roundtrip that was comfortably within the jumpcopter's range. Estimated flight time to the target zone was forty-eight minutes from the time they were airborne.

Sage glanced around at the men seated on the small transport benches, then spoke on private frequency to Terracina. "Going in heavy."

"Intel suggests that this is a big drug lab. Or maybe a biopirate harvesting station." Terracina glanced at the datafeed juicing through his faceshield. The letters and numbers glowed gently on his features but remained encrypted, indecipherable to anyone viewing them from outside. "Either way, the bad guys put that much hardware on the ground, they're going to protect it. Out here, we go in hot, ask questions later."

Sage nodded and sat back against the throbbing bulkhead. He started going over the terrain maps of the area and felt they were woefully limited. "Lot of undiscovered territory out there."

"Trust me. Even if you map an area out in the Green Hell, you can wait a week and go back only to find that everything's changed. The environment constantly develops and shifts. This planet is one big stewpot of vicious plant, insect, and reptile life-forms that takes no prisoners. Some new species of tree or brush or grass or foliage can crop up and kill out the other plants—or us. And that's without the offplanet stuff tracked in by the corps and the pirates causing all kinds of hybridizations and mutations with the work they're doing."

The jumpcopter shuddered as the engines powered up, then it leaped into the air with screaming jets. Sage felt like he'd gained thirty or forty kilos, then the pressure lifted as the jumpcopter leveled off. He flicked onto the command frequency allowed in his helmet and streamed in the audio and visual feeds from the jumpcopter and the three scout drones that searched the territory ahead of the craft.

The jungle below them passed in a haze of dark greens and ochre steeped in dark shadows. Leaves and branches swayed beneath the jumpcopter's whirling rotors, looking like ripples spreading across the surface of an ocean.

Sage leaned back and waited, mesmerized by the wealth of trees that paraded across his faceshield. It was no wonder the planet was so oxygen rich or that mineral strikes were turning up veins of iron and other precious metals that could be used to manufacture weapons and vehicles on asteroid-based plants. Makaum was a deadly paradise. All the Terrans or Phrenorians had to do was get those resources offplanet to make a fortune.

Or to supply a war.

West-southwest of Makaum City
0356 Zulu Time

The jumpcopters made good time, beating the ETA by a few minutes. The pilot kept the craft low, barely skirting the tops of the tallest trees as she closed in on the target site. Dronecraft ahead of the jumpcopters streaked through the airspace above the lab area and sent back video, audio, and radar scans.

Sage flicked through the drone data streaming to the

jumpcopter, assessing the images quickly. Ramshackle prefab buildings blended into the surrounding jungle, almost absorbed by the encroaching vegetation. Several trails snaked through the jungle and showed bare patches of ground that were the result of defoliants. However, even those were starting to be reclaimed by the verdant growth.

The main building that Sage could see measured one hundred meters by forty meters, but he was certain more structures or huts for personnel existed under the fringe of the trees.

There was no sign of vehicles, and that was the second thing that alerted Sage to the trap. The first was that innate sense of his that always came to life on the battlefield. Whenever something wasn't quite right, even before he could identify what was wrong, unease drifted over him and pricked at the nape of his neck, putting him on alert.

"Break off the approach." Sage spoke over the private link he had to Terracina, unable to communicate directly with the jumpcopter pilots.

Terracina turned his head to look at him, but he was already giving the order. Confusion knotted his eyebrows. "Pull up. All aircraft, pull up." He focused on Sage and used their private link. "What's wrong?"

Sage was going to point out that no thermal signatures had registered on the drones' sensors, that nothing human was there, and that the lab was a ghost town and probably bait in a trap. He'd figured out that much by then.

But that was when the surface-to-air missile slammed into the jumpcopter and turned the world into whirling maelstrom of cracking thunder and fiery lightning. The aircraft's warning systems had flared red, sending the same warning lights into Sage's helmet. He'd prepared himself for the hit, knowing they were vulnerable.

Knocked on its axis by the blast, the jumpcopter flipped

end over end at least twice by Sage's estimation, the ablative armor plating holding together and responding with counter-explosives to absorb part of the missile strike. His senses whirled, cotton filled his ears from the multiple detonations despite the helmet's dampening program, and the feeling of free-falling spiraled in his stomach.

Sage held onto the restraining straps and planted his boots solidly to brace his back against the hull. Some of the soldiers slid free of the restraints and dangled by straps or slammed into other soldiers or the floor or ceiling of the jumpcopter.

The aircraft jerked and shuddered as the pilots fired the jets in an effort to gain control of the rotation. A moment later, the jumpcopter stopped spinning and went into another minor free fall that made Sage think they were about to crash. Instead, the fall halted at the end of fifteen or twenty meters and the craft sprang back like a yo-yo at the end of a string.

Terracina cursed and freed himself from his restraints. He brought his rifle up and charged for the cargo door at the back of the jumpcopter.

Shrugging free of his restraints, Sage followed the sergeant across the slanted floor. Soldiers fought free of the benches to join them. Several of them were panicked, filling the commlink with useless chatter.

"What's going on?" Sage cycled into the jumpcopter's external cams and pulled up images that flickered through his faceshield.

"We hit a web." Curling his left hand into a fist, Terracina banged the cargo hatch's release button.

Servos cranked into motion with pneumatic hisses and the cargo door fell open, but only partially. Something held the door tilted at a sharp angle.

The darkness outside the jumpcopter made vision difficult. If they'd lit up the aircraft, they'd have been spotlighted for their attackers. The drones were already buzzing around, tracking enemy fire back to their origins and marking the spots. Barely visible, the strands of the massive orb web that had caught the jumpcopter came into view.

Spiders on Makaum were huge. Sage had read that. However, the reading—even the video—hadn't prepared him for the creatures' immensity. At the far end of the web, the arachnid scrambled forward, causing the web to dance under its weight. The spider was fifteen meters across, from front legs to rear legs, and almost that wide. Stiff, coarse hair covered the reddish black body as well as the inky black legs. Yellow-green ichor pearled on the mandibles in the moonlight. The spiders, called *kifrik* in the Makaum language, carried deadly, paralytic venom that could down a man in less than twenty seconds. If an antivenin wasn't delivered, the victim's lungs stopped working and he suffocated within minutes. Provided the spider didn't crack open the AKTIVsuit and drain him dry before he expired.

Shifting on the treacherous web, Sage brought the gauss rifle to his shoulder and aimed at the *kifrik's* center mass. He pulled the trigger and the accelerated uranium round struck the creature's abdomen just beneath the quivering mandibles and tore through. The *kifrik* staggered only for an instant, then lunged forward again.

Sage fired once more and watched as smoke rose from the half-meter-wide wound. The *kifrik* gathered its limbs and sprang, leaping over Sage and Terracina to land on the jumpcopter lying half on its side. Bending down, the predator grabbed a soldier by her head and shoulders with one of its front legs, then caught another soldier by his left arm with the other.

Swiveling, Sage fired again, scoring another hit but not doing any appreciable damage because the spider continued its attack undeterred. Slinging the gauss rifle as the *kifrik* sank its fangs in the first soldier's body, Sage drew the .500 Magnum and aimed at the spider's head.

The smartlink built into the Magnum's butt connected with the helmet's targeting system and a silver reticle formed on the faceshield. Sage fired quickly, sending all five hollow point rounds into the *kifrik's* face, shattering the exoskeleton and pulping the head.

The *kifrik* shuddered, then sagged and went limp atop the jumpcopter. The soldier held by his arm tumbled free, tried to get up, and fell through the widely spaced web strands. As he plummeted into the leafy darkness below, the man's screams echoed through the commlink.

Balancing on the crossed strands of the web, Sage shook the empty brass from the .500 Magnum, refilled the chambers with a Speedloader, and leathered the pistol. He pulled the gauss rifle into his arms again and looked at Terracina. "Do they come one to a web? Or do they have bunk buddies?"

"One web, one spider. Like back on Terra." Terracina cursed and knelt by the injured soldier lying under the collapsed spider. She wasn't moving. As soon as Terracina touched her, her stats flowed into his data, then into Sage's.

Her heart and respiration had crashed. Terracina reached into the medpack he carried and pulled out a slap patch filled with antivenin. He slid the woman's helmet off as a rocket flared through the sky and took out another of the jumpcopters. Flaming soldiers blew free of the stricken aircraft, arms and legs pinwheeling as frantic cries filled the frequency. Terracina applied the slap patch to the woman's neck.

Sage pulled up the datafeed streaming from the drones. Suspended ninety-three meters above the jungle floor, the soldiers on the web were sitting ducks for the ambush team swarming through brush below. He roared orders. "Get lines out of the jumpcopter. We need to get down on the deck. Now."

The soldiers reacted slowly, trying to figure out who was supposed to take charge. Sage realized they hadn't been prepared for extraction teams or triage effort. Their attention was divided between the ambushers closing in on them, the dead *kifrik*, salvaging the supplies in the jumpcopter, and the soldiers that had been injured during the landing.

Sage strode forward, picking out individual soldiers' names from the datapack that had been dumped into his helmet. Some had been trained as combat medics and others had been through survival training that included rappelling.

The antivenin slap patch didn't stop the poison. The venom-stricken soldier's KIA status blinked into place on Sage's HUD, accompanied by several others.

Terracina abandoned the dead soldier and turned his attention to the survivors. He bellowed orders, calling on many of the soldiers who he'd identified from the intel he had. "Schaub, get your unit together. Lay down suppressive fire. Hoyer, evacuate those jumpcopter supplies. Dasgupta, get the wounded clear of this web."

The team knew what to do, but the training wasn't second nature, the way it should have been. Sage watched the jungle, knowing that whoever had attacked them wasn't just going to walk away when they were exposed.

Then a jumppak-equipped enemy rose up out of the darkness and targeted Terracina with a rocket launcher. Sage's HUD screamed the alert, but he was almost out in front of it, alerted by his own visual, already tracking the attack.

Wheeling with his rifle, Sage took aim and put three gauss bursts into the man's face, burning through the lightweight armor with the first two and cooking the man's brain with the third. Jumppaks were designed for individuals, snipers with minimal armor.

Out of control, the jumppak-assisted corpse shot skyward briefly before being targeted by the jumpcopter's AI-driven onboard machine guns. Seven-point-sixty-two millimeter rounds shredded the dead man's body and blew up the jumppak in a bright blister of yellow-white flame.

Terracina staggered back as the initial rocket blast knocked him backward. He slipped through the web strands and fell, but somehow managed to grab hold with one hand. The AKTIVsuit augmented his strength and helped him hold on, but he dangled helplessly, unable to recover. His biometric readouts revealed he'd been grievously wounded and couldn't be coherently tracking.

A nearby soldier crossed over to Terracina and reached down. "I got you, Top. I got you." The soldier's voice sounded young and scared.

As Terracina turned his head to look up, Sage spotted the pitted damage left from the first explosion, but he also spotted the glistening four-millimeter tube that had penetrated the sergeant's faceshield and bloody cheek. The rocket had been a sabot, designed with a secondary charge meant to breach the armor and deliver a lethal finish to the soldier inside the suit. Somehow the faceshield had managed to prevent full penetration.

Sage held the rifle in one hand and drew his burner as he lifted his voice. There was no time to clear the sabot because they operated on a three-second delay, which had to be almost gone. "Get away from him! Stay away!" The crosshairs fell over the web strand Terracina held. Sage pulled the trigger and the laser beam cooked through the strand.

With a look of shocked surprise or betrayal, Terracina

fell. A heartbeat later, the sabot round detonated, splitting the sergeant's fractured helmet into shrapnel, part of which blew up through the web strands. Terracina's life signs darkened in the datastream Sage viewed and KIA rolled up onto his stats. The concussive wave slapped into the soldier and knocked him off balance, causing him to fall into the hole left by the burned strand. Sage managed to throw himself forward and slap a hand against the man's AKTIVsuit. Juicing his glove with an electrostatic charge, Sage managed to hang onto the man and save him from the long fall waiting below. The soldier twisted frantically and grabbed onto the web.

"Warning!" The jumpcopter's auto systems blasted into Sage's hearing. "Incoming!"

Disengaging from the man he'd saved, Sage looked up just in time to see another surface-to-air missile slam into the jumpcopter. The bright flash temporarily overpowered the filter protection built into his faceshield, and shrapnel from the destroyed aircraft bounced off his armor as the web beneath him tore free of its moorings.

He dropped into the Green Hell, knowing the ambushers weren't finished.

NINE

Tree branches collided with Sage's hardsuit, knocking him around as he fell, making it impossible to control the descent. The AKTIVsuit absorbed most of the damage, but the jolting impacts scrambled his awareness. Everything outside the faceshield was blurred, but part of that was because the filter was still compensating for the flash. He concentrated on the HUD intel, anticipating the collision with the ground and knowing even with the hardsuit's compensation measures that he was going to hit hard.

The jungle floor was 10.7 meters below and rising fast. And something was moving down there. The jerky movement told Sage it was alive, not an inanimate thing. It was also big, not as large as the *kifrik*, but definitely something to be wary of.

Everything in the Green Hell will try to kill you, Sergeant.

Sage tried to track the moving life signal, wondering

how he had missed seeing an enemy on the ground. Heat signals could be masked for a time, but only through expensive tech. The Terran military didn't offer that capability as standard issue. Right now, Sage knew he was lit up for any opponents that wanted to come for him.

The suit's altimeter showed him at 4 meters as he tried putting out his hands to grab onto anything that came within reach. He closed his hands around two branches, both too thin to support his weight, and they didn't slow his descent before tearing free.

He landed on his face. The AKTIVsuit absorbed most of the impact, but the sudden stop still wrenched the air out of him, emptying his lungs in a rush.

Breathe. Remain calm and breathe. The HUD displayed the suit's instructions. *You are in enemy territory. Breathe. Recover. Get to your feet. Move.*

Sage cleared the script with a curse, letting the hardsuit's near-AI know he was functional and in control. He took a breath, knew from the familiar pain that he had probably cracked or broken a rib.

Pain stressors are evident in your body. Do you require medication?

The hardsuit was still leaving him in control of his body instead of automatically pumping pain blockers and stimulants into his bloodstream. That was good. He'd dialed his autoblockers down, choosing to decide for himself when push came to shove.

"No." Sage didn't like the chems in his system unless he really needed them. They eroded a soldier's natural survival instincts, took the edge off the adrenalin. He pushed himself up, tracking the movements he'd spotted earlier. "Where's my rifle?"

The hardsuit's HUD lit up and showed him the Roley assault rifle lying six meters way.

Sage lurched toward the weapon, fighting to keep his balance and against the disorientation that flirted with his senses. The panicked shouts and questions of the soldiers around him became brief focal points. Three of them winked out, dead stars with KIA above them. The battle and the killing continued. Whoever their attackers were, they weren't done.

"Is the rifle functional?"

Affirmative.

"Track my team. Notify them of my location." Senses still pinwheeling from the impact, his breathing not quite right, and the pain still shooting fire down his side, Sage sprinted toward the brush to the rifle.

Immediately the HUD pinged white stat reports of the team scattered across the landscape. Two more winked out almost as soon as they flared to life and KIA replaced them.

"Identify enemy troops." Sage rounded a tree, distracted only slightly by the orange flares that marked the individual troops and vehicles. Red triangles marked unidentified targets within the hardsuit's sensor range.

Cannot confirm identities of combative forces.

"How many of them are out there?"

Thirty-seven confirmed.

"Keep them lit up." Sage intended to find a defensible area, but he wanted to go on the attack. As long as the ambush team felt like they had the upper hand, they wouldn't go away. He had to figure out a means to bloody their noses, shake their confidence.

The wide tree towered in front of Sage. His armor brushed up against the trunk bark as he powered around it. Three vines lashed out at him, startling him because he couldn't remember anything like them being mentioned in the downloads he'd seen concerning the plant life. One of the vines smacked into Sage's faceshield, spreading wide to reveal a throat covered in hundreds of spikes, which unleashed a torrent of bubbling venom.

The HUD flared, providing a brief translucent image of the vines as it downloaded information from one of the nearby soldiers' onboard systems. *Strof, also called vampire vines, are a predatory species that live on blood. Although they regularly feed on reptilian blood, certain strands have evolved to seek out mammalian blood provided by the Makaum people.*

Makaum didn't meet strangers. The world adopted them, turned every new life-form into something it could use. One of the earliest science teams had noted that. The planet took in all forms of diversity and adapted to them, either subjugating them or creating something to destroy them.

Actually, only two of the vines were plant life. The other was a winged snake that had nestled up to the tree. The HUD identified it as an *oskelo*, noting that most of them tended to be three meters long and that they killed by constriction as well as with venom. They didn't fly so much as glide from treetops because the meter-wide wings were actually hood flares, skin that stretched out on either side of the massive wedge-shaped heads and tapered down to half the length of their bodies.

"Stop unnecessary info." Sage seized the *oskelo* as it tried to wrap around his right forearm. The pressure the snake produced was amazing, threatening even the integrity of the AKTIVsuit. He juiced electricity through his left glove as he gripped the snake's head, hitting the reptile with enough of a charge to kill it or render it senseless. Pulling the thing from his arm, he flung the limp body away.

The rifle lay just ahead of him. He reached through the darkness for it just as a meter-wide section of the ground came up and enveloped his head and shoulders, pulling tight. Instinctively, he pushed back against his captor, thinking maybe he'd stepped into a foolie left by one of the ambush teams, only instead of cutting into him or blowing up as he'd feared it might do, the substance wrapped him more tightly.

"Identify." Sage pushed again, using the AKTIVsuit's servo muscle.

The membrane gave way reluctantly but didn't release the hold it had on him. The mass oozed and slipped, changing shape slightly to accommodate his efforts without letting go.

Kukweed is an indigenous spore that feeds on living things.

Sage pushed an electric blast through the hardsuit, expecting the hostile organism to crumple away. Instead, it held on just as tightly and started to spread over more of his body.

Kukweed is impervious to electricity, cold, and fire. Blooms from the—

"Does it have a central nervous system?" Sage interrupted.

Affirmative.

Cursing and curbing the small tremor of claustrophobia that trickled through him, Sage triggered the hardsuit's finger blades and speared the kukweed with both hands. He heaved and pulled his hands in both directions like he was swimming. The curved six centimeter long blades sliced easily through the kukweed, shredding it.

Hunks of the spore organism dropped to the floor of the jungle and writhed as though in pain.

Sage reached down for the gauss rifle just as the massive beast he'd been tracking crashed through the trees and brush behind him. He spun and tried to bring the Roley up, but he knew he was already too late when he spotted the huge creature bearing down on him. Even without the HUD, he recognized the lizard as a *slor*, one of the most dangerous land-based predators on Makaum.

Massive and covered in thick, heavy scales, the *slor* stood almost three meters high at the shoulder. The blunt head looked like a battering ram mounted between broad shoulders. The curved mouth was a meter across, filled with serrated fangs as long as Sage's forearm. Horns crested the head like a thorny crown. The exact color was hard to make out in the darkness, but whatever that hue was didn't matter because the lizard's dappled skin shifted, changing tints and altering patterns.

Before Sage could draw a bead on the swiftly moving creature, the *slor* ran into him, knocking him back a couple meters. He landed on the ground, skidding through the underbrush, but held onto the Roley. The *slor* sprinted after him, banging into trees and tearing through bushes as it sought him out.

"Sergeant Sage?" A woman's voice called over the comm, sounding panicked.

"I'm here." Sage pointed the Roley at the charging *slor* and squeezed the trigger, then rolled to the side, barely avoiding the huge lizard's full-on attack. The creature's foreleg clipped Sage and knocked him into the brush.

"Sergeant Terracina is dead. We're awaiting orders. We *need* orders." The hysteria in her voice was barely controlled.

Sage rolled to his feet and brought the gauss rifle up with him, pointing at the *slor*, which had sunk to the ground, muzzle buried in the soft earth. The lizard huffed and tried to get its forelegs under it, but the disorientation caused by the electromagnetic charge scrambling its brain made that difficult.

"Fall back to Delta Two and set up a defensive perimeter, Sergeant Thindwa." Sage strode over to the *slor*, put the Roley's barrel right behind its right jaw, and squeezed the trigger in a prolonged burst. The rifle vibrated in his hands as the charge leaped free and sizzled whatever neurons remained inside the lizard's skull.

Brain-dead, wiped of even autonomous control, the *slor*'s systems shut down. The big creature shivered and lay still, the gray-black tongue lolling from its mouth.

Turning from the dead *slor*, Sage called up the map on the HUD as he plunged through the jungle. D2 was a promontory 250 meters on the outside of the lab compound. Natural rock formations gave the area some cover and created a defensible position.

On the HUD screen, the surviving members of the assault team hustled toward the designated region.

Sage pulled up the list of snipers left to the combat team. There were three: Anton Jaworski, Elyssa Dumervil, and Kjersti Kiwanuka were still alive and operational. Sage called for a secure signal to the three snipers, lighting them up on his HUD as purple blips.

"The three of you fan out from D-Two. Grab cover and put down as many of these people as you can. You're in a target-rich environment." Sage marked the spots by calling out site designations, placing the snipers in a pincer in front of D2 so they could cover retreating soldiers as well as pick off aggressive enemy.

"Roger that," Kiwanuka responded. A quick look at her field report revealed that she had the most experience of the team. She was a master-class sniper and had put in seven months on Kimos, a planet that had seen plenty of action against the Phrenorians. The official report was that she was currently on Makaum rehabbing a cyberarm. There had been extensive other injuries as well. There was also another note, but Sage didn't have clearance for it yet. Judging from past personal experience, Sage guessed it was a reprimand of some kind.

Sage sprinted through the jungle, avoiding the trees and thick brush when he could, crashing through the undergrowth when he couldn't. With the nightvision on, the jungle became a frenetic layer of greens—strips of dark and light hues. Wind stirred the leaves and branches. Four-winged mothlike insects called *lerlor* fluttered from a nest to his right, exploding out from a disturbance less than a hundred meters away.

For a moment, all Sage saw were the insects hammering against his faceshield, then he spotted the two armed men near the tree bole who were taking aim at him. Reacting immediately, Sage threw himself to the ground, taking advantage of the tall undergrowth.

Laser beams cut through the brush above him, leaving burning leaves and small branches in their wake. Sage rolled again, knowing the men were already adjusting their aim. Their suits would be picking him out just as his was doing for him. He held onto the Roley with his left hand, plucked a thermite gel grenade from his tactical harness with his right, flicked the pin to activate the explosive, and threw the grenade at the two men.

The grenade struck one of the men on the head, sticking to his faceshield. Sage knew he'd been as lucky as he'd been good. The throw hadn't been entirely blind, or without the hardsuit's input, but it had sailed true.

The stricken man stopped trying to shoot and stood suddenly, afraid of what was going to happen next. His armor might have lost some circuitry, crisped in the ensuing blast, but the faceshield wouldn't save him. He wiped at the grenade and the gel smeared across his helmet as he turned to his companion.

Startled, the other man backed away, wanting no part of his partner's fate. The thermite flared to white-hot life and burned through the faceshield. Freed from the helmet, the man's hoarse yells echoed over the surrounding area for just an instant. Then the heat slagged the man's face and melted his skull.

The bright light of the detonation lit up the other man's armor and lifted him from the darkness. The glow illuminated the man's horrified features for a moment before his faceshield compensated to block out the light.

By then Sage had the Birkeland coilgun in hand, locked on target, and pulled the trigger. The blue-tinted beam stabbed through the air and pierced the man's chest armor. As the man staggered back, his suit's med systems already dosing him with chems, stims, and pharms that would perhaps keep him viable, Sage stood and put another beam through the man's faceshield.

The man fell backward as his dead companion slumped to his knees with his head and upper torso on fire, cooking down while in a pose of supplication.

"Locate all operational powersuits." Sage ran, skirting the lab compound. He needed the raw power and weps the powersuits could provide. Whoever they were facing in the dark jungle had a lot of firepower.

The near-AI responded at once, marking the five powersuits that had survived the fall from the jumpcopters. All of them had landed in separate areas. One of them—controlled by Corporal Owen Banda—was only 73.2 meters away and taking heavy fire.

Sage changed course for the man, burning energy from the AKTIVsuit as he raced across the broken terrain.

TEN

A re you still with me, Banda?" Sage called as he crashed through the brush.

"Roger that, Top." Banda's accent hadn't strayed far from his native Malawi. "But I am taking a lot of damage."

"Understood, Corporal. I'm going to do something about that." Sage overrode the automatic controls on the surviving seven drones that had come with the jumpcopter he'd flown in on. He called them down, then assigned them to coverage over the immediate battlefield, spacing them out so there were overlapping zones.

Banda's position was nearly overrun. Several laser beams chipped away at the powersuit's armor, keeping the corporal off balance so that he couldn't effectively return fire. Powersuits contained an arsenal of weps, but they needed time and space to employ them.

Seven armed men in hardsuits pursued Banda's stumbling retreat through the jungle. He would have been able to hold his own against them, but two enemy powersuits closed in on the corporal's position. Once they reached the battle, Banda wouldn't last more than a few seconds.

"Kapito," Sage called. "Do you read?"

Corporal Anson Kapito was the nearest powersuit operator. He also was taking fire, but his situation wasn't as serious. He was 170 meters distant. According to the stats Sage could see on his HUD, Kapito still carried seven missiles, half his machine-gun ammunition, and was equipped with two shoulder-mounted laser rifles.

"Five by five, Top." Kapito sounded tense but focused.

"Rendezvous with Banda."

Only a moment's hesitation came over the comm and Sage knew the man had checked Sage's own position. "Roger that. On my way."

Cresting a small hill, Sage peered down at the battle taking place below.

Banda's powersuit stood eight meters tall and three meters wide, built like a block with arms and legs. The unit was sealed and the thick polycarb hide protected the operator within. His HUD relayed the outside environment.

The ambushers had taken advantage of the terrain, demonstrating their knowledge of the landscape. The attack had been coldly calculated and the designers had planned on using everything they had at their disposal. They'd herded Banda toward the river, cutting off his retreat, and were now closing in.

The powersuit could have entered the water, could have remained submerged for days, but it would have been an easy target in the river because Banda's mobility would have been greatly reduced in the mud. The enemy powersuits would have reduced the Terran military unit to scrap metal, and Banda would have died either inside his armor or as soon as he'd jettisoned it.

They weren't there to take prisoners.

Banda stood his ground, taking concentrated hits that made returning fire with any degree of success almost impossible. Enemy lasers ignited the jungle around the powersuit. Flames gleamed against the polycarb armor. The powersuit's onboard systems were overwhelmed by the assault.

"Banda, I'm patching in a drone to your suit. Use it to triangulate your attacks." Sage overrode the drone's programming and slaved the feed to Banda's powersuit. With the new information source, the corporal would have a better chance of targeting his opponents.

"Roger that."

An instant after the response, Banda's chest-mounted machine guns opened up and sprayed a wave of 7.62mm rounds into the jungle. Two hardsuited attackers got knocked down. Only one of them tried to get back up, and Banda's next swath of machine-gun fire dropped the attacker before he could scramble to safety. Banda yelled in triumph. The powersuit shifted, gaining more solid footing. "Now we are going to see—"

Two missiles scorched through the air and slammed into the powersuit, cutting off Banda's words. Flames erupted around the powersuit and chased away the darkness.

Rocked back on its heels, the powersuit started to tip over. Banda twisted, getting an arm down under his body to keep himself from tipping over and sprawling helplessly before his enemies. The powersuit's four fingers plowed into the soft earth, ripping deeply and skidding toward the riverbank as it threatened to spill Banda into the churning water reflecting the flames.

The two enemy powersuits crashed through the jungle, closing in on Banda.

After a brief check on Kapito's progress, Sage turned his attention back to the second drone he'd called down to his position. Powered by magnetic capacitors, the drone hovered in front of Sage. The disc-shaped craft was eighty centimeters across and nine centimeters thick, covered in armor and filled with the drive unit, comm relays, and vid/aud pickups capable of magnifying and enhancing images as well as sound bytes.

The drones weren't designed as weapons, and the top brass considered their replacement expense too high to be used as such. They were supposed to stay out of harm's way as much as possible during a hot engagement, and to return to base with local intel if the troops were lost or compromised.

The gauss rifle wasn't strong enough to take out one of the powersuits and Sage knew he needed a way of striking back. He pulled his remaining five thermite gel charges from his gear, linked them to the same detonator, and set that for a command that would be issued by him. When he had the charges adhered to the drone with ordnance cling, he stepped back and surveyed the ongoing battle.

Banda had shoved himself erect again, but that had only drawn immediate fire from the ground troops as well as the two powersuits ripping through trees and brush to close in. The Terran powersuit seemed to wilt under the explosive barrage but Banda's health stats held steady.

The two attackers in their powersuits shoved forward confidently, pouring on their weps batteries, filling the air with flames and noise. Banda struggled and reeled, unable to get himself set to return fire.

Sage targeted the rear powersuit and inputted the approach path to the drone, then commanded it to take flight again. Immediately, the drone flashed forward, staying low and taking a circuitous route behind the powersuits. Banda's powersuit slipped as its rear leg tore through the loose earth and slid down toward the riverbank.

Flashing through the trees, the drone hurtled toward

the rearmost powersuit. Leaves and branches clipped by its approach tumbled to the ground in its wake.

Inside the AKTIVsuit, Sage kept his breathing steady, tasting the faint burning trace of chem smoke through his helmet's filters. Information on the battlezone filled his HUD in transparent overlays, each of them tinted a different shade so he could differentiate them. It was still a lot of information to take in at one time.

The general parameters of the battlefield lay farthest back and showed the Terran troops massing at D2. They were taking severe fire there, but they were holding their own. Enemy KIA lay along the jungle where the sniper team had started taking out a blood price for the men who had pursued the Terrans.

Kapito climbed a steep rise to the west, coming up on the two powersuits closing on Banda.

And the drone streaked through the jungle and plowed directly into the powersuit Sage had targeted. Although armored, the drone shattered against the powersuit's polycarb skin. The gel thermite charges smeared across the powersuit's back as the unit staggered under the impact. Before the onboard gyros could stabilize the powersuit, Sage detonated the thermite.

The massive explosion hurled the powersuit forward, battering it against the unit in front of it. Slammed by thirty metric tons of armor, the lead powersuit swayed and the operator fought for balance and control. He turned and shrugged away from his companion, stepping back from the conflagration that consumed the other powersuit.

Armor buckled and broken from the collision with the drone, the powersuit's handler was left vulnerable to the thermite fire. Obeying emergency protocol, the powersuit dropped to its knees and positioned itself for evac of its pilot. The top half of the powersuit broke open and the pilot shot out in his seat, propelled by a jet assist. Flames wreathed the man, and when the parachute popped open high overhead, his burning corpse drifted toward earth until the shroud lines charred through and dropped the body.

Unnerved by the attack, uncertain where it had come from, the aggressors broke off their assault and took stock. They didn't have much time to assess. Sage put the Roley's reticle over the nearest man, squeezed the trigger, and moved on to his next target as the first one dropped. He squeezed the trigger again but knew he'd missed the shot when the man pitched himself to the side.

The surviving powersuit spun and Sage's HUD warned him that enemy sensors had locked onto him. Abandoning his position, Sage dodged to the right, leaving the tree he'd concealed himself behind for a low stand of rock jutting up from broad-leafed undergrowth. Lasers slashed through the tree and it toppled, then exploded into splinters as a pair of missiles slammed into it.

Sage hunkered down, head shielded by his forearms as fiery debris rained down over him. Patching into one of the drones, he scanned the battlefield as Kapito lunged up over the ridge twenty meters back from the surviving powersuit.

The enemy pilot tried to turn his suit around, but the soft ground and his own anxiety betrayed him. The massive feet tore through the soft earth and threw his balance off. He launched a pair of missiles anyway, but they didn't get anywhere before Kapito's missiles hammered him. The explosions buffeted the enemy pilot and knocked him backward. He lost broken polycarb armor like a duck shedding water, weaving helplessly as Kapito came toward him.

Lasers flickered and burned into Kapito's powersuit, but the reactive armor kept the beams from penetrating.

Sage got to his feet and hauled the Roley to his shoulder as Kapito hammered his opponent with one massive fist, then repeated the attack with the other. The blows clanked fiercely, the high-pitched shrill of contact echoing over the immediate vicinity.

Kapito lifted one foot and drove the other down into his opponent's powersuit, something that truly impressed Sage. Not many powersuit pilots could manage that and remain balanced. The leg of the opponent's powersuit shredded, coming apart in squealing shrieks. Without stopping, Kapito brought both fists down onto the other powersuit's missile launch systems, crushing them before the enemy pilot could bring them online to fire.

Defeated, his powersuit hemorrhaging and falling apart, the pilot hit the eject button and blew clear of his failing unit. High overhead, his parachute opened and he drifted away.

No longer under attack, Banda hauled himself back onto solid ground, then lit up the surrounding jungle with his lasers and machine guns. The surviving attackers broke and ran.

"We good?" Kapito asked over the comm.

"Good," Banda replied.

"Maybe so," Sage said as he stepped from behind cover. "But we're not done yet. Move out." He took off into the darkness, heading for the next skirmish line.

"Haqqani, move your squad into position." Sage monitored the three-pronged attack he had put together over the last few minutes. The Charlie Company recon team had stepped up and gotten themselves together after the ambush. They'd had no choice. But they were still running ragged, not smooth, not together as a unit.

If the enemy they faced had been more dedicated to the outcome—*if they'd been Phrenorians*—a lot more of his team would have been dead. That was a sobering truth and Sage kept it at the front of his mind. The soldiers, most of them anyway, were still too green to be truly effective. However, in the jungle that night, they fought for their lives. There was no question about motivation. Desperation rather than professionalism showed in their movements.

Sergeant Haqqani moved his powersuit toward the drug compound. Corporal Leary followed behind and to the right, keeping a clear fire zone for himself. Five soldiers in combat armor trailed them.

Kapito strode in front of Sage and the group he'd assigned to his sweep of the compound.

A number of dead men and women lay scattered in front of D2, proof of the snipers' ability. Sergeant Kjersti Kiwanuka had proven decidedly lethal. She'd racked up sixteen of the confirmed kills, and she had added to that tally as Charlie Recon had marched toward the compound to take possession of the buildings. Her service report image showed her to be a beauty: dark chocolate skin from her Ugandan father and platinum-blonde hair from her Norwegian mother. She'd grown up in Africa but had opted for offplanet military service.

The ambushers had pulled back into the jungle. Evidently they'd gotten a bellyful of actual fighting. Given the toll of the dead they'd left strewn across the jungle floor—and in some cases, the trees—there couldn't have been many of them left.

One of the things that bothered Sage was the lack of personal vehicles that should have been fleeing the scene. Whoever had survived among the ambushers was on foot out in the brush. He considered attempting to track those people down, but that might have played into the crosshairs of another ambush. He held his team together, promising himself that if there was any way possible, all who had been involved with the ambush would see a day of reckoning.

"Alpha Four is empty, Sergeant." Private Petrov had only been on the ground on Makaum for the last two months. He was a new recruit, and as such he was lucky to be alive after the attack. Despite being from Moscow originally, his Russian accent was faint. He was tall, brown haired and dark eyed, with pinched features.

"Go easy, soldier," Sage growled. He pulled up vid access to Petrov's suit, laying the translucent image under his HUD, seeing what was before him as well as what the young soldier was seeing. "None of this is what it's supposed to be."

Petrov peered into the small building. Like the other structures in the compound, the building had been slapped together out of planks cut from the thick trees of the jungle. Sage figured whoever had put the lab up had plopped down a small group of crude engineering bots that had manufactured building supplies out of the native resources.

The rough planks held knotholes and other imperfections and showed no evidence of any kind of real finishing. They had been cut and thrown into place as makeshift shelters. More planks had been used for the roof and thin shingles extruded from leaves and mulch prevented the rain from coming in.

More planks covered the floors, most of them scarred and covered in dried mud tracked in from outside. The buildings remained small, just big enough to get the job done without wasted space. There was no running water, no plumbing, and no electricity, though there were marks in some of the buildings that showed where generators sat at one time. Oil leaks marred the wood and indentions showed where the supports had been.

All of the buildings were empty now. Like a giant spiderweb, long sheets of camouflaged netting hung over the structures to provide a passable disguise that would fool most drones doing a flyover.

Petrov's vid relay lit up as the soldier switched on his exterior light. The illumination instantly attracted a plethora of insects that swooped at Petrov like attacking fighters. The private cursed and doused his light.

"These men were living hard," Kiwanuka commented. She stood to Sage's right, covering his six while Sage ran the op.

"Wasn't just these men." Sage walked along the narrow path that ran between the compound's buildings. "There were others."

"What do you mean?" Kapito asked.

Sage pointed at impressions of bare feet that showed in the dried mud of the walkways. "With all the venomous bugs and lizards in the area, I don't figure the people who made the drugs here would go around without foot protection."

"You wouldn't catch me out here in anything less than an AKTIVsuit," Petrov said. "Or not carrying a flamethrower." He stepped inside the empty building and explored further. There were no rooms in the building, only load-bearing posts that helped support the roof.

Pausing, Sage captured images of the bare feet.

"You think these guys had slaves working the operation?" Kiwanuka asked.

"Yeah. Either Makaum people or offworlders. With the war going on, some of the corps that use slave labor find the pickings easy. There are a lot of displaced people getting Gated from worlds the Phrenorians have taken over."

"I'd heard about operations like that, but I've never seen any."

"Then you're lucky," Sage said. "I've worked operations where we had to recover people displaced from their homeworlds who ended up in a slaver's ship. You don't recover them all. A slaver gets wind that he's hit somebody's screens, he'll jettison the slaves to the nearest planetfall and hope they burn up during an uncontrolled reentry. Or he'll cut them loose in space without heat and air. Those people freeze to death long before they starve to death." He indicated the five-toed footprint. "These appear to be human."

"You think the traffickers took them when they left the compound."

"I hope so. Otherwise, this is going to get worse."

"Worse than losing a third of our team?" Kiwanuka's voice took on an edge, but Sage chose to ignore it. They were all running on nervous energy and fear right now.

"Yeah. Worse."

Kiwanuka snorted softly in disagreement, but she kept the effort mostly to herself.

SAGE STARED AROUND the long main building that was the centerpiece of the camp. In addition to the usually roughhewn walls and floor, several long tables occupied the center of the space. Stains and old burns scarred the surfaces of the tables, and a lot of those markings came from chems, not tools.

"They weren't working cheap labor," Sergeant Roy Thindwa stated flatly. He'd been born and raised in Malawi, splitting his time between village life and the sprawl. He kicked a long wooden beam that ran the length of the nearest table only a few centimeters above the floor.

All of the tables had the same kind of poles on both of the long sides.

"They were working slaves."

"How do you know that?" Kiwanuka asked.

Thindwa growled a curse. "Take a look at those beams."

"I see beams."

"He's talking about the marks on the beams." Sage knelt and ran a finger over the irregular grooves. He'd seen low-tech like this on other planets, and had seen the slaves that had been attached to them. The stench of those conditions and the hopelessness of the people had left an indelible mark that always made his gut cramp. "Those were made by chains. Whoever ran this lab chained the workers to the tables and kept them here." He stood. "The question is whether they were locals."

"Does that matter?"

"It does. An operation this big, whoever was behind this had a lot of slaves working product. The Makaum would know if they were missing this many people. It stands to reason they would tell somebody."

"They don't trust anybody," Kiwanuka replied.

"Then maybe they just wrote these people off," Thindwa said. "Acceptable losses."

Sage took a tighter grip on his rifle. "When it comes to people, there are no acceptable losses. Not in my book." He turned and headed out of the building, wanting to get away from the inhumanity that the beams and the chain marks represented, and from the memories such treatment dredged up. The war was bad enough. Soldiers got killed and families mourned. But what went on behind the war—or under it—was often a lot worse. As a soldier, he'd seen what had taken place on the battlefield when things were hot, and when people tried to pull themselves together later.

"Sergeant Sage."

The HUD identified the speaker as Private Adrian Delome, one of the new recruits who had come in on the dropship with Sage. He was currently walking patrol around the compound, making sure the traffickers didn't return without being seen.

"What is it, Private?" Sage accessed the private's vid

feed and opened it onto his HUD. He bumped one of the four surviving drones into position over the private to maintain aerial recon.

"Found something really bad."

Delome stood on a small ridge and peered down at a depression that looked like it had been filled in a few days ago. Rain had filled in some of the cracks with mud and softened most of the hard edges of the earth that had been moved.

Whoever had filled in the depression hadn't done a good job, though. The covering had been light, and as much as the rain had done to fill in the gaps, it had also washed away the ground covering the corpses underneath.

ELEVEN

Sage stood at the edge of the depression and gazed down at the mass of bodies, partially covered more by debris than by honest effort. Hands, feet, arms, legs, and faces showed in different places across a twelve-meter spread. Charred flesh clung to splintered bones in many cases. Fire hadn't gotten them all. The ages ranged too, from young adults to the elderly. He also saw at least two children and he had to steel himself for more of that. War took victims everywhere and left no one untouched. Especially the soldiers who witnessed the atrocities.

This was the real cost of war: the people who got caught in between and died, and those who survived and carried scars that most people never saw. It took a survivor to recognize a survivor, and even they tended not to talk.

Soldiers fought and killed each other, but both sides expected that. The civilians just wanted to live their lives. Unfortunately, in hot spots they didn't have anywhere to go. They couldn't run far enough, fast enough.

The Makaum jungle wasn't going to let the dead go anywhere either. Not without a fight. Roots already threaded through the loose earth, and in some instances, through the bodies of the dead as well, already making moves to cover the disturbed area with new growth. Makaum treated the dead like mulch, taking from them what it needed and shifting what was left into soil. The odor of rot and decay that Sage had expected was sweeter and less noxious than he had experienced in the past. Maybe the oxygen-rich atmosphere was partly responsible for that, but he suspected it was something else, some process that was unique to the planet.

"You wanted me?"

Sage turned around to face Captain Karl Gilbride, the recon team's most senior medical person. Like the other soldiers, Gilbride wore an AKTIVsuit, but his was emblazoned on both shoulders with a bright red caduceus to indicate his role. He was tall and brown haired with gray eyes and an attitude. He was forty-three, slightly older than Sage.

"I did," Sage said. He remained respectful. The captain's rank Gilbride wore meant more back at the fort than it did in the field. Here Gilbride was chief medical officer. Sage was ranking command of ops. "I need you to take DNA samples of the people here."

Gilbride shot a disgusted glance at the corpses. "Those people are dead. I can't help them."

"No, you can't. But maybe we can help their families."

"They're not military issue, and they're not my problem."

Sage kept his voice calm despite the anger he felt stirring in him. "I'm making them your problem, Captain." He put the rank out there so Gilbride would know he was aware of it, and he put the fire in his voice to let the doctor know who was in charge.

Gilbride's jaw clenched. "I'm not crawling in there like

some kind of ghoul. I don't know where you come from, but disturbing the dead isn't something you should be doing."

"They're dead," someone said. "You can't disturb them any more than they've already been disturbed."

Sage ignored that and concentrated on Gilbride. The man was a captain, an officer used to command, and he bridled at the assignment he'd been given. And he'd probably come closer to losing his life in the past hour than he had in a long time.

"We need to know who these people were," Sage said. "Their families need to know what happened to them, and we need to know where they came from. They're intel that we may need."

"It doesn't matter. They're dead. I've got living people that need me. I don't need some johnny-come-lately-to-command to tell me how to do my job." Gilbride turned to go.

"No." Sage's voice sounded loud and sudden as a whip-crack, and the authority it carried brought Gilbride up short. The soldiers nearest the captain backed away un-consciously, leaving him naked before Sage's wrath. "You don't have patients that need you. They've been taken care of and you've done an excellent job getting that done. I know because I've been tracking your work."

The med reports had come in on time and had been well-articulated. Gilbride had considerable combat experience and it showed in the way he conducted his work. He was fast, thorough, and compassionate to the wounded. Sage wasn't sure what the man was doing on Makaum, but it wasn't because he didn't know what he was doing.

Gilbride stopped short, then turned around and walked back to Sage. "I don't know who you think you are—"

"The soldier in charge of this operation," Sage cut in.

"—but the only man I take orders from died when you

blasted him off that *kifrik* web about an hour ago." Gilbride turned and walked away again.

"Private Petrov." Sage stared at the departing man's back.

"Yes, Top?" Farther up the hill, Petrov shifted uncomfortably.

"If Captain Gilbride reaches you, take him into custody."

"Top?" Petrov gripped his assault rifle uncertainly.

Gilbride kept walking.

Sergeant Kiwanuka stepped in beside Petrov and her
meaning was clear. "Understood, Top. If the captain
reaches this point, we will take him into custody."

Gilbride stopped and stared at Sage. "Are you serious?"

Sage dropped his faceshield so the man could look at
his face. He didn't say a word.

Cursing, Gilbride walked back down the hill and approached the bodies. He unslung his medical kit. "You
can bet this will be in my report."

Sage ignored the threat. "As long as you get me the information I want, Captain, you can put anything in that
report that you want to."

"Do you know what kind of disease can be in these
corpses?" Gilbride demanded.

"I do," Sage replied. "As well as any biological agents
whoever killed them might have used. That's why I want
you on this detail. I don't want some greenie handling this
and getting himself killed. Or worse yet, letting us track
something back to the fort. Get the identification done.
We don't have much time before the inbound jetcopters
arrive."

"I'll need help sorting through this many people." Gilbride shoved his hands into the sanitary sealant extruder
affixed to the front of his uniform and a thin, bright blue
layer of steri-cling climbed over his hands and up to his
elbows.

"You know your team best. Call in whomever you like." Sage tapped into the doctor's comm and watched his HUD as the medical people were reassigned. He walked away to continue his inspection of the camp.

FINDING THE SOLDIERS who had died during the ambush took time, even with the HUD marking their locations. Security was paramount. Sage didn't want to leave anyone unprotected.

He also didn't want to leave the dead behind. They deserved better than that. That was something the newly arrived exfil team didn't want to deal with.

"Sergeant, our orders are to evac you and your people as soon as possible." On the comm relay through Sage's HUD, the jumpcopter pilot was a young second lieutenant, maybe twenty years old. He glanced nervously at the surrounding jungle in the darkness and Sage had to wonder how many times the pilot had been out in the wilderness.

"*As soon as possible* will be when we finish recovering our dead, Lieutenant. We're not leaving one minute before. Neither are you." Sage carried the body of a slain private over his shoulder through the brush. Kiwanuka carried another as she followed him.

Four jetcopters hung in the air over the battlefield. Blue beacons marked off the area and staging zones had been set up in a clearing near the main building. Baskets lifted wounded up to the jumpcopters. Drones from the new arrivals buzzed through the air and cycled at a farther perimeter in a loose security web swarm. So far there had been no sign of the ambushers. They had disappeared as quickly as they had struck.

The pilot contacted the fort. "Charlie Base, this is Raptor Nine on the evac op. I need authorization to leave the area *without* Charlie Recon. My team and I are exposed to hostile forces and the *sergeant* in charge is refusing to comply."

The response was immediate and brimming with crisp authority. "Negative on the return, Raptor Nine. You are to hold your position until you are cleared by the *sergeant*. Is that clear?"

Sage's HUD identified the speaker's voiceprints as Colonel Nathan Halladay, the officer in charge of the fort in General Whitcomb's absence. From what Sage had learned of the colonel, Halladay was a straight shooter, a career Army man. He'd ended up on Makaum as a special attaché to Whitcomb, who had pushed for his recent promotion to colonel.

"Sir, that's crystal." The lieutenant sounded put out and possibly a little frightened. He cleared the frequency.

Sage deposited the dead man he'd carried in a large cargo basket. Kiwanuka passed the man she'd carried off to the two soldiers handling the dead. Three other teams arrived shortly afterward, finishing off the casualty list.

The last of the wounded had already been reeled up.

Another pile of dead ambushers lay nearby. Most of them appeared to be mercs, offworlders with histories of violence that had been carved into their flesh by bullets, lasers, knives, and other weapons. But a few of them were cybered up too expensively to simply be street talent. They represented the corp, or corps, that had staged the ambush.

The reports Sage had reviewed while in his quarters showed that Terracina and his teams had been aggressively pursuing the drug ops out in the jungle. Their efforts had gotten costly, taking a cut out of the black-market profits the corps had been making.

Maybe it wasn't one corp. It was possible that more than one corp had joined together to push back and bloody the Terran military. Terracina's people had gotten a tip about the lab. It was apparent now that the tip had been bait for the trap, but the actual architects who had masterminded the ambush hadn't yet been revealed.

"You know we were set up, and it had to be one of Terracina's local assets. One of the people he'd made deals with to watch the jungle for him." Kiwanuka walked at Sage's side as he returned to where Gilbride was still cataloguing the dead there.

"Yeah. Do you know anyone who might know the identity of tonight's tipster?"

"No." Kiwanuka hesitated.

"Talk to me, Sergeant. If you don't say it, I don't know it. And I can't investigate a possible lead."

"Like I said, Terracina had a few assets he used for intel, but a lot of what we acted on came from Major Finkley. He *liaises* with the corps any time we have friction. Have you met him?"

"Haven't had the pleasure. Sergeant Terracina picked me up at the drop point and gave me the cheap tour. We were supposed to meet the brass this morning." Sage pulled up the major's service record. Anthony Finkley came from Boston, Massachusetts, and was the son of a congressman. He was in his mid-forties and had made major a year ago after twenty-three years in service, so he was a slow promoter, moving up outside the zone. Sage had the feeling that if he dug into the major's jacket for a deeper look, he'd discover that the promotions came through "supplemental recognition" rather than through effort.

"Meeting him won't be a pleasure."

"Like to clear that up?"

"No. Just giving warning. Take your time making an opinion."

"Fair enough." Sage scanned his troops, watching as

they continued their grid searches. "Did you recognize anybody back there?"

"No, but some of those guys are bashhounds. Sec muscle for the corps. The others are just meat. Cheap enforcers you can pick up anywhere. We get a lot of traffic in those for various corps. Warehouse sec. Personal protection. Sec for exploration teams out in the jungle. They cycle in and cycle out regularly."

"Yeah, I noticed that too. Only the guys that attacked us didn't get picked up anywhere on this planet. Someone brought them in and paid their freight."

"You think they were just a layer of deniability?"

Sage shook his head. "I think whatever corp is behind this wanted to go cheap. Figured they could take down our op easy enough since they lured us out here."

"They were wrong about that."

"Yeah, but not by much."

Kiwanuka cursed softly. "Whoever they were, they brought in those people they buried and treated them like animals before killing them. Then they brought us in to kill us and send a message. Now they're going to get away with it."

"No, they're not going to get away with it." Sage ignored the sergeant's apprising look and the question that she hesitated asking while he stopped along the ridgeline and focused on the dead there.

Gilbride and three medtechs gingerly pulled bodies from the makeshift pit. All of the med personnel wore orange hazard suits.

"You better stand back," Gilbride warned as he tugged a dead man from the loose soil. "All of these people are testing positive for Chehgar influenza."

Sage turned a little dry-mouthed at that. Chehgar influenza was a Phrenorian bioweapon that had first seen use nine years earlier. Although Terran military had quickly come up with a vaccine, the sickness had spread throughout several combat zones across solar systems. Getting enough vaccine made to support troops had been difficult.

For five months, Terran forces had had to sit back, unable to engage along perimeter systems for fear of contracting and spreading the disease throughout the troops as well as having the Phrenorians use it on civilian populations. Three star carriers had gone dark with the disease before they could be salvaged or before proper decontamination units could be upgraded. DECON was imperative while coming into contact with so many worlds.

Making enough vaccine to give to civilians was impossible. None of the pharm corps would put up that much free product. Nor would they part with their reverse-engineered cures. The med corps of the Terran military had created a somewhat universal vaccine a couple months after the civilian pharmaceutical corps had, but the mil-developed vaccines didn't work on everyone, and the expense was again an issue when trying to tailor it for other planets.

Posting instructions on how to make the vaccines hadn't worked either. Too many physiognomies were in play. Nervous systems, endocrine systems, respiratory systems, and blood were all too different to make a general cure-all. Sending in military med teams to help other worlds behind Phrenorian lines had only resulted in hostage situations and execution videos that had ripped through the allied worlds. The Phrenorians had never signed the Hawking Convention to establish rules of engagement.

Several outbreaks of the flu continued to present in pockets of civilizations that hadn't yet received the vaccines. Or, in the case of the Rothangu, those that chose not to accept them due to religious practices. Those planets didn't allow anything "alien" to be introduced into their bodies. That didn't stop them from buying goods, though. Business had boomed for the merchants, until they'd contracted the flu and populations had died off.

Other planets had succumbed to the flu because their bodies hadn't been able to utilize the vaccine. There were still worlds that had been declared off-limits until the disease ran its course, which generally left those planets vulnerable to Phrenorian invasion.

Although Sage had never seen the disease up close, there had been plenty of vids of the victims on various planets in the news and cycling through MilNet. The images tended to stay with anyone who saw them. Sage had a few memories of the flu he wished he could get rid of.

In the years before and the years since, the Phrenorians had continued their efforts to create bioweapons. Most were less successful, and none of them had stricken as quickly, deeply, or lethally as the Chehgar strains.

Gilbride laid the corpse on the ground and played a light over the body. The dead male was humanoid but had pronounced occipital ridges that covered nictitating membranes, elongated ears that reached to his jawline, and an orange tint to his skin that wasn't the result of death or sickness. His clothing was simple, probably Makaum made, but now hung in rags.

"Torgarian?" Sage asked.

Torgari had been one of the perimeter worlds hit by the flu. Sixty-three percent of the world population had died within a month and others were continuing to die, unable to stop the cascading illness. Some planets had created quarantines to separate the sick from the healthy. On more than a few worlds, anyone who had caught the disease was put to death.

The Torgarians concentrated on trade, moving goods from one planet system to another. When they couldn't trade, they smuggled. Business went on. Once they'd been exposed to Chehgar, though, free trade with the world was suspended. Many of the Torgarian ships caught out in space had been orphaned and had turned into freebooters, more or less. They hauled honest cargoes and dealt with everyone but the Phrenorians, but they also carried black-market freight. In the ensuing years, they had learned to kill or be killed, vicious vagabonds with no home.

Every now and again, a Torgarian vessel became a plague ship after picking up family survivors from the homeworld. Second- and third-wave Chehgar offered permutations, often turning survivors into carriers.

Unable to catch the flu themselves, the Phrenorians had closed in, set up shop on Torgaria and her four moons, and started producing munitions factories and low-orbit manufacturing stations to churn out warships, stripping the planet of mineral resources. That process hadn't taken overly long. By that time they were good at what they did.

That was how the Sting-Tails operated, converting each planet they took into a stronghold or raw materials. After a few years, the Phrenorians had moved on, but the planet had been so deeply behind enemy lines that the Terran military hadn't been able to ship in vaccine. Sage suspected the only reasons there were Torgarian plague ships these days was because some of the merchants brokered deals with the Phrenorians in an attempt to rescue family.

Kneeling, Gilbride waved a small flying drone over to the dead man's body. The med-drone wasn't much larger than Sage's thumb. Moving nimbly, the med-drone alighted on one of the dead man's open eyes. A needle lanced out, stabbed into the unblinking eye, and pumped out readings.

Sage accessed Gilbride's feed and brought up the medical reports on his HUD. He didn't understand a lot of the information, but he understood enough of it to know his guess had been right.

"He was Torgarian," Gilbride confirmed as he waved the med-drone away from the body. He ran a hand over the corpse, scanning it with his suit's magnetic resonance spectroscopic field. "From what I see here, he was in the last stages of the sickness. There's a lot of lung scarring, liver damage, throat damaged by stomach acid—probably from throwing up—and weight loss. I don't think whoever had him out here was getting much work out of him at the end."

One of the medtechs hauled another body out of the hole and laid it beside the others. The second dead man looked as wasted and emaciated as the first.

Gilbride glanced at the new body. "All of them were dying."

"That explains why whoever set this trap didn't take these people with them," Kiwanuka said. "The work force was perishing. The site was compromised. They burned them to keep the flu from spreading. Using the compound as bait to reel us in was an easy decision because they weren't losing anything." She paused. "Could be whatever drugs they cooked up out here are compromised too."

Sage made a note of that because that had occurred to him too. An outbreak of Chehgar could decimate the Makaum people. If it got loose in the orbiting space station, a lot of civilians who might not have had the vaccine would die and the military would lose access to the intel the station offered. He pulled up files on the planet, looking for medical records.

"The Makaum have all been given the Chehgar vaccine," Gilbride said. Evidently he'd anticipated Sage's concerns. "Command thought it was essential because Charlie Company was cycling rehabbing veterans into the mix that might have been exposed to carriers. It didn't take a lot to convince the Makaum natives they needed the vaccine. They've had experience with vile sickness pumped out by this world." Gilbride pointed back at the bodies. "These people show no signs of the vaccine antibodies."

"Our people are protected too," Sage agreed. "Probably most of the upper echelons of the corps because they don't like to leave much to chance. But there are a lot of people in harm's way if whoever put this operation together didn't contain their people."

"What I'm seeing here are antibodies from the fifth-generation flu strains," Gilbride said. "It's a lot weaker because the Torgarian immune systems were starting to fight it. Probably the sickness was dormant in these people and it wasn't until they were subjected to these hostile conditions—maybe contact with alien flora and fauna—that the sickness presented again. By the time whoever enslaved them had a clue about what was really going on, it was too late."

Sage cursed and glanced back at the empty buildings, thinking about the death all around him and how it probably wasn't going to stop.

Unless he found a way to stop it.

"Let's pick up the pieces here. If we look close enough, maybe we can figure out who was behind this."

TWELVE

Y ou've got to pack it in, Top." Colonel Nathan Halladay's
image ghosted on Sage's HUD. He looked neat and fit
and in his early fifties. Thin strands of gray flecked his
short brown hair and lent him the air of a distinguished
university professor or a CEO.

Given the job Halladay had of placating General Whitcomb and maintaining the fort on Makaum with boots
on the ground, as well as the various contingents of the
Makaum populace and the corps, the colonel probably
had the skills of both.

Sage walked through the buildings, going over terrain
he'd already covered a half dozen times. He'd shot vid of
the compound as well, intending to go over it again later.

The sun hung in the eastern sky. The slight green tint
deepened the emerald jungle's hue and made the bright
flowers stand out in vivid colors. A cloud of jewel-winged
insects lifted from the tall tree tops and buzzed him,

plinking against his faceshield behind Halladay's grim face.

"We need a little more time, sir," Sage said. "The answers are here."

Halladay's green eyes narrowed. "You're all out of time, Sage, and I'm confident you've found whatever answers were there. We're going to have trouble containing intel about the Chehgar flu, and when that gets loose among the Makaum people, I don't know how their leaders are going to react, despite the fact they've had the vaccine."

"We didn't bring the flu here, sir." Sage tried to curb the anger he felt at being able to finish the mission as he saw fit, but the lack of sleep was catching up to him. As well as the post-combat stress. Some of the surliness threatened to emerge. During combat, he was cool under fire, but afterward he liked to take time for himself, to think about things.

With a third of the recon team dead, he had a lot to think about. And then there was Terracina's death and the handoff of the fort to consider. He was going to walk into that as the guy who shot the sergeant off the *kifrik* web. The story wouldn't always include the sabot round that had penetrated Terracina's face and was about to go off.

The already troublesome situation had become even more prickly.

Halladay knew it too. Sage suspected that was why the colonel was barking so loudly.

"I know we didn't bring the flu here," Halladay growled. "I also know that the general is going to be up soon, and he's not going to be happy with my report. I want to at least tell him the remaining soldiers and hardware that went out into the jungle last night are safe."

"Understood, sir." Sage read between the lines, knowing that Halladay had told him more than he'd wanted to, revealing that the general kept himself at arm's length from the day-to-day ops at the fort instead of staying in the know. Whitcomb was effectively ROAD, retired on active duty, just marking time.

He wasn't going to be allowed the luxury of keeping tonight off his desk. Whitcomb was going to have to deal with the Makaum people, the diplomatic corps, and Command. With this many soldiers dead, the fort would need reinforcements soon.

If the general's discomfort hadn't come with the deaths of the soldiers, if only Sage's neck had been on the chopping block, Sage would have called it a fair exchange for causing Whitcomb problems.

Sage glanced over at the impromptu burial site. Vid had been shot of all the dead, DNA samples taken, and the bodies had been burned. Black and gray coals filled the wide area above the depression. Flames from the chem burn still flickered in the freshly dug soil that lay scattered.

Forty-three dead had been taken out of the depression. Shallow graves containing nineteen more dead had been discovered by Gilbride's cadaver bots. Those had been exhumed as well and tossed into the flames.

"Don't just understand me," Halladay said. "Get on a jumpcopter and get back here. We need to figure out how we're going to square this."

"Yes sir."

Halladay's voice softened only a little. "Give the order before I do, Top. I don't want to undermine your authority before I've even put you into your position."

"Yes sir." Sage tamped down his anger, knowing it was more from frustration than anything else. He cut the private comm, then addressed the soldiers around him, letting them know they were shutting down the op and leaving.

Unhappy with the situation, Sage strode back out into the narrow paths between the buildings and walked to the outer perimeter to watch over his soldiers as they pulled out of the area. Kiwanuka joined him. She hadn't strayed far from his side since they'd been on the ground together.

"Did the brass pull rank?" Kiwanuka asked.

"Halladay did." Sage's response was clipped and final.

"Don't hold that against him, Top. Halladay's a good officer. He puts his people first because he cares about them. Not because he wants to look good for the general's reports."

"I'll take your word for that."

"Do that. But he'll prove himself to you."

Sage let that go. Halladay's eventual palatability as a commander wasn't something he wanted to talk about. He held the Roley at the ready and watched over his troops. Magnifying his vision, he scanned the tree line around them. Now that it was daylight, everything seemed bigger and more open. The netting overhead blocked the sun except in the places gaping rips had been made during the attacks.

Teams aboard the hovering jumpcopter reeled in a cargo basket holding two powersuits.

Movement fluttered along the tree line. Sage called for more magnification and made out a young, lean face gazing down at the compound. At first Sage thought the watcher might have been one of the ambushers returning to the site, maybe with others in tow who would have shoulder-mounted missile launchers that would take down the jumpcopters. Then he saw that the young man was Makaum and dressed in camo gear so effective it made Sage use his suit's thermographic imaging to pull him out of the brush. He was short and slender, sleekly muscled, not an ounce wasted on him. But his face still held a little of a child's roundness.

Accessing the AKTIVsuit's digital recording app, he captured an image of the young man's face and ran it against the database he had of Makaum people Charlie Company did business with in some capacity.

Nothing turned up.

In addition to the camo gear, the young man carried a short composite bow and wore a low-grade Tschang beamer at his hip. The bulky pistol looked out of place on the young man.

"We're being watched," Sage said.

After a moment, Kiwanuka replied, "I see him."

"Recognize him?"

"No. Probably one of the local hunters. The Makaum keep their own exploration teams in the jungle to find food."

"They seem pretty well set in their sprawl."

"They are, but over the years they've had crop failures. Blights and disease have struck their fields and their fruit trees, killing them out in a season."

"How did that happen?"

"They tried to modify the original plants and trees, make them produce more of the kinds of fruits and vegetables they wanted. You hear the scientists tell it, Makaum plant and insect DNA is extremely rigid and won't tolerate outside modifications. You hear a *tianban*—a shaman, more or less—tell it, then it's just the planet striking back, lashing out at anything that would imprison it. They say the planet has 'Live Free or Die' embedded in its genetic makeup."

"The scientists ever find that in the DNA?"

"Not to my knowledge, but I don't talk to the scientists much."

"Is the recurve bow indigenous or did he buy it from someone?"

"The bow is indigenous, made of two different kinds of

wood, horn from hellbeetle, and glue strained from a *ki-frik's* web. Within fifty meters, those guys are lethal, and some of them make kills out to a hundred meters. They can be really effective in the hands of a Makaum hunter who knows what she's doing."

"Women hunt too?" That didn't surprise Sage, but he liked to have information.

"There's no real gender specification here. Anybody can do any job. But the Makaum tend to have more female *Quass* than males."

"*Quass*?"

"Political leaders. Think of them as something between a house parent and a full-blown congressman. They serve the needs of the locals on a smaller scale and talk directly to the Makaum ambassadors. It allows them to deal more effectively with the needs of the community."

The young Makaum man turned his head and stared at Sage. The contact only lasted a moment, then the young man was gone, fading back into the jungle like smoke.

0629 Zulu Time

When the cargo basket drew even with the underside of the jumpcopter, Sage threw a leg over the basket's side and clambered out onto the vibrating floor of the cargo area. He slid his Roley over his shoulder and looked at the men and women who had survived the night with him.

"You people did good," Sage said, and broadcast his words over the comm. "Sergeant Terracina would have been proud of you."

No one responded.

Sage let it go at that. Now wasn't the time for a lot of words. Soldiers needed time to recover and absorb their wounds and losses. And pushing any more rhetoric down their throats might have inspired insubordination over his role in Terracina's final minutes.

The soldiers remained secured in their AKTIVsuits, totally closed up. They would stay that way until they'd been through DCon.

"Clear for evac, Sergeant Sage?" the jumpcopter lieutenant asked.

"Clear. Take us home." Sage grabbed the support post in the center of the cargo space. Fatigue chafed at him and made him feel slightly off balance as the jumpcopter heeled in the air and came around. He was slow enough to react that the near-AI almost took over adjusting for him till he backed it off with a sharp command. He kept his faceshield locked. All of them did in an effort to stave off any more exposure to the Chehgar flu than they'd already had.

Most of the soldiers sat on the low benches along the walls and held on to the cargo netting. They talked among themselves, chatting through suit-to-suit comm, putting their heads together to make the connection. A few of them—the more experienced members among them— lay back and caught forty winks in case the chance didn't present itself after their return to the fort.

The dead mercs that had been recovered lay in the back, stacked like cordwood with nanogel layers between them to fashion a crude shelving system. Cargo netting hung from ceiling to floor in front of them, hooked into place so they couldn't come forward if they hit turbulence or had to take evasive action.

The jet turbine ran loud now. There was no reason at this point to hide their position. The steady hum of the engines offered Sage a calming backdrop. Noise like this meant a soldier was almost safe, almost home. He lipped the AKTIVsuit's built-in water reservoir and took a couple swallows of cool, electrolyte-charged liquid.

Since the suits ran at full charge in daylight, the cooled water was a perk.

After a final swallow, feeling some of the parched sensation abating, he stared at the dead men on the other side of the cargo netting. One of the men's profiles looked familiar. Giving in to his curiosity, Sage went forward and slipped through the cargo netting.

The dead man's chest had been ripped away by heavy caliber rounds, leaving gaping holes in the middle of torn tissue. Flesh and blood had sheared away easily, but some of the cybernetic infrastructure and artificial organs remained, including one of the lungs, which looked like a glossy bubble filled with blood veins inside the man's chest.

The man's face hadn't been touched but was partially concealed by the helmet and faceshield he wore. His gear was top of the line and looked like it had been well cared for up until the time he died.

Sage knelt beside the dead man, knowing he was drawing curious stares. He ignored that and focused on the dead man. Reaching for the man's helmet, he tabbed the releases and popped the emergency faceshield, removing the whole front the way a medtech would have to do to give emergency treatment.

The man was handsome, too handsome to be in the line of work he was in. Death had revealed the facial reconstruction he'd undergone at some point, leaving the old skin grafts slightly visible as waxy patches now that the blood had drained. His hair lay smoothly in place. His eyes were open, the pupils of both blown in death.

"What's the sarge's deal with the dead guy?" someone asked.

"I don't know. Don't know him or any of those guys we blew up last night," someone else answered.

Kiwanuka came to a halt by Sage. "Is there a problem, Top?"

Sage nodded. "I know this guy."

"How?" Suspicion colored her question.

"Didn't know him well. Met him in the Azure Mist Tavern night before last."

"This was one of the guys you got into the fight with?"

Sage wasn't surprised people knew about that, but it was good to find out that the fort grapevine was in working order. "This was one of them."

"He worked for DawnStar?"

"Maybe. I'm going to need to find out about that." Sage shoved the faceshield into one of the dead man's thigh pockets, leaving his features bare.

THIRTEEN

Enlisted Barracks
Charlie Company
Fort York
1014 Hours Zulu Time

olonel Nathan Halladay stood awaiting Sage's arrival outside the DCon chamber in the med center when the sterilization cycle finished. The colonel's face was clean shaven, his cheeks gleaming, and he went armed, a coilgun sheathed in a shoulder rig under his right arm and another at his right hip. He held a PAD in his left hand.

Sage came to attention immediately and raised his arm in a salute. "Sir, Master Sergeant Frank Sage."

Halladay seemed to be taken aback a little. He was slow off his marks returning the salute, but when he did, it was textbook perfect. "At ease, Top."

"Thank you, sir." Sage dropped into parade rest, the Roley slung over his left shoulder. "I was on my way to turn in my after-action report."

"I appreciate the diligence." Halladay acknowledged

the other soldiers filing from the DECON chambers and heading off to the mess hall. "I'll expect that report soon."

"Yes sir."

"In the meantime, I want to know what happened out there."

"We were ambushed, sir."

"In detail. Come to my office and we'll talk."

Sage fell in step with the man. A four-man personal security detachment walked in two-by-two formation around them. All of the members of the PSD appeared competent, but they were too relaxed after an ambush for Sage's taste. He watched Halladay as they walked, taking some measure of the colonel, noting that the man was in good shape and watchful. Halladay wasn't a fool, and he was attentive. That alone could keep a soldier alive.

Colonel Halladay's Personal Quarters
1030 Hours Zulu Time

"Coffee, Top?" Inside his office, Halladay held up the coffeepot.

"Yes sir." Sage sat in front of the man's desk, eyes forward, picking up everything with his peripheral vision.

Halladay poured. "You want to add anything to it? The Makaum people have refined seventeen different sugars from various plants, and there's at least a dozen different kinds of honey."

"No thank you, sir. Black is fine, sir."

Halladay handed Sage a cup of brew that was black as sin and smelled rich, then the colonel sat behind the modest metal desk.

Sage sipped the coffee and discovered it was surprisingly good. He set the cup on his knee and waited.

In addition to the efficiency desk that was clean and

neat, holding only his PAD, Halladay's office supported only a few items. A shelf along the back wall held print copies of field manuals. Sage kept a few in his kit himself on various pieces of armament that he was not well-versed on because PADs and Net connections were not guaranteed things and a man needed to know what he needed to know when he needed to know it if he was going to stay alive. Evidently Halladay felt the same way.

There were also pads of actual paper, but they looked different than anything Sage had seen before and he thought maybe this was locally produced paper. Boxes contained pens and pencils, and those appeared to be homegrown as well. Beside them was a sliderule, and Sage was truly surprised to see that. Not many people knew how to use them.

Halladay held his cup in both hands and peered over the brim. "The ambush, Top. Tell me about that."

Sage did, in a no-nonsense fashion, not glamorizing any aspect of anything that had happened, though he did mention the work done by the powersuit pilots and the snipers. They had been the backbone of the retaliation Charlie Recon had delivered.

"Did First Sergeant Terracina tell you much about the recon work he'd been doing out in the wild?" Halladay asked when Sage fell silent.

"Not much, sir. He was familiarizing me with the fort. He did mention that he had a network of assets that provided him intel about the drug traffickers working in the jungle."

The colonel grimaced. "We can suppose that particular well has finally been poisoned. The sergeant has, under my orders, been trying to thin the traffickers and serve notice to those who might want to haul contraband through this sprawl that that merchandise wasn't going to be allowed. Terracina had a thin network at best."

"Sergeant Terracina told me Major Finkley had more luck turning assets, sir," Sage said.

Halladay's eyebrows rose slightly. "Yes. That's true. Major Finkley has managed a few coups around here regarding relationships with the locals and the corps. His father is a congressman."

"I'd heard that, sir."

"Do you know who told the sergeant about the drug lab you people raided?"

"No sir. That never came up. We were more focused on the mission." Sage paused just for a second, then hurried on before Halladay could pick up the slack in the conversation. "In fact, I'm not certain that Terracina was acting on information he'd gotten himself or someone had gotten for him."

"That's going to have to be something you look into."

That surprised Sage. "Me, sir?" He'd figured one of the officers would have been assigned to the task.

"Yes, you." Halladay breathed out a little, just enough to push and hold before taking up trigger slack on a sniper rifle. Sage trained men on exactly that kind of breath. "As you probably know, most of the officers here are greener than grass. That's why I was relying on Sergeant Terracina so heavily. Now that he's gone, I'm going to be relying on you. If that's too much, I need to know so I can plan on your replacement."

"There's no reason to do that, sir."

"Really?" Halladay shot Sage a calculating look. "Because the scuttlebutt about you is that you don't want to be here."

Sage decided in an eye blink to be truthful with the colonel. The man had heard about Sage's protests about staying back as a trainer, and there was nothing to be done but to get those protests out into the air. "I want to be on the front line of the war, sir. That's where I belong."

Halladay regarded Sage for a moment, then nodded. "I understand your feelings. I wasn't exactly thrilled to be reassigned here either, but this is where the general wanted to be. And, for the moment, I go where the general goes."

"Yes sir." Sage sipped the coffee.

"It's just possible I can help you get your wish, Sergeant."

Sage waited without commenting.

Halladay gave him a thin smile. "The general's not going to be happy with you even though Sergeant Terracina led this mission, and despite the fact that we've got standing orders to shut down the black-market ops wherever we find them. You've got a lot of men out there who are going to hold you accountable for the sergeant's death."

For a moment Sage considered defending his actions regarding Terracina, then decided not to. It wouldn't matter.

"I know what you did and why you did it," Halladay went on. "I've already reviewed the vid on Sergeant Terracina's death. You saved a handful of men around you by cutting him free of the *kifrik* web. Maybe more. If that web's integrity had been compromised, that jumpcopter could have gone down, as well as the soldiers that had survived the initial attack. It's no consolation, but if Sergeant Terracina was conscious there at the end, I'm sure he approved of your actions."

All Sage could remember was the look of shocked betrayal that had been on Terracina's face. "I don't think he knew about the sabot round, sir." He hadn't realized he'd spoken his thoughts until the colonel responded.

"Maybe not. Sergeant Terracina was hit pretty badly. Probably already dying."

Sage closed his eyes and banished the image of the sergeant's face. That memory would return, but for now he needed it out of his head.

"If he had known," Halladay stated firmly, "Sergeant Terracina would have approved what you did. If the situation had been reversed, he would have cut you loose too."

That didn't matter, though. On his first night at his new post, he'd killed one of his own team.

"Some of the soldiers out there will realize what happened. Word will spread. And I'll make sure to get the word out too."

Sage nodded, but he didn't think that would much matter. He was still new to the fort, and he was going to be in charge of a lot of the training. He would have been going against the grain to begin with.

"Can you still do this job, Sergeant?" Halladay's voice turned hard and cold. "I need a man who can run this fort, get these men into fighting shape so they can stay alive out there. I don't need a man who's going to spend his time feeling like he needs to be elsewhere. Are we clear on that?"

Anger flared inside Sage and he kept it carefully under control. "Crystal, sir."

"Good. Because the work that Sergeant Terracina had been doing isn't finished." Halladay turned and waved a hand over his desk. In response, a holo fired up and painted images in the air over the desktop.

Makaum sprawl glowed in the center of a vast, deep jungle. Fort York and the Terran embassy sat at one end of the sprawl and the Phrenorian embassy, marked by the hivelike buildings the Sting-Tails preferred, sat at the other. A third embassy, smaller and made of the elliptical construction favored by the (ta)Klar, sat due east. Opposite the (ta)Klar embassy, stalks of prefab buildings housing the corps stuck out of the ground like arrows. All of the structures looked artificial against the jungle.

Halladay leaned over the holo and nodded at Sage to

join him. Sage took his coffee to the opposite end of the desk and peered down.

"Sergeant Terracina gave you the ground view of the situation. I'm going to give you the overview." Halladay pointed at the fort. "Here we sit, in potentially hostile territory, depending on how close the war with the Phrenorians comes. Intel suggests that Makaum may be of more importance to the Sting-Tails than we initially thought. The brass is thinking the natural resources here are starting to look good to the Phrenorian commanders. Or maybe they'll target us because we're a supply line to Terran forces. They'll gear up to fight us for the planet, or they'll rain fire down on us. Either way, this planet has generated enemy interest."

The theories had circled the grapevine, but Sage hadn't put any trust in them. Command had a tendency to overthink situations. Right now, the war was still out in space, not here. "Doesn't the Makaum government understand that, sir?"

"Our diplomats are endeavoring to bring that understanding into sharp focus every day, Top. There's a lot of resistance on part of the Makaum people. For one, they don't want anything to do with the war—or with us, for that matter. For another, the Makaum people have split over offworlder presence among them, and Terran military presence in particular."

"Sergeant Terracina had mentioned that, sir."

"Drop the 'sir.' We're talking right now. I don't need a yes man at this moment. I've got green lieutenants and a major who's more interested in furthering his political career than in paying attention to this fort. And a general—" Halladay stopped himself and took a breath. "The point is, I need a man who can think for himself. Especially after what happened last night." He locked eyes with Sage. "Looking at your service record, you're supposed to be capable of that."

Sage nodded. "I gathered that the locals don't much care for offworlders."

"Some of them don't."

"Is the fort what split the populace?"

"No. In the beginning, I'm told, the Makaum people enjoyed interstellar trade. Some of them, very few, even joined ships when they could. Makaum doesn't manufacture enough trade goods to bring in commerce."

"The corps seem to be mighty interested in things here."

Halladay grinned ruefully. "A few of the corps were already here, stealing what they could, but those efforts were at a minimum because nobody wanted to build a Gate to more easily reach this planet, and the Phrenorian patrols shot them down. When we built the Gate, when Terran soldiers built the fort here, that's when the majority of the corps set up shop and went into business above and under the table. We constructed the road for them to travel, and we provide the protection from the Phrenorians as well as the anti-offworlder contingent among the Makaum. We seeded our own problems."

"Then why allow the corps to be here?"

"Militarily, we'd shut them out. But corps presence here is also political. The corps have a lot of weight back on Terra. Weight that can't be ignored. So we were *encouraged* to help the corps engage with the Makaum. On one hand, they pay taxes that help fund the war effort. Of course, they make profits from that *help* as well. Corps always do. On the other, the corps own several key politicians in the Alliance who control our purse strings. We allow the corps here, they continue our funding. Of course, without us using the munitions they provide, demanding more and better, they wouldn't have the profits they do."

That was always the situation for a military man. War depended on munitions and weapons that were supplied by defense contractors, but those same contractors depended on soldiers using them out in the field. War was a flame that fed itself when it came to profits. As long as those corps remained on a winning side.

"So we're stuck with them here." Halladay took a breath. "They go about their business under relative protection from the Phrenorians, and they conduct their black-market enterprises under the same umbrella."

"What do the Makaum people think about the black market?"

"Many of the Makaum have learned to appreciate profits as well as the offworld goods—legal and illegal. Several of the Makaum have gone into business for themselves, becoming outlaws among their own people. We're blamed for that as well, for providing the temptation and for not being able to control the situation. Dealing with the Makaum black marketers is tricky. Unless we can prove they're pursing illegal business, we can't move against them. Ultimately, though, they view the corps as interlopers, parasites on a business they can now run without outside interference since they've learned how to manage it. They, and the corps, tend to play us in the middle. We defend the corps' legitimate business interests, and we take out the Makaum black market."

That had happened on other worlds Sage had served tours on, and that clash had resulted in spectacularly difficult situations for a soldier simply trying to get the job done.

Halladay pointed toward the jungle. "Out there, in millions of square miles of jungle, small battles take place on a regular basis. Sergeant Terracina and his people have discovered bodies of the Makaum people as well as offworlders where they fell. If we don't find the bodies quickly, there are carrion feeders enough out there that the evidence disappears pretty readily."

"Are there villages out there?"

"A few. Not many. And those communities tend to be travelers living more like hunter/gatherers instead of villages. Those people live lives of desperation. This sprawl is the first place the Makaum people have successfully put down roots."

"What makes this place so special?"

Halladay shook his head. "I don't know. Our scientific division can't explain it."

"Can the corps?"

"No. And I've talked to several sympathetic Makaum who have been forthcoming, and they don't know either. Some of them think that the planet has finally started to adapt to them and is allowing them to become part of the ecology. But only in this place. One of our ecology specialists believes the planet is allowing the Makaum people to live and gather here to shape them—or to find a way to develop something nasty that will kill out human life once and for all."

"How?"

"Maybe by creating a new predator that's smarter and faster than anything we've seen. Maybe by growing some new biological strain."

"Sounds like they believe the planet is sentient."

"Live here for a while. Maybe you will too. The possibility crosses my mind more than I'd like it to."

Sage stared out into the almost impenetrable jungle, remembering what it had been like last night to battle the ambushers. "What kind of support can we count on from the Makaum people?"

"Not much. Those who resent offworlders in general aren't going to help in any way. Those who do support the presence of offworlders are mostly waiting."

"Waiting for what?"

"To see who can give them the best deal. Either way it goes, the Makaum know that Terra or Phrenoria or the (ta)Klar want them as a source of labor. The way they look at it, their days of governing themselves are probably over. At the very least, their world will never be the same again."

Sage nodded.

"Sergeant Terracina and I were waging war against the corps as much as we could." Halladay looked at Sage. "The general isn't in favor of that action and isn't exactly supportive."

"Why?"

"Because it can be problematic. If we step on the toes of the corps, we could lose access to the space stations that orbit this planet. Command isn't prepared to replace those space stations. Losing them would make our job of policing Makaum a lot more difficult."

"Why don't we have our own space stations?"

"They're expensive, and Command hasn't yet decided if Makaum is important enough to defend. Right now all of our heavy space stations are out there shipping weapons and supplies to different units."

"This planet supplies a lot of raw material to the war effort."

"You and I know that. So do the Phrenorians, which is why they're trying to win over the Makaum people diplomatically." Halladay looked at Sage. "With the Makaum people split the way they are, putting a military space station in orbit might be a waste of resources. Why put a space station out there only to lose the ground war if the Makaum people decide to stand against us? Any space station Command puts up there would become a target the instant Makaum decides we're not who they want to support in this situation. You can bet we'd be the last to find out."

Sage rubbed his fingers over the stubble on his chin. "Yeah. But the corps can put up space stations because they're making profits—legally and illegally. The civil war here promotes a smokescreen for them."

"Exactly, and we're providing protection for them while they do it."

"We know what the Phrenorians are here for. Why are the (ta)Klar onplanet?"

"To keep things stirred up between us and the Sting-Tails. As long as Terra stands against the Phrenorians in these sectors, the (ta)Klar don't have to commit assets."

The (ta)Klar Consolidation had a reputation for engaging mercenaries to fight their battles, but they won most of their conflicts through finesse, through seizing control of trade or politics—usually both—and raising the stakes so high that war became too costly for worlds that committed military and materials to the effort. They had a history of walking into star sectors depleted by interstellar war, raising up armies dependent on them, and sorting through the detritus of what was left to manage a profit. No one on Terra knew for certain how large the (ta)Klar Consolidation was, but it was immense.

"The Makaum *Quass* friendly to Terran interests appreciate the efforts we've made to keep the black market and biopiracy under control," Halladay said.

"But the general doesn't agree with those efforts?"

"On paper, sure. In practice?" Halladay shook his head. "General Whitcomb thinks it's too risky. The diplomats rain heat down on us because they believe a course of action further splits the Makaum people."

"What do you think?"

Halladay's face hardened. "I think that the criminal element on this world needs to be brought under control if we're going to help these people. And if we're going to protect ourselves. Whether we're out in the jungle pursuing those cartels and biopirates or sitting here, we've got targets pinned to our backs." He paused. "I don't like being a target."

"Neither do I."

"Good." Halladay waved his hand and the holo vanished. "Then get a good night's sleep, Top. Reveille comes early."

FOURTEEN

At least Charlie Company had plenty of water on Makaum, and access to it as well. Sage had been on several planets where water had been in shortage and bathing had been low on the list of priorities. He luxuriated in the shower despite the hostile stares of the other soldiers, letting the heat soak the aches from his body, then he dried off and returned to his quarters.

Dressed in boxers, skin still tingling from the shower, Sage went through a combination of martial arts and yoga to finish loosening up his muscles and to relax. Even though he'd been up for over twenty-four hours, discounting the attempt last night at sleeping, he couldn't relax. Despite his best efforts and the fact that he was practiced in all of that, he couldn't let go of things. His mind kept reliving the ambush and Terracina's death. He'd seen holos of the man's family, and he'd written emails like the ones Terracina's wife and children had already gotten.

Sage had lost men before, but for the last six years he'd worked in training. Out in the field, a soldier knew that men died on a regular basis. That was accepted. A soldier learned how to compartmentalize, to wall away the confusion and the hurt that might have prevented him or her from doing the job.

During his time in training, Sage knew he'd lost some of that distance he'd learned to insulate himself with. On top of that, he'd liked Terracina. The man hadn't deserved what had happened to him. His family had needed to have him back with them, safe and sound.

Terracina's face reappeared with the sabot round sticking out of it. Then he fell into the Green Hell. Over and over and over, till the sight and sound of his death hammered Sage's mind. He'd come to Makaum to make a difference, to get away from the soldier mill he'd been stuck on, churning out cannon fodder for the front line.

Occasionally a few soldiers were lost in civilian accidents, a few more in suicides or drug overdoses, but Sage hadn't lost any like he'd lost last night in a long time. And he'd never lost anyone the way he'd lost Terracina, never taken up a weapon against a fellow soldier like that.

Every time he closed his eyes, Sage saw Terracina clinging to the *kifrik* web again. The sabot round stuck out of the sergeant's face through the shattered shield and time ticked away.

Again and again, Sage burned through those web strands and watched the man drop into the dark jungle below. The explosion replayed in an endless audible loop, till Sage lay on his bunk covered in an ice-cold sweat.

We've got targets pinned to our backs. Halladay's words resonated in Sage's mind.

Sage focused on that, and he realized what he needed to do. Terracina had been assassinated last night. The sniper with the jumppak had been assigned to take out the sergeant. The only way Terracina could have been found so quickly in all the confusion of the attack was if someone had supplied him with Terracina's DNA or the AKTIV-suit's unique identification code.

Either way meant Terracina had been betrayed. Ultimately, Sage had been the man's executioner, even though Terracina was already dead.

Abandoning his bunk, Sage dressed quickly, choosing camo gear with built-in bulletproof armor that wasn't anywhere close to being as protective as an AKTIVsuit, but would offer some defense against small arms and not be as noticeable. Where he was going, he wanted surprise—at least temporarily—as an advantage. He left his Roley in his locker and strapped the big .500 onto his hip, adding a couple of Speedloaders to his thigh pocket. He left the helmet too, but slipped on an ear/throat setup in case things went worse than he anticipated.

Then he went out, sealing his quarters behind him and wondering if he'd ever see them again. If he was going to be ineffectual here, he didn't care. Makaum was just a way stop for him. Either he'd get moved along to the front line, or his presence here wouldn't matter.

But he wasn't going to quietly sit back. Those days were over.

Oral Statement of Corporal Ralph Schmeltzer to Colonel
Nathan Halladay
Re: Master Sergeant Frank Sage
Charlie Company
Fort York
0356 Hours Zulu Time

*There was no stopping him. I want to make that clear. I
got the impression that if I had tried to interrupt Sergeant
Sage, he would have put me in the infirmary.*

[Colonel Halladay: Sage told you that?]

*He never told me that, there was no threat, but he had
this look in his eyes. If you'd have been there, you would
have known. Same as me. Wasn't nobody gonna stop him.*

*I was manning the desk at the morgue, which is pretty
boring. You stand at security post for eight hours, check
in bodies, make visitors sign in and out, make sure all the
paperwork is done correctly, make sure stuff stays where
it's supposed to unless somebody's supposed to take it.
Like most posts around the fort. Just a null-sweat detail.
I was looking forward to getting a beer and catching up
on the gossip. There were still a lot of stories about the
ambush that I hadn't heard.*

*I knew Charlie Recon had taken a beating out in the
jungle. Everybody knew that before the jumpcopters
came back with all the dead. My squad mates were talking about it while I was getting ready for my sec detail.
A lot of soldiers got killed. I was lucky. I haven't been
on Makaum long and I didn't have anybody outside of a
handful of soldiers that I'd gotten close to. I didn't know
any of the dead soldiers.*

*It's kind of hard to get tight with anybody at a billet like
Fort York. Not everybody here operates on the straight
and narrow. Command is soft.*

Crap, sir! I didn't mean to say that! I wasn't thinking!

[Colonel Halladay: Keep going, Corporal. Just tell me what happened.]

I don't mean any disrespect, Colonel Halladay. I know what you're up against here. I just been places where everything ran tighter. You got guys working their own deals with the corps, doing things off the books. That's what I'd heard happened to Charlie Recon. That's what everybody was talking about. That somebody had burned First Sergeant Terracina. Set him up for that ambush.

Anyway, enough about that. You wanna know about last night. When First Sergeant Sage arrived.

I was at the check-in desk reading a fantasy novel a buddy had loaned me. That late at night, the morgue doesn't get much action, you know? So I was sitting there not expecting nothing when the sarge shows up.

I didn't know him. Hadn't laid eyes on him. But I'd heard about the dustup he'd had with the corps bash-hounds on the DawnStar space station. Heard it was DawnStar sec he'd gotten mixed up with, but I still don't know if that was true.

You know how stories get told at the fort. I liked that the sergeant had stood up to them. We take a lot of crap from those guys.

The sergeant buzzed me through the comm and identified himself. I'd heard he was a stickler from a couple guys that he trained who are here now. The sergeant is the reason they're here instead of on the line somewhere facing the Sting-Tails. Those soldiers, they don't know whether they have him to thank for being on Makaum, or whether they're supposed to hate him for scoring them so low in boot camp. He's a real by-the-numbers guy. That was why I was so surprised by what he did. But I'm getting ahead of myself.

I made him show me his bonafides, checked them out, then I buzzed him in.

He was wearing light-armor camo and a sidearm. A revolver, I think. That was it. No other weapons that I could see. I was surprised that he didn't have his rifle. You're not supposed to go anywhere without it. I thought about saying something about that, thinking maybe after last night he'd just forgot it because that can happen, then I caught myself and stopped. Probably a good thing. I didn't have no business telling him his business. Given what happened, I figure I saved myself a beating.

He looked at me with those eyes. Man, I've never seen eyes that cold and hard. I reached for my rifle before I'd even noticed it.

"You're not gonna need that weapon, son." That's what he told me. Just as calm and as rational as you could imagine.

I nodded and took my hand back, then asked him what could I do for him.

"I've got a requisition," he says.

I told him sure and could I see his paperwork.

"Paperwork will be coming later," he says.

I told him that wasn't how things were done. I got to admit, I was even wondering if this was some kind of test.

He stepped around my desk, looked at the computer, and got the information he was looking for.

Or maybe I should say who *he was looking for. Turns out he wanted a corpse of one of the guys that was brought back when Charlie Recon came back from the field.*

Dead guy's name was Andresik, Shannon. I don't know much about who he was, other than a dead guy, I was told, who attacked Charlie Recon, but DawnStar Corp was handling the funeral arrangements. They'd already put in the paperwork to reclaim the body. Quartermaster just hadn't cut the body loose yet. I figured it would be sent along through channels in the morning with the rest of the mercs Charlie Recon found out there.

Andresik wasn't on the books as an employee at Dawn-Star. He was a freelance bashhound. Not working for anybody that anybody knew of. I'm friends with one of the intel techs that tracked Andresik, and she told me you had requested whatever information she could find on the dead guy, Colonel Halladay.

Master Sergeant Sage looked over that information too. I saw him draw it up on my workstation.

Then he went back and got the dead body out of the freezer. Just humped it up over his shoulder like it was a duffel and went on out the door.

I didn't try to stop him. You want my opinion? Nobody was gonna stop him. Or what happened later. He was like a heatseeker, and he was locked and loaded.

END OF STATEMENT

Nelumbo
Makaum Sprawl
0017 Hours Zulu Time

The Nelumbo sat like a jewel in the darkness, outshining the other offworld clubs that sat across the streets from it. The premium location showcased the laser show that climbed the exterior, presenting hundreds of colorful images rendered in off-white. Most of them were of offworld sights, objects and environments and people the Makaum natives had never seen.

Sage thought he recognized some of the images, but he wasn't sure. The programming controlling the visual display rendered the images in fantastical proportions, stretching and distorting everything. Some of them might have been erotic. Others might have been completely fabricated. All of them together created a sliding kaleidoscope of shifting visual effects.

Music blared from the speakers, underscoring the otherworldly effects of the building's skin. Like the visual presentation, the audio was a stew of hundreds of tunes that poured like a waterfall into the night and drowned out all other sounds. Sage suspected a lot of white noise went into the sound mix as well, because he felt vibrations running through his body and the night insects hovered outside an invisible barrier at least a hundred meters distant.

The club was named for a variety of Terran lotus fossil that had been found in North Dakota, in the pre-Terran Alliance territory that had been known as the United States. DawnStar had recreated the extinct lotus and chosen it as the icon for their pharmaceutical corp, making the statement that they could, in a sense, resurrect the past, or the dead.

Sage pulled the crawler in next to the curb in front of the club. Now that he was in motion—had a chosen plan of action—he felt calmer. What he was doing had a real good chance of getting him killed, but he knew he wasn't going to get any rest until he followed through on it. Good soldiers had died out in the jungle as the result of an ambush, and that event was getting swept quietly aside by everyone involved.

He wasn't going to let that happen.

Three bashhounds stood outside the club. They eyed Sage warily and he got the impression they already knew who he was. He slid out from behind the crawler's controls and they noted the pistol strapped to his hip. They were armed as well.

Crawlers and bicycles drove by on the streets, but the eyes of the drivers and riders were on the shifting mosaic that continually climbed the building's exterior.

"Hey." One of the bouncers held up a hand. "You can't leave that vehicle here."

Sage looked at the man as he went to the crawler's cargo deck. He never broke stride. He harnessed the anger inside him and used it to fuel his actions. "Are you in charge out here?" His tone was hard, unflinching.

Stepping back unconsciously, the bashhound glanced at one of the other men.

Before the man could say anything, Sage fixed the second man with his gaze. "I guess that makes you in charge."

"What are you doing here, Sergeant?" The bashhound was nearly seven feet tall, amped up on organic growth hormones as well as cyber. He didn't look totally human anymore. Either he felt confident in his abilities or he decided he needed to mark his territory.

"Making a delivery." Sage reached into the cargo deck and shifted the bodybag to his shoulder. The dead man's weight was considerable.

"There are no deliveries scheduled."

"This one's a surprise." Sage nodded toward the club. "Is Kos inside?" He started toward the group, managing the dead man's weight easily.

The bashhound narrowed his eyes and frowned. "Kos isn't one of your fans."

"Not a big fan of his either." Despite the coolness of the night, sweat trickled down Sage's back. He knew he could be dead in the next handful of seconds, but he also felt certain that what he was about to do needed doing. He wasn't going to let Terracina die in vain, and he wasn't going to let the sergeant's killers get away with what they had done. A line had to be drawn. That was what soldiers did when they were in enemy territory and were supposed to occupy an area. They drew a line.

The three bashhounds gathered in front of Sage, bringing

him to a halt. They wore half-meter-long shoktons, fighting clubs amplified with electrical charges, but he didn't doubt for a moment that they had more lethal weapons hidden on their person. The two surrounding the leader drew their shoktons and shifted into ready positions.

"I'm going to see Kos." Sage kept his voice steady, not threatening, but determined.

Around them, a number of passersby halted to watch the obvious confrontation. A few of them were Makaum wearing offworlder clothing. Most of them appeared to be corp execs and personnel, clerks and middle management. Some of them were Terran military, and some of them were Phrenorian warriors.

Sage felt the tension radiating from the standoff and realized that it might break off in more ways than he'd planned on. He hadn't considered that because he'd been so focused on what he was going to do. If things went badly, he knew he was going to kill the men standing in front of him. He hadn't gone there to back down. He reached into his pocket and took out the other thing he'd brought with him. The familiar fist-sized egg shape held his body heat and almost felt calming.

The bashhound grinned. "You're not seeing Kos, but you are going to see the infirmary."

Sage activated the tangler grenade and hurled it at the feet of the three bashhounds. As soon as the device exploded, a dozen strands of plaswire leaped out of the housing. Controlled by a nanobot guidance system, the strands wound around the bashhounds and pulled them into a flesh-and-blood bundle that stood unsteadily on six legs. The strands wrapped tight, but not so tight that they cut into flesh because Sage had set the grenade for nonlethal. Trapped against each other, the men struggled to get free.

One of the men managed to pull a coilgun, but he couldn't point the weapon at Sage.

Striding forward, Sage yanked the pistol from the man's hand, then threw his shoulder into the center of the man's chest.

Knocked backward, the three bashhounds strove to remain on their feet, but it was a lost cause. One of them fell and brought the others down with him.

Another tried to use his in-head comm but the tangler's anti-communications countermeasure kicked in and silenced the channel.

Shouldering his burden, Sage kept walking, climbing the low steps toward the club's door.

FIFTEEN

A re you sure you should stay in here with that madman coming?"

Velesko Kos looked with distaste at the corp exec sitting beside him. For the past ninety-three minutes, they'd shared one of the VIP tables at the back of the club. Even though he loved the luxury that being around people like his companion afforded, Kos's patience was wearing thin. People like his companion were lapdogs, bred and kept for a single skill. Kos was a predator, a man used to taking what he wanted.

For a time, he had done exactly that, on a dozen different worlds, before he had come to the attention of the corps. They had seen what he could do, what he was willing to do, and they had made him offers that he couldn't refuse.

Unfortunately, he occasionally got stuck with men and women like his present companion. It wasn't all bad, of course. The fringe benefits given to people like his companion tended to trickle down to those around them. After all, largess couldn't be adequately enjoyed without the presence of little people.

Herman Kiernan was an important cog in DawnStar Corp's public relations department. The CEO believed that Kiernan had a handle on the Makaum pulse and was keeping the locals pacified. Maybe that was true. Kos just hadn't seen any of Kiernan's brilliance in play, although the man did command more attention from the *Quass* than any other corp Kos knew of. Of course, Kos didn't make it a point to find out what other public-relations people were doing.

When Kos was called into play, he deleted resistance. He didn't try to pacify it, as Kiernan and his ilk did.

"I'm sure I'm not running from that man." Kos watched the club's front door. He opened his jacket and loosened the Rudra Tech plasma burster in his holster, then pulled on special gloves that linked with his suit. Wires crawled from his jacket sleeves to seal the gloves seamlessly to them, then more joined those to reinforce the gloves. His suit was an advanced design from Dawn-Star's fall fashion line and sported interlocking nano-armor weave that was something short of a powersuit. Kos played the corp man for the most part, but he didn't stint when it came to personal weapons. Rudra Tech made excellent armament.

Kiernan reached for his glass and finished off his drink. He was a corp drinker, swilling only DawnStar's best. Tall and lean, but only because his nanobot-modified metabolism kept him from putting on extra weight, Kiernan looked both impressive and nonthreatening, a model specimen for the public-relations division. His brown hair was carefully coiffed and his skin held an unmistakable glow in spite of the fact that he was a heavy drinker, enjoyed drugs, and did nothing to take care of himself. His gold one-piece suit stood out in the club.

Two beautiful women, one on either side of him, sat quietly, awaiting his attentions. They were the best in their particular fields too, and their scant clothing left little to the imagination. Kiernan had originally brought six women and two male counterparts with him. The others were now off with clients he'd been talking business with.

"I heard this guy just survived an ambush out in the jungle that your people had set up for him." Kiernan set his empty glass back on the table. "I'd say he's pretty good at what he does."

"He was lucky." Kos ignored the PR man and focused on the door. He subvocalized commands to the six bashhounds inside the club, calling them over from their various pursuits but telling them to give Sage room to move. Kos was interested in learning what Sage had planned, and in how far the sergeant would go. Kos didn't plan on dying, but he would give Sage enough rope to hang himself.

Kos intended to kill the man if the opportunity presented itself. He should have killed him two nights ago. The encounter in the Azure Mist still rankled Kos's pride. No one in DawnStar's sec forces dared stand up to Kos, and the man intended to keep it that way. The fact that the Terran sergeant had walked away from the encounter unscathed might send the wrong message.

Not only that, but watching Frank Sage in action that night had revealed that the sergeant was a threat. Anyone who could move like that, take on those kinds of odds without blinking and come out on top, was either courting death or entirely convinced of his own prowess. Either way, Kos had resented the orders he'd gotten that night to allow Sage to walk away.

His superior, Zahid Karzai, had ordered Kos to stand down instead of engaging Sage that night, thinking he was preventing the debacle from becoming worse. Dawn-Star liked to operate under the guise of working with the Terran military. General Whitcomb was a frequent guest at DawnStar functions and enjoyed exec privileges on the space station.

Otherwise, Kos would have already dealt with Sage by now. Kos wished he could have taken part in the ambush that killed the previous first sergeant. Terracina had been a thorn in the side of the black-market ops. However, orders had come down from on high that Kos was supposed to stay free of such outlaw behavior so that he could remain working as a public force. Kos had considered ignoring the orders. Sometimes he did that, just to remind his employers he was there by choice. Knowing Sage was going to be there would have tipped the scales.

Now Karzai was busy entertaining Makaum *Quass*, ensuring DawnStar's representations at the local level, gently pulling them onboard with corp goals. Kos hadn't been in the loop to deal with Sage. He looked forward to the confrontation.

"Lucky or not, I'm not going to hang around. A guy like that has an agenda. I don't want to be on it." Kiernan stood and the women stood with him.

"Giving up front-row seats?" Kos smiled.

"Leaving fallout territory is how I see it." Kiernan walked away. "Good luck, Kos."

"I don't need luck." Kos stared at the doorway as Sage arrived carrying a large bundle over one shoulder. Kos sneered. The idiot hadn't even brought more than one weapon and wasn't wearing much armor.

This was going to be easy. Kos looked forward to it.

"Look, Jahup."

Seated at the bar and sipping a fruit drink that cost almost a week's scouting trade chits in the Makaum markets, Jahup glanced over at Noojin, then followed the girl's sharp gaze toward the club's entrance.

Jahup recognized the Terran sergeant immediately as the man who had been at the black-market site that morning. He even knew the man's name. Frank Sage.

Last night, Jahup had led his scouting party out into the jungle to search for offworlder drug labs. The *Quass* members, and his grandmother especially, didn't want the scouts directly engaging with the offworlders because they were so outmatched when it came to firepower. But that didn't stop Jahup from occasionally attacking and destroying small labs, material shipments, and killing personnel who worked at those enterprises. He had seen firsthand what the offworlder poisons could do to his people.

He and his team made it a practice not to tell his grandmother or any of the other *Quass* members everything they did out in the jungle. There were some things the *Quass* didn't need to know. He didn't want to worry his grandmother, and he didn't want to be pulled from his position on his scouting team. Not that he would give up his efforts against the offworlders. He would never do that.

Standing idly by while the offworlders took over Makaum was impossible. He would sooner die. He and Noojin were here now as they often were in order to get to know the faces of the offworlders. They scouted in the club almost as much as they did in the jungle, and both environments were deadly. Knowing the faces of the offworlders helped paint a bigger picture of who was doing what in the jungle.

"What do you think the sergeant is doing here?" Noojin stared raptly at the Terran military man.

Young and pretty, Noojin had always captured Jahup's attention, though he was not certain she was as attracted to him as he was to her. Her dark hair held a slight greenish tint, the product of their environment, and was cut short, lying against her head. She was slim-hipped and didn't possess a woman's full figure, which saved her from the attentions of many of the offworlders.

Like Jahup, she wore casual clothing instead of her scouting clothes. She had two knives hidden somewhere on her person. She always went armed.

Jahup wore long knives strapped to his calves that were hidden by the loose folds of his pants legs. He was certain the club's guards knew that he had the weapons and had just discounted them as ineffectual against their armor and weapons. That was only because they had never seen Jahup use them.

"I don't know what he's doing here, but don't be staring so." Jahup focused his attention on another group but kept the Terran sergeant in his peripheral vision. "You look like an *euvi*."

She grimaced at him, started to say something, then settled for looking away. The *euvi* was a squat amphibian as large as a man's fists together with eyestalks that allowed it to peer above the water while submerged. Any kind of motion attracted an *euvi's* attention, making it an easy target for *uskit* and other flying reptiles desperate for prey. *Euvi* didn't taste good and they reproduced rapidly. The only reason they didn't overpopulate was because they became cannibalistic if their food source ran short and they were reluctant to leave an established area.

Jahup knew that he would pay for the comment. Noojin wasn't known for her forgiving nature. She gave as good as she got.

"The guards in this place will kill him if he tries anything."

"He's not going to do anything here." Jahup said that because engaging the enemy so openly while outnumbered was foolish. Still, part of him hoped that the Terran sergeant was there to get some kind of vengeance for the soldiers that he had lost. Jahup was certain the man knew the corps were behind the ambush. It would be interesting to see how far the man pushed the corps bashhounds.

"He didn't walk in here just to have a look around."

Jahup knew that was true too. After his return to the sprawl, he had heard stories of the combat that had happened at the lab, and of the ambush that had claimed Sergeant Terracina's life. The Terran military didn't know what to make of Sage.

When Jahup had learned of Terracina's death, he'd been saddened. Jahup had always liked Terracina and found him to be a fair and just man, for an offworlder. While hunting out in the jungle for meat to bring back to the families he served, Jahup had always told Terracina of discovered drug labs the scouts could do nothing about, and the sergeant had attacked and destroyed those illegal enterprises.

In exchange, Terracina had helped Jahup and his people keep the offworlder weapons they'd claimed during their raids in top condition. The sergeant had never gone out of his way to promote friendship, always observing the line between the Terran Army and the Makaum people as he'd been instructed by both sides.

Thirty meters away, Sage started forward, heading directly for Kos. There was no doubt about Sage's destination. Jahup searched the rest of the bar to discover where the sergeant's team might be. Surely the man did not intend to confront DawnStar on his own.

But no one else moved in tangent to the sergeant. Jahup would have seen them. He was used to looking for flock and herd and other group movements out in the jungle. Frank Sage was there alone.

"Fool." The word escaped Jahup's lips before he could stop it.

"Why do you think he's a fool?" Noojin narrowed her eyes at him reproachfully.

"Because he's going to get himself killed." Jahup watched more openly now.

"He's not a fool. You saw what was left from the battle last night. A fool would not have survived that ambush." Noojin smiled in appreciation. Her unfettered support of the sergeant's actions irked Jahup. "He is here for revenge."

"He should not be here. If he had any sense, he would wait till Kos was out in the jungle and kill him there from a distance. Revenge should be a safe thing. This is suicide." Jahup knew about killing. In the jungle he and his band often had to bring down large predators they could not afford to meet on equal terms. Sage was confronting DawnStar on less than equal terms.

"Kos seldom goes out into the jungle."

That was true. Although Jahup knew that many of the men operating the drug labs and biopiracy camps out in the jungle worked for DawnStar under Kos's direct supervision, Kos didn't often leave the sprawl.

Jahup watched and felt the tension ratchet up inside himself, making it feel like his heart was suddenly in a cage that was much too small.

Noojin pointed her chin at the club's security people. "Kos is keeping his guards back."

The bashhounds Jahup had identified as Kos's personal sec team stood to the side and watched Sage approach their leader. The only way they would do that was at Kos's direction. Jahup cursed his lack of attention. Noojin had seen whatever passed between the DawnStar bashhound leader and his guards.

Jahup sat up straighter. "That's because Kos wants the pleasure of killing the sergeant for himself." He thought that was too bad because he'd liked the way the sergeant had handled himself.

That morning he had watched the sergeant and observed how well the man commanded his troops, how thorough he'd been while investigating the lab, and the way he'd made certain his wounded soldiers had been cared for immediately. Jahup respected those things in a leader. Those skills were what kept a scout band alive and well.

When he had learned Terracina was going to ship out from Makaum, Jahup had feared for his people. The Terran military was the only force capable of keeping the Makaum free. If they were not there, Jahup was certain the Phrenorians would already have conquered his people.

Or they would have killed them so that the Terrans could not have worked out trade agreements for the bounty Makaum had to offer. Without Terracina, Jahup—and some of the *Quass*—had believed that no one would take up the fight on behalf of the Terran military.

This morning, Jahup had been hopeful again after seeing Sage in action.

Now he was certain he was only going to watch the man die.

SIXTEEN

Nelumbo
Makaum Sprawl
0028 Hours Zulu Time

'm not saying you overstepped yourself when you slew
Yuburack yesterday. I only say that killing him might
have come at a better time. Perhaps when there was less
risk."

Feeling the effects of the native liquor coursing
through his bloodstream, so much sharper since he had
gone through *lannig* so recently, Zhoh GhiCemid gazed
at Mato Orayva and grimaced. His chelicerae quivered
in barely restrained rage. Only his kinship and years of
friendship with the warrior stayed Zhoh's hand from
reaching for his *patimong* and spilling the other's blood.

"Have a care, Mato, that you do not overstep the bounds
of our *spyrl* bond and risk insulting me." Zhoh kept his
voice level with effort. So soon after the *lannig*, his anger
ran as an undercurrent through his body.

"I would never do such a thing." The statement was not
an apology. Phrenorian warriors did not apologize. They

did, however, reassess situations. "Our *spyrl* bond is a sacred thing. Your mother was sister to my mother."

Mato Orayva was tall and proud, a splendid example of Phrenorian warrior breeding. His scales held a variety of deeply purple hues, marking him as one of Raltu Eytuk's lineage. Only that great warrior's offspring bred so true. He got that on his father's side and Zhoh couldn't help but be envious of that breeding, though he would never tell Mato that.

"Yuburack attacked me." Zhoh twirled his empty glass and swished his poison-tipped tail in warning when one of the Makaum natives walked too closely behind him.

The Makaum male ducked his head and darted away, momentarily drawing the attention of the people at the nearby tables. There were not many people nearby. Everyone in the club gave the Phrenorians a wide berth. The corps might have been inclined to bar Phrenorian attendance, but they didn't because they knew that would have incited attacks. So now the corps tolerated Phrenorian presence and even tried to spy on them from time to time. That would not work because no Phrenorian warrior would ever speak of something that he was instructed not to. Failure to comply would result in death.

"I know that he attacked you, but you could have let him live."

Zhoh fixed Mato with his gaze. "Would you have let Yuburack live had he attacked you?"

Mato hesitated, then relaxed in his chair in disgust. "No. Of course not."

"Then why berate me?"

"Because you are not me, *triarr*."

Triarr was a term of affection, *family of my family*, and recognized special relationships with the *spyrl*. Such a thing was not supposed to be so easily recognized while on a mission.

Secretly, Zhoh appreciated the acknowledgment of
their closeness, but he knew he should castigate Mato for
such a transgression. He chose, instead, to sip his drink
and pretend that the address had not happened.

"I do not mean to offend." Mato's chelicerae curled and
straightened irritably. "Nor do I wish to bring up unwel-
come topics, but your star has diminished in the Empire.
Everything that you do outside of given parameters comes
with risk."

"Because that *ang'pol'eag* I was mated with is of in-
ferior bloodstock and her sire had enough wealth and
political pull to make those *ther'ril'eel* blighted spawn
disappear before steps could be taken to denounce her as
worthless to continue the Phrenorian race." Zhoh finished
his drink and felt the alcohol zip through his system.
"Would that I had a chance to depart my home again, I
would do so on different terms. Had I but known I would
end up here, I would have slain that female and prevented
a weakening of Phrenorian blood."

"I would encourage reticence on your part."

"To save me? Or to save yourself?"

Mato made no reply. He didn't have to. Both of them
knew that he was in good standing with the Empire, and
that associating with Zhoh would not change that fact.

Zhoh looked around for another server. The human
waitstaff was notoriously lax in attending Phrenorian
tables. "Trust me, Mato, there is not a member of our
spyrl who does not know about my ill-fated match. Everything I tell you now was voiced in my defense. I spared
no one my thoughts."

"What if the father of your mate decides to prevent you
from talking about his daughter and of his own mistakes
of family?"

Zhoh laughed. "Do you think Yuburack attacked me
only because he thought he would catch me in a moment

of weakness?" His chelicerae snapped with pointed thrusts. "I talked to that stinking *sulqua* as I fed on him. Before he perished, he told me that Blaold Oldawe offered to advance him in rank after he killed me."

"And you told no one?"

"Do you believe me as I tell you now?"

"Yes."

That stopped Zhoh for a moment. He had forgotten what it was like to be around someone who would so easily voice support of him. "Do you think anyone else would?"

Mato fell silent at that.

That lack of response flattened Zhoh's hopes. "No. No one would. All would insist that Yuburack told me the answer he thought I wanted in order that his death would come more quickly." He flicked his tail in annoyance, drawing a squeal of alarm from one of the DawnStar female execs sitting at another table. She and her party got up and retreated to a more distant table though they clearly had not been within reach.

"*Lannig* changes everything."

The saying was the oldest one of the Phrenorian Empire, and it cut both ways as hope and as a warning. *Lannig* could change things for the better, make a warrior stronger and faster and more invincible. But before the strength came the weakness and the vulnerability, an acknowledgment that what was once strong could be made weak.

Zhoh knew that there would never be enough *lannig* phases in his life to give him back what his mate and her father had ripped from him. Only war and risk and triumph could return that to him, and they had made certain he was pushed back from the battles where he might achieve those successes.

Still, he did not want to argue with Mato when the other

was being supportive of him. So Zhoh nodded. "*Lannig* changes everything." He signaled to a server and pierced that young female with his fierce visage, silently ordering her to attend him.

She took their order for more drinks, then hurried in retreat. By the time she returned, Zhoh noticed the Terran sergeant striding across the open floor of the club with the large bundle over his shoulder. Despite the alcohol brewing in his system, Zhoh's mind cleared and his focus sharpened.

He knew the man from the briefings in the daily reports the Phrenorian intelligence services provided. He was the new sergeant, the one who was said to replace Terracina. Zhoh did not know the man's name or his background, but he recognized in the man a sense of purpose and a disregard for rules.

Zhoh sat up straighter and watched in anticipation, sensing the almost out-of-control anger swirling within the man. In this moment, they were almost kindred spirits. The *lannig* opened him up to the emotions of others for a short time and he let himself be consumed by the familiar and welcome rage.

SURPRISED THAT HE had walked across the club floor without being challenged, Sage didn't break stride. He knew that Velesko Kos had made that call to allow him to walk without being stopped, and that the DawnStar bashhound leader obviously thought he could take care of himself.

Kos came to the edge of the raised area of the floor and blocked any attempt Sage might have made to step up into the private area. Kos had claimed the high ground for himself.

Sage stopped at the bottom of the steps, choosing to remain on solid footing.

"Sergeant Sage." Kos's cybered eyes glittered and his body stood taut, all of his amped abilities online. "This is . . . unexpected."

Sage kept his anger under tight control, feeling it squirming and trying to burst out of him. There were a dozen DawnStar bashhounds at his back. If things went badly, all of them would be gunning for him.

"I came to return something to you." Sage spoke in a level voice and he knew that every eye in the Nelumbo was watching him. "Call it a down payment on more yet to come."

"I don't need—"

Sage threw the body bagged corpse on the steps, pulled a combat knife from his boot, and slit the bag from top to bottom. When he stood, he yanked on the bag and the contents spilled from within.

The dead man, burned and torn, lay stiffly on the steps.

Several people yelped and cried out, shocked at the brutality revealed before them. The reaction further irritated Sage. Soldiers had died out in the jungle and the clientele inside the club acted as if those events never happened.

The sight closed Kos's mouth.

"This one's yours." Sage stepped back from the corpse, wishing he had his helmet because he missed the 360-view right now and he felt the coldness of sniper eyes between his shoulder blades. "His name's Shannon Andresik, but I figure you already knew that, because he worked for the same corp you do."

Kos shook his head slowly, but his mouth was a hard, firm line. "I don't know this man."

"Yeah, you do. I saw him with you that night at the Azure Mist."

"If that's true, if this man worked for DawnStar, then you have a history of attacking corp personnel and charges will be leveled."

"I didn't kill this man. I would have been glad to. He was part of the ambush that killed several fine soldiers last night. Men and women who laid their lives on the line to stand against criminals who hope to gut this sprawl." Sage grew conscious of the bashhounds moving behind him. His hand itched for the .500 Magnum, but he refrained. He hadn't come here to initiate a shootout in a public place. He'd come to draw a line, to serve notice, and to validate himself.

"I think you're mistaken, Sergeant Sage." Kos smiled. "This man doesn't work for DawnStar."

"You're lying."

"I'm not." Kos flicked his fingers and a holo jumped out from the wristcomm he wore. The flat image of the dead man rendered in blues took shape in the air between them. "This man *used* to work for DawnStar, but the corp terminated his contract nine days ago."

Sage didn't bother reading the script. DawnStar had written it either two days ago or just now. "Say what you want, Kos, but Shannon Andresik's contract with Dawn-Star was terminated last night, courtesy of the Terran Army. And I'm here to let you know I'm just getting started. While I'm on Makaum, I'm going to shut down every one of your illegal operations out in the jungle that I find. You let your people know they're taking their lives in their hands working for DawnStar at those labs."

"Is that a threat?" The holo blanked and Kos's face turned hard, like it had been lasered out of titanium.

"That's a promise," Sage replied. "Come on out to the jungle and see for yourself."

"You don't just threaten me and walk away." Kos remained standing where he was, but the bashhounds behind Sage closed in another step or two.

Sage remained focused on Kos. "If one of your people

puts a hand on me or points a weapon in my direction, I'll kill you."

Anger flickered in Kos's metallic eyes. "Now *that* is a threat, and since this club is under DawnStar's protective services, I'm required to act in its best interests. You're under arrest, Sergeant Sage. Hand over your weapon."

"Come take it."

Kos shook his head. "No, I have people who do that for me." He gestured to the bashhounds behind Sage. "Take him alive."

Sage turned toward the bashhounds, dividing his attention between them and Kos. Although he'd known the situation was going to get tense, Sage hadn't figured things were going to get to this point so quickly.

Or that Kos would order his men to take him alive. Sage was comfortable risking his life. He'd known he was doing that the instant he'd picked up the body at the morgue. He hadn't thought Kos would escalate the situation to the point of bloodshed. Delivering the body was supposed to put Kos, and DawnStar, on notice.

Several of Nelumbo's patrons scattered, clearing the immediate vicinity around Sage, Kos, and the approaching bashhounds.

Sage cursed, uncertain how to proceed. Standing against the bashhounds wasn't going to do more than delay the inevitable. The odds were against him. And he doubted he'd survive being taken into custody after his performance. DawnStar would want to send a message of its own.

He'd made a mistake, and it rankled him that he'd brushed off one of the basic tenets in military ops in hostile territory: never go anywhere alone. He had acted just as green as a recruit, complacent in his own safety.

But he'd also been unwilling to risk anyone else's life.

The unmistakable high-pitched whine of an energy weapon powering up froze the bashhounds in place. That was immediately followed by a half dozen other weapons powering up or clacking into readiness as safeties were flicked off, and that initiated another wave of energy weapons.

SEVENTEEN

Nelumbo
Makaum Sprawl
0039 Hours Zulu Time

Gut churning, his mind whirling, trying to make sense of everything that was going on, Sage watched, perplexed, as the events unfolded around him. He stood still, knowing the balance between calm and violence was a fragile thing.

The bashhounds turned around slowly, suddenly realizing they were on dangerous ground as well. Beyond them, several Phrenorians stood with hot weps, ready to rock and roll, but none of those weapons were directly pointed at anyone. All around them, several club bashhounds were powering up arms as well.

Kos stood his ground and stared at the Phrenorians. "Put down those guns."

One of the Phrenorians laughed, and the sound was cold and harsh. "No."

"Do you want to start a bloodbath?"

The Phrenorian laughed again. "If I had, I would have

already blasted your ugly head from your too-thin shoulders, human. You would never have seen what happened after that."

Kos's hands stayed within millimeters of his weapons. "What do you want?"

Tail flipping languidly, the Phrenorian tilted his head slightly and his chelicerae twitched. "I would like all of you offal-eating creatures offplanet. Since that's not going to be so easily accomplished, I want Sergeant Sage *not* in your custody."

Kos looked at Sage.

Sage returned the man's gaze and hid his own surprise at the Sting-Tails who had stood to back him. They were the enemy. Nothing was going to change that. Then he recognized the lead Phrenorian as the warrior he and Terracina had encountered in the street during his first night on Makaum. Zhoh GhiCemid.

So what was going on?

"What business do you have with Sergeant Sage?" Kos maintained his stance, but Sage knew the man's mind was working, sorting through the odds.

Sage was doing the same thing, and he didn't like how they kept coming up.

"I've never met Sergeant Sage, but I like the way he delivers messages." Zhoh pointed one of his large claw hands at the corpse lying on the steps in front of Kos. The Sting-Tail laughed again, and the sound was inhuman in the club.

"You're Zhoh GhiCemid, captain of the Brown Spyrl." Kos advanced slowly, stepping over the dead man. "We have an arrangement with your people."

"You do. But only if you're representing DawnStar. If you're representing the illegal labs out in the jungle, we don't have an agreement with you. I will kill you just as surely as Sergeant Sage has promised." Zhoh's chelicerae coiled and uncoiled restlessly. "If DawnStar represents the criminal organizations on this planet, then our agreement with that entity is also null and void. So what is it to be? Is this dead man one of yours? Do you wish to claim your property and your guilt?"

The question hung in the air. Most of the club's patrons were down on the floor now, seeking shelter wherever they could.

Sage's mouth was dry. He wasn't afraid. Years of combat had taught him to put all emotion aside during an engagement, and this was most definitely an engagement. He just didn't like thinking of all the collateral damage that might result. He hadn't intended that.

Kos spoke without taking his eyes from the Phrenorian. "Let the sergeant go."

Slowly, the bashhounds stepped back. They had their weapons in their hands, but nobody raised them.

Sage stood there.

"It's your move, Sergeant." Kos's voice was cold and distant. "You're the one who brought this storm into the club. How do you want this to end?"

Without a word, Sage headed for the door. Getting others—innocents—killed wasn't part of the plan. He walked with his eyes forward, but the skin across his back was tight, expecting a bullet or a beam or a blast. When it didn't happen and he was once more outside the building in the cool night air carrying scents of dozens of trees and bushes, he was surprised.

Someone had released the three bashhounds that had been captured by the tangler grenade. They stood with their weapons ready, but they weren't pointing them at him. Evidently Kos had broadcast his orders to allow Sage passage.

One of the bashhounds spat at Sage's boots, missing by centimeters. "You're lucky, army boy. Make sure you watch your back from now on. Doesn't matter, though. We'll find a grave for you."

Sage started for the crawler he'd driven to the club. Other military vehicles, these packing armor, raced up to him and soldiers in AKTIVsuits debarked, moving out into position with Roleys at the ready.

"Stand down from that vehicle, Sergeant." The command was given in Terran and carried an officer's crisp authority.

Sage stood down.

An AKTIVsuited man walked toward him from the crowd of soldiers and the swagger was pure officer. The man was tall and good-looking, clean shaven, but his features held a hint of las-surgery, which had smoothed them out and made them too perfect. His black hair lay neatly in place. He wore his helmet strapped to his hip. He was a guy used to being looked at, and he enjoyed the attention.

"Major Anthony Finkley," the man announced.

Sage snapped to and held a salute. "Sir."

Finkley didn't respond in kind. He simply looked at Sage, then at the club behind the sergeant. "Had yourself quite the night, eh, Sergeant?"

Sage knew there was no way to correctly answer that, but he said, "Yes sir."

"Well, it's over now."

"Yes sir."

Finkley strode past Sage and headed for the club. "Surrender your weapon, soldier."

"Yes sir." Sage took the .500 Magnum from its holster and handed it, cylinder popped out, to one of the two soldiers who approached him. One of them relieved him of his weapon while the other pulled his arms behind his back and locked restraints onto his wrists. Then they pulled him toward one of the crawlers and stuffed him into an improvised rear cargo deck.

Sage sat on the narrow bench inside the cargo area. There wasn't enough room to sit up straight. He slumped forward, feet spread, to take up his weight. Hours of prolonged fatigue crashed down on him like hammers. The cargo doors slammed shut and he was alone in the darkness. He sat and he breathed. Sometimes that was all a soldier could do. One way or another, he had changed the status quo.

He was also lucky no one had gotten killed.

BLASTER IN HAND, Zhoh walked toward the club's doorway. Mato was at his side and a dozen Phrenorian warriors followed in his wake. All of them were tense and ready for action. The spicy scent of their aggression hung in the still air.

"What did you think you were doing back there when you interfered?" Mato asked.

Zhoh watched the gathered Terran soldiers and the corp bashhounds circling each other warily. Violence thrummed between them and he knew it wouldn't take much to set it all in motion. He was tempted but he set aside his own feelings and concentrated on staying alert.

"What *we* were doing was taking advantage of the situation." Zhoh walked down the steps to the aircar that had delivered them to the club. "The Terran military and the corps are at odds on this planet. They don't like each other, but they're trapped in a symbiotic relationship. The military needs the space station support, and the corps like the free security the military provides on this planet. They will never work together, but I would rather they work more aggressively against each other. That will serve our efforts and give us time to deal with our own agenda. By backing Sergeant Sage against DawnStar tonight, we drove a larger and deeper wedge between those two groups than the ambush did last night. We need to keep our enemies fragmented and at each other's throats. That will make them more vulnerable to us. And it will allow us to move more freely to accomplish our own goals."

"Sage has been taken into custody by his own people."

Zhoh glanced at the transport where Sage had been taken in restraints. "Yes, but the wedge still exists. Dawn-Star made a mistake last night in killing this Sergeant Terracina."

"He was well-liked by his men and by the Makaum people."

"Yes. DawnStar obviously thought they were sending a message to the military and to the natives, and they were doing it in a manner that wouldn't be for all to see. Terracina's tactics had enjoyed limited success out in the jungle. The corps didn't want to tolerate further any such activity. Terracina's execution was supposed to scare the new sergeant and the new recruits, as well as the Makaum informants. This Sergeant Sage knew that as well."

"He could have gotten killed tonight."

"He knew that, and he was willing to accept the risks." It was something Zhoh admired about the human. During the war, he had come to respect humans as an enemy. "He also came without anyone watching his back. He is without a *spyrl*. A being alone. Ultimately, he is doomed to failure. I believe he knows that."

"Then he is a fool for coming here."

Zhoh considered that, but he didn't believe that was the truth. "No, this is a dangerous being. Whatever drives him, it does not release him."

"DawnStar will seek him out and kill him."

"Perhaps. But until such time, we can use him."

"How?"

"Sage is eager to strike against the corps. We have information about their activities out in the jungle. We can ensure that the locations of those operations reach Sage. We can keep him busy striking against our enemies, and they in turn will occupy the military."

Mato opened the aircar's door. It was a long rectangular vehicle outfitted with heavy armor. The magnetic drives whined as they took on Zhoh's extra weight, then Mato's and the other Phrenorians.

"You do realize that Sage may no longer be in a position to act on any information we can give him." Mato settled into the seat and strapped in.

"If Sage is permitted to continue doing the work he has undertaken, we will use him." Zhoh watched through the bulletproof observation slit as the ground dropped away under the aircar. In seconds, the club was a small oasis of bright lights in the relative darkness of the tree-studded sprawl. "Have our intelligence teams find out everything they can about this sergeant."

EIGHTEEN

S age occupied a private cell and sat on a cot screwed into the wall. Besides the bed, and that term was both doubtful and generous, the cell contained a toilet and a sink.

After he'd been locked up, Sage had stripped down to his skivvies, turned off his mind, lain down, and slept, allowing all the fatigue to catch up with him in a rush that pulled him into blackness. This time he wasn't a witness to Terracina's recurring death and the ambush. Delivering the body to Velesko Kos hadn't changed anything, but at least Sage felt as though he'd put the man and the corp on notice. He slept soundly for six hours, then awoke, bathed himself as best as he could in the sink, dressed, and waited.

Last night's interaction with the corps would hurry things along. Sage figured he'd more than likely be booted out on the first dropship flaring into the heavens, then Gated to the front line or back to his training assignment. Maybe if the Terran Alliance hadn't been at war, the confrontation with Velesko Kos would have ended what remained of his career.

If there had been a chance that he would get booted out of the military, he thought he might not have pushed the situation so aggressively. Even as he considered that, though, he knew he'd had no choice. Terracina's death was unacceptable. Especially when Sage knew who was responsible. What he'd done had to be done. Someone had to take a more deliberate stand than the diplomatic liaisons would.

Sage hadn't become a soldier so that good men could die at the hands of murderers and thieves hiding behind corp protection. He could not abide that. If he was unable to prevent those deaths, then he would up the cost of such actions.

Other soldiers slept in the cells around him. The combined stench of boozy breath and body odor mixed with the scent of chemical cleaners and artificial fragrance to become a foul fog that had been present to a lesser degree in the barracks.

The brig was old fashioned, constructed of prefab blocks dropped from low-orbit cargo ships. The pieces had been towed into their present configurations, then snapped together. In some areas, the joints hadn't fit quite smoothly. Plascrete covered seams that had allowed the jungle to wriggle in.

A soldier came by with a backpack flamethrower and spat fire over the delicate tendrils that had crawled in overnight. Scorch marks showed the process had been done time and time again. The soldier entered one of the cells, hosed a patch of growth, and endured the curses of a female soldier still in the throes of hangover.

Breakfast arrived a short time later, wheeled in on a cart with squeaking wheels.

Sage accepted and ate the unappetizing fare: toast and soymeal and some kind of processed protein-sub, and drank the weak tea.

Then he waited.

1137 Hours Zulu Time

Two military policemen arrived just as Sage was beginning to think he was going to have lunch in the brig before he heard anything from the brass. The other soldiers had woken or gotten roused and were sent on their way. Most of them had studied Sage with sullen and suspicious stares. Many of them had whispered Terracina's name.

Sage didn't address any of them, just sat on the cot and waited, elbows resting on knees, eyes forward. He didn't try to guess what would happen to him.

Both MPs were big men who looked well-versed in violence. They worked well as a team, moving fluidly and staying out of each other's way as they dealt with Sage.

"Hands," the shorter one said. He had broader shoulders than the taller man and his nose wasn't quite in line anymore. Scar tissue clustered under his eyes.

Sage approached the cell door and turned to present his back to the men. The taller man clamped on the restraints.

"Step forward and clear the door."

When Sage did, the shorter man waved a keycard in front of the reader. The red light on the locking mechanism switched to green and the door rattled in its moorings as it slid to the side. Sage waited.

"All right, Top, you can join us."

Sage stepped forward.

The shorter guard faced him but stayed out of range of a kick. "Are you going to be a problem?"

Sage quirked his lips at that. "If I was to break out of this place, Corporal, somehow get past you and your buddy—"

"Ain't gonna happen," the taller man promised.

"—where would I go?" Sage finished.

The shorter guard nodded. "Just wanted to make sure we were on the same vector."

"We are."

"I'm Culpepper. That's Tobin."

Sage nodded.

Culpepper shrugged. "This ain't personal, Top. Just doing our jobs."

"No sweat, Corporal."

Culpepper grimaced. "If it was up to me, I wouldn't have you in restraints. Those are the major's idea. I would have told him they weren't necessary, but the major, he don't listen when he don't wanna listen. And he don't wanna listen most of the time. Truth to tell, me and Tobin like what you did to DawnStar last night. We heard that the corp was behind the ambush that killed Sergeant Terracina."

"They were." Sage didn't want to go into it.

"Yeah, everybody knows it, but we ain't been able to call them on it on account of the diplomatic oversight committee we got watching every move we make."

"Don't we have somewhere we have to be, Corporal?"

Culpepper nodded. "We do, Top. Just wanted you to know that more than a few soldiers here at the fort appreciate what you tried to do last night." He put a hand on Sage's shoulder and guided him forward. "Gotta take you to the major, and that's not gonna be a fun time. You get out alive, I'll stand you to a beer."

Office of Major Finkley
Charlie Company HQ
1206 Hours Zulu Time

Even though Sage knew Major Finkley was waiting for
him and was undoubtedly looking forward to the encounter, the major kept Sage and the two MPs waiting for ten
minutes before the receptionist passed them through to
Finkley's office. If the waiting was supposed to unnerve
Sage, the tactic failed.

"Corporals Culpepper and Tobin reporting with the
prisoner, Major." Culpepper brought Sage to a halt ten
feet from Finkley's large desk. The corporal and his partner both saluted, but Finkley ignored them.

The office was large, spacious, and was decked out in
furniture several grades above military standard. Instead
of metal, the desk was inlaid wood, a striking piece of
deep purple and cream woods lacquered to take on a dark
luster. Someone had tucked the hardware seamlessly into
the grain so that the holo seemed to rise from the wood.

The two chairs in front of the desk were equally impressive, concoctions of comfort and elegance. Everything sat on a wooden floor that overlaid the prefab metal.
Light maple panels covered the walls except where built-
in shelves stood and held several items that Sage couldn't
identify.

Finkley's gaze raced over the transparent holo hovering
over his desktop. Three or four screens of information lay
open to him. He manipulated the screens, quickly shifting through datastreams and images, which disappeared
in muted flashes.

From the other side of the holos, Sage couldn't see the
information, but he thought most of them had to do with
Terran Alliance trade data, not MilNet intel. Images and
videos accompanied some of the personal missives, and

most of those were from attractive women that looked like corp execs.

After a few more moments, during which Finkley worked with impressive speed and certainty, the major planted both palms against the desk and the holos turned into pixel dust and disappeared. The lights faded from Finkley's too-perfect features.

"Sage." Finkley spoke the name like it was something foul. "Do you realize what that stunt you pulled last night has done?"

"No sir." Sage knew that pointing out DawnStar's involvement in the ambush that had killed so many Terran soldiers wasn't an acceptable response.

"I'll tell you." Finkley placed his hands together before him and rested his elbows on the desk, leaning into them in a theatric pose. "You've got DawnStar up in arms, and their powers-that-be are eagerly reminding us that we have satellite intel *only* by their good graces, not to mention space-station accessibility. A space station, I will add, that not only adds support to Fort York, but also provides offices to the Terran Alliance Diplomatic Embassy, giving them a certain cachet over other political rivals on-planet, a cachet that those people appreciate. Therefore, not only is our military presence threatened aboard that space station, but so is that of our embassy personnel."

Sage stood silently, thinking that his assignment to Makaum was possibly going to be the shortest post he'd ever been on. He considered, only briefly, of speaking out against DawnStar and about the ambush, but he knew such an effort was doomed to failure.

"Not only that, but you somehow triggered a certain amount of saber rattling on the part of the Phrenorians, which has everyone nervous." Finkley's eyes narrowed. "Can you explain to me what that was about?"

"No sir." Sage knew he had nothing to do with that,

and he remained curious about the Phrenorian involvement himself.

Dropping his hands, Finkley leaned back in his chair. "Well, you'd better figure out what happened, Sergeant Sage, because there are a lot of people—*important* people—who woke up this morning and want to know."

"I have no idea, sir."

Finkley scowled even more darkly, but it was all theatrical posturing. Sage got the sense that the man didn't care, that Sage was just a bump in the career path Finkley had chosen and would be summarily dealt with.

The major shook his head. "You're lucky those Dawn-Star bashhounds didn't burn a hole through your head."

Sage didn't mention that he didn't think that would happen, with Velesko's life hanging in the balance as well.

"And you're even luckier that an all-out war didn't break out last night." Finkley took in a breath and let it out. "There is some speculation about your relationship with the Phrenorians, Sergeant. Our intel division is checking through your past involvement with them."

"The only past involvement I have with the Phrenorians is killing them, sir. I got really good at it till I got sidelined."

Finkley grimaced and shook his head. "I've been through your field service report. You weren't sidelined. For the last six years, you were given a hero's posting as a drill instructor in recognition of your efforts."

"I didn't request that posting." Sage clamped his jaws in order to keep from cursing. "I didn't want it. Sir. All I wanted was the opportunity to serve with my fellow soldiers."

"Your fellow soldiers had a bad habit of getting themselves killed around you. I've seen the after-action reports. Analysts were torn between declaring you the luckiest soldier to ever take the field, or a master survivor. Now, after last night, some of them are wondering if you'd been protected by the Phrenorians. And why."

Sage barely bit back a scathing reply. Protesting his innocence would have just been a waste of breath. Finkley had already chosen his course of action.

"On all of those worlds where you served, the Phrenorians have penetrated our communications and were privy to information they shouldn't have known." Finkley regarded Sage with suspicious speculation. "Given the situation that occurred last night, some of those analysts are reevaluating the possibility that you are working with the enemy."

"That isn't true." Sage couldn't keep himself from responding even though he knew the major's words were designed solely to elicit a response from him.

Finkley splayed his hands across his desk. "Perhaps not, but people are asking questions. Rest assured, Sergeant, that you have pretty much ended your military career."

The statement hit Sage like a particle blast. He suddenly felt dizzy, like he was weightless and being sucked into a black hole. He couldn't be released from the army. There was a war on. And if he wasn't a soldier, he wasn't anything.

"General Whitcomb has been apprised of your activities. I have made the recommendation that you be dishonorably discharged for insubordination and conduct unbecoming a soldier." Finkley stared at Sage with a calculated gaze. "There is also some talk of holding you accountable for the murder of Sergeant Terracina given the actions on the night of the sergeant's death. In addition to getting kicked out of the military, you may spend the rest of your natural life in a military prison."

Sage kept silent with difficulty. He wanted to know what Whitcomb had to say, and he reeled while trying to comprehend how much pressure was coming back on him. This response was above and beyond anything he'd expected.

The office door opened.

Finkley growled a curse. "Corporal Rusch, I told you I wanted everything held until—"

"Corporal Rusch was ordered to stand down." Colonel Halladay strode into the room.

Finkley stood with obvious reluctance that was a couple degrees short of actual insubordination and saluted. "Colonel, I didn't know you would be joining us."

"Neither did I." Halladay's tone was hard. "I thought you understood that Master Sergeant Sage was supposed to be brought to me. Immediately. Those were the instructions I'd given. I even checked them after I discovered Master Sergeant Sage was brought to you first. I was very clear."

"Yes sir. I thought I would help you clear your calendar."

Halladay's sharp reply cut like a nano-whip. "When I give instructions, Major, I have already done all the thinking that's required."

A dark flush crept up Finkley's face from his neck. His jaw worked for a moment, but whatever he was on the verge of saying was swallowed. "Yes sir."

"You and I will discuss this at a later date."

"Yes sir." The threat caused Finkley to pale a little.

Halladay turned to Culpepper and Tobin. "Remove the master sergeant's restraints."

"Yes sir." Culpepper keyed the shackles and they opened, releasing Sage's wrists. At the same time, turning so that neither of the officers could see him, the corporal winked.

Sage understood then how Halladay had found out about the visit to Finkley's office.

Halladay gazed around the office. "It's been a long time since I've visited your office."

"Yes sir."

"It's more elegant than I remember."

An uneasy look filled Finkley's face and he reddened. "It's been a while, sir."

"You've acquired a lot of things."

"Yes sir. Gifts from the diplomatic team, the Makaum *Quass*, and others who appreciate the work I—*we*—do. As you know, I see a lot of those people here. I've made modifications to make the office more amenable to receiving those guests."

Halladay fixed the major with his gaze. "The next time I'm in this office, which will be within the next twenty-four hours, I promise you, I expect it to be returned to military specs. Those accommodations are fine for the people you see."

"Sir—"

"I trust that *order* left no possibility of confusion."

Finkley's nostrils flared. "No confusion, sir."

"Good." Halladay turned to Sage. "You're with me, Top."

Not certain if he was jumping from the frying pan into the fire, Sage nodded. "Yes sir." He followed Halladay from the room.

NINETEEN

Office of Colonel Halladay
Charlie Company
Fort York
1219 Hours Zulu Time

Halladay led the way into his office and tossed his cover onto the hat rack in the corner with a casual flick of his wrist. Walking behind the desk, so much smaller than the one in Finkley's office, he took a seat.

Sage stood at attention in front of the colonel's desk.

"Take a seat, Top."

"Yes sir." Sage slid into the nearest seat.

Halladay narrowed his eyes in thought. "The general is not happy with you."

"I expect not, sir."

"You've caused him a lot of trouble this morning. I've spent the last few hours listening to him chew me out."

Sage didn't know what to say to that, so he said nothing.

"There was some talk of putting me on report for not having better control of my people."

"That was not my intention, sir."

"I know that, but I'm irritated, because if I'd known what you were going to do, I would have been prepared for it. As it was, I ended up blindsided and scrambling. Just so you know, that's not a good place to be with General Whitcomb, who intends to ride out his glory years as quietly as possible."

"That was not—"

Halladay held up a hand. "Stow the apologies. We're where we are. Let's deal with the fallout."

Sage lapsed into silence.

"I could have gotten you from Finkley's office sooner. I chose not to because I wanted to you to see the grinder that was waiting on you. I trust he told you that there was some talk of a dishonorable discharge?"

"Yes sir."

"For the record, that option was brought up. I blocked it." Halladay's blue eyes flashed. "In fact, I told the general that your presence at that club last night was on my orders. Needless to say, that extended our little chat throughout most of the morning, and I got a sharply worded letter in my personal file."

That surprised Sage. "Why would you do that, sir?"

Halladay opened the bottom drawer of his desk, took out a bottle, and two glasses. He poured dusky amber liquid into both glasses. "Because Sergeant Richard Terracina was a good man and didn't deserve what those animals did to him. And because standing up for what you did was the right thing to do. Not the smartest. I want to be clear on that." He pushed one of the glasses across to Sage. "I joined the military because I wanted to make a difference. My father died fighting the Phrenorians on Ralkko Nine."

"That was a bloody bit of business, sir."

"It was, and when we're drinking together, Sage, drop the sir." Halladay held up his glass. "To Sergeant Richard Terracina, one of the finest soldiers I've known."

Sage raised his glass as well, and they drank. The potent alcohol tasted smoky and Sage knew it hadn't been locally produced. The drink hit his stomach like napalm and settled into a warm glow.

Halladay poured them another round. "I'm here with General Whitcomb because I know serving under him will fast-track my career. It already has. I'm not just doing it for me. I'm doing it for the Alliance and for the soldiers I serve with. I'm good at what I do, Sage. I just haven't had much of a chance to do it here." He picked up his glass. "Until now. After that ambush, the gloves are off. General Whitcomb agreed with me, reluctantly, but the corps went too far. They're about to find that out."

Hope started to blossom inside Sage. He'd wanted something to do for six years. Maybe it wasn't fighting Phrenorians on the front line, but weeding out the black market and the criminal franchises around Makaum would be a worthwhile task. He could live with that. For now. "Sounds good."

"But just so you know, if you do something like what you did last night again, I'll throw you under the bus."

"Noted." And if the colonel wasn't in agreement about something, Sage figured he could find a workaround they could both live with.

"I also want you to know that if you'd come to me last night, I would have joined you and placed a rifle unit behind you. A soldier in my unit never goes anywhere alone. See that it doesn't happen again."

Sage knew the surprise he felt must have registered on his face.

"The night before last, the corps pushed us." Halladay rolled the glass in his fingertips. "You were right to push back. You were wrong to do it alone."

"I figured I was alone."

"You were. But you're not alone anymore. Sergeant

Terracina was following my orders to unseat the drug ops out there in the jungle. We were doing it slow and consistently, making certain of ourselves, being careful not to step on any toes or rock the boat." Halladay locked eyes with Sage. "Those days are over. Complacency on this post is over. We may not be engaged in the war with the Phrenorians, we may even be sharing a DMZ with the Sting-Tails, but we're not going to tolerate the black market in any area under our control, and I view the Makaum sprawl as under military protection. Maybe I can't do anything about what the corps do on their own grounds, but I can shut down known offenders in the DMZ."

"All right."

"The corps are going to know we're coming now, though, and they're going to be more dangerous than ever. The soldiers we've got are green and lax. Some of them are even involved in those illegal ops, and some of them are using their products. I want you to train these soldiers, break them and remold them if you have to, and I want you to ferret out whoever is involved with the black market. You find those soldiers, I'll get rid of them, ship them directly to the front line with warning labels so those commanders don't get caught flat-footed. Word will get around. I don't know how fast we can get recruits here, so be aware that you're going to be whittling down our manpower as you go."

"It's better to have people like that outside the fort than in."

Halladay nodded. "I agree, but as we cut people here, they may opt to desert and join the corps' illegal activities if I can't get them on a ship fast enough. We'll be stacking the odds against us, and we're going to make a lot of enemies."

"The odds are already stacked and it's better to know

who the enemy is. We'll just make sure we know who is on what side of the line."

"Finkley is going to be a problem." Halladay rubbed a big hand over his lower face. "His father is a career diplomat and he put Finkley here. The general allowed it as a favor, but I think he suspects he made a mistake. The major plans on following in his old man's shoes, and he's using his stint in the military to shore up relations with the corps and the local politicos. Scuttlebutt even suggests that he's working with some of the (ta)Klar, providing them information and access to our movements. I can't touch Finkley because he's too well connected. Even the general is leery of uprooting the major without good reason, because doing so would trigger an avalanche of political repercussions. Alliance Senator Aldous Finkley watches out for his only son."

"You mean, uprooting the major without evidence."

"I do mean without evidence. And lots of it if we can get it. Like I said, the major is well connected." Halladay's blue eyes hardened. "I suspect Finkley had something to do with Terracina's death. Or someone close to him did. But I don't think we'll ever be able to prove that."

Perhaps not, but Sage resolved to try.

"Therefore," Halladay continued, "you're going to be working directly for me. Through a lieutenant who will be theoretically in command of your team."

"My team?"

"I want you to find out who you can trust, and I want you to train them to be fast and lethal out there in the jungle. I want a special-ops task force dedicated to removing the drug labs, corps sponsored and domestic, and start squeezing the black market that's currently flourishing here. When you're not training, I want you and those people out there busting heads. And when you're not out there busting heads, I want you training."

The immensity of the operation staggered Sage, but it excited him as well.

"In order to be successful, you and your team are going to have to operate independently of the rest of the fort. That's going to trigger some bad feelings among the other soldiers, and you're going to need to be sure of the people you pull onto your squad."

Sage knew the task was harder than Halladay was saying. Sage was new to Fort York. He didn't have anyone there whom he shared history with.

Halladay evidently knew what was going through Sage's mind. "Check the files. Some of the soldiers here are people you've trained with. Start small and build as you go, as you're sure of the soldiers you want on your team."

That was, if the attrition rate of the amped-up effort out in the jungle didn't kill soldiers faster than Sage could recruit them.

"Is that something you're interested in?" Halladay stared at Sage over the top of his glass.

"It is."

Halladay grinned. "Then finish that drink. We've got a lot to do and this isn't going to be easy or safe."

"I didn't sign on for either of those things."

Special Ops Conference Room 3
Fort York
1307 Hours Zulu Time

A knock sounded at the security door.

Sage sat in the private conference room with Halladay at a table where a holo hovered in the air between them. Halladay brushed aside the holo of the jungle surrounding the Makaum sprawl, dumping it off view for the moment, then punched up the camera overlooking the door to the room.

A man wearing second lieutenant bars and carrying a Roley stood at the door. He was average-looking, black hair and doe-soft brown eyes, with a cleft chin. He wore neatly pressed camos and he looked young enough to be a college student or just out of officer candidate school.

"That is Lieutenant Hadji Murad. He's going to be the acting officer on your unit. He's good. Dedicated. But he's greener than grass. Thankfully, he also takes orders well. And, as far as I can determine, he's not involved with the corps or the black market. Your job is to train him and keep him alive while you're out there." Halladay flicked a hand against the holo and the door's locking mechanism clicked open.

Sage got to his feet and stood at attention as the young lieutenant entered the room.

Murad was a couple inches shorter than Sage, and his skin was a couple shades darker. The lieutenant was also easily a dozen years younger. The young Russian moved well though, compact and fluid. His watchful eyes flicked from Halladay to Sage and stayed there, sizing Sage up.

Sage held his salute until Murad returned it.

"Have a seat, Lieutenant." Halladay waved to one of the chairs. "I don't think you've met Sergeant Frank Sage."

Murad sat in the chair next to Sage and studied him briefly. "I have not met him. But I have heard about him."

"You're going to hear more." Halladay pulled the view of the jungle back onto the holo projection. In terse sentences, the colonel outlined the plans for the special team.

Sage watched the younger man to see if there was any hesitation or reluctance.

"As I understand it," Murad said when Halladay finished, "I'm going to be serving more or less as a rubber stamp to Sergeant Sage's operations." He didn't appear flustered or put out, just interested in clarifying things.

"No, sir," Sage said before Halladay could respond. He locked eyes with the younger man. "The colonel explained to me that you're an intelligence specialist, that you haven't been on many ops like this before, but you've been trained on the hardware we'll be using. He also told me out of all the junior officers in the fort, you've been the one most often out in the jungle."

Murad blinked in surprise.

"The colonel said you had an interest in the flora and the fauna." Sage grinned. "You may have mustered out of college as a second lieutenant, sir, but your field of study was xenobiology."

"It was. I wasn't aware that anyone knew that."

"We are, sir," Sage said. "This team is going to need both of those pools of information. The intelligence, the cybernetics knowledge, and the xenobiology if we're going to last more than a few days. In order to effectively hunt our enemies, we're going to need to know how to trap them, and how to stay alive out in the wild."

Murad leaned into the holo then and interest stirred more keenly in his liquid eyes. "This is going to be a very dangerous enterprise."

"Yes, sir, it is." Sage stared into the transparent depths of the jungle, watching as fierce reptiles and giant insects moved through the trees and brush.

"We need to set up base camps outside the fort." Murad took out his PAD and took notes with his stylus. "The team will need to get acclimated to the jungle. I assume we're going to be staying out on patrol for extended periods."

Halladay nodded as he poured coffee and pushed cups through the holo to Sage and Murad. "Once we start this, the black marketers are going to want to know who's raiding them, and they'll want to strike back. Men who go on these missions are going to be marked."

The words the colonel spoke only yesterday rattled through Sage's mind. *We've got targets pinned to our backs.* That was true, and they were about to outline those targets in neon.

"We need places that are clear enough to train in." Sage sipped his coffee. "Places where the water is good, where we can defend ourselves from natural predators, and where the enemy can't sneak up on us."

Reaching out with his stylus, Murad shrank the topography surrounding the Makaum sprawl and marked a few areas with bright red dots. "I know a few places."

"We're going to have to move around a lot." Sage studied the topography and the dots. "More than that. Those areas are too close together."

Murad shifted the stylus and marked more areas.

"You've been to all of these places?" Sage asked.

"I have. And I've got field notes on those areas." The lieutenant looked slightly embarrassed. "I've been working on articles regarding Makaum's eco-structure . . . in my spare time, Colonel."

Halladay nodded. "Understood, Lieutenant."

"Have you published any of those articles?" Sage asked.

Murad glanced at Sage in confusion. "A few."

"Then you'll need to take those places off the map. Once those black marketers figure out you're part of this, which will be soon, they'll study you and find those articles. They'll start guessing where we might be, and they'll be right enough to cause us problems."

"Of course." Murad tapped some of the dots and they extinguished. Several of them were removed. The lieutenant obviously stayed busy, and Sage felt more confident about Halladay's choice of officers.

Sage traced the lines of dots. "These are all along the rivers."

"You said you wanted fresh water."

"I do, but those rivers are going to be roads that lead right to us. These areas by the rivers, we'll use those for quick stops, resupply places where we can get what we need and get gone again."

Murad's face brightened in understanding. "You want places that have springs."

"And places where we can dig wells." Sage nodded. The fort had portable automated digging equipment they could use to set up wells. "We need to have sources of water, but they can't be in any predictable order."

The lieutenant's lips twisted in a smile. "Roger that. You've really thought about this operation."

Sage looked at the holo map. "This isn't an operation, Lieutenant. This is war."

TWENTY

Dressed in clean camos and fresh from the shower and from a solid night's sleep, ignoring the stares of the soldiers that followed him down the training facility, Sage strode down the hallway to Holo Deck 13. A lot of times the number was left out of rotation because soldiers still equated 13 with bad luck. As a result, Holo Deck 13 throughout the Terran military tended to be underutilized.

Pausing at the door, Sage peered through the viewscreen. Inside, Sergeant Kjersti Kiwanuka was lying on a raised dais, shooting again and again into the green void that lay around her at targets only she could see. She wore multipocketed camo pants that she had altered herself or had gotten altered, because they fit her well, and a white tank because the holo decks tended to run hot, simulating the mugginess of the Makaum jungle. She was trim and fit, her dark skin shiny with a sheen of perspiration. Her platinum hair fell over her shoulders.

When Sage pressed his palm against the biometric plate at the side of the door, the door slid back and the program running on the holo deck froze. He stepped through the doorway as Kiwanuka turned to look at him. She rested the stock of the heavy sniper rifle on the skeletal butt-stock. Including the oversized silencer, the weapon was almost two meters long, a nasty construction of black matte steel.

"Sergeant." Sage nodded at the woman, who still lay prone.

"My time isn't up."

"No, it's not."

"So that door should be locked."

"It was." On Halladay's orders, Sage had gotten special clearance to nearly every structure at the fort.

"I guess it's not anymore."

"Not for me."

Kiwanuka paused for a moment to just stare at him. "I figured you would be in the brig." Anger sounded just under the surface of her attitude.

"I was. For a while."

"What changed?"

"Colonel Halladay had me released."

"I didn't think they would give you time to say good-bye."

"Why would I say good-bye?"

Kiwanuka regarded him suspiciously. "You're not getting kicked offplanet?"

"I'm not leaving."

"You threw a dead body at a DawnStar employee and claimed they were responsible for the ambush that killed Terracina."

"I did."

"Then why aren't you gone?"

"Circumstances have changed."

"What circumstances?"

"That's what I'm here to talk to you about. When you have time." Sage raised his voice. "Holo Deck 13. Resume program."

The green interior disappeared in an eyeblink and was replaced with the ruins of a city Sage didn't recognize. Alabaster buildings, most of them broken spires of wreckage, stood against rolling crimson hills that led down to a sparkling azure sea. Several ships sat in a natural harbor, and most of those vessels had flaming sails and men fighting to the death on the heaving decks.

Kiwanuka settled in behind her rifle and took shots at shaggy combatants. At first Sage thought the enemy were soldiers dressed in some kind of tribal hides, then he saw that he was wrong, that they were excessively hairy beings wearing equally hairy armor that looked like part of their bodies.

Sage held his hands up in front of his eyes and the holo program dutifully provided a pair of vector laser rangefinder binoculars. He scanned the landscape, piggybacking Kiwanuka's view through the sniper scope.

The rifle tracked smoothly across the buildings and picked up a group of five shaggy soldiers sprinting across a rooftop with anti-tank weapons obviously headed for use against the Terran armor group smashing through the buildings on street level.

"Who are they?" Sage asked.

"Iracko." Kiwanuka's voice was almost neutral, but Sage detected the hint of emotion there.

"I've never heard of them." Since the Gates had opened, Terra had been exposed to a lot of new planets and races.

"It's from a small war on a planet most people have never heard of. Command wanted to keep it for pride points. The Iracko are from the Tavamox system. They're violent and bloodthirsty, but they can be cold and calculating. Think of them as Romans without any sense of remorse. They live to conquer and they feed on human flesh. This world is Jufonu. My brother, Kasule, was a Terran medical support person onplanet. He died there defending a hospital. We never got his body back. The Iracko tend not to leave much of their defeated enemy behind, and they don't take prisoners. Not to keep."

Kiwanuka took up trigger slack and the rifle kicked against her shoulder. She rode the recoil out and shifted to her next target, the Iracko warriors at the end of the single line spread across the rooftop. She fired the second round before the first round cored through the leader's neck and almost decapitated him.

When the leader sank into an uncoordinated stumble and fell, then began sliding for the rooftop's edge, the other Iracko warriors halted and immediately turned around to retreat.

Kiwanuka's second shot slammed into the last warrior's head just beneath the helmet, which looked like a skull from some exotic creature. Dead on his feet, the Iracko warrior slumped into a boneless heap while the other three surviving warriors froze in indecision.

Coolly, like she had all the time in the world, Kiwanuka killed the other three warriors with quick, well-placed shots, no wasted bullets, no wasted movements. The economy of skill was as precise as Japanese haiku or Omrayund ale. The range to the rooftop was 2,027 meters. Movement of even a fraction of an inch would have made Kiwanuka miss her target by centimeters at that distance. All of her shots had gone precisely where she had wanted them to.

Kiwanuka's biometric readout hadn't fluctuated in the slightest. She'd remained totally focused throughout the encounter, her heart rate steady and her breathing regular.

"You come in here and kill Iracko warriors often, Sergeant?"

"I do. Freeze program." Kiwanuka lowered the weapon to rest its butt on the ground, which in the holo was a craggy promontory that overlooked the besieged city.

The battleground locked into place and the whole room shifted from vibrant life to an artificial quality that had always jarred Sage. The 3-D quality lost its edge. When the holo was running, everything looked real. But when things stopped, the sudden stillness left his senses slightly rolling.

Kiwanuka sat up and looked at Sage. "You come around to watch soldiers in holo much, Sergeant?"

Sage ignored the question for the moment. "What are you carrying?"

Kiwanuka answered without looking at her weapon. "Cheytac ten point four millimeter semiautomatic. Caseless ammo. You have to clean it often, but it's the most reliable sniper weapon I've ever used. It makes kills out to two thousand meters plus. It comes with a standard seven-round detachable box, but when I have a secure sniper perch and a target-rich environment, I bump up to specially made thirty-round magazines. I load my own rounds."

"Why not a beam weapon or a particle blaster? There's no recoil on those, and you don't have to worry about reloading."

"A sniper doesn't have to worry about reloading. She's there to take a shot, a key shot. If I've got an assigned target, or even three, usually that's all the shots I take, then I have to move. The only time I use a thirty-round box is when I'm there to punch holes in enemy combatants and disable their vehicles. A sniper who stands her—or his—ground too long gets killed there."

Sage nodded. "A slug thrower like that generates a lot of recoil, takes time off of follow-up shots."

"I like the psychological effect the physical damage has on the enemy. They get beamed, they tend to just fall. If you see someone's head, or limb, suddenly turn into bloody mist, that leaves an impression. Especially when you're thinking you could be next. Plus, even if you miss hitting a target squarely, the hydrostatic shot of an impact can incapacitate an enemy and sometimes kill them." Kiwanuka narrowed her eyes. "You didn't just decide to drop by and talk about weapons."

"Yes and no. We'll get to that. What are you doing on Makaum?"

"My job."

"I checked your file. You've tried to go offplanet since you got assigned here seven months ago to rehab an injury."

Kiwanuka frowned. "Until I saw you in action at the ambush, I thought you were just a sergeant killing time here till retirement."

Stung, Sage had to work to keep from putting steel in his words. "I came to Makaum under protest. This isn't where the war with the Phrenorians is."

"That's where I want to be." Kiwanuka nodded. "Instead, I drew this place."

"Why?"

"If you've seen my field service report, you already know why."

Sage had seen the full field service report after Halladay had cleared his access. Kiwanuka wasn't on Makaum just for rehab.

"The notation regarding your . . . disagreement with Lieutenant Swarton seems diluted. And usually striking a superior officer will get you dumped out of the military in a heartbeat."

"Swarton led my unit into an area we knew to be questionable. He didn't wait till the minesweepers gave us a green light, just ordered us through. I was in the lead crawler. An IED took out my team, killed two of them and maimed the third." Kiwanuka's nostrils pinched as she inhaled in a controlled fashion. "I lost my right arm." She held up the limb and made a fist.

Sage couldn't tell any difference between that arm and the other. "The medtechs did a good job patching you up."

"I chose bionic replacement over organic."

"They tend to be problematic and don't last as long as organic replacements." They also tended to remind a soldier of his or her mortality, and they distanced them from other flesh-and-blood soldiers at times too.

"That's fine. I wear this arm out, I'll go get another. If I got a chance to hit Swarton again, I wanted to drive my fist through his face. I went through the spinal reinforcement too."

That surprised Sage. Spinal enhancement surgery like that took longer to recover from, and when the body rejected the bionics, as they sometimes did, temporary and even permanent paralysis could result. The neural linkages weren't guaranteed, and if they failed, it was a lot of misery to go through.

"I gave an arm in service to the Alliance, for a war I believe in. I wanted something more back."

"What about Lieutenant Swarton?"

Kiwanuka wrapped her arms around her bent knees. For a moment her dark gaze was somewhere else, then she looked back at Sage. "After the explosion, after I saw that my team was dead, after I made sure the medics were taking care of Corporal Naqsh, I did my best to put Lieutenant Swarton in the morgue. I only got him as far as the hospital."

"With an injured arm?"

"With a missing arm. The AKTIVsuit clamped the wound just past the shoulder and pumped me full of meds. The others pulled me off of Swarton before I killed him. If I'd had two arms, they wouldn't have been able to do that."

"Swarton was in intensive care for four days, then had to undergo facial reconstruction."

"That was a waste of time. That man was ugly even after they finished with him." A cruel smile framed her lips.

In spite of the grave nature of the conversation, Sage laughed.

Kiwanuka hesitated at first, then joined him.

"You were lucky Command didn't cut your psychiatric discharge papers and send you on your way."

"I'm a great sniper, a great soldier. They need people like me more than they need Lieutenant Swarton. The way the system's set up, favoring politicos and corps, the military ends up with a lot more Swartons than soldiers like me." She studied Sage in open speculation. "If you're here instead of on a dropship headed offplanet, I guess somebody figured they needed you too."

"Colonel Halladay has a special assignment for me. I'm putting together a team. I thought I'd ask if you were interested."

"Tell me about it."

"Let me buy you breakfast and we'll discuss it."

0752 Hours Zulu Time

Several pedestrians blocked the streets as Sage guided the crawler toward the bar Kiwanuka had recommended. After he'd come to a stop several times, he was beginning to think he and Kiwanuka would have made better time on foot. He swept the street, looking for a way through. Already on alert, he spotted the assassin on top of one of the vine-encrusted two-story buildings that lined the street to his left. The man wore patchy green clothing that helped him blend into the surrounding vegetation, but the barrel of his rifle with its straight lines looked out of place.

"Down!" Sage jerked the crawler to the right and floored the accelerator.

The sniper's bullet caromed through the thin padding that covered the back of the driver's seat, missing Sage by millimeters. The vibration of the impact shuddered down Sage's spine. He pulled the crawler into an alley and stopped. With the people in the streets, there was no way they could escape in the vehicle.

"Sniper's nested on the building across the street." Kiwanuka bailed from the crawler and reached into the back for her rifle. She'd left her sniper rifle in its case in the cargo deck. The Cheytac was too unwieldy, close up like this, and the bullets were too powerful for a densely packed urban area with no proper place to set up.

"Roger that." Sage pushed free of the crawler and grabbed his Roley.

Kiwanuka ran to the corner of the alley. "Is there only one sniper?"

"I don't know. Would you work alone?" Sage sprinted in behind her and kept an eye on the other end of the alley through his helmet's 360-degree vision. Plan B could have included a second team looking over the alley. Sage knew he would have put one there.

"Not if Command wanted to make sure that the target I'd been assigned to terminate got dead. They'd always have a backup team in place."

"That's what I was thinking." Sage reached into his combat vest and pulled out two mini-drones. He activated them through his helmet, assigned them screen overlays that cluttered his vision somewhat, then hurled them into the air.

The mini-drones, nicknamed ParaSights because they were flying eyeballs that could relay imagery and GPS locations, took flight immediately, heading in opposite directions. They were smaller than his little finger, looked like tiny zeppelins with fins at one end, and were solar-powered. Switchblade wings popped out the sides to give them added control.

Sage voice-commanded the ParaSights, overriding their pre-programming to map out the surroundings and to focus on the nearby terrain, searching for hostiles. Almost immediately, one of them picked up the sniper lying atop the building across the street.

"Mark and continue surveillance."

On the transparent overlay of ParaSight 01 the sniper was outlined in orange, painted as a recognized enemy. Meshing all three views, the 360-degree configuration as well as the incoming feeds from the mini-drones, was problematic and took a lot of training. Sage had mastered it, couldn't manage more than two of them at a time while on the move, and always had a headache for a couple hours after any time spent working with the mini-drones.

"Sniper's still on the roof." Sage opened a comm channel to Fort York.

Kiwanuka paused at the corner of the building and peered out into the street. She tilted her head up. "I don't see him."

"If you saw him, he'd be dead by now."

"How do you see him?"

"ParaSights."

"Feed me."

"You're trained?"

"I can handle up to four of them at a time."

Sage placed his gloved hand against the back of Kiwanuka's helmet and pulsed a feed connection to her through
his suit. "Got 'em?"

"Only two?" She sounded surprised.

"That's all I can handle."

"You need to practice more."

Before Sage could respond, the comm opened to the
post. "Fort York Command."

"This is Master Sergeant Frank Sage. I've got a Condition Red. I need a couple of jumpcopters in the air now.
Send them to my location." He pinged his GPS location.
"Sergeant Kiwanuka and I are taking hostile fire from
unknown assailants."

"Roger that, Top. Unfriendly bogeys at your twenty."
The comm operator's voice sharpened but remained professional. "Sending two birds now that are weps hot."

"Understood."

"Notifying Colonel Halladay."

Sage returned his attention to Kiwanuka as she turned
and planted a shoulder into his chest, knocking him back.

"Grenade! Move!"

Sage turned and ran with Kiwanuka at his heels. Para-
Sight 02 relayed the image of the gel grenade that had
plopped onto the corner of the building where they had
been taking cover. There was no time to attempt to re-
trieve the crawler.

The helmet filtered most of the explosion, lowering the intensity to something just short of thunder that
would have ruptured their eardrums. The concussive
wave knocked them flat. Sage's faceshield hammered
the ground as debris thudded against the AKTIVsuit
hard enough to leave bruises that would last for days. His
senses swam at the edge of a giant black hole that was
trying to suck him in.

TWENTY-ONE

et up! Sage made himself move, made the neurons connect the synapses and got his body in motion. He forced himself to his feet with his left hand while his right found the Roley and pulled it to him. The armor's near-AI punched stims into his body and his mind started clearing at once as his senses sharpened and the world seemed to slow down around him.

He turned to Kiwanuka and found her lying bonelessly beside him. Some of the stone shrapnel stuck out of her AKTIVsuit and he wondered if one or more of them had gotten through the armor and killed her. They had practically been on top of the grenade when it detonated. He laid a hand against her shoulder and accessed her biometrics.

The heartbeat and respiration were there and she didn't appear to be losing blood. She was just unconscious. Sage accessed the suit's near-AI. "Stims online."

```
Warning. This soldier is comatose. Stim
should only be administered by med
personnel or if in enemy territory.
```

Sage cursed. "We're in enemy territory. Stim her now." He tracked ParaSights 01 and 02. ParaSight 01 still had eyes on the initial sniper, who had taken advantage of the explosive distraction to abandon his sniper's nest atop the building and was now swapping out the sniper rifle for a heavy-duty particle-beam pistol as he ran toward the alley where Sage and Kiwanuka were.

```
Stims administered. Soldier responsive.
```

Kiwanuka's biometric readings surged and she regained consciousness with a sharply indrawn breath.

"Report hemorrhaging, internal and external." Sage pulled on her shoulder and helped her to her feet. Even half out of it, she retained the presence of mind to pick up her rifle. "Broken bones. Any threatening injuries."

```
Soldier appears physically stabilized. No
danger of further injury from movement
imminent.
```

Sage pushed his faceshield into Kiwanuka's, peering through his HUD and the ParaSight overlays to see her face. "Are you with me, Sergeant?"

Kiwanuka nodded slowly at first, then got it together. Her eyes focused on him and she took a breath. "Roger that."

"Can you move?"

The ParaSights tracked a small group of gunners crossing the street. The Makaum citizens struggled to get clear of the area, ducking into buildings, alleys, and running to get away as quickly as they could. Three Makaum citizens lay dead or wounded at the impact site. The corner of the building looked like a predator had taken a bite out of it. The wood hung in splinters.

"Yes."

"The other end of the alley."

Kiwanuka lifted her rifle and opened fire just as a group of armed assailants started shooting at them. A laser bean scorched the front of Sage's AKTIVsuit but the armor held even though it grew uncomfortably warm before he could dodge to the side.

"This way." Still firing, Kiwanuka headed for a nearby building where a door stood wreathed by branches from the trees and bushes that grew through the wall.

Sage followed her and triggered the Roley as he went, aiming for the center of the crowd. Their bursts knocked down three of the gunmen and dispersed the others.

The door at the back of the building was locked when Kiwanuka reached it. She turned sideways as bullets and beams ripped through the foliage in front of her. She used her bionic arm as a battering ram, hammering the wooden barrier.

Sage stepped into place beside her and took aim at the ruined end of the alley as the first of their attackers from that direction put in an appearance. Squeezing the Roley's trigger, Sage put two bursts of accelerated magnetic force into the man's center mass, staggering the dead man back into his companions as they came up behind him. Before they could recover, Sage hurled a tangler grenade at them.

The grenade bounced in their midst, then a half-dozen strands shot out and wrapped everything they touched. Several of the attackers were caught up in that. Mercilessly, Sage opened up the Roley on full-auto. The trapped attackers stopped struggling, dead or unconscious.

Kiwanuka's second effort at the door nearly ripped it from its hinges. "Let's go." She took up her rifle and stepped through the doorway.

Sage rolled around the edge of the door and slid inside just as another gel grenade plopped onto the ground out in the alley. He spun and closed the door, hoping the heavy wood was thick enough to offer some shelter from the coming blast. Sage turned and ran, following Kiwanuka as his helmet switched over to infrared to deal with the darkness trapped within the room. They were at the back of some kind of shop, shoving through crates and climbing over racks of clothing.

When the grenade detonated, searing fury slammed into the door and finished ripping it from its hinges. The door followed them into the room and smashed into the overturned crates they'd left in their wake. Flames from the incendiary charge flared in after them and clung to the building on the other side of the narrow alley.

Sage pulled down intel from the fort and spotted the jumpcopters en route, two klicks away and coming hard. All he and Kiwanuka had to do was stay alive for a few more minutes. He pulled up area maps as well, pinpointing them, the attackers the ParaSights had identified, and where they were in the sprawl.

The transparencies from ParaSights 01 and 02 showed their attackers pouring into the alley after them. The fire inside the building spread quickly, taking advantage of the natural wood that had gone into the construction. Fire was a huge concern in Makaum's populated areas because of the building materials. Wildfire was a problem out in the jungles during the dry season.

"Is anybody in the building?" Sage asked as he smashed another crate out of his way.

"No. I saw two men running through the door when I

entered." Kiwanuka shoved through the overturned crates that had spilled across the narrow stockroom. Clothing and sundries littered the floor. She reached a window that held only shards of glass after the concussion from the grenade had finished with it. Using her rifle muzzle, she knocked the remaining glass from the window and crawled through.

Sage followed her, stepping out into another alley paved in hard-packed mud. The alley ran in the same directions as the one they'd quit. Another alley opened up behind the buildings in front of them.

"Which way?" Kiwanuka crouched beside a tree that bore red ovoid fruit that Sage had eaten before. The flesh tasted savory but had the consistency of a melon. Kiwanuka's suit's white noise generator drove away the bees working the fist-sized pink-and-white flowers.

"Across. Through that alley. We should be able to take cover at the well house." The ParaSights' transparent overlays showed their attackers pursuing them. Some of the assailants had sprinted up to the doorway and were held back by the fire that was already spreading throughout the structure. "They'll head us off at either end."

Fire alarms screamed for attention, adding to the din and promising even more confusion as business owners in the nearby buildings abandoned their shops. Some of those people went down under the anxious guns of the attackers hunting Sage and Kiwanuka.

Sage hated leaving the civilians behind to fend for themselves as they got caught up in the firefight, but he and Kiwanuka were focal points for the aggression. The people were collateral damage in the effort being made to kill him and Kiwanuka. Whoever was trying to kill them was pulling out all the stops.

DawnStar Security Center
0758 Hours Zulu Time

Standing in the observation room, Velesko Kos cursed Sergeant Frank Sage and the team he had sent to kill the man. The operation had been simple. Sage had been found and marked, and the sergeant's route through the sprawl had been straightforward. The market had been deemed the ideal spot for the assassination. A one-shot kill would have guaranteed anonymity in the wave of confusion that would have followed.

Now there was only confusion and several of the people Kos had hired to do the job were dead or wounded. Or still in pursuit of their quarry.

The dead and those mercenaries who were captured would be annoyances, but Kos had stacked a defensible layer between himself and those people. Perhaps the Terran military could suspect who had sent them, but they would never prove it to the Makaum *Quass* that DawnStar had sided with.

There might even be some flack passed down from the exec level, but Kos knew he could weather that easily enough. DawnStar needed him to arrange their less-than-legal enterprises. As long as he brought big profits to the bottom line for the corp, he was golden.

Perhaps it would have been better to let Sage walk, but after last night, after the way the sergeant had so directly challenged him, Kos couldn't do that. Sage had to die to prove that crossing Velesko Kos was not something anyone would want to do. Sage was to be an example.

Instead the man insisted on living and causing even greater problems.

Kos stared at the screens and watched as Sage and his companion ran through another alley and kept going, not allowing their pursuers to catch up.

"Do you have them painted for the mercenaries?" Kos tapped another screen and brought up a map of the area, trying to figure out where Sage was headed.

"Yes. They're painted." The sec technician gestured in the 3-D control field, managing the spy cams and the communications among the mercenaries. "They have Sage and the other soldier."

Kos swallowed a curse. The mercenaries didn't *have* Sage. That was the problem. Kos thought again that he should have done the job himself, but getting caught and identified by someone would have been costly to his employment at DawnStar. That was the downside of becoming management: he didn't get to solve the day-to-day problems that cropped up in his job.

"The military has two jumpcopters in the air," the technician reported. "They're en route."

"Monitor them."

"Yes sir."

After a brief look at the map, Kos thought he knew where Sage was going. The old well house was located in the center of the Makaum sprawl near the market. That structure was made of stone and would offer more protection than the wooden houses. There was also room for the jumpcopters to maneuver.

Kos lifted the small mic at the side of his head and opened the encrypted channel that connected him to the mercenary leader. "Jozef."

"Yes?" Jozef Sasnal sounded out of breath or wounded.

Kos spoke in Polish, the native language they shared. "Sage is headed for—"

The comm channel went dead at the same time the vidscreens filled with gray fuzz.

Kos turned to the technician. "What happened?"

"Fort York's intelligence teams found our signal array." The technician gestured like a man suffering palsy, trying to bring the feeds back online. "They've shut down our comm to the field team."

"Can you reconnect?"

"I can, but if I do, we're going to risk being found out. If they don't already have us."

Cursing, Kos stripped the comm set from his head and threw it away. Sage's luck continued to hold. Still, there was a chance that Sasnal and his team would succeed.

0801 Hours Zulu Time

Holding his position at the corner of one of the shops in the market, Jahup lifted his rifle and took aim at the men pursuing the Terran sergeant. When the sights rested on a man's throat, where there was no armor, Jahup took up trigger slack and pulled through. The rifle stock banged against his shoulder as the 7.62mm round tore through the man's flesh and sprayed crimson over his chest plate and the back of the man in front of him.

The dying man stumbled and dropped his weapon, grabbing his ruined throat with both hands. He spun, looking for help, his eyes wide behind the protective mask.

The sight froze Jahup for a moment. Before the offworlders had come to Makaum, Jahup had never killed a person. There had never been any need. Crime had been relatively unknown on the world. The Makaum people had been outsiders on the planet since the generation ship had crashed. They'd needed each other to survive.

Now crime had spread, and the Makaum people took up arms against each other to chase profits that had never been realized before they'd had connection to the offworlders. Life on Makaum had not been perfect. It had been filled with danger and desperation, but at least there had been no evil within.

Jahup pushed his breath out and forced himself to focus. There would be time to think later. He sighted down his rifle again.

Behind the mercenary Jahup had shot, another man took one look at the blood pumping from his companion and recognized that a new threat had materialized. He stepped behind the dying man, using him as a human shield as Jahup tried to track him. Jahup's second round smashed into the dying man as the man sheltering behind him opened fire.

Jahup flattened behind the corner of the building as laser blasts charred the structure and crisped the tree leaves in front of him. One of the branches caught fire and blazed merrily.

Noojin slammed an angry fist into Jahup's shoulder. "What do you think you're doing?"

"They're trying to kill the Terran sergeant. The one who challenged Velesko Kos."

"So? This is not our fight."

"I could not stand by and let them do that."

"You idiot! You can't stop them from killing that man if that's what they want to do. The offworlder means nothing to you."

Jahup didn't have time or the words to make Noojin understand. The Terran sergeant had impressed him with his courage. Jahup had fully expected the man to die two nights ago. Now here he was, still on Makaum and still fighting the Terran corps that sought to hollow out Jahup's world like *krayari* worked a dead thing. Jahup couldn't idly stand by and let the man just die at the hands of the carrion feeders.

"Come on!" Noojin pulled at his sleeve. "Before you get yourself killed!"

Peering around the corner of the building, Jahup checked the sergeant's attackers. Three of the men had peeled away from the group racing along the shopfronts and were now approaching Jahup's position. Jahup pulled his rifle to shoulder again and took aim. He knew that the bullets he fired couldn't penetrate the attackers' armor, but Terracina had talked to him once and pointed out the armor's weak points—in case he ever faced armored men out in the jungle. Perhaps the bullet wouldn't penetrate the armor, but the expended force would still strike home like a sledgehammer.

Aiming at the lead man's knee from thirty meters away, Jahup pulled the trigger. The bullet didn't penetrate, the armor stopped it, but the knee beneath the covering twisted violently sideways in a way nature had not intended. Jahup had no doubt that bones were broken, or at the very least the knee had been dislocated.

When the man collapsed, yelling in agony, his companions ran for cover, thinking perhaps that Jahup was firing armor-piercing rounds.

"Jahup!" Noojin pulled at him again.

Knowing that if he stayed there she would remain with him and become a target as well, Jahup wheeled, grabbed her hand, and sprinted for the end of the alley. He wished the Terran sergeant well, but he'd done all he could do for the man.

0802 Hours Zulu Time

"It appears you were correct."

Zhoh stared at the vidfeed streaming from one of the Phrenorian spy cams planted in the Makaum sprawl. This one was from one of several that monitored the market area. A lot of business was done there by the Makaum people because their economic system was primarily based on barter and co-op production.

Anything worth having could be gotten at the market. Including information and alliances and secrets that could be used for blackmail. Phrenorian intelligence agents had acquired all three and continued to do so.

On the vidscreen, a group of armed men chased two people, one of whom, the intelligence division had assured Zhoh, was Sergeant Frank Sage. Zhoh had known he was correct about the Terran sergeant's ability to draw the hostile attention of the corps he'd challenged. Dawn-Star could not sit back and take such an affront. They were currently the dominant corp onplanet and they wouldn't want that pecking order to change.

Seated at his desk, Zhoh brought up other screens and played back the beginning of the violence. He noted with satisfaction that he'd also been right about Sage being a dangerous man.

"He should have died in that first attack." Zhoh glanced up Mato, who stood in the doorway. He had been the one to bring Zhoh the news about the gun battle.

"You sound like you are glad he did not." Mato's chelicerae twitched. Zhoh knew that Mato was troubled.

"I am glad. It proves my judgment of the being was sound. And as long as this soldier remains alive, he's going to be a distraction to DawnStar, and the sergeant will be forced to focus on staying alive. Just as I predicted." Zhoh waved at the screens. "This attack may heal some of the civil unrest and uncertainty between the Makaum people and unite them against common enemies. They will pull back from the Terran corps and the Terran military both, and they will look for more stable forces to partner with."

"You think they will turn to us."

"I am certain of it. The escalation of enmity between the Terran corps and military will give the Makaum natives no alternatives. They will recognize the need for structure and security. They will also recognize that we can offer those things." Zhoh watched as flames claimed one of the buildings, bringing it down and spreading to the next. The damage mounted and the Makaum fire suppression methods would be hard-pressed to control the blaze. "We are here and we are not going away. Makaum will have to come to us for protection and stability."

"They could always go to the (ta)Klar."

Zhoh stood up from his desk and adjusted his armor, then reached for his weapons and strapped them on. "The (ta)Klar will not stand against the Terrans. Not directly. They are not a species that will openly oppose a challenger. They behave cowardly."

"Do not discount them so lightly because they have different ways of achieving their ends."

"I do not discount them at all. They will be a problem we must, in time, deal with. The (ta)Klar depend on worlds they bend to their will to stand up to anyone who would pull them away. The Makaum are not strong enough to stand against us. Only the Terrans are, and we are better served if the Terrans are divided against themselves." Zhoh moved toward the door. "One enemy at a time, Mato. Let us conquer the Terrans and force them offplanet first. Then we will rid ourselves of the (ta)Klar."

"Where are you going?"

Zhoh smiled. "To act the part of benefactor. Those fires in the marketplace need to be controlled. It's easy to see they're beyond the meager abilities of the Makaum people. They would never have built so many structures so close together had it not been for the Terran corps, and they had never counted on that kind of destruction taking place there. They need help, and Phrenoria will provide it. Today we will be saviors. On another day, we will be conquerors. Do you wish to come?"

TWENTY-TWO

There." Sage pointed to a community well house covered in cut stone.

The natural cistern was fed by an underground spring and was located in the center of the Makaum sprawl. Judging from the age of the buildings nearby, the sprawl had grown around the well house as the initial community had gotten larger. If Makaum had an "old town," this was it. Sage guessed that the spring had become a meeting place for the Makaum hunters and gatherers in the beginning, then had become the cornerstone of the sprawl as the wandering tribes had put down roots. The *Quass* councils were held there, as were celebrations.

Built of cut rock, the skeletal well house had been arranged in the shape of an insect called an *ypheynte*, a winged creature that reminded Sage of a Terran dragonfly. The long body of the insect formed the main building and the rocks had been cut to balance on six thick, arched legs over the cistern. Special vines grew up and along the roof of the well house, stretching out to flare into wide wings. Other vines threaded through the stones, making up the legs, and helped hold the structure together. The craftsmanship that had gone into the construction had been time-consuming.

Domesticated *ghakingar*, a miniature version of *kifrik* that had been patiently bred into a separate and distinct species by Makaum geneticists over generations, lived in the vines and wove fine orb webs that caught the green sunlight and looked like a field of brightly colored jewels from a distance. Few insects were caught in the webs because they were so distinctive and not hidden, which was a drawback that would have killed the species in the wild. The Makaum people put crumbs of delicacies in the webbing for the spiders to feast on so they would not starve. The *ghakingar* were totally dependent on their benefactors and did not successfully leave the area. Evidently they were content to be kept as pets.

According to the intel Sage had on the place, peace treaties for the early tribes had been worked out there. Family lines had been recorded there so that marriages could be arranged to keep the Makaum gene pool healthy. With such a limited population that had come from the generation ship, care had been taken to keep inbreeding from occurring.

There wasn't any religious rule against such mating, from what Sage had read. The decisions were all based on knowledge that if the gene pool became too streamlined it would only take one strong sickness to kill the whole population. Or at least enough of the population to doom the rest of them. Makaum's human species had been balanced on a knife's edge since they had crashed there.

Sage felt guilty taking up a position in the well house, knowing that the attackers that followed them wouldn't hesitate to destroy the structure. Still, the well house offered more protection than anywhere else, and he and Kiwanuka were exhausting options where they could run.

He glanced at Kiwanuka, who stood behind one of the two-meter thick insect legs. She caught him looking and nodded her readiness. They had nowhere else to go. Sage hoped the jumpcopters arrived in time. It was going to be close.

The cistern was a natural stone bowl twenty meters across that had been cut into the earth. The water pressure was enough to keep the supply full at all times. A low stone wall ringed the cistern, but it was more for decoration and for seating than to hold the water in. The water level never came up to the wall. Lily pads and other flowering plants grew in the water. Bright yellow and purple blossoms floated above the water's smooth, glasslike surface.

Back toward the market, thick black smoke coiled toward the green-tinged sky. As Sage watched, another building suddenly tumbled down and scattered sparks in all directions. Some of them would land on the roofs of other structures and set those on fire as well.

Their attackers crept up through the buildings, firing again and again. At least for the moment, Sage and Kiwanuka were ahead of them, but that wouldn't last long. There was too much open space around the cistern. If they tried to run, they would be cut down before they reached any kind of shelter. Shadows of the *ghakingar* crept across the thrumming webs, which were also mirrored on the ground.

A crawling sensation prickled across the back of Sage's neck. He had to remind himself that the AKTIVsuit wouldn't allow any of the creatures ingress. And if one of them happened to get by the hardsuit's defenses, the near-AI would alert him.

Sage peered out at his foes. He felt bad about all the damage cascading through the sprawl even though he knew it wasn't his fault. But that was war. All it took was two sides. The Makaum people weren't going to have the luxury of remaining neutral for long.

"You ready, Sergeant?" Sage asked.

"Yes."

"Then pick your targets." Sage stayed locked onto a man even though bullets ricocheted from the stone pillar he stood behind and laser blasts cracked the rock. He breathed out half a breath, held it, and squeezed through the trigger.

The gauss blast caught his target in the face and pitched the dead man backward. At the same time, Kiwanuka dropped another attacker with an ankle shot, then put a blast through the man's throat as he struggled to get back up.

Two crawlers roared at Sage from the side. A hail of laser beams and particle bursts hammered the ground and the stone column as Sage slid around his cover. Coolly, he put the Roley's sights over the face of one of the drivers and pulled the trigger. Even if the head armor kept the gauss blast from piercing the man's skull, the impact of energized particles batted his head back.

Dead or dazed, the driver lost control of his vehicle and turned sharply. When the front wheel caught the rugged ground, the crawler flipped onto its side and slid toward Sage in a cloud of dust. A blue gel grenade suddenly popped into existence on the stone pillar a meter above Sage's head.

Knowing his defensive position had been compromised, Sage yelled a warning to Kiwanuka and sprinted toward the sliding crawler. The passenger got caught under the vehicle and was reduced to meat jelly despite his armor.

The other two attackers riding in the rear of the open vehicle hit the ground and tried to stay ahead of it.

Sage shot one of the men at almost point-blank range, knocking him from his feet and leaving him easy prey for the oncoming vehicle. On the run, Sage intercepted the only other attacker on his feet, yanked the grenade launcher from the frightened man's grip, and kicked his opponent's feet out from under him.

Whirling, slinging the Roley over his shoulder, Sage dodged the oncoming crawler by centimeters and stepped into the trailing dust cloud, counting on it for a moment of disguise. He shifted through the HUD's display, tied in his optics to ParaSight 02's vid signal, and took aim with his newly appropriated grenade launcher. He rapidly pumped two blobs of gel explosive into the knot of men taking cover inside a building fronting the well house forty meters away.

The resulting explosions ripped the attackers and the building to pieces as the skidding crawler smashed one of the well house's supports. The insect cover and the tapestry of spider webs came apart in a rush. Kiwanuka managed to get away from the avalanche of rock and ripped vines.

"Sergeant Sage, this is Blue Leader," a crisp voice called over the comm. "Be advised that you have aerial support at your twenty."

Glancing up at the sky as the dust thinned around him, Sage spotted the unmistakable shapes of two jumpcopters screaming toward him.

"Roger that, Blue Leader. Do you have eyes on Sergeant Kiwanuka and me?" Sage took cover behind the overturned crawler and reached for a resupply pack for the grenade launcher. Taking advantage of the lull in action, he fed the ammunition into the weapon's reservoir.

"We do. Can you mark our targets?"

"I can." Sage accessed the ParaSights and fed the information through to the jumpcopters.

"Thank you. Take a breather, Top, and let us do the heavy lifting."

By the time Sage was reloaded, the lead jumpcopter swooped out of the sky and opened up with the heavy particle blasters mounted on the stubby wings. The searing burst caught another group of attackers and punched them into the ground. None of them lived through the assault. Broken bodies littered the wreckage of the building where they'd hidden.

The survivors chose to break off the attack at that time. Even then, snipers aboard the jumpcopters and Kiwanuka managed to take down stragglers.

A moment later, a jumpcopter hovered over Sage. One of the crew tossed out a line. The other jumpcopter did the same for Kiwanuka. Sage stepped into the loop at the bottom of the line and held on with his free hand as he fisted the Roley in his other hand. Kiwanuka did the same.

"Ready." Sage braced himself, then strained to hold on as the jumpcopter's cargo line reeled in. Holding onto the line, he spun dizzily as he shot up to the waiting aircraft.

Hands grabbed him and hauled him aboard. Getting his feet under him, Sage whirled around and searched for the second jumpcopter. In the other jumpcopter, Kiwanuka got to her feet and reached for the overhead support.

The cargomaster opened his comm. "All good back here."

"Roger that." The jumpcopter pilot spun the aircraft around and headed back toward Fort York.

Gazing down through the open cargo doors, Sage studied the battlefield that had taken shape throughout the heart of the sprawl. The well house stood in spite of the damage it had taken, but several of the jeweled webs were burning. A few of the Makaum people hesitantly left their shelter and ran for the well house with buckets. In seconds, they were sloshing water over the flames and forming lines for a bucket brigade to the buildings that had caught on fire. Smoke curled up into the air and wafted in through the cargo door.

Sage opened a channel to Fort York. "Colonel, are you there?"

"I am." Halladay sounded grim.

"These people need help putting the fires out. Maybe we could—"

"Negative, Top. If we send out vehicles against an enemy that we haven't fully ascertained—"

"It was DawnStar, sir."

Halladay ignored the response. "—then all we're going to do is send up targets for them to knock down. We can't do that. Soldiers and materials are too hard to replace out here. If we were able to secure that area, the situation would be different."

Sage knew that was true, but he still felt torn as the jumpcopter carried him back to the fort. This wasn't what he was on Makaum to do. He'd wanted to make a difference, to fight the Phrenorians. Silently, he cursed DawnStar and whoever it had been that had made the decision to kill him and Kiwanuka this morning.

0807 Hours Zulu Time

Jahup grabbed the wooden bucket that was handed to him, dunked it into the cistern to fill it, then passed it back off to the second line. The buckets came in on one line, then passed back to the fires along another. Jahup was soaked and cold from the well water, and his boots were filled. His back and shoulders were starting to ache from the constant, rapid motion.

He grabbed another bucket, dunked it, felt the cold water swirl around his hands, and lifted it to pass to the man in the second line. He tried not to think about the black clouds that filled the sky above the market. Buildings were lost. Goods were lost.

Lives were lost.

He had seen the dead dragged out into the street so the bodies didn't burn with the buildings. He had dragged four of them himself. One of them had been a small girl, surely no older than his little sister. He couldn't imagine that happening to Telilu.

And it had all happened so *fast*.

For a moment, his breath caught and he was looking into the dead girl's eyes again. They were clear and glassy, empty of everything she had been.

"Jahup!" Noojin banged the empty bucket against his shoulder.

Drawn out of the waking nightmare, Jahup looked at her.

"Fill the bucket!" Angrily, Noojin thrust the bucket into his hands.

Goaded back into motion, Jahup took the bucket, dunked and filled it, and handed it off to the next man.

"Do you still think you should have involved yourself in that fight?" Noojin handed him another bucket.

Jahup didn't answer. He knew Noojin well enough to recognize that she was looking for an argument. He gripped the bucket, slammed it into the water, felt the cold eat into his flesh again, then lifted and handed.

"If those Terran soldiers had been killed, the violence would have been ended sooner. So many of our people wouldn't have been killed." Noojin thrust another bucket at him.

He took it and said nothing, dunked it and handed it on.

"Those soldiers you sought to save probably started the shooting."

"No."

Noojin glared at him over the next bucket. "How do you know?"

"They would not have attacked so many. They were the ones who were attacked."

"You do not know that."

The heavyset man standing next to Jahup took the filled bucket from Jahup's semi-numbed hands. "The Terran soldiers did not start the shooting. They were fired upon first. I saw this with my own eyes."

Noojin glared at that man too and he stared back at her.

"I *saw* this." He passed the bucket on and took the next from Jahup. "The Terrans are not all evil. The soldiers are better than the Terran corps. And I do not trust the Phrenorians."

Silently, Jahup agreed. The Phrenorians kept to themselves and dealt harshly with anyone that got in their way. He plunged another bucket into the water.

"That sergeant, Sage, started this two nights ago when he brought that body into the club." Noojin handed Jahup another bucket, a little too forcefully. "He begged for this fight."

"No." Jahup surprised himself by arguing with Noojin. He tried never to do that because he could never win an argument with her. "Sage brought that body to Kos because that mercenary worked for DawnStar. Sage was standing his ground, shoving back at those who pushed him."

"That sergeant just got here. What does he know of what's taking place on this planet?"

Jahup thought of the sergeant's face that night, of the pain and weariness and the anger that had been etched on it. Then he also remembered how Sage had dealt with the drug lab out in the jungle, how he had treated the dead soldiers with respect. "He knows, Noojin."

"So you say."

"I do." Jahup caught the bucket that she might have been aiming for his head, and suddenly he could no longer hold in the anger and frustration that rattled around inside him. "I *do* say."

"Then you are a fool." She shoved the bucket at him and nearly knocked him from his feet.

"Stop!" The man standing beside Jahup put a heavy hand on his shoulder to steady him. He looked at Noojin. "If you are here to help, then help. If you are here to argue, go somewhere else."

Bright tears gleamed unshed in Noojin's eyes. For a moment Jahup thought she was going to explode in anger, but she turned without a word and walked away. She looked embarrassed, but she couldn't deal with that either.

Jahup felt like he should go after her, but he knew that would do no good. He could help more by holding his place in line and filling the buckets.

"She is angry." The heavyset man took the bucket that Jahup handed him.

"At me."

"No. She is angry with what has happened to our world, at the fact that what she grew up knowing no longer holds true. She has lost some of her innocence. We all have. Things will never again be the same." The man took another bucket and passed it along, then turned back to Jahup, who handed him another. "However, we cannot allow ourselves to stay focused on what we have lost, on how our world has changed. We must remain clearheaded as we make our next moves and save what we can of our lives, and of the lives we will hand on to our children."

Jahup looked at the man with greater respect. "I am Jahup."

"I know who you are. You are a scout. Your grandmother is *Quass* Leghef." The man nodded and smiled. "I am Warlye, a harvester."

"We have not met." Jahup only knew a few of the harvesters. They stayed to themselves and fought the jungle for space to grow crops to help feed the sprawl.

"No, but I know you through your grandmother. She is a most intelligent woman."

Jahup knew Grandmother Leghef was also obstinate and could be hard to get along with when she chose to.

Warlye looked up as he lifted the current bucket from Jahup's hands. "Now we have the Phrenorians."

Glancing up, shading his eyes with a hand, Jahup watched five Phrenorian aircars glide through the sky and pause above the twisting flames clinging to the roofs of the burning buildings. Moving quickly, the Phrenorian warriors tossed objects into the flames. Only seconds later, explosions went off.

White foam suddenly jetted from the doors and windows and broken walls of the buildings. The flames vanished and the twisting black smoke thinned and blew away in the breeze.

Cheers from the bucket teams suddenly filled the street.

Slowly, the aircars floated across the sprawl, trapping the fire and turning it back on itself with the fire suppression bombs. Jahup noticed two of the air cars floated higher than the other three and the Phrenorians there carried weapons or manned deck guns.

"Perhaps the Phrenorians are not so bad," the old woman who had taken Noojin's place said as she pulled wet hair back from her face.

Warlye shook his head in disgust as many of the Makaum people shouted their thanks to the Phrenorians. "They are fools. They do not realize they're just pieces in the games the Phrenorians play with the others."

The old woman straightened her bent back. "So you say, Warlye, but we must believe someone is here to help us."

The bucket lines broke up as the people gathered to watch the Phrenorians suppress the fire.

"None of them are here to help us." Warlye bent and swept up burned bodies of *ghakingar* from the ash-filled cistern water. "They are here only to help themselves."

Knowing he was no longer needed to help put out the fires that the Phrenorians defeated so easily, Jahup walked from the cistern. He looked for Noojin, but she was nowhere to be found.

TWENTY-THREE

Do you know any of these people?" Halladay stood to one side of the holo that hovered over the conference table. The colonel's irritation was evident in the hard lines on his face, but it wasn't directed at anyone in the room.

Standing on the other side of the table and the holo, Sage studied the five faces that hung in the air. Four of them were men and one was a woman. All of the images had been recorded during the attack by the ParaSights, and their vid records had been uploaded to Fort York's databanks.

Sage shook his head. "I've never seen them before."

"They weren't there that night at the club?"

"I didn't see them, sir. They might have been there. I was more concerned about Velesko Kos."

Halladay shifted his gaze to Kiwanuka, who stood to

one side of Sage, while Lieutenant Murad stood on the other. All of them gazed intently at the holo.

"No sir." Kiwanuka shook her head. "I haven't seen them before either."

Halladay shoved his hand into the holo stream and gestured. The five faces spread out across the holoscape and neatly spaced columns printed out below them. Names and backgrounds glowed in green font. Two of them had long histories throughout several systems serving as mercenaries and assassins, and there were a few outstanding charges on a number of planets. As yet, there was no extradition allowed from Makaum, which made the world even more attractive to lawbreakers.

"They're all outlaws and mercenaries," Lieutenant Murad observed.

Halladay nodded. "Exactly the kind of people corps like DawnStar want to employ when they need to distance themselves from an illegal operation."

Sage made himself remain calm, but that was difficult because he was ready to strike back. He'd seen the casualty lists that had run before Halladay had called up the collection of faces the intel techs had managed to get from the vids.

Seventeen Makaum people had died in the attack. Another forty-plus had been wounded. Both numbers were expected to grow as the debris was sorted through. Several buildings and goods had been lost, and that was going to leave an economic footprint in the sprawl that would take time to recover from.

"None of these people can be tied back to DawnStar?" Sage asked.

"No. Not directly." Halladay gestured in the holo stream again. The face of the woman glowed a little brighter, and her name stood out more sharply. She had dark hair and dark eyes, and Sage knew that the unearthly beauty had come from a laser scalpel. "But we have some history on this one."

```
HODGKINS, ELLEN.
WANTED FOR MURDER, BLACKMAIL, AND
TERRORIST ACTIVITY IN THE KIBUR SYSTEM.
CONTACT INTERSYSTEMS INTELLIGENCE BUREAU.
BOUNTY OFFERED BY ELDSNY CORP.
```

"What history?" Sage asked. He hadn't seen the woman during the attack, but he'd seen her since in the vid files. She was sleek and deadly, no wasted effort as she'd pursued him and Kiwanuka. When the time had come to abandon the attack, she'd thrown down her weapons and promptly disappeared inside a nearby building. Since the military drones hadn't picked her up again, she'd probably been wearing a change of clothing under her hardsuit. Once she'd shed the hardsuit, she was just another person on the street.

Halladay gestured again and more information scrolled under Ellen Hodkins's face. "She's worked for Velesko Kos prior to her appearance here. They were strikebreakers for Domanska Mining Corp in the Awver system. Some of those communities that DMC rode roughshod over still have bounties offered on Kos and Hodgkins. The situation there got pretty bloody. A lot of innocent people were killed."

The strike had made news that Sage had seen. By the time it was settled, DMC had gotten all the concessions they'd wanted and were still in the process of picking the planet clean.

"Will that connection be enough to go after Kos?" Sage asked.

"We can chase Hodgkins, provided we can find her, but we can't prove that Kos was behind the attack on you and Sergeant Kiwanuka," Halladay replied. "Command isn't comfortable with acting aggressively on the soft intel that we have at the moment, and the diplomacy teams are dead set against any kind of action in the sprawl again. I've got people who are running the intel down, hoping to improve what we have."

"Then we're going to just be targets for DawnStar's bashhounds and mercs?" Kiwanuka's displeasure was evident, just barely a notch down from insubordinate.

Halladay gave a thin smile. "No, Sergeant. I don't have to tell you that the general wasn't happy with this turn of events. He doesn't want the fort or its personnel causing any kind of diplomatic kerfuffle, but he's not going to let his soldiers be attacked without striking back, and he's not going to wear a black eye over strained diplomatic relations. General Whitcomb knows this strike was designed to elicit the effect it has. He's working through channels to do damage control." He paused. "We're going to be cutting back on our presence in the sprawl, keeping closer to home to keep our people safe, but"—he smiled—"that leaves all of the jungle open for us. We're still going to police those areas and take down the illegal lab operations we find out there. We're going to hit them where they'll feel it most: in their illegal-profits bottom line. If you're still interested."

"Yes sir," Lieutenant Murad responded, but he didn't look as confident as he had yesterday.

Sage folded his arms. "Out in the brush, we're not going to run the risk of civilian casualties. We can better control what goes on at those sites."

"You're also going to be a long way from support teams." Halladay blanked the holo with a gesture and looked at the other three members of the team. "I'm not going to sugarcoat this for you. Once you're out in the jungle, separated from the fort, you're going to be more on your own. And Kos, if he *was* behind this, is going to be gunning for you just as hard as you're looking for him."

Let him come, Sage thought.

"In the meantime," Halladay went on, "we've got another problem. The Phrenorians appear to be intent on making the attack today a soapbox for them to gain points in the eye of the Makaum public." He gestured above the holo and a new image took shape.

Anger tightened the muscles in Sage's jaw as he watched the Phrenorian aircars float over the burning buildings and heave out suppression bombs loaded with chembots that unloaded fire-quenching foam.

The vid moved quickly forward in jerks, showing the Phrenorians putting out fires. Some of the buildings had been reduced to skeletons consisting of rock and burned timbers. One of the aircars floated to a landing in the middle of the empty market near the sagging well house.

A tall Phrenorian warrior stepped out onto the ground and gazed around. "Greetings. On behalf of the Phrenorian Empire, I am hereby offering assistance to your wounded. Bring them to our facilities and we will treat them. We are saddened that you got caught up in an act of violence that was not your problem. In days to come, if we may offer our materials and labor, we will help you rebuild your dwellings."

Several Makaum natives came cautiously forward, then cheering broke out.

"The Sting-Tails didn't waste any time stepping in to grab the glory, did they?" Kiwanuka pursed her lips in disgust, and Sage noted the same grim intensity in her eyes as he'd seen in the holo training. She wasn't just looking at the Phrenorians, she was peering at them through a sniper scope.

Halladay froze the image. "Do you recognize this Phrenorian warrior, Top?"

Sage studied the Phrenorian.

"His name is Zhoh GhiCemid, captain of the Brown Spyrl."

Halladay looked a little surprised. "That's right. He's an important warrior in the Phrenorian Empire, from a family just a step down from their primes. From the intel we have on him, he's always been on the forefront of the war."

"Then what is he doing here?" Sage asked.

"We're not certain, and, frankly, when Command learned of his presence here, we became concerned." Halladay stared at the Phrenorian warrior. "At first the covert ops division thought Zhoh's presence here indicated some kind of coming buildup, maybe a play for Makaum, but that hasn't presented itself. There hasn't been any buildup of warriors or materials. Our intel people are tracking down a rumor that Zhoh has fallen out of favor with the Phrenorian primes."

"I did some of the prelim backgrounding on Zhoh," Murad said. "Zhoh's family has always been the next tier down from the primes. They've always occupied a position of respect and authority. We weren't able to make any sense of his presence here."

Halladay stared at the Phrenorian warrior. "Whatever his purpose here is, Zhoh apparently has an interest in you, Top. He backed you against Kos."

Sage shook his head. "I don't know why."

"Just watch yourself out in the jungle, Top. We know the Sting-Tails are out there too. We just don't know where, but you can bet they'll be looking for ways to improve their situation on Makaum."

"Yes sir."

Personal Quarters: Sage
Enlisted Barracks
Charlie Company
Fort York
2228 Hours Zulu Time

A knock sounded on Sage's door while he sat at his desk and went through the files he had been going over with Lieutenant Murad and Sergeant Kiwanuka for the last two days. Over the last three days, they'd assembled the small platoon he'd chosen and eight fireteams, two of them equipped with powersuits; as well as ground-troop carriers, drivers, and mechanics.

Sage knew their numbers were small, but trying to field a group any larger than that would allow others to know where they were. Small but invisible, large enough to make an impact. That was the desired goal.

The Phrenorian influence in the sprawl had continued to increase. Zhoh GhiCemid had provided warriors to help rebuild the personal dwellings that had been lost, and they'd ended up working side by side with some of the Terran corps engineers. Peace was a fragile thing in Makaum these days, and all it would take was a spark to set it off.

Glad for the break, Sage glanced up at the door and stretched the kinks out of his back and shoulders. "Come in."

Kiwanuka entered with meal packs in her hands. The smell of spices tickled Sage's nose and his stomach rumbled in anticipation.

She looked at Sage and held up one of the boxes. "I checked at the mess. They said you hadn't been in."

"I forgot." The maps and the intel had consumed Sage. He'd worked to transfer and organize everything to his

PAD, adding in maps, geological surveys, and even Net chatter uploaded by military personnel during their free time as well as civilians working for the corps.

"I thought you might have." Kiwanuka glanced at the desk, which was covered with Sage's gear. In between studying the field service reports of the soldiers he was taking, he'd been working on his personal equipment, cleaning it and speccing it out. "I think you've got a desk in there somewhere."

"Let me find it." Sage stood and cleared the equipment from the desk onto a plasteel locker at the foot of his bed. He took the food cartons from Kiwanuka and set them on the desk. "Smells good."

"It is."

"That's a lot of food."

"I haven't eaten either. I thought we could eat and talk." She glanced at him for a moment. "I can go back to my quarters if you'd rather be alone."

"I don't mind the company." Sage pulled a folding chair from beside the neatly made single bed and set it up on the other side of the desk.

Kiwanuka sat and gazed around the room, focusing on the bed. "You haven't slept in three days?"

"I've slept six hours every night."

She raised an eyebrow. "You made your bed this morning? Expecting a surprise inspection?"

"I make my bed every morning. No inspection should be a surprise. You should be ready to go at all times."

Kiwanuka smiled and shook her head. "I only make my bed when I know there's going to be an inspection."

"You run your barracks."

"I do, and I schedule the inspections." Kiwanuka smiled again as she shrugged out of a backpack and set it on the floor. "That's how I know it's an inspection day. So, the army taught you to make your bed every day."

"No. My mother did that. She was born in Argentina, in a border town that was constantly caught up in one skirmish or another. She never had a home till she met my father and he married her and took her away from that. She always promised herself if she lived long enough to have a house and possessions, she would take care of them. She always did. I learned to appreciate what I had through her."

"Sounds like you have a good mother."

"I did." The old pain tweaked through Sage but he quickly pushed it away.

" 'Did?' "

Sage reached into a small cupboard on one wall and took out two acrylic plates and flatware. "My father and I lost her a few years after I joined the military."

"I'm sorry."

"Yeah. Me too."

"You're close with your father?"

"I lost him three years after we lost my mother. He was in action on Serack."

Kiwanuka's face darkened. "Serack was a bad place to be."

"It was. My father was one of several soldiers that didn't make it back." Serack was one of the first major Phrenorian offensives. Military historians likened it to Chosin Reservoir during the first Korean War.

For a moment, Kiwanuka was silent. " 'I'm sorry' doesn't seem like enough."

"Sometimes it's all we have." Sage passed over a plate and flatware. "I'm hungry, Sergeant. Let's eat."

Kiwanuka took the plate and set it down on the desk. "This is kind of fancy. I thought we'd eat out of the boxes." She held up chopsticks. "I'm not one to insist on atmosphere."

"I like to eat off a plate when I get the chance." Sage

felt a little uncomfortable at the admission. "Tonight we have the chance."

"Your mother teach you that too?"

"No. I've eaten enough meals out in the field that got mixed with dust and other debris that I learned to appreciate having a meal that's going to stay the way it was prepared and taste the way it was meant to. Where we're going in the morning, there aren't going to be many opportunities for a sit-down meal. Or plates."

"Next time I'll bring a picnic basket. However, there is an upside. I might be lacking in etiquette, but I brought beer." Kiwanuka opened her backpack and brought out a six-pack of locally bottled beer that was chill enough to start sweating. She split the beers, then they worked together to dump the contents of the food cartons onto the plates.

Sage inhaled the aroma of the foods. "Fujian style?"

"Jiangsu, actually. One of the entrepreneurs who set up shop just outside the fence is from Nanjing, China. He's an old man, but he likes to travel and ended up here. The place is small, but the food is good and the price is pretty decent."

"How much do I owe you?"

Kiwanuka laughed. "That wasn't a hint for you to reach for your creds. This is on me. Next time you buy."

"You'll have to recommend a place. I haven't exactly gotten to know the neighborhood since I've been here." Sage put the fork aside and sharpened a pair of the chopsticks Kiwanuka had brought.

"I will." Kiwanuka opened one of the beers. "The menu isn't as robust as it could be. Mr. Huang grew up on the Yangtze River near Nanjing. He conscripted into the military, but retired."

"To open a noodle shop?" Sage grinned.

"Every noodle shop he's ever opened has been on some frontier." Kiwanuka took a long drink of beer.

Sage grinned, understanding then. "I take it Mr. Huang doesn't just sell noodles."

"He doesn't. If he did, Mr. Huang would not be able to continue to afford his grandchildren the lifestyle to which they've become accustomed."

"So he's a spy."

"Mr. Huang trades in . . . secrets. He's very good at keeping them, and he's good at finding them out."

"Does the top brass know this?"

"No."

"You're holding back?"

"I am." Kiwanuka set her beer aside and used her chopsticks to pick up a morsel of spiced meat. "I have found, in my career as a non-com, that it's often beneficial to have intel sources the officers don't have access to. It allows a more rounded view of things as they shape up. A system of checks and balances. I don't always have to know only what Command wants me to know. And I don't want to be limited to their intel sources."

Sage picked up a sliver of meat. "I've eaten Jiangsu food before. They do a lot with beef and pork. This is neither of those."

"Jiangsu cooks also use a lot of fish and turtle meat, both of which Makaum has a lot of. Different than what you might be used to."

"And this is?"

"*Jasulild.*"

"What is that?"

"It might be better to tell you after we finish eating."

Sage popped the meat into his mouth and chewed. The flavor was tangy and the spices enhanced the taste. "Okay."

Kiwanuka eyed him in idle speculation. "Do you want to know?"

Sage plucked up another morsel. "We're about to go out into the wild, maybe be cut off from support for long periods of time so we can disappear into the jungle and look for those labs. I think it would be helpful to know more about what we can find to eat out there in case we run low on supplies and don't want to return to the fort, or we get cut off for a while by enemy forces."

Kiwanuka pointed her chopsticks at a chunk of meat lying atop a pile of seasoned rice. "*Jasulild* is a kind of cuttlefish. They're ugly and they smell bad, and one of them is big enough to eat you if you don't eat it first."

"I guess if you catch one, there's plenty to go around." Sage picked up another piece of meat and chewed.

"There is." Kiwanuka smiled. "Mr. Huang buys *jasulild* from the Makaum fishermen. He told me that if I really want to know what's out in the jungle, I should talk to one of the hunters that forage out there."

Sage had been thinking the same thing. Having the local hunters as scouts would be a bonus, but after the attack in the marketplace, gaining the trust of the locals would be hard. "Did he give you any names?"

"He did."

"Do you know any of them?"

"I don't. I tried to talk to them, but they weren't interested in anything I had to say." Kiwanuka took another bite, chewed, and swallowed, then frowned. "It's hard to get to know these people. They prefer to keep to themselves."

"And they don't trust any of us. Especially after today."

"We haven't given them any reason to. Even before today. The corps are here to exploit them and their planet. The (ta)Klar want the same thing, only they use a more passive approach, like a terminal illness." Kiwanuka's eyes narrowed in distaste. "The Phrenorians and Terran military see Makaum as a potential prize if the war pushes in this direction, which in all likelihood it might. You can't blame the Makaum people for walling us out as much as they can."

"I understand it, and I've seen it before. The people in my mother's town had the same feeling toward the peace-keeping forces."

Kiwanuka tilted her head to one side. "You went to your mother's town? I thought you said she left there."

"She did. But she went back to see her family. She had two sisters and a brother there. Nieces and nephews."

"You weren't close to them?"

"No." Sage picked up more food and ate. "My mother married my father. He took her away from there."

"They resented your mother?"

"No, but they pretty much hated my father. They weren't too fond of me either. Both of us represented ties to a world they wanted no part of."

"Then why did you go?"

"To protect my mother. There was a lot of insurrection there then, and it remains now." Sage shrugged. He tried to put away the memories, but only succeeded in dulling them. The mixed scents of spicy food and underlying layer of gunpowder haunted him. "Some places never know peace."

"I know." She was quiet for a moment, picked at her food, then talked without looking at him. "I was born in Kampala, Uganda. You've heard of it?"

"I have." Sage was glad of the distraction. He was never comfortable talking about himself on a personal level, and he didn't want those old memories rattling around inside his head now. He had enough on his plate.

"My father serves with President Walukagga as a dip-lomatic attaché."

"Sounds like he's an important man."

"He is, but he's also an inflexible man, and not very giving when it comes to family. I don't know what my mother sees in him, except maybe the fact that being married to him affords her a lot of political standing, which is unusual for a woman in that country. She went to Uganda on a medical-relief mission. She's a surgeon and has done a lot in the field of nano-meds. She's created a few patents, then given them away to charities to help in Africa."

"That's a good thing. Most people I know aren't that generous."

"Wealth has never been one of my mother's goals. She's always wanted power and recognition. That's why she married my father."

Sage sipped his beer. "Given that kind of background, you could have had a choice of careers."

Kiwanuka looked at Sage and smiled ruefully. "So how did I end up in the Terran Army amid all the other possibilities?"

"Something like that."

She opened another bottle of beer and took a sip. "Because my brothers and sisters did those things and I wanted to go my own way. I grew up in a large family. My mother and father, and most my siblings, are comfortable with Terra and a couple of the outer systems. I wanted to see more. So did my brother who died on Iracko."

Sage remained silent, sensing that wasn't the only answer. There was pain and fire in Kiwanuka that hadn't been put there by her parents. She hesitated for a long time, obviously trying to figure out how much to talk about. Sage let the silence stretch. The decision was hers, and he didn't want to take on any more weight than he had to. Once a private thing was shared, it couldn't be taken back.

"And because of Phiromera." Kiwanuka put the bottle

aside and her hands shook just a little. "She was a friend of mine in Kampala. Her mother is one of my mother's best friends. Phiromera and I grew up together. We were always different from the other children, planning to go out into space as soon as we turned eighteen. Her parents designed colony ships and had come to Uganda to help manage the displaced people. Phiromera and I wanted to be on one of those ships." She took a breath. "Only that didn't happen. When we were twelve, Phiromera was raped and killed by one of the terrorist gangs in Uganda. They took us both, but I got away before I was killed." She halted for a moment and gathered her thoughts, but there was a lot told in that silence, a lot that was left unsaid. "By the time I got help, the men who had taken us were gone and Phiromera was dead."

"I'm sorry for your loss."

A hard gleam glittered in Kiwanuka's gray eyes. "We've both lost people, Sage. We know what that's like. These people on Makaum, they're just starting to learn about loss on a scale they've never considered before. Until we arrived, they didn't have any of the problems they have now. They had to worry about natural predators, putting food on the table, raising their kids right in a way that made sense to them, but that was all."

Sage sipped his beer and knew she was speaking the truth.

"I know you want to find a way to get off Makaum and get back to the front lines of the war. That's no secret. I felt the same way when I first got here, so I don't begrudge you any of that. But this planet is as innocent as Phiromera was. It'll never be the same now that everyone is here, but I want to rescue what I can of their way of life and their identities. I don't want Makaum just to be a ticket to someplace else, just a stepping-stone or a resupply outpost." Her chin thrust out defiantly, challenging him.

"What we're going to be doing out in the jungle won't just be for a ticket out of here." Sage met her gaze with his, let her see the truth in his eyes. "I don't know how much of a difference we'll make, Sergeant, but I intend to make all the difference that I can while I'm here, and we start making that difference tomorrow." He held up his bottle in a toast and Kiwanuka touched the neck of his bottle with hers.

"To the difference," she said.

Sage nodded and they drank. "So what else did Mr. Huang tell you?"

Some of the heavy emotion lifted from Kiwanuka's shoulders and she smiled a little more easily. "He gave me a location of what is potentially an illegal DawnStar lab site. If it's still there."

"Let's have a look at that then." Sage reached for his PAD and opened the map function.

TWENTY-FOUR

Jahup shifted his pack, settling the weight more comfortably across his shoulders, and walked through the market with his spear in hand. Despite the damage that had been done only a few days ago, the merchants had set up shop again and trade was brisk. Prices were called out by vendors, shot down with derogatory remarks by potential buyers, and other amounts suggested as the constant haggling resumed.

It was almost as if people had not died there. Except for the remains of the buildings that had burned and two of the vendors that Jahup had known who were now being readied for funerals.

Offworlder equipment, noisy and large, snorted and pawed the ground like a male *dafeerorg* going through his spawning cycle. Tracked divots stood out across the hard-packed earth, making the way hard. The offworlder lifter crawlers shoveled up debris in great mechanical maws and dumped them into waiting cargo crawlers that hauled the wreckage away to the fire pits that had constantly burned outside the sprawl for the last three days. Makaum children with bright eyes sat hunkered atop the nearby homes and watched the offworlders work.

Jahup could remember feeling wide-eyed with astonishment after the first ships had landed less than three years ago. The Terran soldiers in their polished armor had impressed him. He envied their guns and hardsuits because at that time Jahup had carried only a bow, spear, and knife, and knew the dangers he faced in the jungle. The few hand beamers and rifles that had survived the crash all those years ago remained in the possession of the sec details appointed by the *Quass*.

He wasn't wide-eyed anymore. And he felt guilty over his part in prolonging the attack on the Terran sergeant. Perhaps Noojin was right. If the corps' assassins had killed the sergeant and woman soldier quickly, maybe not all of the deaths and destruction would have resulted.

Guilt over his own part in the attack had settled firmly into Jahup's mind. Aiding the sergeant had seemed only natural. The man was one against many, and the military did not take so much from the planet as the corps did.

Yet.

Noojin's word and prophecy haunted Jahup. Although he had searched for her in all the places they sometimes went, he had not seen her since she'd left him that day. He had never gone so long without seeing her, and her absence cut like a knife.

Head down but still wary because he now knew that violence could break out again at any moment, Jahup skirted a pair of *dafeerorg* heavily loaded with trade goods. He needed to hunt. He knew that. It wasn't just for the meat the sprawl required. He also needed to be out and away from all the people to properly clear his thoughts. He had always been a solitary person. He let his imagination go, and for a moment he was among the wild things in the jungle, living in the instant between heartbeats as the role of predator and prey shifted. One mistake and predator turned to prey in an eyeblink.

"Jahup."

The familiar voice jerked Jahup from his reverie. He looked and spotted Leghef standing near the spice merchant's kiosk. Despite his anxious and unsettled mood, seeing his grandmother put a smile on his face.

Changing course, he crossed the thoroughfare behind one of the offworlder crawlers loaded with wreckage and strode toward her.

Leghef was dressed well for the day, probably for the meeting of *Quass* that was scheduled later. She wore a traditional gown made of *kifrik* silk dyed in brilliant greens that made her stand out against the dirt and wreckage of the market. More silks covered her head to prevent bugs from alighting there. She was short, only coming up to Jahup's shoulder, which was not an overly high distance from the ground itself. Her black hair held thick threads of gray these days, but Jahup didn't know if age had caused those or if it was her dealings with the offworlders. Her face was lean and brown, only marred by a few wrinkles.

"Good morning, son of my son." Leghef curtsied slightly in the Old way. Despite her years, she remained physically able and exercised vigorously. In the whole time that he had known her, Jahup had seldom seen her ill.

"Good morning, mother of my father." Jahup bowed as well, but felt awkward in his protective hunting clothes. The bow across his back and the short spear in his hand made him stand out as well. He did not care for the Old manners, thought they were annoying and limiting. That was one of the reasons he seldom went to meetings of the *Quass*.

"You have not come to see me in a long while. I have missed you." His grandmother regarded him.

Guilt assailed Jahup but he pushed it aside. With all the problems that faced his grandmother, his lack of visiting wasn't a main concern. With the invasion of the offworlders, they all had more pressing issues. "I have been busy. I apologize for my inattentiveness. I will amend that as soon as I am able."

Grandmother Leghef took him by his free arm, and though she was old, her grip held steel. "Walk with me for a while and I will let you return to your day."

"Of course." Jahup paced beside her. Several merchants and passersby acknowledged her presence with polite greetings. She wasn't just *Quass*. She was also a woman who was a friend and mentor to many.

"You are preparing to go back into the jungle?"

"People do not stop eating. We need meat, and with the offworlders now forever poking about in our jungles, scaring away the creatures we take for our food, we have to go farther to get it."

"I know. I worry about you ranging out in those far reaches. I used to hunt there myself and it was always dangerous."

Jahup grinned at her. "You always worry about me."

"It is the task your mother and my son left to me after they passed."

"I can take care of myself."

"So you think."

His grandmother's words stung even though Jahup knew she did not intend for them to, and he spoke somewhat brusquely. "I help feed the people, *Quass*. I am capable of taking care of myself."

Leghef squeezed his arm in warning. "Careful. Even if you do not disrespect a *Quass*—"

"I would never."

"—you still run the risk of hurting your grandmother's feelings."

"I would sooner throw myself upon the thorns of a *gimumigu* tree filled with stinging *wovoro* that could burrow into my skin and nest along my bones." Jahup gave her the saddest look he could summon.

She frowned at him in mock despair. "That is positively horrid."

Enjoying the humor they always had between them, Jahup grinned and felt a lightness of heart he had not experienced in days. "I am inspired by the stories you used to tell me as a child."

"I did not tell you those stories. Your father did."

"He always assured me they were true because he'd gotten them from you."

"He blamed me for his excesses, though he chose to give into them." She smiled at the memory, and the sadness that clung to her was stamped deeply into the expression. "I still worry about you."

"I worry more about you." Jahup kissed the top of her head, choosing to treat her as his grandmother and not as *Quass*. "After all, I am only combatting creatures we have known all our lives. You, on the other hand, are being forced to contend with the offworlder conquerors whom we may never truly know."

"I am intelligent enough to recognize the dangers they pose, and wise enough to pick my battles among them." Leghef nodded to a group of children who called out greetings to her as they passed by under their mother's watchful eyes. "I have been talking to Noojin."

"She adores you."

"And well she should."

"She also always seeks you out when she wishes you to influence me." Jahup kept bitter words and a remonstration about that irritating habit to himself. That argument would be with Noojin, not his grandmother. With Noojin he at least stood a chance of being heard.

"I talked with her last night. She said she has not seen you in a few days."

Jahup grew more frustrated at Noojin. The girl was a meddler when she thought she could get away with it. "I have not seen her because she has not wished me to see her. She is well?"

"She is. She said she has chosen to make herself scarce."

Jahup said nothing because it was a time for listening. He could not always be certain of those times when his grandmother first began speaking, but he knew them when she revealed them.

"You and Noojin have a difference of opinion about the offworlders." Leghef looked up at him. "She thinks you have become less wary of them."

"No. They are all bad. I wish they would climb into their ships and vanish back into the stars. Or that we were strong enough to drive them from Makaum." That was the truth. Especially after the attack in the market.

"Even the Terran sergeant you seem so interested in?"

"I am not interested in him." Jahup replied without hesitation, hoping in vain to avoid further discussion of the sergeant and his interest in the offworlder.

"Noojin told me you killed some of the men that were trying to kill the sergeant during the attack."

"Noojin had no business telling you that."

She shot him a look filled with rebuke but softened by a grandmother's love. "Am I not *Quass*? Am I not responsible for our people and therefore need to know such things?"

Realizing he had entered an argument he would never win, Jahup remained silent and walked slowly in step with his grandmother.

"And of equal importance, I am your grandmother and would not see you do something foolish."

"Helping the sergeant was not foolish."

"Why would you do such a thing and risk your life as well as Noojin's?"

"We escaped without harm."

"You did, but perhaps you were luckier than you wish to admit, and that does not tell me why you involved yourself in the first place."

Jahup shook his head. "It does not matter. I will not make that mistake again."

Leghef stopped to inspect a tiny wagon of *corok*. The small melons were the size of two fists together and stayed in season most of the year. They were filled with sweet yellow meat. The juice could be fermented and turned into wine, and was one of the major exports Makaum vintners shipped offworld. The merchant stepped forward and greeted Leghef. "Good morning, *Quass*. As you can see, I have many fine fruits today. For you, I will make a special price."

"Thank you, Lunajo, but I have no need for a special price. I am *Quass*, as well as a woman of means. I can pay your price." She and Jahup's grandfather owned large tracts of cultivated land, earned because they had been successful in agricultural endeavors. When the sprawl had first been established, only those who were prosperous tenders of the land were given property to manage.

Even though Jahup was not certain he'd ever seen the merchant before, he was not surprised his grandmother knew the man's name. She was *Quass*, and as such she was part of the bond that held the people together. When the survivors had first stumbled from the wreckage of the generation ship, they had recognized the need for negotiators, and for people who would not forget the lessons of what had gone before. Telilu, his younger sister, was already in training to become *Quass*.

His grandmother made a few *corok* selections, paid for them, and shoved the melons into the catchall net she carried for her purchases. Jahup asked if he could carry them for her and she allowed it. They continued on their way.

"Do you know who sent the assassins after the Terran sergeant?" Leghef asked.

Jahup wondered why his grandmother was so interested in the topic. "No."

"But you think you do."

"Yes. I think Velesko Kos was responsible."

"No one can prove this because there is no solid information, but I believe you are right." Leghef sighed. "The offworlder let his anger get ahead of him. He views the business with the sergeant as a personal thing and he is loath to let the matter go."

"I think so too."

Leghef glanced up at Jahup. "The night the Terran sergeant carried that dead body into the offworlder club and threw it at the feet of Velesko Kos impressed you."

For an instant, Jahup hesitated, and in doing so knew that he had already given his grandmother the answer she was looking for. He had never been able to hide anything from her. "I have never seen a braver thing."

"Nor a more foolish one," his grandmother said sharply. "The Terran sergeant could just as easily have been killed."

"But he wasn't. And if I think Velesko Kos had tried to kill him, the sergeant would have sold his life dearly."

"That act that night inspired the violence that has disrupted this place and left so many of our people dead or hurt."

Jahup could not argue that because he knew it was true, and he felt guilty for having felt so enamored of the sergeant's actions at the time. Still, doing such a thing had been brave and . . . defiant. No one had treated Velesko Kos in such a manner.

"In all the years that we have lived on Makaum after losing our homeworld, we have known peace and left behind the war that chased us to this place. More or less," his grandmother said.

Jahup knew that was not entirely true. The civil war that had raged on the world their ship had come from still held echoes in the Makaum population. History was a hard thing to forget, even if that world no longer existed.

His grandmother continued. "Part of our peace is because of the wisdom of the *Quass*. But part of it is because we knew we only had ourselves to lean on for survival. When the initial groups kept growing so large they could not effectively hunt and forage for themselves, they fragmented, always beginning anew and not able to forge a unified community. Once farming was instituted and successful, they started banding together in this place. They knew they would become targets for the predators in the jungle, those who would come forth to hunt. But they took that chance because they felt they had enough numbers to make that happen."

The old stories danced inside Jahup's memories. As a child, they had sat within the Tale Circle and listened to the *Quass* relate stories about the Beginning Days. Those stories, handed down generation after generation after generation, had bound the young together. The lesson was simple. Together, they stood. Divided they would become little more than creatures again, the way they had been after the Fall. The old, the young, and the weak would be easy prey for everything that would hunt them. Many sacrifices had been made before the

people were able to better fend for themselves against
the hostile jungle.

"Over the years, there has been some unrest within
our people," Leghef went on, "but never did we think we
would confront what we are now facing."

"The offworlders?" Jahup shook his head. "We do not
have to accept them."

"But some of our people do accept them." Leghef came
to a stop beside her personal vehicle, a wooden box on
wheels that was pulled by two *dafeerorg* in harness. "Like
you, some of our people see things in the offworlders that
they respect. Or desire. For some it's just as simple as
having a way to other worlds, to other experiences. Many
of our people wish for simpler, easier lives, and they believe it lies out there among the stars."

Old Pekoz stood near the beasts and looked like a
withered reed the wind could blow away at any moment.
As long as Jahup could remember, Pekoz had served his
grandmother. Jahup's father had related stories of the old
beast handler when Jahup had been a child. If the stories
were to be believed, and Jahup thought they were, Pekoz
had been a formidable warrior and hunter.

Silently, respectfully, Pekoz opened the riding area of
the vehicle and wooden steps swung out to allow Leghef
to board. Despite his focus on the *Quass*, the driver remained attentive to everything that went on around them.

"The greatest threat we have facing us now is not the
offworlders, but the choices their presence here allows us
to make." Leghef accepted Pekoz's hand and stepped into
the vehicle. The *dafeerorg* stamped restlessly and made
the harness jingle.

"You have always supported choice," Jahup reminded
her. "You wanted me to become a blacksmith, remember?
Or a craftsman? Not a hunter. But when it came time to
stand before the *Quass* and be Counted and declare my

vocation, you supported me." The Counting was an important part of Makaum culture. It allowed the community to identify and supply trades and positions the people needed. During some years, there was not much latitude and positions had to be filled. Jahup had been fortunate during his Counting year and been more able to choose. Of course, with the high attrition rate among the hunter parties, becoming a hunter was easy enough.

Leghef smiled at Jahup. "I did support your decision, but it was the most fearful thing I had done in a long time. I had not considered your father dying while you were yet so young, nor your mother's death so soon after." She reached out and stroked his cheek as though he were a child again. "I want you to be careful, son of my son."

"I will, mother of my father."

"Good luck on your hunt. Give Noojin time to find her own feet along the path you have chosen. She is an independent young woman, and you will want one like that. She cares about you very much."

"I care about her."

"It may be that your paths divide."

"If she so chooses." Even though he stated that so lightly, Jahup knew that such a decision would pain him. He could not imagine a time when Noojin was not at his side. Yet, here he stood now without her.

Leghef smiled again in a way that Jahup did not quite understand. It was as though she knew something he did not, and that made him feel irritable because he was certain of what he was doing. "Her path has not been so easy either."

Shrugging, Jahup doubted that. Noojin had always done as she wished, and most of the time she'd gotten him to do as she wished as well. But that was not going to happen now.

"Do you know the noodle maker? Huang?"

Surprised by his grandmother's change of subject, Jahup nodded. He enjoyed many of the dishes the old man made in his shop, and Jahup often traded meat for meals.

"If you want to know where to find this Terran sergeant out in the jungle, talk to Huang."

"Why would I wish to do that?"

Leghef arched an eyebrow. "In case you so choose."

"What will a cook know about the sergeant?"

"Ah, son of my son, you are still so young. You still believe people wear only one face, when the truth is that they wear many. Talk to the noodle maker and tell him I sent you."

"Perhaps I am not interested in this sergeant any longer." Jahup couldn't help feeling rebellious. He did not like being so easily read in this matter.

"Then there will be no reason to talk to Mr. Huang. Be well and safe until I see you again." Leghef nodded to Pekoz, who let off the brake and urged the *dafeerorg* into motion. The lizards lurched into the harness and plodded down the street.

Feeling confused, Jahup watched them go and waved to his grandmother. Feeling angry for no good reason that he could think of, he glanced up at the sky and saw the rim of dark clouds starting to gather. It was going to rain before morning. He could smell it and feel it in his bones.

"We could always wait until the rain blows over," Noojin suggested.

Jahup turned toward the sound of her voice and spotted her standing next to a cart of candied *keval* berries. The small crimson fruits stood out against the soft dark green cushion of fresh-pulled *lekeher* leaves that could wrap a man's head.

"How long have you been there?"

Noojin shrugged and ate from a small basket of berries she had purchased. "Not long."

"You talked with my grandmother."

"Many people talk to Leghef. She is *Quass*." Noojin looked obligingly innocent as she popped another berry into her mouth.

Rain came down without warning and many people around the carts cursed the weather as they always did even though they knew it was normal. Water ran through Jahup's hair and trickled down his face, threading through the sparse hairs on his chin. "Do you wish to hunt?"

"You are still going now? Even though it rains?"

"Rain will not hurt me, and I've had my fill of the sprawl. I will hunt. People need meat."

"Do you wish me to accompany you?" Challenge glinted in Noojin's gaze.

For a moment Jahup almost let his anger have its release so that he would tell her she could do as she pleased, but he knew that he did not wish to hunt without Noojin. She was good, and she knew how to hunt with him. "I do. I want to be out there, not trapped in the sprawl."

She shrugged and stepped out in the rain to join him. "Then I will accompany you. Have you told the others?"

"We will tell the others as we go." Jahup hesitated, wondering how much Noojin knew about his grandmother's talk with him. He thought that chances were good Leghef would have told Noojin about the noodle maker as well. Leghef and Noojin did not have many secrets from each other. It always seemed to Jahup that he was the last to know of what passed between them. "First I must stop at old Huang's."

Noojin cast him a sidelong glance as she adjusted her hunting jacket and pulled a hood over her head. "For breakfast?"

"No. I have eaten." Jahup felt certain she knew why he was stopping at the noodle maker's, and for a moment he feared that she might leave him.

But she remained in step with him. He accepted that and turned his mind to hunting. Anything to keep his thoughts from the sergeant. He hoped they stayed on separate paths. Huang's information would help him do that.

TWENTY-FIVE

The lab occupied a small cave at the bottom of a broken mountain amid thick trees. According to the lidar readings Sage's scouting team had taken earlier, no tunnels led out from the cave. The cavity was a pocket scraped out of the mountainside by rain. The biopirates working there had trapped themselves, trading escape routes for an extremely defensible position. Since they were tucked out of the way and not likely to be found unless someone knew where to look, the trade was a good one.

Twilight settled over the jungles and filled the empty places between the trees with deep purple darkness. The lizards had gone quiet as the light green sun had sunk below the tree line. Before that, they'd been busy. The predators had sniffed out the soldiers, but short bursts from microwave emitters around their defensive perimeter had turned aside whatever rudimentary interest they'd

had. Getting a meal somewhere else was easier. The biopirates holed up in the cave used the same kind of aver-
sives to lizard and insect intrusion.

A small stream poured from the top of the mountain
like a broken-backed snake. The water reflected small
coins of light from the lab operation. The drug lab operated behind a camo veil that obstructed view and kept
most of the illumination within. From what Huang had
said, the group—maybe working for DawnStar Corp—
had been there for months.

The biopirates had become lax. Evidently they'd
worked the location for a time and had grown complacent
because no one had ever bothered them. All of the pirates
were armed, but some of the members were designated as
guards and wore full combat armor.

Kiwanuka used burst transmission to speak with Sage
over their private channel. Her words appeared printed
across the inside of his faceshield.

LOOKS LIKE THE NOODLE MAKER KNEW WHAT HE
WAS TALKING ABOUT.

YEAH. BUT THIS IS STILL GONNA BE DANGEROUS.

GUY WHO RECRUITED ME SAID DANGER IS WHAT
I SIGNED ON FOR. PROMISED ME THE ARMY
WOULD TEACH ME HOW TO BECOME INVISIBLE AND
INVINCIBLE.

THEY PROBABLY TAUGHT THAT GREEN LIEUTENANT
THE SAME THING IN OCS. I BET HE DOESN'T
AGREE TO DO THIS THE EASY WAY.

I'M NOT TAKING THAT BET. I'M SURE THE
COLONEL HAD HIS REASONS FOR PICKING THIS
GUY, BUT I'M NOT SOLD YET.

Huddled behind a rocky outcrop three hundred meters distant from the lab, Sage leaned over to Lieutenant Murad and used the touch comm permitted by the helmet contact. "Your call, sir, but the easiest way to deal with this situation is to mine that mountain and bring it down on top of the pirates. Shut down the lab in one strike without risking our soldiers."

"You're talking about just executing those people." Murad sounded like he couldn't believe Sage had suggested that.

Sage didn't flinch from the truth, didn't attempt to soft sell it. "Yes sir, I am. We've got green soldiers. Some of them haven't been under anything more than small arms fire situations inside the Makaum sprawl before. What you've got over there is a hornets' nest waiting to explode if we don't take it down sudden. We're here to send a message, and killing them would send a strong one."

"You're talking about murder."

Sage held the man's gaze through the faceshields. "Killing an enemy isn't murder, sir."

"These people aren't enemies."

Making himself breathe, Sage waited, knowing he had to let the officer work through the problem for himself. Personally, Sage wanted to end the confrontation as decisively as possible. And as quickly. In his mind, the biopirates were the enemy. They definitely wouldn't hold back if it came to a firefight. If the soldiers held back at the beginning, expecting an easy victory, some of them were going to die.

"Also, if we do as you're suggesting," Murad went on,

"we lose any chance of recovering testimony that these people are working with a corp. Proving complicity is part of what we agreed to do, Top, and I don't see anything in that cave that screams DawnStar to me. We tie the illegal activities to the corps and let the diplomatic channels handle the fallout on their level."

"There might not be any proof. Those people inside that lab may not know who their ultimate employer is. The corps use cutouts to insulate themselves from people like this." Also, Sage wasn't convinced the Terran diplomats would draw a hard line against the corps even if they were given irrefutable proof of their involvement. The diplomats might try to leverage DawnStar with the information instead of trying to push them offplanet. A lot of people enjoyed the space station parked in orbit around Makaum.

"I would rather try to save the proof, Top."

"Yes sir." Sage bit back a curse. Murad's lack of experience wasn't his fault. The young officer was as green as most of the soldiers he led, and he wasn't as coldhearted as he would have to become in time to survive against odds like these in a situation like this.

"Is your team ready?"

"They are."

Murad's helmet dipped a little as he nodded. "It's time then. Those harvester crawlers should be en route." His voice sounded dry and hollow. "Let's get this done. We'll see what we have when we finish up."

"Yes sir." Sage checked the chron readout on the faceshield and saw that it was 2116. The three scavenger teams would be inbound to the lab now with the latest harvests they'd taken. They'd done that the last two days the team had set up watch over them. He opened the private channel to Kiwanuka.

YOU READY TO COVER ME IF THIS GOES SOUTH?

READY. I TAKE IT WE'RE NOT DOING THIS THE
EASY WAY?

NEGATIVE. WE'RE DOING MY SECOND-FAVORITE
PLAN. YOU GOT A HEAVY PLASMA LAUNCHER
THAT CAN BE "ACCIDENTALLY" FIRED INTO THAT
MOUNTAIN IN CASE THIS THING GOES SIDEWAYS?

I DO. BETTER TO ASK THE LIEUTENANT'S
FORGIVENESS LATER THAN PERMISSION NOW?

YEAH. JUST DON'T FORGET TO SHOUT OUT A
WARNING FIRST BEFORE YOU HIT THE TARGET.
I DON'T WANT TO BE INSIDE WHEN THAT
MOUNTAINSIDE COMES DOWN.

ROGER THAT!

Sage eased up out of the darkness and moved through
the jungle back toward the rutted trail that led to the cave.
The deep furrows left by the crawler tires were almost
hidden by the fast-growing grass, but an unwary soldier
could trip over them. He opened the channel to his attack
squad, two four-man fireteams that had the most experienced soldiers on them.

YOU PEOPLE READY?

A chorus of affirmative answers lit up his faceshield,
ticking off the list he'd planned and engaged as he moved
into position. Each fireteam consisted of a sergeant and
corporal, who served as team leaders; two riflemen; two

grenadiers armed with gel grenade launchers slung under their Roleys; and two soldiers carrying fully automatic Birkeland light machine coilguns capable of unloading a maelstrom of destruction in seconds.

Team 1 took up a position on the north side of the rutted road, hiding in the brush. Team 2, with Sage accompanying them, took up positions on the south side.

Sage settled in and waited, put his thoughts on hold, and let time slide by.

2122 Zulu Time

The harvester crawlers returned late. They were boxy-looking vehicles on eight wheels, 4 meters tall and 3.5 meters across. The front cab held a driver, a navigator, and a plasma mini-cannon operator sandwiched between them on an elevated seat. The cannon could sweep 160 degrees and rotated 270 degrees top to bottom.

The electromagnetic turbines growled thinly, not quite silent, as the crawlers hurtled through the jungle. Infrared lamps lit up the scenery in front of the crawlers, invisible to the normal eye, but turned the nightscape into almost day for the drivers and anyone equipped with an optics system.

To Sage inside the AKTIVsuit, the lamps threw out a large pool of light that pushed back the night. He closed his eyes.

"Look away from the lights," Sage ordered. "Keep your optics clear. Wait till they pass. Snipers ready?"

"Ready."

"Ready."

"Fire at will." Sage remained hunkered down, but he reached inside his combat harness and freed two Para-Sights. He accessed them, bringing them online, then flung them into the air. They were small enough that the crawler systems wouldn't notice them, and there was no way the unaided human eye could pick them out of the darkness.

The crawlers thundered by on wide tires, crunching through the grass-covered ruts.

As soon as the infrared lamps passed over him, Sage rose to his feet and took off at a run. The crawlers were moving faster than they'd estimated. He swung his arms at his sides, whipping them to gain speed, using the amped-up abilities of the hardsuit.

Crashing through the brush, Sage launched himself in pursuit of the rear vehicle. Four other soldiers fell in beside him, all of them chasing the crawler like a pack of wolves.

The crawlers had rear gunners as well. They occupied gimbal-assisted exterior blisters that allowed them to operate their plasma mini-cannon in different positions horizontally and vertically. Taking those men out, *before* they could fire or get word to the rest of the crawler teams or the base camp, was imperative.

Sage ran, telling himself the suit could withstand some of the plasma fire if things didn't work out as designed. Getting fired upon would mean getting spotted, and that would send out an alert to the pirates. Taking the lab would be more difficult if the plan didn't go as expected.

The rear gunner's infrared lamp swept across Sage in a blinding arc. He didn't break stride. There was no time to get the momentum going again. Then the lamp started tracking back, coming out of the jungle and rolling toward the group of soldiers catching up to the crawler.

Come on! Sage thought at the snipers. *Get your target!*

Amplifying the magnification on the faceshield, Sage watched the rear gunner. The man had been only halfway paying attention during the lamp sweep, but he sat for-

ward now, taking control of the lamp to bring the beam
back onto the trail. If there had been any chatter over the
pirate channels, the comm operator monitoring those frequencies would have let him know.

Sage barely recognized the gunner as a Wedoidian, one
of the heavily muscled denizens of the Whallath system.
Only two planets in that system supported life, and both
of them produced squat and ponderous humanoids capable of dealing with the heavy gravity.

Before the man could adjust the lamp, two armor-
piercing bullets starred the impact-resistant glass, coring
through and punching into his face. Partially flattened by
the bubble, the rounds almost tore the man's head from
his shoulders. Limp in death, the gunner jostled in his
harness, swinging and rocking in a macabre dance.

Since the crawler didn't deviate from its course, Sage
felt certain no one aboard knew that anything had gone
wrong. He stretched his stride a little more, then hurled
himself for the crawler's rear bumper. His right hand
caught the underside of the crawler, but his left missed.
He flailed for a moment, then grabbed hold with his left
hand as well. After he caught hold with both hands, he
went limp, dropping prone to the rutted trail and stretching out. The rutted ground banged against him repeat-
edly, and he felt like a stone skipping across a pool of
water. Others joined on either side of him.

Reaching under the crawler, Sage caught hold of
the chassis and pulled himself underneath the vehicle. Bouncing and hammering against the ground, he
climbed forward till he could lock his feet into place.
Then he lifted himself from the ground and held on like
a parasite. Two other soldiers climbed up beside him,
then all five of them were secured as the crawler rolled
toward the hidden base.

"Penetration Team in place." Sage glanced forward,

feeling the crawler shift as the driver applied the brakes and started slowing.

"Roger that," Murad replied.

Sage controlled the ParaSights, sending them high and slow, creeping into the cave and taking up positions that gave him a look inside the operation. He relayed the information to the rest of his team.

Guards stood behind the camo veil that masked the entrance to the cave. Behind them, long tables filled with chemicals and equipment lined one side of the cave under the tracked rows of soft illumination. On the other side of the cave, processing vats and kilns took the raw product from its natural state to the gummy tar boiled and chemed down to its essence. The tar could be converted to other states that could be smoked, ingested, and injected, all with different levels of strength.

The drug was called *lexoti* by the natives, who had used it for pain management, but the black-market trade had branded it as Third Eye because of the out-of-body-experience high-quality forms often created. Not only was the drug supposed to expand the consciousness of whomever was taking it, the effects also enhanced sexual experiences.

The three crawlers came to a stop in the center of the cave. The doors opened and the crew in the cab got out to meet the people still inside the lab.

Sage used the ParaSights to do a quick head count. The operation had more manpower than he'd thought. Twenty-seven men and women ran the lab, working the raw harvest into finished product. That was eight more than they'd estimated. Boxes of Third Eye sat at the back of the cave.

"Somebody grab me a beer." The driver stepped from the first vehicle and caught a bottled beer from one of the men standing at the sidelines.

"How did you do?" The speaker was a middle-aged Asian male with a shock of black hair that sported a blue stripe on the right side. He wore armor and appeared alert.

Sage captured an image of the man with the ParaSights and recognized it from the database they'd set up for the operation. During their surveillance, they'd gotten several hits almost instantaneously. Most of the pirates were high-end criminals with long histories of violent behavior.

Suthep Worachaisawad had been born in Thailand, but he'd shipped out only a few years later to follow in the footsteps of his career-criminal father. Suthep had outstanding warrants on several planets, and had been thought to be somewhere on Hejar, in the Cha'ard system. DawnStar had a large presence in the Cha'ard System, taking advantage of cheap local labor to manufacture products they Gated to other systems. All four planets in that system were known for poverty and crime.

The database confirmed the presence of three other people—Ivan Lebedev of Moscow, Oora Uito of Turbel, in the Cha'ard system; and Darrd Kycus of Ineestend, in the Zardet system—before the driver of the third crawler opened his door and said, "What's wrong with Hobed? He's not answering his comm."

Sethup hammered the side of the third crawler with a fist as he walked to the rear of the vehicle. "Hobed. Are you asleep again, you pox-ridden *ton'or*?"

Hobed was evidently the Wedoid male slumped at the plasma mini-cannon in the third crawler. As big as he was, he nearly filled the gunner blister. Blood painted the back wall of the compartment, but that was hardly visible in the darkness trapped in the blister. If it weren't for the fact that Hobed's head was MIA, people might have thought he was merely relaxing in the self-adjusting seat.

At the rear of the crawler, staring at the blister, Suthep cursed in his native language, which Sage's hardsuit near-

AI translated easily, and swung his Vais plasma subgun up. "Weps ready! Now! Somebody's—"

Sage released his hold on the crawler and dropped to the hard stone floor with a thump. He peeled a couple of anti-personnel grenades from his combat harness, activated them, then fanned his arms out to the sides to throw the grenades out into the cave.

"Fire in the hole!" he called out in warning.

TWENTY-SIX

The penetration team stayed put in their position under the crawler, waiting for the explosions, but they readied their weps. Sage took up the Roley and counted down.

"There's somebody out there!" One of the guards at the front of the cave took cover and lifted her Iseld needle rifle. "I saw someone out there!"

Most of the pirates in the cave carried Iseld weapons. Iseld was a knockoff munitions corporation that specialized in reverse engineering weapons. The corporation was one of Green Dragon Industrial Trade's shell businesses. Sage thought maybe the weapons were carried to create confusion as to who the lab belonged to. On the other hand, GDIT was good at getting illegal weapons out to different systems.

"Grenade!" someone yelled as one of the anti-personnel munitions Sage had thrown bounced off the leg of a table.

By then it was too late. The grenade exploded and a cloud of shrapnel filled the cave. A few of the sharp metal shards slammed into Sage's hardsuit with tiny *pings!* but the armor held. His helmet blocked the sound of the detonations.

Several of the biopirates went down as the razor-edged shrapnel tore through their light armor and flesh. Some of them were ripped to pieces and others went down flailing at wounds.

"We're inbound," Murad radioed.

"Roger that," Sage replied as he readied the Roley. "Confirmed there are no civilians on-site. All are hostiles, and there are eight more than we counted."

"Understood."

"Pen Team go!" Sage rolled to his right, coming to a rest in the prone position on his elbows with the Roley up and ready. He settled the sights over the man in front of him, squeezed the trigger as the guy tried to swing his weapon around. Plasma bolts singed the air over Sage's head and cooked the crawler's side. Then Sage squeezed the Roley's trigger and the gauss burst short-circuited the man's heart and blew it through his back.

One of the other fireteam soldiers rolled into position behind Sage while the other three took up positions on the other side of the crawler.

Sage swung his rifle around and picked off two more traffickers. Getting to his feet, he kept track of the enemy forces through the overlapping vision provided by the ParaSights.

He checked the soldier behind him and saw that she was moving as well, staying on his six, and headed for the lab equipment, intending to seek out shelter there. His armor held up against most of the small-arms fire, but some of the plasma bolts tore into it, peeling away layers that would have to be regrown by nanobots later. His suit gyros helped him withstand the hydrostatic shock of solid ammo rounds slamming into him, but he was dodging and moving, putting lab tables and other equipment between him and his opponents.

A plasma bolt struck a chemical canister atop one of the tables. The canister's contents erupted and flames splashed in all directions. A hot concussive wave slapped into Sage and nearly knocked him from his feet.

Relying on the hardsuit to keep him safe even though part of the spill had enveloped his arms in fire, Sage sighted in on the female pirate who had shot at him and squeezed the trigger. The blast hit her dead center and hammered her body over one of the tables. Shifting the rifle, Sage aimed for one of the pirates manning a heavy plasma cannon at the cave mouth and squeezed the trigger again. He slid the Roley slightly to the right and picked up another gunner standing at the cave entrance, then squeezed the trigger.

He turned on the suit's PA and started the pre-recorded address as he pulled back to look for more targets. "This is the Terran Army. Drop your weapons and surrender."

The warning only drew a sudden salvo of firepower that chased Sage into brief retreat behind a loading mech. Private Charity Fleming went down under the barrage of hostile fire.

Trapped for the moment, Sage searched his surroundings. "Fleming? You still with me?"

"Yes." Her voice sounded thready and distant. "I'm leaking blood and I can't feel my legs."

"Hang in there and keep your head down, Private. Help's on the way."

"Roger that."

Sage didn't know how badly wounded the private was, but he was pinned down and couldn't get to her. He spotted a ten-liter canister of the same chemicals that had nearly exploded in his face earlier, which sat on a shelf within arm's reach. Holding the Roley in one hand, he grabbed the canister by the looped handle, set himself, then heaved the ten-liter container in the direction of the group of traffickers taking cover behind the lead crawler's nose.

The canister banged into the side of the crawler near the front and ricocheted only slightly, starting to fall toward the ground. Sage fired by instinct, placing a blast into the canister, which erupted into cascades of flames that fell over the traffickers, setting them ablaze. As they broke cover, Sage dropped three of them with quick bursts. Two fell, succumbing to the fire that clung to them.

The other three soldiers took up positions on the other side of the crawlers and used the equipment there for cover as they opened fire. Return fire chopped into the equipment and Private Pete Bowden went down as a near miss from a gel grenade launcher blew him off his feet.

Two pirates fired at Sage as they ran between the ends of two tables seeking cover. Sage rounded the other end of one table, put a hand on it, and shoved, getting the AKTIVsuit's muscle behind the effort. The table zipped across the floor and smacked into both pirates, trapping them between that table and the next.

Sage fired at them point-blank. He grabbed another canister from a nearby shelf and slid it along the seven-meter table, knocking lab equipment and other containers out of the way. Less than a meter from the two struggling pirates, he shot the canister and detonated the contents in a liquid, fiery rush.

Suthep clambered into the rear crawler and slid behind the steering wheel. The electromagnetic turbines cycled to life and he engaged the transmission. Once he had it in reverse, he floored the accelerator and backed over his own people in his rush to get out of the cave. Other pirates had the presence of mind to leap onto the escaping vehicle, or at least get out of the way.

Stepping out around the table he'd shoved, Sage sighted on the crawler's windshield and hammered it with bursts from the Roley. The impact-resistant clearplas fractured but held.

Sage opened the comm to his team as he stood over Fleming and guarded her. All of the pirates inside the lab were down. Sage and two of his team remained standing.

"Meacham," Sage called.

"Here, Top."

"You've got one crawler headed in your direction."

Outside the crawler was taking fire from Murad's advancing team. Some of the pirates clinging to the vehicle's sides returned fire, but they weren't accurate as they struggled to hold on to the crawler. A coilgun burst ripped one of them away. Before the pirate could get back up from the ground, Suthep backed over him.

Pulling on the steering wheel, Suthep cut hard to bring the crawler around, then he engaged the forward gears and plunged through the surrounding brush. Small trees went down before the crawler as it gained speed.

"I see him, Top." Brittney Meacham was a grenadier on one of the fireteams Sage had led into battle. She carried a gel grenade launcher. She'd seen combat against the Phrenorians on Kimrilu before the Terrans had been forced to retreat from that system. She'd seemed like a solid soldier, but she'd been rotated to Makaum because she was good with languages and had specialized in working with agrarian worlds.

The crawler raced along, picking up speed rapidly and leaving a hole chewed through the jungle. White scars showed on the dark trees where bark was torn away and brush splintered.

"There are no friendlies on the vehicle." Sage turned and went back to Private Fleming. He signaled to the other two members of his team inside the cave and had them set up a defensive perimeter.

"Roger that. No friendlies." Meacham sounded totally calm.

Kneeling beside Fleming, Sage placed a hand on her suit and kept watch on the fleeing crawler through the ParaSights.

A line of gel grenades suddenly plopped onto the crawler. Two of the biopirates clinging to the vehicle recognized the danger they were in. One of them dropped from the crawler and the other tried tearing the gel grenades free.

Linked for detonation, the gel grenades exploded all at the same time, ripping a hole in the crawler's side and tipping it over. The crawler skidded for a few meters and smashed to a halt against a rocky outcropping, leaving broken tree stumps in its wake. Flames sprouted up and gray smoke lifted into the dark sky.

Meacham and the remaining half of the fireteams advanced on the stricken crawler. A pirate covered in flames struggled to crawl from the cab, didn't quite make it, and tumbled over the side to lay still.

"Fleming, you still with me?" Sage brought up the soldier's vital signs on his faceshield, then glanced through the damage reports.

"Still with you, Top." Fleming sounded pained.

"Relax, soldier. You're going to be fine."

"You'd tell me that even if I was dying."

That was the truth. Sage had been forced to do that before. The young ones always seemed to know they were dying and often remained calm about that. Older, more seasoned soldiers who'd seen a lot of action tended to deny dying until the end.

"I would," Sage agreed. "But that's not the case here.

Looks like a couple nerve clusters in your back are traumatized. Swelling's cutting off nerve relay."

"I can't move my legs, Top."

"Once we get the swelling under control, you'll get your legs back. I've seen this kind of injury before. In the meantime, I'm going to have your suit give you something for the pain and release nanites to work on the injury." Sage sent those commands into her suit.

"Okay."

"Until we get ready to transport you out of here, I want you to lay still and just breathe."

"Roger that."

Sage checked her bio readouts again and saw the meds and the nanites were already at work. Her respiration and heart rate dropped steadily toward more acceptable levels. "I'm going to check on Bowden."

"I'll be here, Top."

At the front of the cave, Murad and Kiwanuka secured the perimeter.

"Top?" Murad called.

"Yes sir." Sage knelt down beside Private Bowden. The man's left leg had been taken off just below the knee. At first Sage thought the suit had amputated the limb, then he saw there was no blood. Even with the hardsuit shutting down the bleeding, there would have been some blood.

"Are your people all right?"

"Two wounded, sir. Working on them now." Sage put a hand on Bowden's scorched hardsuit and tapped into his med info. "You with me, Private Bowden?"

"Affirmative, Top. Just catching my breath."

"It appears you've lost a leg."

"Look around. Maybe you'll find it."

Sage glanced at the boot and armor encased lower limb lying under a pile of lab equipment. "Found it."

"Still in once piece?"

"Looks like it."

"If you don't mind, maybe you could bring it over here. If it's not damaged too badly, the bionic nanites might be able to reattach it."

"Either way, you're going to need another boot."

Bowden laughed, but the effort was strained. Despite the fact that the limb was cybernetic, the young private had suffered a lot of blunt force trauma. "Yeah, I will, Top."

"If I give you something for the pain, can the leg still heal?"

"Roger that. System runs itself. Give me a few hours and, since the joints are still pretty much intact, and I'll be good as new."

"Glad to hear it." Sage released meds into the young soldier's system, then fetched the cyber leg and guided it back into place. He twisted it so that the ends fit together, more or less. As he did, a message crawled across his HUD.

```
CYBER REPAIR BOWDEN, PRIVATE PETER RINGO
ONLINE. IMPLEMENT PROGRAM?
```

Sage acknowledged the question and watched as gleaming strands suddenly started drifting between the two sections of Bowden's leg. In just seconds, a web of cyber muscle and tissues were woven into a gleaming latticework.

"You good, Private?"

"I'm good, Top." Bowden sounded slightly dreamy from the meds in his system.

"I'm here if you need me." Sage patted the young man reassuringly on the shoulder and stood.

```
DIAGNOSTIC SUGGESTS REPAIRS ARE NECESSARY
TO HARDSUIT.
```

The near-AI's announcement scrolled across Sage's HUD.

IMPLEMENT?

"Roger that," Sage commanded. "Implement."

Nanites programmed into the hardsuit began patching up the armor, pulling replacement materials from resource packs in the combat harness. Sage added an item on his post-combat to-do list:

RESTOCK ARMOR MATERIALS.

Murad stood in the center of the cave and started breaking the area down into search grids, assigning personnel from the team to cover the sections.

TWENTY-SEVEN

Following the successful op out in the bush, after the spec ops team was blooded, Sage turned part of his attention to the training ground and started pushing the soldiers at Fort York. Terracina had broken up the PT units and left the soldiers to their own devices. As a result, many of them weren't as organized and diligent about drill and training.

Sage broke the schedule down himself, settling the soldiers into three sections, and he oversaw it all himself, mixing the original drill instructors in with the squads. Some of them would come back out to resume their roles with a stronger work ethic. Others would be rotated back down to grunt status.

When he finished, there would be no slackers.

The hardest part of the schedule was the mornings. Sage arranged for early reveille for the day shift, got them up at 0500, put them through their paces, had breakfast with them, then took the soldiers from night shift and trained with them at 0800.

He got up at 0300 himself to tend to the fort's paperwork. Major Finkley didn't like the fact that Sage wasn't there at his morning briefings and made an issue of it on the first day. A call from Colonel Halladay set the major straight on that.

In the evening, Sage met with his spec ops team and they pooled intel, then planned and executed strikes within the jungle, taking down targets as they found them. Most of the labs were small, not like the big one they had hit first. But all of those operations added up. Tension ratcheted up in the black market.

The drug profiteers, and the corps working with them, wanted Sage dead, but none of them dared attack him. Halladay had insisted on a personal security detachment around Sage anytime he went into the sprawl. Sage didn't like it, but acquiesced, bargaining to take only his own people to watch over him.

Mostly these days, he trained the troops, pushing and pulling, breaking and building.

Those back-to-back drills in the morning were draining, in the planet's humidity, and Sage often discovered he'd lost between two and four kilos of water weight during those times. During his training post, Sage had kept himself in better shape than any of the soldiers he'd instructed. Some of the young ones tried outrunning him during the hikes, but by the time they hit the end of the 10K, Sage was passing them up.

"Becoming an effective soldier is about dedication and stamina," Sage told them later as they stood around huffing and puffing. He wouldn't allow them to fall out immediately. "And you want to be an effective soldier because an effective soldier is one who lives longer."

The grunts hated him. He saw that in their eyes as they watched him. He was pushing them past their endurance, taking time out of their day, and he was breaking them down psychologically, making them see how lacking they were.

They had to at least keep pace with him when they ran, and he varied his speed so they couldn't lock into a solid effort. He knew what he was doing, and he knew what he could do.

After the second day of keeping up with three sessions of PT and drills, they not only hated him, but they were in awe of him as well. Whispers started to circulate that he was strapped with bionics and enhancements. Captain Gilbride, as medical officer, put them straight on that: Sage was not augmented in any way. He was as organic as they came. The captain still wasn't a fan of Sage's, but he was fair.

Starting on the first day, Sergeant Kiwanuka joined him, restructuring her day so that she was with him for all three drill periods. Sage hadn't been too surprised about that. Even though he and Kiwanuka got along, she would want to get the measure of him. Not just physically, but mentally as well. Knowing how far he would go, how much he would push, how hard he would come down on soldiers who didn't come up to the bar he set—all of those were important factors for her to learn.

What did surprise him was Lieutenant Murad's attendance during the 0500 drills. Murad had been somewhat out of shape and was paying for it, but he kept up with the middle of the group.

During water break, Sage had looked at the lieutenant, wondering what had brought him out to the drills.

Bathed in sweat, obviously hurting, Murad returned Sage's gaze and spoke softly. "I am not an idiot, Top. We go out there in the brush the way we are, hunting those labs, if I am out of shape and not sharp, I am a dead man."

Sage nodded. "Yes sir, you are. Glad to have you here, sir."

"I am far from happy about this myself, but I will be here every day."

"Yes sir."

Murad walked away, limping a little.

Kiwanuka joined Sage. "That's an interesting development."

"Not so interesting," Sage said. "He wants to stay alive. Why are you here?"

She grinned at him. "To watch your back, Top. You keep pushing these grunts like that, one of them is going to try to kill you."

Sage grinned back. "They might at that. Until then, they're going to learn to be better soldiers."

1604 Hours

A short distance from the fence that separated the fort's training grounds from the sprawl, Jahup sat on a roof in the shadows of the trees and the taller building behind him. A group of people gathered there to avoid the heat and watch what Master Sergeant Frank Sage was having the Terran military soldiers do.

Soldiers along the fort's perimeter manned gun towers and nonmilitary personnel weren't allowed within the double-deep fence.

Over the last few weeks, the training area had been re-shaped as the sergeant had added more equipment. Soldiers clambered over walls, crawled under barbed wire, slid through mud, ran innumerable kilometers on the track inside the training area, and battled each other on combat arenas.

"I thought I would find you here." Noojin looked up at him from the ground. She was clad in hunting armor and carried a spider-silk bag in one hand.

Today was a day of rest from the hunt. Tomorrow they would be back out in the jungle again.

"I didn't know you were looking for me," Jahup said. Their relationship had seemed to mend, but he was still cognizant of the split that had occurred and didn't completely trust that it wouldn't happen again.

Noojin held up the bag. "Have you had lunch?"

"It is well after lunch."

She lowered the bag. "In that case, I can eat it by myself."

"I haven't eaten," Jahup admitted. He'd been busy cleaning gear, then, knowing the Terrans were going to be training at this time of the day, he'd come to watch. Over the years of hunting, he had learned many things by observing the insects and lizards they took as game, and the Terrans weren't any different. Jahup was learning things from them as well.

"Then it's a good thing I brought enough for both of us. Come down and I'll share with you."

"I want to watch the Terrans."

Noojin glared at the training field. "Watch them do what? Run and sweat and hit each other?"

"There's more to it than that."

"That's all I see."

"Then you're not looking," Jahup chastised. "Come up. Please. I wish to see this."

With a slight pout, Noojin offered her empty hand.

Jahup leaned down, offered her his bow to grab hold of, then hauled her up and caught her hand to pull her up to the low roof. He scooted over to make room for her.

She remained silent as she reached into the bag and took out the food she had prepared. The breaded *croeb* legs and *foech* pudding were his favorites. She'd also assembled two small *corok* melons and a handful of *keval* berries. She shared out the food, placing it on two *lekeher* leaves that spread across his lap.

Jahup watched the soldiers train, but mostly he watched Sage.

"Why are you watching the sergeant so much?" Noojin asked.

"Because I can learn from him."

"Learn what? How to kill people? How to challenge others until they strike back and try to kill you?"

"No." Jahup forced himself to remain patient. He was learning that from Sage as well, but he wasn't going to tell Noojin that. "I am learning how to train people."

"You already know how to train people." Noojin shrugged. "You trained me for the hunt."

That was true. Jahup had been accepted to Chaiq's hunting band a full year before anyone had spoken for Noojin. She'd had to serve in the kitchens till her Calling was finally accepted. By that time, Jahup had become a trainer, excelling over many of those who ran in Chaiq's band. Within three years, only a few seasons ago, Jahup had been split off with his own band. Noojin had come with him.

"I trained you, yes. But training is an ongoing thing. It is as alive as those jungles where we hunt."

"We hunt prey the same way we always have."

"But there is new prey. Makaum stirs the pot out there, cooks up new things to throw at us. Remember the *ashgh*?"

The *ashgh* was a particularly lethal water beetle that had either come from deep within the jungle or had manifested from a previous insect. Two meters long, a meter wide, and a meter tall, the *ashgh* preyed on fish and lizards five and six times its own size.

"We lost three hunters, experienced people, to those

things before we figured out how to kill them," Jahup continued. "And it was a long time before we learned it was the male *ashghs* that carried the eggs on their backs."

The eggs were delicacies among some of the Makaum, provided they were harvested early enough that the embryos were barely begun. They looked like fat globules attached to the dark umber carapaces of the *ashghs.*

"You've listened to the stories in the Tale Circle," Jahup went on. "If there is one constant about Makaum it is that things will change."

Irritably, Noojin crossed her legs and munched on a *croeb* leg. The fried skin and breading cracked as she bit into it to get at the white meat. The skin was edible but tough, but if it was removed the meat simply burned rather than cooked.

"So you are watching the sergeant to learn how to fight the Terrans when the time comes?" Noojin asked. Her tone suggested that she doubted that was the real intention, and he knew part of her was looking for a fight.

"If it comes to that, yes. But in the meantime, I want to learn."

"What is it that you learn?"

"This sergeant is not like the others that I have watched." Jahup had been observing the Terran Army since they had arrived. He had a sharp interest in their weapons and wanted to know more about how to use them as he got his hands on them, and he intended to get his hands on them. Opportunities for raiding came up in the jungles, and sometimes they took gear from the labs they destroyed. "He is stern and enforces discipline, but he helps those soldiers who are actually trying to learn from him. The other leaders yelled at them and punished them. In the end, the commanders ignored the soldiers who would not learn, and all those soldiers wanted in the first place was to be left alone."

"You punish someone in training so they know how to do something."

Jahup looked at her. "Did I ever punish you when you did not learn something fast enough?"

"No," she admitted reluctantly.

"Chaiq never punished me either." Jahup had liked his old mentor and had adopted many of the woman's ways when training his own band. "I thought the constant practice was punishment, but I learned that was wrong. Constant practice, like the sergeant has these soldiers doing, is what saves your life while on a hunt."

"They are not on a hunt."

"He has taken down five drug labs in the last eight weeks with his team."

"Then he should be training with those soldiers."

"He is." Jahup pointed to the training grounds with his chin. "They are out there. All of them. When they are not serving other posts and duties, they watch over him. They know he is in danger from the corps and the black marketers."

"Why have those people not tried to kill him again?"

"Because he is protected, and because if a second attempt is made on his life, the Terran Army and the Alliance will take more direct action against the corps and the black market."

"You figured this out by yourself?" Noojin looked doubtful.

Jahup grinned slightly and shook his head. "No. I was wondering why they were not trying to kill him now as well." Secretly, he had been fearing for the sergeant, which was why he always brought his rifle with him when he came to observe the training. "My grandmother said she and the other *Quass* have made it known to the corps, the Phrenorians, and the (ta)Klar that they would also look upon another such action against the sergeant in the sprawl with disfavor."

"Why? Are the *Quass* now choosing a side?"

"No, but as they have pointed out in the meetings with those people, the inability to keep the peace inside the sprawl reflects on all of them. If the sprawl is not safe for its citizens, none of them have promises she or the *Quass* want to listen to."

Noojin popped a *keval* berry in her mouth and chewed. "That is true, I suppose. Still, the *Quass* might only be able to prevent the sergeant from being attacked in the sprawl, but out in the jungle it will be a different matter."

"I know."

"Also, Ekalu and his band were nearly killed by black market sec last night. Evidently they got too close to one of the hidden lab locations and alerted the sec systems. Reyst was wounded and will not be able to hunt till she heals."

"I had heard," Jahup said. "We will have to be more careful. Those people working the labs have become more wary of anyone they meet out there in the jungles."

"The paranoia of the lab teams is a result of the sergeant's efforts."

"No. The paranoia they feel is the result of the drugs they consume." Jahup thought again of Gogh and how he had gotten himself killed so foolishly. "If the drugs are not stopped, Noojin, they may be the death of us all. You have seen how our people die with that poison in their veins. That is why we destroy the labs when we can." He rubbed his chin as he watched Sage step onto one of the combat arenas.

TWENTY-EIGHT

Stripped to the waist, wearing only his ACU pants and sparring boots, Sage stepped through the ring cables and onto the four meter by four meter combat mat. A thin layer of insulation foam softened some of the falls, but impacts against it still left a person bruised and badly shaken. Sage knew that for a fact because he'd gotten slammed against them for years in training.

Despite Sage's standing orders that soldiers weren't to break training on the different stations during the exercise period, the troops came over to watch the coming bout. Sage decided not to push the issue and concentrated on one thing at a time. If this many people were interested in the outcome of the match, he assumed the soldier who had agreed to get onto the combat mat with him was a ringer. After the first couple of days of "sparring," no one had bothered to challenge him.

"I want you to know, I still object to this." Kiwanuka stood outside the ring and held the sparring gloves as Sage pushed his hands into them.

"Why? You get into the ring and spar."

"That's training."

"This is training," Sage protested.

"No, too much of this is your ego. You can call it training all you want to, but I see the competition in you every time you take on one of these soldiers."

"There's nothing wrong with having a competitive edge. That's part of what makes a good soldier and a good leader."

"If you lose, you're going to lose more than a fight. These soldiers will start a passive rebellion."

"Then I'm not going to lose."

"You can't guarantee that."

"If they beat me in this ring, *any* of them," Sage replied, "then I'm not fit to lead them."

"A leader isn't just a physical entity. You can train them to think like soldiers."

Sage looked out over the expectant crowd. "Later. I can do that later. Right now all I've got to get their attention is this. I run with them, I eat with them. I don't ask them to do anything I won't do. Including stepping into this ring." He drank a mouthful of water, swished it around his teeth, then spat it out on the ground. "Besides, I need practice too."

"You could train with me."

"Is that an offer, Sergeant?" Sage smiled.

Kiwanuka shoved his mouthpiece between his teeth. "No. There are others you could train with. People on *our* team. People that wouldn't see you as a target."

"I don't think you'd hold back. I've got the definite feeling I'd be a target there too."

A hint of a smile showed on her lips. "No, I wouldn't

hold back. Not for a minute. But I'd stop when I had you beaten. I wouldn't cripple you the way some of these people want to." Kiwanuka nodded to the other side of the ring. "Most of the grunts in Charlie Company have put up a bounty on you, bribing the fighters among them to come forward and take a shot at you. Corporal Lai Pai-shih decided to go for it today. He's not like the other tough guys—and women—who have stepped up to take you on."

Since the first couple days of training, when the would-be contenders went down in quick succession, there had been no takers on Sage's offer to "practice" with any soldier who wanted one-on-one combat training with him. During those early fights, when the men and the women wanted to challenge him, Sage hadn't held back, ending the combat quickly and decisively, never carrying the weaker opponents. The faster an opponent learned he or she was up against someone with a superior skill set, the faster that opponent learned that continuing the fight and potentially getting badly hurt was not a good idea. He didn't want anyone getting hurt over a pride issue.

On the other side of the combat mat, Lai Pai-shih was a monster of a man. Lai was young, maybe mid-twenties, and rippled with muscle. His hair was shaved to the scalp and his eyes were dead black marbles. He wore an assortment of scars from laser burns and knives. Since cosmetic surgery to get rid of those was part of the military package, he must have chosen to wear those scars.

Sage rolled his head, stretching his neck, and regarded his opponent. "Is Lai any good?"

"I've never seen him fight, but he's been involved in some bar brawls against superior numbers and managed to walk away under his own power."

"If you deal with amateurs, that's not so impressive."

"He was up against Green Dragon bashhounds. They're supposed to be some of the best."

"They are some of the best." Sage took a closer look at the soldier and re-evaluated his take on the man. "I've fought a few of them myself."

"There's something else I've heard but haven't verified. Corporal Lai is supposed to be some kind of martial arts champion on Terra. He comes from old-school Hong Kong, where they still have bounty fights."

"I've fought a few of those guys too." Sage took a breath in through his nose and blew it out his mouth. "Let's see what the corporal has." He walked toward the center of the combat ring and Lai came off the ropes. Adrenaline surged in Sage and he knew that Kiwanuka was right. Fighting in the ring was not just about proving a point to the soldiers. It was also about winning. "Corporal Lai."

"Top." Lai nodded in an abbreviated bow, eyes constantly on Sage. "I need to know something before we start."

"Sure."

"When I knock you out, maybe break a few bones, how much time am I going to have to spend in the brig?" Lai grinned coldly, like he'd already won the fight.

Sage grinned. "None. I told all of you at the—"

Lai was faster than he looked and he looked fast. Sage guessed the guy had been training under heavy-grav to pick up that extra edge before the fight. There was only a flicker of warning, the slightest shift of weight, then the corporal's right hand whipped toward Sage's gut and connected like a hydraulic ram. The power behind the blow was enough to make Sage question whether Lai was augmented and Kiwanuka hadn't known after all.

Staggered by the punch, lungs empty of air, Sage only managed to turn his head slightly as the follow-up left to his face rocketed on a collision course. Lai's fist connected with Sage's right temple and left his senses spinning. Knocked off his feet, Sage hit the mat on his back and the soldiers gathered around the arena went wild with exultation.

"Get him, Lai!"

"Mess him up!"

Giving no quarter, Lai lunged in and brought up his right leg, then drove his heel down where Sage's head would have been had he not rolled to the side. Even then, Sage retreated on his hands and knees till he got to his feet. Still dazed, he only put up a weak block against Lai's roundhouse kick and found himself knocked over again.

Once more Lai tried the stomp technique, coming in close. This time Sage only slid out of the way, knowing he had to put the corporal down quickly before he had to hurt him. Sage slid toward Lai's planted left leg, wrapped his left arm around the corporal's ankle, and then rolled back on the captured leg before his opponent could turn around. He spun and drove his right elbow into the back of Lai's knee with everything he could muster.

The knee buckled and came down. Lifting his legs, Sage caught Lai's head between his ankles and pulled, yanking his opponent backward. Lai hit the mat on his shoulders, laying his arms out to slap his hands against the surface to lessen the shock. Sage rolled on top of the man, pinning his shoulders against the mat, then powered a straight punch to Lai's forehead that drove his head against the mat and knocked him unconscious.

Head still pounding, his sense of balance still spinning, Sage regained his feet. The cheering had died down and the majority of the soldiers looked disappointed and unbelieving.

The match had lasted all of twenty-three seconds, the fastest Sage had ever disposed of an opponent.

Sweat streaming down his body, his vision still blurred, Sage looked at them. He spat his mouthpiece into one gloved hand. "Anybody else want a shot at the title today?"

There were no takers, and since Lai was on his back unconscious, the crowd drifted away.

Looking impressed, Kiwanuka tossed Sage a towel. "I haven't seen that move before."

"There are a lot of moves you haven't seen."

"I thought he had you with that sucker punch."

Sage toweled off, feeling the wind blow coolly against his sweat-covered body for a change. "He should have. I was careless and didn't think he would try something like that. I let my guard down. And that wasn't all. He's so quick I couldn't stop him."

"The moves were really good."

"Thanks." Sage draped the towel over his shoulder and stepped through the ropes. He gazed around the training grounds and saw that the soldiers had returned to their PT. "Corporal Finnegan."

"Yeah, Top." The soldier was young and redheaded. As medical support for the hand-to-hand combat training, he was tending to Lai.

"Get a detail together and get that soldier to the infirmary. He's probably got a concussion. If he does, keep him out of the roster till he's healed. If he doesn't have a concussion, send him to me when he's conscious."

"Roger that." Finnegan called out three names and the soldiers set to picking Lai up from the mat to lie on a back board.

Sage continued his rounds, walking among the men. He was certain a couple of teeth had been loosened too, and he thought he might have a cracked rib or two, but he wasn't going to let any of the pain show. He wiped at his face again and the towel came away with smears of blood.

"You should probably report to medical too," Kiwa-nuka said.

"Does anything need sealed?"

"No. You've got a couple tears. Nothing that won't knit up on its own. Maybe you're not as tough as you think."

"Thanks for the vote of confidence."

"Hey, I just know how hard that punch was. I felt it over where I was standing."

"Trust me, you have no clue. I don't know if I've ever been hit that hard by anyone who was human standard."

Kiwanuka squinted at him as they walked through the training grounds. "The eye looks bad. It'll probably swell shut."

"It'll be okay. I'm going to tend to PT, then get it checked out."

"Don't be stubborn."

"They can't see that I'm hurt."

"They don't think you're invincible, Top."

"It would be better if they did." Sage glanced over to the row of buildings closest to the perimeter fences. "The kid is back over there."

"I know. I saw him. His name is Jahup. And he's not a kid. He's a leader of his hunting band."

He was also the guy who had helped save Sage and Kiwanuka when they had been attacked. Jahup's actions with his rifle had been picked up by the ParaSights. Sage hadn't noticed the boy until prepping his after-action report on the assassination attempt.

"What's he doing here?" Sage asked.

"Watching. That's what he always does." Kiwanuka didn't glance at the young Makaum man's position. "I think he's watching you."

"Why?"

"Probably to see one of these younger soldiers kick your butt."

Sage grinned at her and the effort sent a stab of pain through the side of his face. "Not going to happen."

"We'll see."

Sage ignored that and watched the young Makaum, thinking about how good it would be to have people in the jungle who knew their way around.

TWENTY-NINE

Personal Quarters: Sage
Enlisted Barracks
Charlie Company
Fort York
1722 Zulu Time

Someone rapped on Sage's door and when he looked up, he saw Colonel Halladay standing there. Sage quickly stood to attention and saluted, wondering what was going on. The colonel was usually good about giving him a heads-up.

Halladay returned the salute. "At ease, Top. This is more of an informal visit."

"Yes sir." Sage dropped into parade rest.

Looking mildly amused, Halladay said, "Permission to come inside, Top?"

"Granted, sir."

Holding his cover in one hand, Halladay entered the small office. "Do you have coffee?"

"I do."

"Could I have a cup?"

"Yes sir." Sage retreated to the stripped-down coffee service and poured a coffee. He served the cup to the colonel and warmed up his own. If the colonel was going to have a coffee, they were going to be there for a while.

"Sit, Sergeant." Halladay waved to the chair behind the desk. "This is your office, not mine." The colonel looked around. "Mine . . . isn't as neatly kept. Yours is positively Spartan."

"I travel light, sir." Taking his seat behind the desk, Sage looked at Halladay and waited.

"That eye looks bad." Halladay touched his eye, mirroring the swollen eye Sage sported.

"It'll heal."

"You should have expected Corporal Lai to try something. With the way you've been knocking guys down in practice, you should have known they would stop fighting fair."

Sage was surprised but didn't say anything.

"I saw the fight," Halladay said.

"I didn't notice you there."

"I wasn't there. Some of the soldiers upped vid of the fight onto the sprawl net."

That irritated Sage. The training they were doing was supposed to stay within the ranks, not be privy to outsiders. "Do you know who posted the vid? If not, Murad could probably find out."

"I know who did it. Murad did find out. I asked him to look into the matter and I've already dealt with it."

Sage sat back in his chair as understanding came over him. "Major Finkley." There would be no other answer except one of the lieutenants, and Halladay would have delegated the punishment to the major if it had been one of them. And if it had been an enlisted, Sage would have been detailed to take care of it.

"It was Finkley. Evidently he's been running a sport

book on some of the fights in the arena. Streaming live vid into bars in the sprawl. It's run on the QT, but a following has developed. Finkley has a cryptographer setting the odds and he's been making a pile. They were pretty good about keeping everything under the radar. I caught your showdown with Lai today because I had a meeting with some of our local civilian labor directors who are fight fans."

"Access to our training doesn't fly, sir. What we're doing here, how we're doing it, the Phrenorians don't need to see that."

"You're not doing anything secret, Top," Halladay said. "You're training your men. Every Phrenorian warrior worth his salt is doing the same thing right now, and probably a lot of that training is the same."

"That's beside the point, sir. What goes on in our house should stay in our house."

"I agree. Finkley has been reprimanded. I alerted the general, and the general is actively displeased with the situation as well." Halladay grimaced. "If I had my way, if Finkley's father wasn't Alliance Senator Aldous Finkley, I'd bounce Finkley to some backwater post where he couldn't do anything."

"Maybe that's what they were thinking when he got bounced here."

"No. When Finkley's father, the senator, requested that his son be sent here, it was as a liaison for the corps. Senator Finkley wanted to make certain his *constituents* got a fair shake out here in the Green Hell. First pick of concessions, etc. Profit margins have got to meet corps' margin expectations."

"So Finkley's been reporting on how you do your job."

Halladay nodded. "As a result, I walk a thin line, Top." He paused. "I'm also getting some pressure on your activities out in the jungles. Command thinks that Charlie

Company is spreading itself thin beating the brush for drug labs. I think you and your team are getting too successful at putting corps labs out of business. Command has voiced the opinion that we should stay closer to home before we ignite a hostile situation between warring lab operations that spills over onto the fort."

"Are they forgetting that our soldiers are being affected by the drugs moving across the planet as well? That our position here is getting undermined and threatened by the black market?"

"They're choosing to ignore that for the moment. Later, of course, they'll claim that we should have been on top of it. I'm documenting the exchanges. When the pressure goes away, and it will, I'll be able to show a trail concerning our activities and our orders."

"So we're going to shut the op down?" The possibility caused the back of Sage's neck to burn in anger.

"No," Halladay said. "We're going to be more choosy about our targets. We've put pressure on the corps at street level. We've killed or incarcerated drug manufacturers and smugglers. We've destroyed materials and raw product. The street price of the drugs has gone up dramatically and profit margins have decreased. Just because the black market ups the price on product doesn't mean that the people they sell it to are going to be able to purchase it."

"I hadn't realized we were having that effect."

"You are. And it's not because the suppliers want the price to go up. They're squeezing out buyers, losing creds at the bottom line. They've had to raise the price just to stay in business. We're hurting them. Rather, I should say you and your team have hurt them."

"This is a team play, Colonel."

Halladay nodded. "I've been running interference on the political end of things, and dodging the brass. However, they've gotten onto General Washburn and pressure there carries more weight. The general wants to finish out a calm billet. So I'm at a catch twenty-two. The drug cartels the corps have established can't deal with the profit loss, and I can't deal with the heat from Command. Something has to give."

Sage thought about that. "You just said you're not shutting down the op."

"I'm not. Not yet. But we're going to have to change the game, Top. We can't keep going after the nickel-and-dime guys. We need a win. A big one. One that I can use to leverage Command into freeing us up."

"They're not going to back off, sir."

"They won't have a choice. The labor director wasn't the only person I saw today. I also saw members of the *Quass* that are sympathetic to Terran military presence. I let them know I need them to back me. If you can get me proof that ties those drug networks into the corps, those *Quass* members are willing to go to bat for us in a much bigger way. They'll push to break charters with the corps and send them packing."

Sage considered that. "You want something that will roll back onto the corps supporting Senator Finkley."

"I do, Top. But I don't want it. I need it. *We* need it."

"I understand, sir."

"I don't want to add any pressure to the situation, but have you or Lieutenant Murad developed any leads on where we can get information about a clearinghouse regarding these drug labs? They may be independent cells, but I haven't met a criminal yet who completely trusts his grunts. Somebody somewhere is keeping an eye on the creds."

"Roger that. Lieutenant Murad has been talking about the same thing. Every lab we've taken down has been tied into a cyber connection. They've always been so heavily encrypted that the lieutenant hasn't been able to crack them."

"I've been reading Murad's reports. He says that those sites have been cybered up pretty tight."

"The lieutenant hasn't given up though, sir. He appears to be as skilled with code as Sergeant Kiwanuka is with a sniper weapon. The problem we've faced so far is that all the operations we've hit have been small. The lieutenant thinks if we can find a larger operation, one that has a lot more raw materials, more shipping channels, then the latest version of his crack coding might suss out the network backing the drug labs. Put a bow on a large chunk of it."

"That's what he said when I talked to him about this."

Sage sipped his coffee. "You should have told me you'd already talked to the lieutenant, sir. I've wasted your time."

"No you haven't." Halladay held a hand up over his head. "Murad explained what he was doing somewhere about here to me. My emphasis was on handling soldiers and materials, training the right people for the right job. Murad told me he'd discussed this with you and Sergeant Kiwanuka."

Sage nodded. "He brought it up last night."

"You followed what he was talking about?" Halladay lifted a skeptical eyebrow.

"Lost me at the get-go, sir. But I believe the lieutenant can do what he says he can do. I just need to find the right target where we can implement the cyber attack."

Halladay smiled. "I may be able to help you with that, Top."

"You know a location?"

"If I did, I would have already told you. No, my talk

with the *Quass* was about more than just pushing back at
the corps given the right ammunition. I also went to them
asking for help."

That bothered Sage and he tried not to let it show, but
he knew he failed.

"I'm not big on trusting someone outside of the fort
either," Halladay said. "Not with the situation being what
it is. As you know from my views on Finkley, I'm not in
favor of trusting everyone here. But some of those *Quass*
have the same agendas we do. One of the elder *Quass*,
a woman named Leghef, knows how to play her cards
pretty close to the vest. She doesn't know where a major
lab is, but she thinks she knows one of the local merchants who will."

"You're going to ask for cooperation?"

Halladay flashed a cold grin. "I was told this merchant
wouldn't be interested in cooperating with anything
that was going to impact his bottom line. And we're not
hoping to do anything less than destroy that bottom line."
He paused. "Asking him isn't going to fly. At least, asking
nicely won't."

Sage nodded. "So we're not going to ask nicely."

"No." Halladay sighed. "And I can't sanction this op,
Frank. If you, and your team, decide to pursue this, you'll
be doing it on your own without any deniability."

"I can't speak for the team, Colonel, but if I can find
the soldiers than can help me pull this off, that will be
fine with me. We just won't get caught. Now give me that
name."

THIRTY

Clad in a lightweight no-see glidesuit that gave up nearly all armor (it wouldn't stop a direct hit from a solid projectile and would only partially block beam weapons) and dumbed the onboard AI functionality down to directional assistance and nightvision only, Sage dropped from the jumpcopter a thousand meters out from the target house. He popped his arms out and unfurled the wings that ran from his wrists to his ankles. The nano-augmented memoryweave stiffened into webbed wings as it caught the wind.

Rolling his body, Sage controlled his rapid descent toward his target. Before he knew it, he was plunging through a cloud of *asnd*, which were bloodsucking mites as big across as his hand. The bulbous insect bodies smashed against him, spreading over him in splotches of bug guts.

Behind him, Kiwanuka hit the insect cloud and cursed vociferously. Her voice carried to him over the limited-range, line-of-sight inner-ear comms they were using for the op.

"It's not anything that won't wash off," Sage said. "Be glad your faceshield holds up against them."

"They've covered my faceshield. I'm flying blind."

Kiwanuka sounded calm, but Sage knew that wasn't the case. He didn't like the glidesuit, and he didn't trust the no-see fabric to "bend" light and other detection systems well enough to keep them hidden while they were without support and in enemy territory. The man they were after, Sneys, had on-site bodyguards around the clock.

Sage had racked up nearly four times as much practice time in the glidesuits as Kiwanuka, and he still didn't care for the rapid descent or the knowledge that his fate depended on skills he wasn't happy with. Glidesuits weren't primary equipment at training, but there had been enough training to make a difference. Sage had never before used them till training.

"Turn your head from side to side," Sage told her. "Let the wind resistance do the cleaning."

With the memoryweave locked out into glide position, Kiwanuka couldn't move her hand in to clean her faceshield. That was another item on the long list of things Sage didn't like about the suits. He couldn't even look over his shoulder to see if Kiwanuka was following his suggestion. He missed the 360-degree view provided in the battle helmets.

The distance to the ground and to the target counted down rapidly inside his faceshield, fogged up occasionally by the heat of his breath against the humid night air.

"Okay. Got it. Most of it." Kiwanuka still sounded tense.

"Confirm target?" Sage asked.

"Roger that."

Below, the private quarters of Sneys the merchant stood tall in a copse of trees. The man had chosen to build on a promontory that overlooked Makaum City. The trees were thin there and Sneys employed a large crew that kept the jungle clear of his private garden.

According to the intel Sage had, Sneys's home hadn't always been so grand. The man had always been successful among the Makaum, following in the footsteps of his family's horticulture business. Before he'd started working as a drug designer for the corps, Sneys had created new strands of fruits and nuts and trees that the Makaum people could train to grow into homes.

The structure Sneys lived in was a labyrinth of dozens of trees that created a protective fortress against the larger predators that stalked the planet. Dozens of rooms had been created inside, and local legend had it that Sneys could coax his home into growing another room within a week.

His privacy had been earned by the fields around his home that grew edible crops. Only Makaum people with a gift for agriculture were given large tracts of land, and Sneys owned enough to put him in the top tier of the sprawl population.

The structure's expansive roof was covered in a flower garden that was lush and immense and beautiful. Sage had observed the garden for the last three days they had done recon on the property. Jumpcopters had already flown over the area regularly on patrol, so getting an up-close look at the property hadn't been hard.

Getting onto the grounds was more problematic. One of the plants that Sneys's family had perfected was *uspkh*, a sensory vine that alerted the merchant whenever anyone approached the main house on foot. Sage hadn't been able to ascertain how the alarm vine was able to do that, but that was how the story went.

Murad had attempted an explanation of the vine that had ended up making Sage's head hurt and he'd finally given in. The only thing that mattered was that the vine worked as claimed.

The road leading up to the house was guarded by tech as well as flesh-and-blood sec provided in the form of off-worlder mercenaries. They didn't, however, provide aerial support to watch over the grounds.

Sage rolled and adjusted his glide path again, and the distance to the garden melted away. He arched his back and spun, putting the microweave against the wind and settling to the ground amid flowers and decorative grasses. He stumbled and almost fell before the microweave went inert and fell slack, then sucked back up into the suit. He cursed the suit again, but looked for Kiwanuka and spotted her in time to catch her by the foot before she crashed into a *keval* berry tree.

Off balance, unable to catch herself and forgetting to relax the glidesuit's memoryweave, Kiwanuka did a face-plant. Luckily the loam was soft and springy, so she didn't do much more than knock the wind out of herself.

Drawing the narco-dart machine pistol that was the only weapon they were carrying on the op, Sage hunkered down beside her while she recovered.

Pete Bowden and Brittany Meacham completed the four-man insertion team. Both of them had a history of covert ops and more time in the glidesuits. They came down almost together, dropping the rigidity of the memoryweave while a meter in the air and coming down like they'd been born with wings. By the time they landed, they had their narco-dart pistols in hand and were spreading out in formation.

Sage gazed around the garden, letting the nightvision prog adjust to the terrain and the light. In a few seconds, the nightvision had acclimated to the environment and Sage could see almost as clearly in the shadows as he could in the light of day.

The only problem was the amount of nocturnal insect life flitting among the night blossoms. Their body heat was slightly higher than the prevailing temperature and they registered like a snowstorm of embers all around Sage and his team.

Kiwanuka stood and drew her weapon.

"Okay," Sage said. "Let's go." He pushed through the thick plants and headed for the house's skylight.

Instead of glass or translucent plascrete, the skylight used tree resin that could be formed into thin, resilient sheets. Getting the tree resin to the right consistency was delicate work, and putting in the decorative imagery was painstaking art. The resin skylight had been formed to fit the two-meter opening. It latched from inside. Occasionally the skylight was opened to allow fresh breezes into the living quarters, but only when white noise generators were on to keep the insects at bay.

Sage sprayed the skylight with a canister of solvent that dissolved the resin. The skylight thinned, became translucent, revealing the dark quarters below, and finally melted to the sides, leaving the opening clear.

Kiwanuka walked the rooftop carefully and shot sonar of the structure. "Okay, I've confirmed the blueprints we received. There aren't any surprises in the home. Layout's just like we were told it would be." She put the sonar pulse reader into her chest pouch.

"Good." Colonel Halladay had gotten the skinny on the house from his sources within the *Quass* members who had been invited to Sneys's estate.

Taking a self-starting piton from his equipment pouch, Sage knelt down and fired it into the thick loam. After making certain the piton was set properly, he hooked his rappelling cable D-link through the eyelet and clambered over the opening in the skylight.

Once Kiwanuka and Meacham were set up, and Bowden had a close cover position to watch over them, Sage launched himself over the side and spun down the rappelling cable like a spider. Eight meters down, he landed on the floor soundlessly. The gel soles of his boots made no noise as he unbuckled the rappelling line and walked away.

He pulled the narco-dart machine pistol into his hands and covered the large room's three exits while Kiwanuka and Meacham followed him down.

The room had become a showpiece of Sneys's wealth. Before he'd inherited the estate, the room had probably been used for the same purpose for generations. The rough wood of the tree trunks that made up the walls had been worn smooth, but the grain showed through. Shelves had been grown in the spaces, not carved as Sage had at first believed. He'd seen some of the work the enviro-shapers had done with the local vegetation to create homes and had been amazed.

Furniture wasn't brought into the home. It was created within the structure, grown from the trees that made up the building. Nano fiber aboard space stations and starships could do the same thing, rise up from the floor and become furniture in seconds. What the Makaum people managed to do, even though such shaping took weeks and months, was nothing short of spectacular.

Meacham positioned herself against a dark wall that gave her an unobstructed view of the home's lower floor and the winding staircase that grew out of the wall.

Sage scanned the house for biometrics and discovered four active humanoid life-forms in one of the second-story rooms. Two of the downstairs rooms each had one life-form reading.

Moving on stealth mode, but quickly as he dared, Sage entered the first room and discovered an elderly Makaum woman sleeping in a bed.

"Domestic help," Kiwanuka said. "Sneys is supposed to have two live-in staff."

Lowering the machine pistol, Sage took a fully soluble slap patch from his chest pouch and applied it to the sleeping woman's exposed neck. She woke for just a moment, but the drug in the slap patch stole her consciousness before she completely roused. The narcotic would guarantee four hours of uninterrupted sleep.

A quick trip to the other bedroom and another slap patch guaranteed the domestic help were accounted for.

Returning to the big main room, Sage crept up the stairway and turned into the hallway that led to the master bedroom, where Sneys slept. Voices and movement sounded inside, conversation and laughter, most of it from a man's voice. Sage sampled the male voice with the suit's limited recording features and compared it to a chunk of Sneys's voice. In short order, the indicator flashed green, letting Sage know Sneys was present.

Another peal of laughter came from the room, and it sounded fake and forced. The man spoke again and there was more laughter.

It would have been better if Sneys and his company had been asleep, but Sage wasn't going to abandon the mission. He was just going to have to be quick.

The door had been equipped with a sensor-fed locking array. Sage placed a foolie on the lock and let it do its work, nervously waiting for several seconds before the locks clicked open.

Machine pistol tucked up under his arm, Sage disabled

his nightvision feature because lights were on inside the room and he didn't want to be blinded when he entered. Then he shoved the door open and followed it inside.

Sneys was a pot-bellied Makaum in his middle years. From the scuttlebutt Murad had dug up with dataminers slipping through the Makaum sprawl net, Sage knew Sneys had been something of a letch even before the corps had made him an even richer man.

Totally naked, Sneys romped in the bed with three off-worlder feminine consorts. One of them was human. Another was *Ehati*, a race that was beautiful and intelligent, passionate in the arts. *Ehati* were expensive courtesans.

The third was a *Youghy*, a massive female who stood nearly three meters tall, massed out at a conservative one hundred and sixty kilos, an Amazon of a woman. The *Youghy* were a warlike race that hadn't achieved star flight on their own, but had been picked up by several interstellar species as laborers, and as warriors.

The *Youghy* spotted Sage first and reached for her *brear*, a tri-bladed throwing weapon large enough and lethal enough to cut through armor or lop off a soldier's head or limb. *Youghy* had a habit of never being far from their personal weapons because they were also their prayer tools to their gods.

The *Youghy* female was quick, managing to grab her weapon and fling it at Sage. The blades fanned through the air and sounded like a fast-beating heart as it closed on Sage.

"Down!" Sage ordered, throwing himself to the floor under the spinning blades and hoping that Kiwanuka managed to do the same. The *Youghy* female had already grabbed her spear, shaking it once to release it, expanding it from the baton-length to three meters of deadly reinforced steel. Blades jutted out of either end.

The *brear* thudded into the wall over Sage's head as

he centered the machine pistol on the *Youghy* female and squeezed the trigger. The machine pistol's slight recoil didn't affect Sage. Phosphorescent fins on the five-centimeter darts glowed across the woman's midsection, injecting her with narcotic.

She flung the spear as a last act of defiance before collapsing to the bed and trapping the *Ehati* female beneath her. As Sage feathered the *Ehati* woman with darts, Sneys vaulted up from the tangled sheets faster than Sage would have given the man credit for.

Getting to his feet, Sage fired another burst of narco-darts at the female and dropped her in a rolling sprawl from the bed, leaving her on the ground.

Sneys wrapped a hand around the portable comm on the floor by the bed and tried to thumb the panic button.

Sage kicked the device from the merchant's hands before the outside mercenaries could be signaled that something was wrong. If the guards had been alerted and brought into the dwelling, Sage wasn't sure if his team would have been able to handle them because they were armored.

Sneys tried to scramble to the portable comm, but Sage kicked the man in the side hard enough to flip him over onto his back. Putting the muzzle of the machine pistol only a handful of centimeters from the merchant's eyes, Sage shook his head.

"Don't try it. For now I want you alive. You don't want to change my mind."

Quivering in fear, Sneys held up his hands. "All right. Don't shoot. Just don't kill me."

"Get up. Slowly," Sage directed. "You're going to get dressed."

"Why?"

"We're going to take a trip."

"I have credsticks here. I can pay you." Sneys's eyes were wide with fright.

"I'm not interested." Sage tapped the man's face with the blunt muzzle of the machine pistol hard enough to get and keep Sneys's attention. "You and I are going to talk, and you're going to tell me what I want to know. Otherwise, I'm going to find a *kifrik* web and tie you to it."

THIRTY-ONE

S age stared down into the holo of the target zone and tried to peel back the jungle to see the large lab site Sneys had claimed was there. Even with the view from the satellite recon, there was no way to push back the trees and brush to get a clear view of the terrain. Dawn-Star had selected the site well. The maps designated the area as the Cer'ardu Heights.

Halladay leaned on the desk and examined the territory with tense anticipation. "What do we know about this area?"

"Not much, sir." Sage had spent the last three hours sorting through the geographical studies and topographical maps Terran military had of the site. Adrenaline thrummed softly through his system because he knew the window of time open on the op was steadily closing. If they didn't move soon, Sneys's disappearance would be noted and it wouldn't take DawnStar long to connect the dots. "Military ops are wide of that area because the Makaum have stayed out of it for the most part. It's a hundred forty klicks out and in rough country according to the reports from Makaum hunters that intelligence has picked up over the past couple of years."

"If we go straight at the people in that complex, they're going to see us coming."

"We can go straight at them, though, sir." Sage had just figured that part out.

"How?"

"You're looking at this as a two-dimensional problem, staying strictly on the ground. We don't have to do that."

"What are you thinking?"

"We can use dropships, launch off the DawnStar space station and hit dirt with soldiers within minutes at the end of a rapid planetfall. The people in that compound won't know where those dropships are heading until it's too late." Sage waved a hand across the holo, triggering the next set of schematics he, Murad, and Kiwanuka had proposed.

A simulated sequence showed two dropships plunging through the atmosphere, burning off landing pads out of the jungle, and hitting dirt within a short distance of what they believed was the outer perimeter of the site.

"We've got troops up on the space station now on leave. We send up more troops with a dropship without alerting anyone, tag it for emergency maintenance, then stack that dropship with the soldiers we send up and the ones we bring back down in a dropship still in orbit. Instead of landing in Fort York, we put both dropships down near the lab."

Halladay pulled up a separate screen out of the holo and reviewed the troop numbers. "Did Sneys give you any indication of how many guards might be stationed there?"

"He said he thinks there are around a hundred Dawn-Star bashhounds," Kiwanuka said, "but those numbers are supplemented by mercenaries and local guards. Maybe a hundred and fifty."

"We've got eight hundred and seventy-two troops cleared for active duty in this battalion." Halladay gazed at the readout panel that glowed against the virtual topography. "I can't leave this fort understaffed."

"I know that, sir." Sage looked into the other man's eyes. "And, provided we can get that second dropship and soldiers up to DawnStar without alerting anyone—because soldiers talk, we can't deploy more than a hundred of our people. We put fifty men in each dropship, fifty on the ground and take fifty from the men on leave at the space station, equip twenty percent of them with powersuits for heavy artillery, and have them hit the east and west ends of the lab and launch attacks."

"We can't just attack that lab without proof of what they're doing."

Sage nodded. "I know that, sir. Lieutenant Murad is going to lead our covert team into the lab so we can get you the proof you need. Then, after we get that to you, you can get authority to launch the dropships and hit dirt."

"If we get clearance to launch an attack like that," Halladay looked at the three soldiers around the holo table, "you're talking about a nine-minute window before I can put troops on the ground even with an emergency fall from low-planet orbit. If you blow cover before those troops arrive, you're on your own until we can get there."

"Yes sir," Sage said. "That's nine minutes that none of us can make go away. We'll have to eat that time. But if we want to break the hold DawnStar and the other corps have on the black market here on Makaum, this may be the only chance we get. Once DawnStar finds out we took

Sneys, they'll know we have more intelligence on them than they were expecting. They'll be more careful, and they'll pump up their defenses and hit back politically if they're able."

Halladay stared at the holo. The grim lines on his face deepened. "We haven't even confirmed the existence of a lab at that site."

"Once we do, things will have to happen pretty quickly if we're going to do anything about it." Sage paused. "If we can make this happen, sir, we'll be out in front of them instead of chasing them for a change."

"I know." Halladay cursed softly. "Where is Sneys?"

"We've got him and his staff on lockdown," Murad said.

"How soon before anyone knows he has gone missing?"

Sage shrugged and the adrenaline inside him picked up the pace. "Hours. Sneys doesn't keep a regular schedule, but people will know when he's not around for a while."

"It would help if we had more control of that."

"Yes sir, it would. But we don't." Sage watched Halladay's eyes and saw the conviction roll into place as the man's gaze turned harder. The mission was going to be a go. Halladay couldn't back off now if they were going to have a chance to strike back. There wouldn't be another opportunity to catch DawnStar as vulnerable.

"All right, let's get it done. I'll get the cavalry in order."

"Yes sir."

Halladay's expression turned grim. "And something else to remember, people. Until you get me the proof that DawnStar is involved in a criminal enterprise, I can't help you. If you're caught on-site there, you're felons, and they won't keep you alive to try you. They'll want to make an example of you."

Sage nodded. "Understood, sir, but once we turn the tables on them, we've got leverage."

**The Cer'ardu Heights
140 Klicks West of Makaum
0117 Hours Zulu Time**

Clad in his combat suit and hidden in a cleft of rock above the black-market drug factory, Sage scoped out the operation. Sneys had told Sage the operation was big, and that it was a clearinghouse for raw materials necessary for processing the drugs in the various smaller labs scattered throughout the jungle.

Most of the complex—and Sage was comfortable thinking of the operation as that because there were a number of prefab plascrete buildings scattered over the site—remained underground. The prefab construction served mainly to control access to the natural underground caverns.

The cursory geological surveys that had been done on the region by the Terran Explorer Division, responsible for mapping out the planet, had given considerable information on the cave systems. Although the initial decision to put Fort York close to Makaum City had never wavered, a number of fallback positions had been designated in the event of Phrenorian aggression.

The Cer'ardu Heights had been in the top ten of those positions. Gazing on the area now through nightvision magnification, Sage understood why the place had gotten such a high rating. He wondered if DawnStar had found the site themselves or if they had discovered it on their own with one of their off-books pharmaceutical teams surveying the planet.

Sage pushed the question aside because it didn't really matter. What he had to do now was get his team inside the installation, get Murad somewhere close to the computers that ran operations, and let the lieutenant gather the intel they needed to rain Terran Army down from space.

Secmen patrolled the darkness below, all of them dressed in combat hardsuits with camo capabilities and nightvision. Their communications were sporadic and heavily encrypted. So far the capture prog software Murad had in his bag of tricks hadn't been able to penetrate the encryption.

In addition to the lieutenant and Kiwanuka, Sage had brought in the eight fireteams they had been operating with on the covert missions. Six of those fireteams had dug in a klick away to the north, higher up in the mountains, and were awaiting orders. They'd been armed with powersuits and light artillery to provide suppressive fire in the event of a forced retreat. If things went as planned, and the order for the assault was given, they were supposed to create a backdoor for the insertion team or provide confusion until the heavy troops arrived.

Two of the fireteams were close in, ready to offer immediate support if they had to. But only if it would do any good. If the probe team got busted during the insertion phase, they had orders to stand down and withdraw.

Sage turned from his observation post and faced Murad and Kiwanuka. "Let's get this done."

Kiwanuka looked at him, her face barely visible through the faceshield of her helmet. "I don't like being left out here. I could go with you."

Sage shook his head. "I don't like the idea of giving up a sniper just to put her inside a situation she could help me get out of. If this goes sideways, if there's a chance I can get out of there, I want you watching my back."

She nodded. "I understand. Just make sure you get back out."

"Roger that." Sage shifted his attention to Murad. "These drones are all automated? All I have to do is deliver them to a comm access point?" His backpack contained a dozen different flying drones equipped with hijacking progs and burst satellite uplink capabilities.

"They're ready to go, Top." Murad seemed a little tense. His vitals were elevated. "I could still come with you to ensure the tech works the way it's supposed to."

"No, sir. The platoon leader stays with the soldiers to take care of the situation. That's why sergeants were made."

"Good luck, Sergeant." Murad offered his hand.

"Thank you, sir." Staying low, Sage went down the mountain.

Dhanvantari Point
0138 Hours Zulu Time

Velesko Kos clambered out of the crawler he'd just spent the last three hours rattling around in. He hated the necessity of ground travel to arrive at the hidden complex, but the operation was under his protection. DawnStar had been adamant about that. Granted, the assignment had its own perks. He got a percentage of the profits, not just a straight salary, which was better than any other contract he'd gotten from the corp in the past.

DawnStar wanted a motivated security chief for the ops on Makaum. In the beginning, the arrangement had been more than satisfactory. Kos had been making more profits than he had in twelve years of being associated with DawnStar. Makaum had turned into a good deal for him.

Now, though, with the losses inflicted by the Terran military's new sergeant, Kos was currently making less profit than he had in those twelve years. As he'd come to discover, when the losses had to be covered by DawnStar, the corp also took debits out of his accounts.

Even as Kos swept the entrance of the hidden complex with his gaze, his thoughts were centered on Terran Army Master Sergeant Frank Sage. Kos wanted the man dead for several reasons now, not just for the confrontation at the club. Sage and his team were cutting into the drug profits.

However, DawnStar had not yet sanctioned direct action against the sergeant. That was coming, though. Kos was certain of that, and he was going to tend to the matter himself when the time came.

Covered in the hardsuit, nightvision systems on, Kos strode from the dust-covered crawler toward the complex's main entry area. DawnStar had listed the site as Dhanvantari Point, naming it after the Hindu physician to the gods. Corps were like that, always insisting on naming things.

If Kos had been in charge of the site, it wouldn't have had a name. No name meant no one talked about it. No one talking about it meant no one ever found out about it.

So far, Sage's jungle raids hadn't come near the site. The location had been chosen because not even the Makaum hunters frequented the area. Saber spiders lived there in heavy numbers, making the Cer'ardu Heights one of the most dangerous regions on the planet.

Kos's comm crackled in his ear. The heavily encrypted equipment was another nuisance. This far out, the encryption became problematic and bogged down the cyberware. The constant feedback gave him headaches. He didn't like coming out to the site, but he did so once a month just to crack the whip. Security only ran smoothly if the head of operations showed up when expected, and also unexpectedly.

This was one of those unexpected times, and Kos hated the fact that the visit wasn't prompted as much by wanting to keep his sec team on their toes as by his wanting to make certain everything there was going well. Days had passed since Sage's last foray into the jungle. Profits from drugs were still down, and sales onplanet were dropping because the street prices had gone up. Kos had been in favor of using DawnStar's deeper pockets to keep the product prices low and drive out the independent agencies, especially the domestic efforts that had sprung up, but DawnStar's board of directors hadn't gone along with the idea.

The board was good with playing the long game against other corps, playing price wars and withholding stock to make competitors exhaust their own resources, when it came to standard profits. But when it came to illegal profits, DawnStar execs wanted that steady flow of credit filling their coffers.

Makaum was a gold mine. The board just couldn't see it. If they were able to lock up the planet's natural resources, control the drug trade on- and going offplanet, they could have had a monopoly.

Kos had almost gotten board members to go for a coup on the drug trade, except that Sage's delivery of Andresik's corpse in the club had triggered an unexpected reaction on the part of the Phrenorians. No one knew why Captain Zhoh GhiCemid had backed Sage that night, and everyone expected Kos to decipher it. Worse than that, the board blamed Kos for the sudden interest by the Phrenorians. The Sting-Tails had been making inroads with one of the Makaum political factions. Especially after the humanitarian aid the Phrenorians had exhibited during the fire in the sprawl.

AGITATED AND SEETHING, Kos wanted to go rattle the cages inside the complex, make the lower echelons scurry, and see the fear in their eyes—and then he wanted a tall drink and the company of some of the women they kept on-site to service the sec squads.

The comm crackled again, but this time a message printed out on the inside of his faceshield:

WE STILL HAVEN'T BEEN ABLE TO FIND SNEYS.
EVERYTHING SEEMS OKAY AT HIS HOME, BUT THE
DOMESTIC STAFF ACTS NERVOUS.

Kos wasn't surprised the domestics at the merchant's home were acting tense around the sec team he'd sent to investigate Sneys's silence that day. They were intimidating people. That was what he'd hired them for.

Sneys was a different matter, though. The man was petty and greedy, qualities that Kos knew on a personal level how to work with. He had managed and manipulated Sneys since the first day they'd met.

WHAT DOES THE HOUSE STAFF SAY ABOUT HIS
ABSENCE?

THEY'RE NOT HERE EITHER.

Kos was certain something had happened. Sneys wasn't a clever mastermind by any stretch of the imagination. But the man could be bought too.

CONTINUE YOUR INVESTIGATION. *FIND* SNEYS.

YES SIR.

At the sec door built into the prefab building, which looked like a fungal growth clinging to the side of the mountain, Kos took off his glove and waved his hand in front of the biometric scanner. The sec system cycled and the airtight door slid open.

Two guards in heavy armor stood inside. They acknowledged him with nods but kept their rifles at the ready. Kos passed between them and took the elevator down thirty feet to the secondary security checkpoint.

He passed through that, lifting his faceshield for the first time, and gazed out at the main cavern, where the bulk of the offplanet chemicals were kept awaiting delivery to satellite sites. All the barrels and crates stood neat and organized on a stone floor that had been resurfaced with mining lasers. The rock that had been removed to enlarge the cavern had been used to shore up defenses in other areas, making the reinforced areas look like part of the natural terrain.

"Good evening, Mr. Kos," a pleasant voice said.

Kos turned and found Frantisek Dubchek bearing down on him, flanked by two heavily cybered sec guards. Kos returned the greeting and meant it. He and Dubchek went back even further than the current relationship with DawnStar. Dubchek had never had a qualm about killing whoever Kos told him to whenever the order was given.

Dubchek stood tall and lanky, and his face appeared baby smooth and much younger than he really was. Over the years of their association, Dubchek had done everything Kos had asked him to do no matter how dangerous that had been. The man had nearly been killed several times, and his face had been reconstructed a lot. Kos couldn't remember what the man had originally looked like, but the features that Dubchek wore now looked alien and artificial because they were so perfect.

"Everything is running well," Dubchek stated. "We have your quarters ready for you."

"Good."

"You're actually in for a treat. The outer perimeter guards caught a group of Makaum hunters getting too close to the Point. The guards attacked them, killing some of them, and managed to capture some of the women. Once I heard you had arrived, I took the liberty of sending for one of the girls taken captive so that you might enjoy her."

Kos nodded but didn't say anything. Although he would not have admitted it, tonight was a night he looked forward to violent pursuits, and the possibility of sharing them with someone not as seasoned as one of the paid women was pleasing. He wanted to break someone, to hear them cry out in pain, and allow the frustration he felt to be given voice.

The suite of rooms was kept for Kos. No one else went there. He stepped into the closet space and the automated valet stripped the combat armor from him, leaving him naked. He pulled on a robe.

Dubchek stood at the wet bar and poured them both a drink. He handed a glass to Kos and asked, "Will you want to go over any of the reports now?"

Kos shook his head. "No. Sometime tomorrow will be fine. How are the supplies doing?"

Dubchek frowned, and the expression looked strangely out of place on that angelic face. "We are stockpiling chemicals at the moment, due to the loss of the satellite manufacturing sites. We are attempting to develop replacement operations, but—given the pressure and scrutiny we're under—we're proceeding slowly so our efforts here aren't compromised."

"We've got to move faster. Nature abhors a vacuum. If we don't get manufacturers to meet the demands for the drugs, the locals or the offplanet independents will take up the slack."

"Agreed. I've been developing more personnel connections. I've even taken the liberty of contacting Miroslav to pull in some of his drug designers. They may not be as savvy regarding the local flora and fauna, but they're fast learners and we already have a number of products they can simply take over the manufacture of."

"Good." The choice was good. They had worked with Miroslav before. The man would cut himself in for a piece of the action, but that could be tolerated for the moment. And they had several designer drugs that had good markets on- and offworld.

The door pinged, announcing the arrival of visitors.

Dubchek put his glass on the bar. "That will be your entertainment." He went to the door and returned with a young woman dressed only in a silky gown.

Kos studied her, immediately drawn to her youth and vitality, and the aggressive tilt of her chin. She couldn't hide the fear that filled her, though, and lent an even sharper edge to the hunger that vibrated through him. She thought she was strong enough to resist him, and that made him desire her even more.

Then he realized he had seen her before. She had been in the intel packet concerning Sergeant Terracina. The girl belonged to one of the Makaum hunting bands that had given the sergeant information about the drug labs. She hung around the young Makaum scout who had become so interested in Sage.

Kos's eyes narrowed as he captured her chin in his hand. "I know you."

She yanked her face away from him. Before she could complete the action, though, Kos backhanded her and knocked her to the ground. She caught herself on her hands, barely keeping her face from smashing into the floor as she rested on her knees.

Kos hunkered down beside her and grabbed her by the hair, yanking her face back up to look at him. Tears swam in her widened eyes. "Tell me your name, girl."

For a moment, pride held her silent, but the fear was too much. She answered in a trembling voice. "Noojin."

THIRTY-TWO

Y ou cannot go down into that place. They will kill you."

As he gazed down on the hidden installation and felt the fear and loss and the pain swelling up in him, Jahup listened to Lyem's argument and knew that what his companion said was true, but he could not agree. "Noojin is alive, Lyem. I cannot leave her."

The offworlders had taken Noojin alive. When he'd passed out, thinking that he was dying, Jahup had seen the offworlder sec man laughing with his companion as he threw Noojin's unconscious body over his shoulder and carried her away.

At least, Jahup told himself, Noojin had been unconscious and not dead. She could not be dead. He would not believe that. He had trailed after them in the direction they had gone, afraid that he would find her body, and terrified that they would keep her prisoner.

Lyem cursed in the darkness and called Jahup all manner of a fool. "Even if she is alive, Jahup, they will kill you. And what use will you be of to Noojin then?"

Jahup did not try to answer that question. That would have meant admitting the answer might exist. No, Noojin lived, and he knew he had to find some way to free her. The horrible stories of what the offworlders did to captured women ran through his head.

These men were as predatory as a *kifrik* or a *khrelav*. They deserved to be killed as such too.

Looking down on the prefab buildings almost hidden in the rough mountainside, Jahup thought desperately, trying to figure out some means of getting inside the underground complex. Noojin was in trouble because of him. They had been arguing over the Terran sergeant again, even though Jahup had deliberately taken them deep into the Cer'ardu Heights in order not to cross paths with the Terrans, and Jahup had missed the warning signs of the drug traffickers in the area until after they had opened fire.

Most of Jahup's band had scattered, miraculously alive, but they had left three dead behind. One of them had been Oesta, who had been almost like a brother to Jahup. Noojin and two other girls had been taken. Jahup blinked his eyes and willed himself to be strong, forcing himself to believe that Noojin would be fine and that there was time for him to rescue her.

"Perhaps we can return with other hunters," Lyem suggested. "Jahup, it is worth trying."

Jahup wouldn't let himself be fooled. They were at the least five days' hard travel from Makaum City by foot. Other hunters, if they came at all, wouldn't risk using crawlers because they would easily be detected. So that would mean another five days' travel back to this site.

That time didn't even include the delay that convincing others to accompany them to attack an offworlder site protected by heavy weapons would take.

If he could convince anyone at all.

And during that time Noojin would be subjected to horrible things that Jahup did not wish to contemplate, but could not keep from his mind either.

"They will not come," Jahup said. "They will not stand against these offworlders for fear of being killed."

"Then pray that Noojin was dead when they carried her away," Lyem said. "That is the greatest favor you can wish for her."

Jahup stood then and faced his friend. "I will not leave her. I will not abandon her. Leave if you wish. Save yourself." He made the last an accusation though he immediately did not like himself for doing so. He could not demand that the others die for his own inability to realize the inevitable.

A haunting look of fear and guilt clouded Lyem's thin face. One of his eyes was partially swollen shut, and he had a puncture wound in his right thigh that needed to be sewn closed. The other eight members of the hunting band were pretty much in the same shape, requiring medical attention as well. Except for bruises and a few lacerations, Jahup was relatively uninjured. The lack of personal damage contributed to his feelings of guilt.

"What can you do?" Lyem asked. "The offworlders have security all around this place."

"I can go to her. The offworlders are in the caves under the mountains. Remember when we were younger and came this way? We explored these lands. We have been down in those caves. There are other ways to get down there. There is a chance I can find her and get her out." Even as he said that, Jahup knew how thin that chance was.

"What if the offworlders have sealed those areas off?

Jahup, even if you can remember where those entrances are, they may no longer exist."

"I have to look!" The entrances had to be there. Anything else was unacceptable. "Noojin would not be with them if not for me." *The others would not be dead!* Jahup pushed that from his mind. There was nothing he could do for the dead, but he might yet save Noojin and the two other women.

He had to try.

"This is not your fault, Jahup. No one saw the off-worlders until they attacked us. If we had been any slower, we would have all been dead tonight."

"I am going." Turning around, Jahup headed down the mountain and stepped into the arms of a shadowy figure before he knew it. He tried to escape, but he couldn't.

0155 Hours Zulu Time

Sage wrapped his arms around the struggling young man and held on tight. He put his mouth close to his captive's ear. "I am Sergeant Sage of the Terran Army. Stop struggling."

For a moment he didn't think the young man—Jahup—was going to desist. Then he stopped and nodded.

"I'm going to let you go, Jahup. Don't run. If you do, you might alert the guards, and if you—if *we*—get captured, that's not going to help Noojin. Do you understand?" Sage gazed at the young Makaum hunters that stood back a few meters away and watched them. He'd spoken loud enough to be heard by them as well.

Gently, Sage released Jahup. He stared at the young man, knowing his mission hung on the Makaum hunter's ability to keep calm and see the big picture.

"Will you help me find Noojin?" Jahup asked.

Sage nodded. "If I can. I think maybe we can help each other. You said you knew another way to get into the cave system?"

Jahup nodded.

"Good, because that's where we need to be."

0203 Hours Zulu Time

"This kid may not even know what he's talking about," Murad objected. "We could be wandering around out here in the dark."

Hearing the young second lieutenant talk about Jahup's lack of knowledge when the Makaum hunter was probably less than a handful of years younger than Murad would have made Sage smile under more favorable circumstances.

"That's true, sir," Sage agreed. "That's why I'm going to go with him, see if we can find that way in that he's talking about. If it's there, then maybe we can get a team inside and improve our chances of finding the information we need to break this operation open. We can spare a few minutes. And this is a better opportunity than the plan we had."

The original plan had been for Sage to take down one of the sec guards and use one of the AKTIVsuit's foolies to mask himself as one of the guards to gain access to the lab long enough to set the hacker drones free. Even if he'd gotten inside, even with most of the site's guards sleeping, the chances of getting discovered were high.

And that was hoping that the geological surveys of the cave system were accurate. Generally the mapping was done by drones, but those maps hadn't taken into account the remodeling DawnStar might have done.

"This is the better chance, sir," Sage said.

Murad nodded. "Then we'll do it that way. Only we're going with you."

"Sir, it would be better if you and the others—"

"Remained out here?" Murad shook his head. "If the two of you can get in there, then the ten of us can get in as well. It won't do any good if you get inside and get discovered before you can deploy the drones. We'll split up the drones and increase our chances of getting the intel we need about the site."

Sage started to object, but he knew that the lieutenant was right, and the look in Kiwanuka's eye let him know she wasn't going to back down either. He nodded. "Yes sir."

0311 Hours Zulu Time

Kos stood in the command center of the complex's security systems and swept the vidscreens where three mercenaries monitored the surrounding jungle. After he'd recognized the woman, he'd felt certain that the Makaum hunters hadn't just accidentally found their way into the area.

"Velesko," Dubchek said, "I assure you, the hunters were just that: hunters. They chanced upon us."

One of the screens played back onboard vid from the powersuit pilots that had attacked the hunters. The Makaum hadn't quite been taken by surprise. They scattered just ahead of the lethal fire that had raked the trees and chopped brush like a scythe.

Kos operated the controls, slowing down the action and magnifying it to better see what had happened. All he saw in the jungle were the Makaum hunters. There were no hardsuits, and the return fire that had struck the mercenary unit pursuing them had been pitifully weak.

"Those people were not armed with anything better than primitive weapons," Dubchek said.

Onscreen, an arrow flew through the jungle and shattered against the powersuit's chest. The pieces fell away.

Everything Dubchek said made sense, but Kos couldn't get memories of the young man who had been with the girl Noojin from his mind. His spies had watched Sage train the soldiers at the fort, and some of them had reported seeing the young man.

Jahup.

Finally remembering the young man's name, Kos accessed files he'd stored on the DawnStar space station and brought up the information on the young man. He pasted the image of the young man into the security footage and initiated a facial recognition search among the faces that the mercenaries' vid had picked up.

None of the men were Jahup.

Kos refused to believe that bad luck on part of the Makaum hunters had brought them into contact with the sec guards. "This wasn't an accident," Kos insisted. "The girl hangs out with a young man who has been crushing on Sage."

"The Terran Army sergeant you've warned me about?" Dubchek asked.

"Yes. It's possible that Jahup and his people began working with Sage. They could have led Sage to this site, and if they did, he's out there waiting."

Dubchek spoke tactfully. "If the army had been out there, they wouldn't have allowed us to simply kill those Makaum. They would have fought to defend them."

A ping drew Kos's attention to the vids displaying the stream from the drones spying around the perimeter. As he watched, one of the drones locked into a stabilized position, then painted a Terran military powersuit almost hidden in a copse of trees and a pile of broken rock. Once limned in a targeting laser, there was no mistaking the shape.

In the next minute, the drone went offline—HARDWARE MALFUNCTION—that Kos felt certain was the result of a sniper's bullet. He turned cold inside, vindicated for his paranoia, and looked at Dubchek.

"Someone's out there, Frantisek. Send a team to see who it is."

0315 Hours Zulu Time

Sage's hardsuit automatically mapped the underground cave system they followed. After Jahup had shown them the entrance, they had chosen the tunnels that led toward the area where Sage expected the underground complex to be located. Some of them had dead-ended, the way made impossible by cave-ins, requiring time-consuming doubling back.

More quickly than he had hoped, however, they located one of the foam construct blockages the complex designers had put up to wall off the caverns they'd chosen to locate in. The plas-trusion looked artificially rough against the smooth walls left by the receding ocean millions of years ago. Geological survey teams had verified that much more of Makaum had been underwater during the planet's cooling phase.

Studying the blockage with the hardsuit's sensors and the nightvision, Sage turned to Kiwanuka, who was inspecting the blockage with a more sensitive scanner.

"I'm not picking up any electronic signatures." Kiwanuka put the scanner away. "This section is inert."

Sage nodded. "Then this is our way in." He glanced at Murad. "If you're in agreement, sir."

Murad nodded but didn't say anything.

Sage put his Roley aside and reached into his combat vest for incendiary grenades. "This plug is probably just here to help control the HVAC. It probably won't be very thick. We can burn our way inside and take a look around. We'll wire it with explosives in case we have to come back this way in a hurry."

Just as he started to place the incendiary charges, his comm crackled to life. "Alpha Team, this is Red Team One. The hostiles have discovered us. I repeat, our position is—"

The rest of the transmission was lost in a roar of thunder.

Murad looked at Sage, the question showing in his eyes but not once uttered.

"We go forward, sir." Sage reached into his pack for heavy explosives.

"They're going to be overrun," Murad protested. "They'll be killed."

"They're dug in tight. The only chance they have is if we can find the information we need and call down that dropship strike." Sage adhered the high-ex gel packs against the plas-trusion. "Now fall back to a safe area."

All ten soldiers and Jahup fell back to behind a twist in the tunnel. Sage joined them, gripping his Roley in his hands. He felt the vibrations of the missiles aboard the powersuits shaking through the tunnel then, and dim echoes of the explosions rolled through the hollows.

Sage readied the Roley. "Things are going to go fast once we're inside."

Kiwanuka nodded. "Blow it."

Sage sent the signal over his comm and the high-ex gel packs detonated, filling the tunnel with plas-trusion chunks, thunder, and smoke.

THIRTY-THREE

Wheeling, Sage turned and charged down the tunnel with the Roley at the ready.

The gel packs had cleared a space three meters across. Debris crunched underfoot and smoke filled the tunnel beyond the opening. Klaxons mounted on the walls inside the underground structure screamed to life, causing Sage's aud dampers to kick in immediately.

He forced himself not to think about the team he'd left out there fighting for their lives now. If they survived the first engagement, they had a chance to set up a holding action. If they didn't, it was already too late.

All Sage could hope to do now was locate the intel Halladay needed to call down the strike team.

The tunnel ran straight for thirty meters. Harsh emergency lighting stripped away the shadows, peeling back the darkness to glint off the granite walls. Prefab walls foamed into the tunnel held doors and created private quarters for the mercenaries billeted there.

As Sage ran, some of the mercenaries stumbled out of the quarters and tried to gear up. He cut them down with quick bursts from the Roley, leaving them dead or dying or heavily injured. The soldiers behind him added to the carnage.

Bullets and beams bounced off Sage's hardsuit, rocking him slightly as the armor's gyros compensated. The onboard AI recorded damage, ghosting into Sage's vision till he cut it off with a curt command. Damage reports didn't matter at this moment. He was going to live or die in the next few moments, and measuring that by degrees wasn't necessary.

Reaching the end of the tunnel, Sage discovered he was on an elevated platform that ringed the storage area below. Crawlers sat between the aisles of crates and barrels, which bore chemical symbols he wasn't completely familiar with.

The AI recorded the rough dimensions of the open space and generated a quick potential map of the area based on probable room configurations.

"Launching hacker drones," Murad called out behind him.

The drones signatures flared to life on the inside of Sage's faceshield as they took flight. He launched his own ParaSights to help scope out the base. Their vid feedback painted translucent images inside his faceshield as well, creating layers of reality that only long periods of training allowed Sage to sift through on the fly.

Vibrations to his left shook the plasteel deck under his boots. Turning in that direction, Sage swung the Roley around as a powersuited mercenary heaved himself up the steps. Ten meters tall, the armored goliath wheeled on him and opened fire. Gunfire cracked and beams hissed

behind Sage, letting him know that the awakening mercenaries weren't completely out of the fight either.

Abandoning the Roley for the moment because the
beams would only ricochet off the powersuit's armor,
Sage dialed up the gel launcher slung under the rifle. He
squeezed off three grenades, which slammed into the
powersuit's head, hoping to break through the thick transplas faceshield.

The grenades detonated in gouts of fire and concussive waves that hammered Sage. If he hadn't locked his
boots down onto the plasteel decking, he would have been
knocked backward. Three mercenaries in hardsuits died
in the fallout of the blasts, crumpling to smoking ruin
around the powersuit.

The powersuit pilot swiveled and managed to keep his
balance, then brought the shoulder-mounted heavy machine guns to bear. A barrage of 15mm rounds chopped
into the wall where Sage took cover. The tremors shivered
through his hardsuit and stone slivers sang as they ricocheted off his armor.

In the 360-degree view he had of the tunnel they'd
entered, he saw that the desperate fight with the mercenaries was almost over. Kiwanuka's sharpshooting skills
picked off the targets harder to get to while the other soldiers kept up steady fire to keep her protected. As calmly
as though she was shooting in a holo deck, Kiwanuka
became a gunsight. Laser beams cored through the heads
of the mercenaries she picked off in rapid succession.

On the platform, the powersuit advanced with pounding steps that shook the floor beneath Sage's feet. He
couldn't duck around the corner without getting shredded, and trying to make it to another position while facing
the heavy fire was tantamount to suicide.

Thinking quickly, he dialed up more gel grenades and
called one of the ParaSights into position. He used the

ParaSight's view to aim the Roley without exposing himself, then plopped three gel grenades onto the plasteel at the powersuit's feet.

The detonations sounded like a solid ripple as they went off. Through the ParaSight, Sage watched as the shattered plasteel platform gave way under the powersuit. Chunks of it fell away and the powersuit tumbled twenty meters down into a stack of barrels. Ruptured and broken, the barrels released their contents in a deluge.

Spotting two mercenaries racing up the next set of stairs leading to the raised platform, Sage brought the Roley to his shoulder and squeezed the trigger twice in quick succession. Their bodies dropped only a second apart. Even if they'd gained the high ground, they couldn't have bridged the broken section, but they would have been able to set up sniping positions. Now they were no longer a threat.

Below, in the debris of the broken platform, the powersuit pilot struggled to get to his feet in the tangle of crushed barrels. His movements only broke open more containers.

"Analyze chems," Sage told his AI as he peered down. He wasn't close enough for the hardsuit's olfactory enhancements to kick in, but the spectrometer in ParaSight 01 tagged the chems as being mostly modified alcohol that he assumed was used in refining the drug products.

Sage fired two grenades into the powersuit. The resulting explosions shook the powersuit, but they also set off the alcohol, igniting a blaze that climbed up the unit in a roiling ocean of blue and yellow flames. Normally the armor might have withstood fire, but the powersuit had either taken some damage in the fall or the artificially enhanced alcohol burned at a higher intensity than the fire retardant could withstand.

The powersuit pilot fought to get free, but the fluids beneath his feet proved too slick to provide traction and he fell back into the barrels, bringing more of them down on top of him. The flames spread quickly across the warehouse, adding to the confusion as the smoke billowed out and filled the area. More explosions rattled the interior of the cavern.

Below, fire suppression drones rolled toward the conflagration. Sage picked off three of them before hostile fire drove him to the ground. He checked the soldiers behind him and found his team was all still intact.

"Kiwanuka, can you do something about those riflemen?" Sage asked.

"Yes." Her hardsuit scarred silver where she'd taken projectile hits, and burned black in other places from lasers, Kiwanuka slithered to the edge of the platform and took advantage of the height there to start picking off targets.

New explosions launched flaming barrels into the air as Sage added his firepower to Kiwanuka's. Below, with the fire spreading and the klaxons shrieking, the mercenaries struggled to maintain order. Sage hammered the cover their opponents mistakenly chose behind more chemicals with gel grenades, setting off even more fires.

Even if they didn't get the information they'd come for, the site was going to be a loss.

The acrid stench of chem fumes burned Sage's nose. Realizing the danger from the chems loose in the air, he opened the comm. "Mask up. You've got bad air in here." His suit flipped over to the hour-long supply of onboard oxygen made possible by the air canisters and the suit's carbon dioxide scrubbers.

The use of the hardsuit's oxygen limited the amount of time they could remain on-site underground, but Sage knew the chances of them catching a bullet or a beam was greater than succumbing to drug fumes or lack of oxygen.

A few meters away, Jahup struggled with stripping armor from one of the downed mercenaries. The young Makaum man hacked and coughed, and he didn't have as much control over his movements as he would have normally, because he was already fighting for air.

Sage dropped back to aid the young man, expertly stripping the dead mercenary's head gear with one hand, then helping pull the mask and helmet over Jahup's head. Returning his attention to the corpse, Sage removed the man's vest from him, providing a little armor and the oxygen supply to Jahup. He helped the young man into the vest and got it operational, filling the appropriated helmet with oxygen.

"Sergeant," Murad called over the suit comm.

"Coming, sir." Sage handed Jahup the dead mercenary's rifle, showed him how to fire it and how to replenish the charge packs, then draped a bandolier of them over the young Makaum man's shoulder.

Jahup nodded thankfully. "I must find Noojin."

"We will," Sage replied. "If she's in here, we will." He didn't bother to tell the younger man that locating the young woman would only be possible if they remained alive, which was looking doubtful. Staying low, Sage returned to the lieutenant, who was staring fixedly at the inside of his own faceshield.

"I've got a lock on the comm stations," Murad said. "The drones have tracked the comm array, but they can't access the network. They're locked out and can't bypass the security."

"Where are they?" Sage asked.

Murad put a hand on Sage's wrist and shared the connection to the drones.

A 3-D map popped into view on Sage's faceshield and blips appeared on the image to show the location of the drones. After a brief consultation, he realized the drones had massed at a room on the lower floor on the east side of the complex.

"I've got them, sir."

"Can you get to them?"

"Yes."

Murad lifted his rifle and added his firepower to that of Kiwanuka and the rest of the team. "Good luck."

Sage pulled himself toward the edge of the platform and studied the floor twenty meters below. He pulled a grappling hook from his combat vest and encircled a support post that held up the safety railing around the outer edge of the platform. When he pulled on it to test its strength, the post seemed like it was strong enough to hold him.

Sage threw a leg over the side, held the Roley in one hand, wrapped one leg in the cable, and slid down to the floor one-handed. He released the rope and stepped away, barely avoiding having Jahup drop on top of him.

"You're not armored," Sage objected.

"Noojin is in here somewhere. I am going to find her."

Sage didn't have time to argue. "I've got drones out scouting. Keep your comm tuned to this channel." He made the adjustment on the young man's helmet comm. "If I find her before you do, I'll let you know where she is and how to get her."

Jahup nodded and hurried off, taking advantage of cover wherever he could.

Staying low himself, Sage ran to the outer edge of the lower floor. The heat from the blazing chemicals and the smoke eddied around him, coalescing into a strong physical presence. Sage stepped into the darkness, and fought to keep his directions straight because the embers flying through the air caused problems with the hardsuit's vid.

Before he knew it, he ran into a wall he never saw until he was up against it. Rebounding, barely able to stay on his feet because he'd been moving quickly, he flailed around and located the passageway's opposite wall and kept himself upright and moving.

Forty-seven meters and three turns later—two right and one left, all marked by his fingertips rather than visually—Sage reached the complex's command-and-control center. Windows took up almost half the walls on all four sides.

Sage bounced a sonar blast off the wall and discovered the transplas was twelve centimeters thick, followed up with a spectroscopic analysis that showed it was fire-resistant and blast proof.

The drones hovered around the structure like fat bumblebees. None of them were any larger than Sage's fist. Two of them sported miniature satellite dishes.

Four people lingered inside the command and control module. All of them were armed, but only two of them appeared to be military people. In his 360-view, Sage saw three men step out of the swirling smoke, then drop down as their heads exploded inside their helmets.

"I've got you," Kiwanuka stated calmly. "Now pull back from that building. The lieutenant found a door opener."

The drones flitted back a safe distance and Sage followed suit. On the other side of the transplas, the guards started arguing. The female pointed at the door and brandished her weapon, and Sage gathered that she liked her odds. Or maybe she disliked the odds of staying inside the room.

A half dozen other mercenaries rushed at Sage out of the whirling smoke. Alcohol-fueled fire wreathed two of them, but they paid the flames no heed.

Sage whirled to face them, knowing he was exposing his back to the mercenaries inside the room. He raised the Roley, but before he could fire, a powersuit lumbered out from behind them.

Cursing his luck and the bad timing, Sage switched targets. He knew the Roley wouldn't penetrate the armor, but he hoped shooting at the pilot would cause some distraction.

As his sights settled over the pilot's chamber, Sage saw that a dead man sat behind the transplas at the controls. He fired anyway and the gauss charge burst created a disturbance in the air over the transplas shield.

"Don't, Sage!" Murad barked. "I've got the powersuit slaved."

In the next instant, the powersuit attacked the mercenaries before it with fists curled into giant hammers. Three of them were dead before they knew anything was wrong. A fourth died before she could do more than turn around and take aim. Sage shifted the Roley over the two survivors and took them down with well-placed bursts.

For a moment, the powersuit froze, surveying the carnage that lay around it. Sage knew the machine wasn't malfunctioning. Murad was frozen, not believing what he had done.

"Lieutenant," Sage called over the command frequency.

"My God," Murad breathed hoarsely.

"It's all right," Sage said. "What you did here, it's all right."

"I did it—*this*—because they were going to kill you."

"I know, sir. I appreciate the help."

"They never had a chance." Murad sounded dazed.

Sage put steel in his voice. "Maybe not, sir, but it was their choice to be here, their choice to do what they've been doing."

"I know."

"Get it together, sir. We need you."

The powersuit stepped over the dead mercenaries, set itself, and drove a huge hand through the transplas shield as the people inside backed away. One of the huge hands curled around a mercenary, squeezed, and withdrew with a corpse hanging from its fingertips.

Sage pulled an entangler grenade from his combat vest and threw it into the room. When the grenade went off, the gleaming monofilament snaked around the room and trapped the three surviving mercenaries.

The drones swarmed through the opening and settled onto the computers like gleaming mosquitos.

Sage took up a position to guard the command-and-control module. He sorted through the vid relayed through the ParaSights, looking for more targets.

"We're in," Murad exulted. "Spinning up the data now. We should know who's arranged for this operation in seconds."

Hurry, Sage thought silently, knowing that Murad wasn't wasting any time, but knowing also that their teams were bearing the brunt of full-scale attacks.

One of the ParaSights hovered over Jahup as he went room to room shouting the girl's name. Someone must have answered him from behind one of the doors, because Jahup then stopped and concentrated on opening the door. He didn't see the two mercenaries step around the corner behind him.

THIRTY-FOUR

The Cer'ardu Heights
140 Klicks West of Makaum
0326 Hours Zulu Time

Noojin! It's Jahup!"

"Jahup!" Noojin's voice was rushed, not understandable.

Frantic, his mind summoning horrible image of things that might have happened to Noojin since he'd last seen her, Jahup stepped back from the door and aimed at the locking mechanism.

"Jahup! Two gunners behind you!"

Sage's voice thundered in Jahup's borrowed helmet. He reacted instantly, like he would in response to a member of the hunting band. He threw himself down and to one side, bringing up the pulse rifle. He aimed by instinct and fired on full-auto, burning through the charge park and leaving a score of carbonized scorch marks marring the walls.

The two smoldering corpses dropped their weapons and fell over in a tight cluster.

"Noojin," Jahup called as he swapped out the spent charge pack for another. "Back away from the door."

"Okay! I'm safe! Hurry, Jahup!"

Jahup pressed the trigger and held it till the locking mechanism burned a bright-cherry red and dripped from the space. He swapped out charge packs again, lifted a leg, and drove his foot against the door.

Shivering, the barrier sank inward. In the next instant, Noojin was in his arms, holding him tight.

"Get her a mask and get out of there," Sage ordered over the comm. "The fire is out of control. It's going to destroy everything in here."

Jahup checked the two dead men, hoping that he had not destroyed their helmets. He had been aiming at their center body mass, so the chances were good. Only one of the helmets had survived, but he only needed the one. He helped Noojin into it. She was racked with coughs, already on the verge of succumbing to smoke inhalation.

He worried about her, about whether or not she had already inhaled too much smoke, and about whether they would get out of the caves alive. More explosions detonated all around them. Rifle in one hand, he wrapped his arm around Noojin's waist and helped her back in the direction of the Terran soldiers.

0329 Hours Zulu Time

"We've got the intel, Top," Murad announced. "Uploading it to Colonel Halladay now."

"Do we have what we need?" Sage asked.

"There are definite ties to DawnStar. This should be enough."

The comm crackled inside Sage's helmet and cleared

up immediately. "Attention, Alpha Team, this is Command. Be advised that we're about to planetfall on your twenty within the next three minutes."

Three minutes? Sage knew then that Halladay hadn't waited for confirmation. He'd launched early, trusting that the evidence they needed would be found, and found in time.

Or maybe the colonel had been planning on taking the heat for the engagement anyway, since he had soldiers on the ground in harm's way. Either way, Sage respected the man for his commitment. Then his thoughts were swept aside as his second ParaSight flashed on a face that he knew.

Velesko Kos was running through a tunnel that led outside of the complex. Four armed mercenaries ran with him. Sage didn't know if the man was abandoning the site or if he was going to take control of the battlefield.

Sage pinged the ParaSight and got the GPS location of Kos. "I'm going after Kos," he said as two members of the fireteam arrived. "You two take over security for the lieutenant."

"Roger that, Top."

Sage ran, leaping over exploded debris, dodging flames where he could, and running through them when he couldn't. He pushed himself, looking forward to the coming battle.

For six long years he had been sidelined, working with young men and women to turn them into halfway-knowledgeable cannon fodder for the war with the Phrenorians. Velesko Kos wasn't Phrenorian, but he was an enemy, one of the worst the Makaum people had known. Sage was determined not to let the man escape.

0331 Hours Zulu

Velesko Vos was determined to escape as he emerged from the underground labyrinth. He didn't know how such a small insertion team had wreaked havoc within the complex, but it had been done. His profits were going up in smoke that very minute, and he knew DawnStar would hold him accountable for everything that was happening. His only choice was to get offplanet as quickly as he could.

But when he saw the dropships plummeting out of the sky through the murky haze of drifting smoke, he knew even escape might be too much to hope for. As he watched, the assault team deployed, spun out into the air like floating seeds. Within seconds, the units were on the ground.

The surrounding landscape looked like it had been carved from old Terran stories about hell. Smoke spewed from craters punched into the earth by light artillery. Dead mercenaries and exploded powersuits lay in scattered disarray, slain and destroyed by one-man barb fighters that had offloaded from the dropships upon reentry into Makaum's atmosphere.

Kos cursed and glanced around in the direction of the drug base, spotting the hidden hangar where Dubchek had housed light aircraft. With all the confusion, Kos thought there was a chance he could get away. He turned and ran toward the hangar, two hundred meters distant.

Without warning, the armored man on Kos's left slammed into him, knocking both of them down. Kos regained his footing. Only then did he see the gaping hole in the side of the man's helmet, which denoted a bullet from a large-caliber handgun.

Fearing what he knew he was going to see, Kos turned

and spotted a familiar figure standing just outside the entry point to the complex. Terran Army Master Sergeant Frank Sage had survived the battle in the underground bunker and had lived to continue his war outside, in the jungle-covered mountains.

"Kill him!" Kos ordered the two men beside him as he lifted his weapon and took aim at Sage.

0333 Hours Zulu Time

When Kos and the two surviving mercenaries turned their weapons on him, Sage threw himself to the ground with the .500 Magnum levered forward. He sighted on Kos, tracking the man, and fired while the man was on the move.

Instead of striking Kos, the big round cored through the faceshield of one of the mercenaries. The inside of the man's helmet turned crimson and his twitching body dropped bonelessly. Sage eared the hammer back and took aim again as he pushed himself to his feet.

Kos ran, dodging behind trees. Two more of Sage's rounds tore through branches and knocked limbs from the trees.

Sage ran, taking advantage of cover himself as his quarry returned fire. He had an easier time of it because he was running forward and firing ahead of him. Kos and the other mercenary had to try to fire behind them. Sage didn't know where Kos was running, but he knew the man had a plan.

When he'd fired the .500 Magnum dry, Sage popped the cylinder open and shook out the brass, slipping fresh rounds into it with a Speedloader. His attention was split for just a moment while he'd worked his reload. The mercenary took advantage of that instant, stopping behind a boulder holding burning debris from a powersuit hit directly by troops from the dropships.

The mercenary swung out with a laser rifle held to his shoulder and fired.

A superheated beam burned through Sage's upper left chest, leaving open wounds in the front and the back.

```
WARNING! YOU HAVE BEEN SERIOUSLY WOUNDED.
YOU SHOULD SEEK SHELTER AND AWAIT MEDICAL
ATTENTION. YOUR LEFT LUNG HAS BEEN
IMPAIRED.
```

Sage ignored the warning and took aim at the mercenary's exposed head and shoulder as the man steadied himself for another shot. Knowing Sage was firing back unnerved the man, though, and the follow-up laser blast sizzled through the air only a few centimeters above Sage's chest.

Sage squeezed the trigger and watched the mercenary's head snap back. On the move again, Sage watched as the stricken man went down, still moving, still struggling to bring his weapon up. Sage took aim, preparing to send another round into the mercenary's head, but before he could squeeze the trigger, a large, chitin-covered thing popped up from the earth, grabbed the mercenary, and yanked him down into the hole it had emerged from. In a heartbeat, the man and the overgrown centipede were gone.

Skirting the hole, Sage ran after Kos. Although the laser had cauterized the wound in his chest, the exertion Sage was putting himself through tore open the wounds. Blood started seeping into his lung, taking away his air space. He told himself that he could survive with one lung and stubbornly continued the chase, despite the pain and the swelling constriction in his chest.

"Med panel," Sage gasped. He was still gaining on Kos, but not as rapidly as before. "Seal the chest wounds and start a drain on the injured lung." He continued running, head spinning dizzily from lack of oxygen, and knew the nanobots in his body would start working on him.

REQUEST PERMISSION TO ANESTHETIZE

printed across the inside of his faceshield.

"Negative," Sage croaked. Then a sharp, gnawing pain bit into the front and back of his chest.

REQUEST CESSATION OF COMBAT.

"No." Sage spotted the hidden hangar ahead of him and knew that was where Kos was headed.

All around them, the Terran Army spilled across the landscape, locked in fierce battle. Powersuits fought hand-to-hand in places, like mythic titans, and sometimes they stood or crouched in firing positions, unleashing machine guns and missiles. Soldiers and mercenaries in hardsuits were locked in mortal combat.

Losing perception of the world around him, Sage reached the hangar only seconds after Kos did. Kos hid inside in the darkness, where three small aircraft sat waiting.

Struggling to stay on his feet at the hangar entrance, Sage put the pistol away and slid the Roley from his shoulder. Activating the grenade launcher, Sage rolled around the doorway and pumped gel grenades at the three aircraft. An instant later, all three aircraft exploded, filling the hanger with heat and light and flying debris.

When the initial concussive blast swept by him, Sage

tried to catch his breath and couldn't, no longer able to
hold onto the Roley and barely yanking the .500 Magnum
from shoulder leather and bringing it up. The pistol felt
like an anchor at the end of his arm. His feet felt like lead
as he lifted them to walk into the hangar. It was possible
that the detonations had killed his quarry.

Black comets swirled in Sage's vision as Velesko Kos
stood up and fired his coilguns. The bursts ripped into the
hangar around Sage and tore through the air.

Sage struggled to sort which image of Kos was the
actual man, trying to remember how impaired vision
worked when a soldier was suffering from hypoxia. He
picked the middle one and pulled the trigger three times
as quickly as he could.

Kos was blown backward and lay on the hangar floor in
the midst of the aircraft wreckage.

Knees going out from him, senses swimming and his
head too heavy to continue to hold it up, Sage walked over
to Kos.

The man lay on his back, pale and panicked as he tried
to breathe through his burst lungs. As Sage watched, life
drained from Kos's dark eyes and left his empty husk
behind.

No longer able to stand, no longer able to keep his
senses together, Sage thought he heard someone calling
out his name, but he didn't have the strength to answer.
The suit's near-AI switched on his emergency GPS loca-
tor and he sank into the darkness.

0341 Hours Zulu Time

"Is the sergeant dead?"

Standing at the display screens broadcasting vid from
the satellite they had above the jungle where Sage had just

defeated Kos, Zhoh flicked his eyes toward the data in the upper left corner. Phrenorian drones flitted through the area, hauling in raw intel they gleaned from light hacks into the Terran hardsuits.

Sage still lived. Barely.

"He's alive," Zhoh said to Mato, who stood behind him.

Mato's primary hands clacked irritably. "It would be better if he were dead."

"Yes," Zhoh agreed. "The time will come soon enough. We'll bring this whole planet to its knees before long." He turned away from the vidfeed, already lost in his plans.

Sage's injuries would slow the man down, and if he was slowed, the Terran Military would be slowed too. But the overall timetable was speeding up and Zhoh knew that, even if the other officers he worked with refused to see that.

Sage was a catalyst, an element of entropy that had entered the carefully constructed blueprint the Phrenorian Empire had for Makaum. The others would choose to overlook the human, not realizing the changes he could make, but Zhoh intended to capitalize on Sage.

In the coming battles, Zhoh would take back honor and glory that had been stripped from him. He would spill enough enemy blood to wash away the disgrace he had been framed with committing. There were plenty of people to sacrifice to reach his goal.

EPILOGUE

Beeping hospital equipment woke Sage. His head felt thick and his tongue felt swollen. He glanced at the displays with blurry vision and tried to remember what all of the numbers meant, but even that grasp of the situation eluded him.

"You survived," a woman's voice told him.

Sage swiveled his head to the foot of the bed and the effort took a lot more out of him than he thought it should have.

Kiwanuka stood there in ACUs. She didn't look battered or bruised, or like she'd just stepped off of a battlefield.

"We're not dead?" he asked.

She grinned at him. "No. Although the colonel tells me that you nearly got to find out what being dead was like."

"It seems pretty *quiet*. At least, that's what I remember." Sage licked his dry lips. "How long was I out?"

"Five days. The surgeon put you in a medically induced coma while they rebuilt your lung."

Sage pulled a hand up to his chest and only felt a little sore.

"They replaced the original with a bionic one. There's not a lot of donor material to be had out here."

"Did we get enough intel to expose DawnStar?"

Kiwanuka nodded. "We did. Colonel Halladay and the diplomatic teams are sorting it all out now. Of course, DawnStar insists that Velesco Kos was running a rogue element inside the corp, which gives them a layer of deniability. We'll have to wait to see how the dust settles on this, but the black market on Makaum has taken a big hit. It's not dead by any means, but it's been shut down a lot. Many of the major operators have been exposed as a result, and the Makaum *Quass* is cracking down harder on its people. Things are changing, Sage."

"But?" he asked. He could hear the *but* in her words.

"The direct action Charlie Company took out in the jungle has split the Makaum people even more. The drug cartels are shutting down, but the civil war is heating up, and we've lost some ground with the *Quass*. I guess you could say they're more sharply divided. There aren't many ambivalent Makaum left when it comes to our presence on this planet. The Makaum left who like us are really supportive, but the (ta)Klar and the Phrenorians have gained support as well. You don't find many fence sitters out there now."

"I take it the general isn't happy?"

"Not even. He's made it known that whenever you're well enough to ship out, you're welcome to go anywhere you want to." Kiwanuka smiled at him. "So I guess you have what you wanted before you got here."

Sage thought about that, thinking of the war that was calling to him out there, but he was thinking about Makaum as well. "There's still a lot here to do, and the situation is even worse than it was when I got here. I learned a long time ago to clean up the messes I made."

"I'm glad you see it that way. Colonel Halladay and I both think that a large part of what we're facing now is due to you, so it's only fair that you pitch in to help patch things up." Kiwanuka took a breath and looked more serious. "Also, we think we know what a high-ranking Phrenorian like Zhoh GhiCemid is doing here." She placed a miniature holo projector on the serving table at the side of Sage's bed. "We just got this a couple days ago from Jahup."

"The kid's okay?"

Kiwanuka nodded. "He's running scouting expeditions for us now. He's brought on a whole group of young Makaum that are definitely pro-Terran military."

"That's good to hear."

"It is. It's working out pretty well. If it hadn't been for Jahup and his hunting bands, we wouldn't know about this." Kiwanuka switched on the projector.

The image was grainy and indistinct.

Sage squinted at it, not certain what it was supposed to represent. Then he saw the unnaturally straight lines that took shape out in the jungle.

"Is that what I think it is?" Sage asked. His thoughts suddenly burned crystal clear.

"If you're thinking this is a secret Phrenorian base hidden on Makaum, roger that. Because that is what we think it is. We haven't gotten close enough to ascertain that, but we're working on it."

Sage stared at the image, seeing it more clearly now.

"It looks like you don't have to go find the Phrenorian War, Sage," Kiwanuka said. "It's coming to Makaum."

IAN DOUGLAS's
STAR CARRIER
SERIES

EARTH STRIKE
BOOK ONE
978-0-06-184025-8

To the Sh'daar, the driving technologies of transcendent change are anathema and must be obliterated from the universe—along with those who would employ them. As their great warships destroy everything in their path en route to the Sol system, the human Confederation government falls into dangerous disarray.

CENTER OF GRAVITY
BOOK TWO
978-0-06-184026-5

On the far side of human known space, the Marines are under siege, battling the relentless servant races of the Sh'daar aggressor. Admiral Alexander Koenig knows the element of surprise is their only hope as he takes the war for humankind's survival directly to the enemy.

SINGULARITY
BOOK THREE
978-0-06-184027-2

In the wake of the near destruction of the solar system, the political powers on Earth seek a separate peace with an inscrutable alien life form that no one has ever seen. But Admiral Alexander Koenig has gone rogue, launching his fabled battlegroup beyond the boundaries of Human Space against all orders.

DEEP SPACE
BOOK FOUR
978-0-06-218380-4

After twenty years of peace, a Confederation research vessel has been ambushed, and destroyers are descending on a human colony. It seems the Sh'daar have betrayed their treaty, and all nations must stand united—or face certain death.

ID2 0513

IAN DOUGLAS's
MONUMENTAL SAGA
OF INTERGALACTIC WAR
THE INHERITANCE TRILOGY

STAR STRIKE: BOOK ONE
978-0-06-123858-1

Planet by planet, galaxy by galaxy, the inhabited universe has fallen to the alien Xul. Now only one obstacle stands between them and total domination: the warriors of a resilient human race the world-devourers nearly annihilated centuries ago.

GALACTIC CORPS: BOOK TWO
978-0-06-123862-8

In the year 2886, intelligence has located the gargantuan hidden homeworld of humankind's dedicated foe, the brutal Xul. The time has come for the courageous men and women of the 1st Marine Interstellar Expeditionary Force to strike the killing blow.

SEMPER HUMAN: BOOK THREE
978-0-06-116090-5

True terror looms at the edges of known reality. Humankind's eternal enemy, the Xul, approach wielding a weapon monstrous beyond imagining. If the Star Marines fail to eliminate their relentless xenophobic foe once and for all, the Great Annihilator will obliterate every last trace of human existence.

IDI 0609